NEUROSHOCK

DIVISION ZERO BOOK 7

MATTHEW S. COX

DIVISION ZERO PRESS

Division Zero: Neuroshock
Book 7 of the Division Zero series.

A DIVERGENT FATES NOVEL

ISBN (ebook): 978-1-950738-48-9

ISBN (paperback): 978-1-950738-49-6

CONTENTS

RIDE-ALONG

Awkwardness haunted Kirsten like another spirit come seeking assistance.

Though her life now had more trappings of normality than she ever expected would be possible, she hesitated to fully embrace it. She feared as soon as she truly allowed herself to be happy, something would go wrong. Dr. Loring, her therapist, thought her anxiety came from the way Mother would often punish her whenever she smiled or didn't seem miserable enough. After all, one could not possibly 'atone for cavorting with the Devil' if they knew joy of any form.

Comments occasionally filtered down from the higher command staff above Captain Eze regarding how impressed they were that a woman with her background didn't show more signs of instability. It sometimes made her doubt her own sanity, but at least Dr. Loring as well as the medical review board's telepaths told her she weathered her past surprisingly well and emerged mentally intact.

Evan thought those Seraphim things had something to do with her mental resilience. Kirsten didn't know much of anything about them other than suspecting they represented the opposite energy of Harbingers. Not that she considered the Harbingers evil. They merely had to deal with darkness. In fact, as of late, she didn't mind their presence as much. How beings utterly saturated in pure dread could seem at times like ordinary coworkers amused her to a point. She liked to think the Seraphim had not been aware of her existence back then, so she didn't have to resent them for leaving her to suffer at the hands of her horrible mother. As far as Kirsten believed, she survived as well as she did because she did not accept the woman's lies as truth and never internalized any guilt. She viewed the woman as a betrayer, damaged, mentally unstable, a hostile outside party... not a frantic parent trying to deal with a demon-sent child.

Most who knew of her past thought she'd been alone most of her life, either locked in a closet at home or hiding in the Beneath... but they got it wrong.

Various ghosts had always been there for her. They kept her company at home and they'd looked after her on the street.

The majority of the National Police Force generally tried to keep psionics at arms' length. Whoever made the decision for Division 0 uniforms, cars, and everything else to be all-black committed an error. Sure, it looked elegant and cool—but it also created a foreboding air of apprehension, making them seem far more dangerous or secretive than reality bore out.

Society as a whole begrudgingly accepted psionics among them but remained distrustful... and of course, idiots like Reverend Harris and his cult actively hated them. Adding to her feelings of not fitting in, even some of her compatriots within Division 0 kept their distance due to her having a 'scary' ability known as Mind Blast. Technically, the lab-coat people named it 'sensory overload burst telepathy-induced neuropathy,' but no one wanted to say that over and over again, even if 'Mind Blast' made it sound like a spell from the Monwyn fantasy world.

No matter what she did, she would always feel at least half a step removed from the world, an outsider. But... she could decide not to care what anyone thought about her. She didn't need outside validation anymore. She had Evan. She had Sam. She'd even found confidence in herself—mostly.

As much as she loved Sam Chang, being with him proved

exhausting. Not for anything he did, but how she constantly questioned herself and everything she said or did around him. It had taken her forever to find someone she might have an adult relationship with who didn't run away screaming the moment they learned about her being psionic. Even though she didn't really expect he'd leave over something as trivial as her not being perfect enough, irrational worry dogged her.

If he wanted perfect, he'd never have looked at me.

She frowned at her reflection on the video display pretending to be the passenger side window of a patrol craft. A gleaming world of silvery plastisteel and grey thermacrete stretched northward to the horizon. Sunlight shining from the east created skyscraper-shaped shadows amid low hanging clouds and fog. Despite the surface in front of her eyes being electronic, it recreated the daylight glare powerfully enough to make her squint. Bots delivering items or flashing adverts coursed along, the scintillating neon blood of West City. Their millions of tiny lights sparkled in the shaded portions of the city. Higher, at level with her, innumerable hovercars flowed in four separate traffic layers spaced ten meters apart.

A small boy in a car beside them stared seemingly at her. The child couldn't see her, yet the gaze he fixed on the patrol craft appeared to gaze into her eyes. To the outside world, the patrol craft's 'windows' were blocky, armored panels. No doubt, he simply found the presence of a marked police vehicle fascinating, as children tended to do.

Only nine-point-four percent of citizens can afford hovercars.

Her parents hadn't been *poor*, though they couldn't have afforded a hovercar. The two years she'd spent living in the Beneath as a child, she'd been beyond poor, not even owning clothes other than what she could forage out of trash. At age twelve, the police found her in a tunic she'd made from a plastic tarp and a power cable for a belt. She'd gone from the upper end of working poor to indigent to comfortable. Division 0 paid well, considering psionics as rare specialists. Being the only operational Astral Sensitive in the west had its perks. If she wanted to, she could afford the payments on a personal hovercar. The insurance would be a burden, but not impossible.

Still, she didn't bother. As long as she remained active duty in

Division 0, she could use her assigned PC. Besides, it had a Dorian attached to it.

Not having him with her at the moment only added to the discomfort of today's ride-along.

Kirsten no longer suffered anxiety about being in public, but every now and then, she ran into someone who reminded her how nice solitude could be. Case in point: Detective Nevi Arun. The woman seated to her left at the patrol craft's controls embodied much of what Command required of its officers: driven, confident, proud, fearless… and a few things it didn't: jaded, opinionated, impatient. She had to be at least ten years older than Kirsten to have made detective the normal way—as opposed to getting handed a rank simply for having a rare psionic ability.

The detective wore her hair in a sharp bob, longer in front, the left side bright red, the right jet black. Bright azure light glowed from the holographic irises of her artificial eyes. Two almost invisible lines of slightly darker brown traced across her right cheek toward her ear and vanished under her hair—nanofilament wires embedded in the skin.

Unlike Division 1 beat cops, the detective wore normal street clothing: a dark grey top, black pants, boots, and a dark burgundy trench coat with armor panels. Six strips of raised material across each of the coat's shoulder pads appeared to contain some manner of electronics.

Compared to the detective, who could pass for a civilian in her present attire, Kirsten's Division 0 blacks, utility belt, and forearm guard added to her sense of awkwardness, as if she'd shown up to a casual hangout with friends in a full evening gown. Captain Eze didn't tell her *not* to wear her standard uniform. It didn't even occur to her not to wear it until she arrived in the Div 2 squad room over at the Regional Tech Center earlier that morning—the only one out of over a hundred people dressed obviously like a cop.

Contrary to the attitude shown by the majority of the NPF, Detective Arun didn't appear to be in any way fearful of Kirsten or psionics in general. She *did*, however, make no secret of her disdain for them. In much the same way ordinary employees of a corporation looked down their noses at an incompetent who got a high-paying job only because they happened to be the child of the CEO, Nevi Arun didn't believe anyone in Division 0 counted as a *real* cop.

At least Kirsten had been promoted to lieutenant.

As a detective, Nevi Arun's rank translated to warrant officer grade one as far as the military hierarchy went, not exactly enlisted but not a commissioned officer either. Kirsten's prior rank of agent would have also technically outranked her as it had a pay grade equivalent to that of WO4, but only jackasses tried to pull rank over someone so close to them on technicalities.

Of course, even the non-psionic divisions within the NPF regarded anyone with the special rank of 'agent' as basically a child on 'take your kid to work day.' Division 0 brass used it to activate people, often teenagers, who had uniquely powerful or rare (and highly needed) abilities. In Kirsten's case, they activated her at sixteen because they had no other astrals to handle a raging spirit.

Fortunately, the woman didn't tease Kirsten about being a 'fake' officer. Her lieutenant bars carried real weight and real authority, even if she didn't fully feel adequate to wield the power or responsibility. Alas, Detective Arun spent most of the morning rambling on about how Division 2 did all the real work and she had better things to do than give a tour to someone from Division 0—as if an operational ride-along happened to be a mere media stunt.

The NPF had a doctrine of interdepartmental cross-training, at least on paper. In reality, Division 2 was overworked and understaffed. Whenever possible, Division 0 got tapped to help out and ease the workload. As psionic incidents still represented a rather small percentage of the city's total crime, they could spare a day or two every few months at least. Unlike Divisions 5 and 6—mostly combat-hardened meatheads—the sort of work Div 2 did required finesse, intelligence, and patience.

Kirsten started the day hopeful that being paired with another detective would be more engaging—and a little safer—than her last interdepartmental day riding with a Div 1 patrol unit. It simply *had* to be better than sitting in a car all day long in hopes of catching someone who disabled their hovercar's auto-drive and flew like an idiot.

"Real investigations can take weeks or months," said Nevi,

breaking a six-minute silence. "Since you're only with me today to get a feel for our process, you're not going to see that part of it."

Kirsten forced herself not to scowl. "I do know the routine. I'm I-Ops, not Tactical. Our investigations are basically the same except for the murder weapon. Your suspects use guns or blades. Ours use psionic abilities."

Detective Arun smirked.

"Mine are usually already dead," muttered Kirsten.

"They got you working on cold files?" Nevi glanced over at her.

"Not exactly. For most of my cases, the suspect died *before* they caused trouble."

Nevi blinked. "You're trying to mess with me. It won't work."

"Didn't read my file?"

"I have actual work to do. Why would I waste time researching the resume of some Division 0 kid they're going to saddle me with for a day? Six and a half hours from now, we'll go our separate ways and never think about each other again."

Here's hoping. "We should be so lucky the day goes that smoothly."

"Don't worry. If it gets too grisly for you, you can wait outside. I work better on my own, anyway."

Kirsten chuckled. "Okay."

Four seconds of silence.

"Why the tone?" asked Nevi.

"Oh, no reason." Kirsten smiled to herself.

Nevi turned to fully stare at her. "Seriously. What? Tell me. I don't appreciate being messed with."

"I'm not trying to mess with you or I'd have said what I thought." Kirsten picked a stray bluish thread from her uniform legging and dropped it to the floor. "There's no way for me to tell you without you dismissing me as talking out of my butt."

"Ugh. Are you fourteen or do you only look like it?" Nevi rolled her eyes. "You're an officer in the NPF—or at least are one on paper—you can say 'ass' without getting in trouble."

Kirsten sighed. "I'm trying to be professional."

Nevi snickered.

"Fine. If there is something at this crime scene bad enough to make *me* nope out of the room, you're going to end up 89-B'd."

The detective burst into laughter. "I'm amazed you could say that with a straight face."

"Because I'm not teasing."

"Uh huh." Nevi shook her head. "If we see something bad enough for me to be put on psych suspension, you're going to be under the bed sucking your thumb for the rest of your life."

"Doubt it," whispered Kirsten.

"You know I can hear you when you whisper." Nevi tapped a finger to her ear. "Augments."

"Figured." Kirsten shivered.

"Got a problem with cybernetics?" asked Nevi in an almost confrontational tone.

Kirsten wiped both hands down her face, then sighed. "I don't have any problem with people who get them. Just... not for me. The very idea makes my skin crawl. I don't even have an M3."

"Wow. Seriously? How the heck do you exist in this world without at least that?" Nevi gawked.

"The same way people did for hundreds of years." Kirsten held up her left arm. "Well, almost hundreds of years. Holo-terminals aren't *that* old."

Nevi tapped at the console. The patrol craft dropped down one traffic lane and shifted all the way to the left. "Oh, right. I remember hearing something about psios hating implants. Some crap about auras or whatever."

"It's not auras." Kirsten shrugged. "Honestly, I don't think anyone really understands it. We do know that adding more and more cybernetic implants to a body has a negative effect on a person's ability to use as well as resist psionic abilities. For example, those giant monsters who are just a brain in a robot body? They're like helpless babies to me."

"Now I know you're full of shit," said Nevi. "You expect me to believe a little thing like you is going to kick the ass of a cyberganger all trucked up to the max?"

Kirsten whistled. "Who said anything about ass kicking? I can make them stand there and not hurt anyone for as long as I need."

"Just a little bit creepy if you're not full of it," muttered Nevi.

"No creepier than those eyes of yours." Kirsten folded her arms. "They're lifeless."

Nevi stared forward in silence.

"Sorry," whispered Kirsten. "You've been confrontational all morning and it's rubbing off. We don't need to be bitchy."

"They're tools. Night vision, ten-x zoom, material analysis... I can see fingerprints on surfaces, locate blood or biological matter in the dark, all sorts of useful shit." Nevi mashed another button before grabbing the control sticks to take over flying from the computer. She pitched the patrol craft left while rolling into a dive, dropping away from organized traffic routes. "I don't own them. Get real, these things are a quarter million creds each. That's way out of my pay grade. They belong to the department. When I retire, they go back."

"Eww."

"Relax, kid." Nevi chuckled. "I've got my bio eyes on ice. Works out. I'll be sixty with the eyes of a thirty-year-old. Won't have to worry about going blind. The cancer or whatever will get me long before my eyes crap out."

"Oh." Kirsten squirmed at the thought of having her eyes removed. "Sorry you have cancer."

"I don't. Just saying. Something's going to catch up to me before the eyes fail."

Kirsten fidgeted at her uniform shirt. "At least you'll get them back."

"If I live long enough to retire. This ain't the cushy vacation job you have."

"Can we stop with the rivalry thing?" Kirsten pinched the bridge of her nose. "To be perfectly honest with you, sometimes, I'd almost rather have your job than mine. The weird things I end up dealing with are far more painful and terrifying than some normal person doing something evil." *Like a demon with six baby-headed serpents bursting out of its guts.*

"You guys just sit around all the time."

Kirsten waved dismissively. "We do have periods of idleness in between cases, especially me... since all the astral stuff is mine. Command wants me available if the spectral shit hits the fan."

"You said a dirty word. I'm telling your mother," deadpanned Nevi.

"Good luck with that. If there's anything left even remotely resembling her, it's in the Abyss."

Nevi brought the patrol craft to a midair halt and stared at her.

Silence became intolerably uncomfortable after ten seconds.

"What?" asked Kirsten.

"The sudden change in your tone, heart rate, and somatic response made me wonder for a moment if you killed her."

Kirsten closed her eyes, searching for calm. "No. I didn't. She died in prison. Other inmates killed her after hearing rumors of what she did to me when I was little. The world's a better place without her."

"Sorry," muttered Nevi before nudging the patrol craft forward.

The unexpected sincerity in the woman's voice made Kirsten feel a little better. Whatever electronics the detective had to read people with evidently picked up on the strength of her mood. Nevi likely assumed her mother had done something truly horrible, but didn't want to 'waste time' talking about it.

Kirsten didn't much care to dredge it up either.

A few minutes later, Nevi veered toward the roof landing deck of a residence tower. "So, if Div 0 has time for you to sit around so much, you guys should absorb some of our caseload. Oh, wait... you aren't trained for this."

Kirsten glanced away, deciding to ignore the remark. It didn't matter to her if this woman took her, or Division 0, seriously.

Another six hours and she's no longer my problem.

Nevi came in to land near a cluster of other blue-and-white Division 1 patrol craft close to the entry doors. Whirring vibrated throughout the cabin, the sound of the car's ground wheels extending from their tucked-up flight position. Billows of water vapor fog engulfed the patrol craft as its weight transferred from ion thrusters to its physical suspension. Pneumatic hisses accompanied the gull-wing doors opening upward.

Nevi got out, peeked under her coat to check her sidearm, then fast-walked toward the building entrance.

Cryomil fumes tickled the back of Kirsten's throat despite her reflexive habit of holding her breath for a bit after getting out of a hovercar. Fortunately, at seventy stories up, the chilly wind pulled the acrid mist away in seconds. She hurried around the front of the patrol craft and jogged to catch up to Nevi.

A short hall led to a room containing six elevators. Once inside a capsule on the way down, Kirsten activated the terminal in her left forearm guard. According to the Navcon, they'd gone to a residence building close to the southern edge of Sector 3422. The two sectors directly south of it, 3370 and 3316, showed as grey zones, as well as 3317, one sector west of 3316. Society already had started to write off three entire five-by-five-mile grid squares as losses.

It could be worse, though. This particular area appeared to have only begun the process of slipping toward grey, evidenced by there not being any disavowed sectors adjacent to them. The worst sectors, colloquially known as black zones because they appeared as blacked-out squares on the map, decayed to the point not even the police would generally go to them.

Grey zones could get rough, but they fell far short of the violent chaos one could find in a disavowed sector. Also, this building didn't happen to be in the grey, only near it. Another ten to twenty years, and Sector 3422 would likely end up grey as well. Honest people tended to leave the area, trying to avoid gang violence and the crime drawn into declining regions. As much as she couldn't blame them for leaving, good people going away only made the decline worse. The absence of a black zone here did offer some hope sufficient effort could reverse the downturn of the region… but that only happened if someone could make money off it.

They rode the elevator all the way down from the roof to the fourteenth story. The doors snapped open with a faint squeak, allowing the scent of carpet shampoo to flood in. A man on the younger side shouted furiously somewhere nearby, accusing another person of being useless.

Close-spaced doors suggested economy-sized apartments, likely a single bedroom with a multipurpose room of modular appliances. Generally, the closer to ground level, the cheaper the apartment. It cost money to go high enough to not have to care about stray gunfire from outside.

Detective Arun headed to the right, taking the eastern hallway out of the central elevator chamber.

Kirsten followed. "What do we know?"

"Not much yet. They found a guy dead in his apartment." Nevi glanced over, her expression the same as the last dozen times she'd made a jab about 'real' police work, but she kept quiet.

The shouting grew louder, seemingly coming from the right up ahead past where the corridor ended at a T. Nevi headed toward the yelling, though didn't seem to notice it. A spiritual presence swept over Kirsten, tickling as though she'd wandered nude into the gossamer caress of a massive cobweb. The feeling had long ago ceased unnerving her. An indefinable quality to the shouting told her it came from a ghost.

Here we go again.

Kirsten paused for a few seconds at the corner to prepare herself for whatever awaited, then strode around the bend, trying to exude the sort of confident authority she figured real lieutenants ought to.

Three Div 1 officers stood at the entrance of an open apartment five doors ahead. Armor mostly concealed their features, though by height, Kirsten assumed one to be a woman. The patrol team got into an easy conversation with Nevi about the scene, suggesting some amount of familiarity or at least comfort with her.

Continuous yelling came from a twentysomething man with a fluffy ball of neon green hair, wearing only loose purple briefs and grey socks. He berated the officers for being worthless, lazy, useless, and so on.

Kirsten stopped a few paces away and pondered inserting herself into the conversation with the living. The Div 1 officers hadn't noticed her yet, and Nevi appeared to have forgotten about her entirely. *Whatever. Finish the day and just mark the interdepartmental cooperation event finished.* She decided to remain where she stood and stare at the ghost until he sensed the weight of her looking directly at him.

The green-haired guy twisted to glare back at her, revealing Asian features. She couldn't tell by looking at him if he'd been born with that appearance or stopped by a Reinventions, not that it mattered much.

"They can't hear you." She waved him closer. "Come talk to me. I can help you."

The spirit rushed over, flailing his arms. "You can see me?"

"Yes. The other officers can't. Other people usually can't." Kirsten summoned her most comforting tone of voice. "I'm afraid you're dead. Being a spirit can take some getting used to, but you might not have to linger here."

"Oh, I do." He waved around frantically. "And yeah, I know I'm dead. I watched that son of a bitch kill me."

Kirsten blinked at him. "Oh, sorry. I saw you yelling at the cops and thought you might not understand why they weren't listening."

"I wasn't trying to talk to them. I was yelling at them for just standing there doing nothing." The ghost scowled. "They've been here for almost an hour. All they did was walk around my place, say 'yep, he's dead' and leave."

"They had to wait for a homicide detective." Kirsten activated her terminal screen and introduced herself. "Let's start with the basics. Who are you?"

"Jun Nakami, but almost no one calls me that. They just call me Aesir."

She tapped at the holo-panel floating above her left arm, entering notes. "Aesir? You're online a lot?"

"Yeah." Jun grumbled. "It's my character in Monwyn Online, Aesir188."

"All right. You know who killed you?"

"Asshole's name is Hiro Tanaka."

Kirsten typed it in, then tapped it to open a secondary window looking for the name in the system. "Any idea why?"

"Yeah. We were friends for a while, but the dickbag stole Amina from me... so we kinda ended up hating each other."

"Amina..." Kirsten glanced up from the panel screen at him. "Is that a name or something else?"

Jun folded his arms. "Name, yeah. My former girlfriend. Amina Kuro. She left me for Hiro a couple months ago."

"He killed you over the girl?"

"No. He was serious-pissed at me for winning a loot roll on the Bow of Embers. But that's just like the last thing that really pushed him over the edge. He's been harassing me for months, threatening me and shit." Jun paused. "Oh, sorry. It's a game… Monwyn Online. We were in the same raid team."

Kirsten gawked. "Are you serious? The Bow of Embers actually dropped? I've been trying to get that for months."

"You play?" Jun seemed ready to laugh.

"Yeah. When I can." Kirsten exhaled into a whistle. "So, you think this guy killed you over game loot? I mean… I know people take it seriously and all, but are you sure?"

Jun pointed out two exit wounds from bullets in his chest. "Do I look like I'm confused? He broke into my place middle of last night, screamed about the bow, and shot me in the back."

Kirsten bit her lip. *Sounds like this Hiro guy is upset about more than just the game. He's probably been jealous for much longer than he showed it.* "Do you know where he is now?"

"Yeah. He went home. He's probably in the game right now on his assassin, Chōrōki."

Kirsten scrunched her nose. "He plays as an assassin and he rolled on the Bow of Embers?"

"Seriously." Jun stared straight up for a long few seconds, heaving a great sigh before looking back down at her. "The guy's a total asshole. He only wanted it because I wanted it and it infuriated him that I won the roll anyway. Like it wasn't bad enough he set me up to lose Amina."

"Guy's got some serious issues with you."

Jun stared. "Do all cops love saying obvious things?"

"Yeah. It's in the rules." Kirsten sighed at her terminal screen. "Do you have any relatives or friends you'd like me to pass any messages or information to?"

"Umm." Jun gazed down. "My parents… I'd like if you could tell them I will miss them and I'm sorry for getting killed. Also, I'd love it if you can find Amina and convince her the girl she caught me kissing, I thought it was her."

"How?" Kirsten tilted her head.

"In the game. Hiro gave a bunch of gold to this other girl to pretend to be one of Amina's other characters. But when Amina logged on and caught us together, the bitch denied claiming to have been Amina's character. I thought I was fooling around with my girlfriend, not some other person."

Kirsten fought the urge to roll her eyes. The Monwyn Online game got close to feeling like reality even when she used a senshelmet. Someone jacked in directly via cyberware wouldn't be able to tell the difference between game and reality unless they witnessed obviously unrealistic things like magic, goblins, dragons, and so on. As stupid as it sounded on the surface to 'cheat' with a video game character, it probably did count given the extreme realism of cyberspace. If both people plugged in using M3 ports, the brain couldn't tell the difference between virtual sex and real sex.

Some GlobeNet sites even existed solely for the purpose of providing virtual sex services, including many options that would be considered illegal, unethical—or impossible in reality.

The thought sent a shiver down Kirsten's back. As depraved as some people could get in the real world, they went a hundred times worse online where they couldn't get in trouble for it... at least most of it. Beyond even sex, some of the darker sites allowed people to commit virtual murders or do other depraved acts to 'relieve stress.' While some people, even doctors, thought the outlet might defuse potentially unhinged psychopaths, Kirsten worried it only let them rehearse for the real thing.

"All right. Give me their contact info." She forced the bad thoughts out of her head.

Jun gave her the PIDs and physical addresses of not only his parents and former girlfriend, but of his killer, Hiro Tanaka.

"Okay. Wait here a moment." Kirsten gestured at the cluster of cops. "Since your death was not in any way associated with the paranormal or a psionic crime, I can't claim jurisdiction. She'll be handling it."

Jun scowled at the patrol officers. "They're just standing there. Where'd the woman go?"

"She's inside studying the crime scene." Kirsten tapped the button to close the holo-panel projected from her forearm guard. "Give me a few minutes to save her a few hours."

"Okay." Jun grabbed two fistfuls of his neon green hair and paced around. "Dammit! This sucks! I didn't even get to use the Bow of Embers."

Wow. He's dead and he's more upset that he can't play the game anymore. Never thought I'd run into anyone more obsessed with Monwyn than Evan. She cringed. *Please don't ever let him get this bad.* The worry passed as soon as it manifested. The boy she'd adopted was far too pragmatic to ever think a video game mattered more than reality.

Kirsten approached the apartment door. Jun trailed after her, still muttering about not getting a chance to use the bow.

The patrol officers eyed her warily. None appeared overtly afraid of her, merely tense. Their reaction might have come simply from her being a lieutenant. All three saluted her, confirming they feared Division 0's reputation.

She returned the salute. "We aren't all self-important prigs. I'm just out here trying to do the best I can, same as you guys."

One guy nodded. The other two kept staring.

Kirsten smiled despite feeling a bit of a pariah, and headed into the apartment.

It wouldn't take a forensics team long to go over the place, as it consisted of two rooms. The first room contained modular furniture and appliances allowing it to shift between bedroom, living room, and workstation area. The smaller, secondary room served as kitchen or bathroom depending on which way the wall panels rotated.

Jun's body slumped forward over a small desk against the left wall, a wire still connecting the M3 jack behind his right ear to a white cyberspace deck festooned with cute anime stickers and big red kanji. Someone left a bathrobe draped over him, concealing the bullet wounds in his back. Given the lack of holes in the robe, it must have been placed there by whoever found the body.

Nevi crouched beside him. A grid of blue laser lines crept over the dead man's skin, projected from her artificial eyes. "Oh, there you are. Thought you were going to sit this one out. Actual dead guy."

Kirsten walked over. "I know. Seen plenty of dead bodies before."

"Okay, hotshot." The blue grid pattern disappeared an instant before Nevi peered up at her. "What do you think happened here?"

"The deceased is Jun Nakami, known online as Aesir188. He was shot twice in the back by his former friend turned rival Hiro Tanaka last night between midnight and one in the morning. The two men had a dispute over a virtual item Jun acquired in an online game. Tanaka also evidently stole the deceased's girlfriend, a woman named Amina Kuro who might be able to offer some testimony about the nature of the relationship between the deceased and the killer."

Nevi's right eyebrow twitched. "You're messing with me. I don't know how you kept a straight face through all that... or fooled my soma."

"Your what?"

"Somatic response detection system." Nevi tapped the faint wire lines on the side of her head. "It constantly monitors pupil dilation, sweat response, facial emotion signals, breathing, and heart rate. The thing's telling me you aren't lying."

"Because I'm not." Kirsten gestured at the corpse. "If you lift the bathrobe off him, you'll find two entry wounds near the center of his back. My guess is class 1 or 2 ballistic handgun. The exit wounds in the chest are too small to be anything bigger. Slugs are probably embedded in the wall or somewhere in the next apartment."

"You seriously expect me to believe you got all that just from looking at the scene?" Nevi shook her head. "You haven't been in here yet, much less lifted the body to see any possible exit wounds."

"The victim's ghost is standing right next to me. I can clearly see his injuries. He told me what happened. Check the geo-ping logs for the NetMini belonging to Tanaka and it will show him being here at the time of the killing. Check the logs for Monwyn Online and you'll find at least a couple months of antagonistic private messages from Tanaka to Nakami's character. Look for exchanges between Chōrōki and Aesir188."

Nevi rubbed her forehead, groaning. "You're serious?"

"I am." Kirsten glanced at the ghost. "The spirit of the deceased is genuinely right beside me. He told me everything."

"Wow. If you guys can do this shit in twenty seconds, why do we even exist? It would have taken me weeks to even make my way through everything else in this guy's life before I even considered something as random and fucked up as a damn video game."

Kirsten sighed. "Yeah. I mean… it *was* the Bow of Embers."

Nevi stared at her as if she'd spoken Russian. "What the heck does that mean?"

"Whoa, really?" asked one of the Division 1 officers, poking his head in the door. "That damn thing like *never* drops. I can see someone getting angry enough to kill over it."

Jun screamed in frustration. "Kill my character, sure. But actually kill me? What the hell?"

"I agree," muttered Kirsten.

"Wow." Nevi pursed her lips.

"Oh." Kirsten scratched her eyebrow. "I wasn't agreeing with the officer. Jun's spirit said it's stupid to kill over video game loot."

"Right." Nevi gazed at the ceiling. "Still… if you're right, you just did in a couple minutes what would've taken me months. Why does Division 2 still even exist?"

"Because…" Kirsten closed her eyes and let out a labored sigh. "Judges don't believe in ghosts. The legal system does not admit psionic anything as evidence for an inquest. Also, not every ghost of a murder victim sticks around long enough to talk to. Another thing, and not that you care, astral sensitives like me are really damn rare. There are only three of us in the west that I know of. One's a child. One's a civilian completely uninterested in doing this job. So, that leaves me."

A distant, unfocused expression washed over Nevi.

"You okay?" asked Kirsten.

"Fine. Just entering notes. Oh, that's right. You type everything manually." Nevi put on a pair of sterile gloves, then gingerly lifted the bathrobe to peek under it. "Well, damn. Look at that. Two holes. Guess it's worth at least starting off with your info. Maybe it will save me a ton of work."

"Unless the ghost is lying to me." Kirsten shifted her gaze to Jun. "It will check out."

"Why would I lie?" asked Jun. "I'm already dead."

"Being dead is no guarantee of truth. Spirits can be mischievous. But... you feel sincere." Kirsten faced Nevi. "I'm reasonably sure Hiro Tanaka is the killer here. Sounds like a hot-headed idiot. I doubt he put much effort into concealing what he did. Acted in a rage."

"Right." Nevi examined the wall behind the desk. "Think you're right about class 2. Holes are pretty obvious."

"They are?" Kirsten raised an eyebrow.

"To me, they are. You'd think half a mil worth of electronic eyes would be good for something." Nevi leaned forward, projecting the blue grid from her eyes on the wall. "The slugs are in the floor of the next apartment. Shooter was standing. Victim was sitting. Yep. There they are. I can see them."

"Impressive." Kirsten raised both eyebrows at the imagery in the woman's surface thoughts. The detective saw a glowing blue wire-frame outline of a suspected shooter standing behind the desk. Other neon lines traced estimated bullet paths through the deceased into the next apartment.

"Jealous?"

"Nope. I don't want cyberware." Kirsten gazed at the rest of the apartment. "Shooter just walked in, shot him, and left. You won't find anything of interest anywhere else in here."

Nevi smiled at her—for the first time that morning. "Seems you are useful after all."

"Thanks." Kirsten smirked.

"You guys over in Zero *do* understand humor, right?" Nevi winked. "I'm trying to apologize for being a dick to you all morning."

"Oh. Sorry. Just... there's a somber energy here." Kirsten bowed her head.

"Yeah, I get it. Respect the dead and all. They can handle a bit of black humor. I respect the dead by finding the people who killed them." Nevi resumed examining the body. "If the ghost is here, tell him I'll get the guy."

"He can hear you."

"Thanks." Jun tried unsuccessfully to unplug the M3 wire from his body's head as his fingers had no substance. "Be nice if you can hurry it the hell up."

Kirsten almost smiled. "He's grateful for your help and a bit impatient."

"Late for an appointment?" asked Nevi without looking up.

"Something like that." Kirsten let a silent sigh slide out her nose. *Hope we aren't going to be standing around here all damn day.*

2

OFFLINE

Kirsten stood a little off to one side watching Nevi conduct her investigation, mostly trying to distract Jun from obsessing over his remains.

Eventually, the detective walked over and simply stared at her, close to expressionless except for a mild hint of nervous disbelief.

"Is something wrong?" asked Kirsten.

"Tech just got back to me. They confirmed Hiro Tanaka's NetMini was in this apartment last night around the time the victim would likely have died. They also found records in the PubTran system of his trip here and back home."

"Wow." Kirsten whistled.

"You're surprised what you told me appears to have been correct?" Nevi widened her eyes, making the electronic irises seem to glow brighter.

"No." Kirsten shook her head. "I'm stunned a guy would take a PubTran directly to the place he intended to kill someone. I mean... at least walk a couple blocks so there isn't a direct connection."

Nevi chuckled. "No doubt. Confirms your theory, the killer acted in a blind rage. Or he did it on purpose expecting to be caught and hoping to plea crime of passion."

"Ugh." Kirsten rubbed her forehead. "The judge is going to laugh in his face if he tries to claim that over a virtual item. So, umm, why are you staring at me like that?"

The detective glanced down at her hands as she removed her blue gloves. "I'm trying to process you pulling all that information out of nowhere and being accurate. Never really worked with a psionic before. Do all of you just know stuff?"

"Very few of us 'just know' things. Jun's spirit has been here the entire time."

"Damn." Nevi tossed the gloves into a waste receptacle. "They should have you guys doing these cases. It would have taken me a long time to get this close to done on my own the usual way. If you can solve every murder in five minutes, Zero could catch up our backlog."

Kirsten winced. "Sorry. It's not quite that easy. If you'd gotten a clairvoyant for a ridealong partner, they might have been able to see some things about the killing, but I'm pretty much the only person Zero has in West City who can talk to ghosts. And a ghost can only give me all the details of who killed them if they happen to still be around."

"Oh." Nevi gave a heavy sigh. "Well, thanks at least for making this one easy."

"I'm sure you'd have found the killer pretty fast. He took his NetMini into the room."

The detective chuckled. "You're right. I should waste fewer brain cells on being annoyed and more on the case."

"Sorry," said Kirsten in a voice barely over a whisper.

"For what?"

"Annoying you."

"It's not you personally." Nevi swiped a hand through the red half of her hair. "I'm annoyed at the backlog of cases, not having a permanent partner, Command throwing this interdepartmental cooperation crap at me like it's actually good for anything."

"Oh, well..." Kirsten smiled. "This case did go faster with me here."

Nevi laughed. "Yeah, but you know how it works. I'm gonna go back to doing what I did before. You're going to go back to do the same thing you did before. I don't see the point of these one-day things except as a PR stunt."

"Can't be a PR stunt." Kirsten overacted looking around. "There aren't any cameras following us. Probably an internal morale building exercise."

"Heh. Yeah, you're probably right." Nevi raised an eyebrow. "Is it working?"

"Is what working?"

"Do you feel the morale improving?" deadpanned Nevi.

"Oh." Kirsten chuckled. "A little. Much more now than this morning."

A tech approached. "Excuse me, detective."

Nevi faced him. "What's up?"

"We're done here. Deceased is on the way to the RTC. Building manager wants to know if he can clear the place out or if we still need it."

"What's gonna happen to my stuff?" asked Jun.

Kirsten glanced at him. "You're worried about your stuff?"

"Not like that. Just don't want that jerk to steal it and make money off me. My parents should get it."

She nodded at him, then looked at the tech. "What's going to happen to the deceased's possessions?"

"Well…" The tech poked a few buttons on his tablet. "The manager is probably going to post the required notice in a small GlobeNet site no one will ever find, then sell off everything here in forty-eight hours when no one claims the stuff."

"Keep the apartment a secure scene for twenty-four hours." Kirsten frowned. "I'll notify the family."

Nevi raised both eyebrows. "You guys still do notifications?"

"You *don't*?" Kirsten gawked.

"By the time we get in contact with the next-of-kin, they've already gotten a hundred notifications from adbots trying to sell funerary services, or the decedent's NetMini sensing death and alerting anyone in the contact list who had frequent communication. We have so much to do, we ended up just letting the system deal with the notifications. Been like that for at least fifty years now."

Kirsten exhaled. "Oof. No wonder there are so many angry spirits around here. I'd be pretty pissed off if my family heard about my death because an advert bot showed up trying to sell them a spot for my urn."

"Got it. Twenty-four hours, lieutenant." The tech saluted her and walked off.

"We're done here," said Nevi. "Hungry yet? Lunch?"

"Sure." Kirsten started for the exit.

"You're going to eat?" Jun wandered along beside her. "Just leaving?"

"There isn't much else we can do right this second. It will take a little while for a judge to review the inquest notes and issue an arrest warrant. Relax, it won't be long."

The ghost sighed, but gave a reluctant nod.

Nevi led the way down the corridor back toward the elevator chamber. After rounding the corner at the T junction, Kirsten found herself drawn to stop and stare to the right down another hallway. An inexplicable urge pulled at her to go that way instead of straight, as if some external force called out to her.

Nevi kept walking for a few steps before turning to peer back at her. "What?"

"Need a minute." Kirsten headed to her right. "Feel something strange coming from this direction."

"Psionic stuff?" Nevi followed, keeping a few steps back.

"I think so." She projected mental energy forward in a telepathic sweep, searching for any possible source of her sudden desire to go down the hallway. Thirty or more living minds existed within her range, though not one of them resonated with the temptation to investigate this part of the building.

"Does crap like this happen to you often?" whispered Nevi. "Like a psionic hunch something bad's going down?"

"This feeling? No. Not really. Usually, it's hanging dread or sorrow." Kirsten paused to probe the area using Astral Sense. "This is not evil or dreadful or sad. It's more like... I dunno. As if something paranormal drew a picture and really wanted people to see it."

"A ghost?"

"Maybe." Kirsten resumed following the urge, creeping past apartments on both sides.

Here and there, sounds came from inside the dwellings: movies, music, the whirr of cleaning bots, and the occasional voice. All of it created an overwhelmingly normal ambiance for a residence tower straddling the upper end of poor and the bottom end of middle class.

The inclination led Kirsten to another T junction and left. As if going home, she instinctually selected the fourth door on the right side. However, she did not live in this building, nor was her apartment the fourth door in the hallway. Within seconds of her coming to a stop in front of apartment 14-49, the strange pull ceased. In its absence, a noticeable heaviness rolled into her awareness. Something felt *wrong* about this place.

She swiped her hand at the silver panel, activating the doorbell.

"Lieutenant?" asked Nevi. "Wanna clue me in on what's going on here?"

"As soon as I know." Kirsten buzzed again. "A sudden desire to go down a hallway to a specific door has never happened to me before. Feels like there's something not right."

"No one's home," says Nevi. "We should have at least gotten a 'fuck off' by now."

"Ugh." Kirsten fidgeted.

"What's wrong?"

"Getting an unexplained, possibly psionic pull to this door is a bit flimsy to use as justification for overriding my way into a random apartment."

Nevi chuckled. "I didn't think they let psionic abilities count for anything legal."

"Zero has *some* leeway. If I was chasing a phantom and they ducked in there to get away from me, I could barge in." Kirsten looked at Jun. "Hey, would you mind going in there and looking around? If you see anything strange, don't go near it."

"Umm, sure." Jun shrugged and walked through the door.

"You weren't talking to me, were you?" asked Nevi. "I could say we heard a strange noise inside, thought the occupant might be in medical distress. As long as there's no damage, no one gives a shit."

Kirsten squirmed. Sure, Division 1 often played kinda loose with the regs. It seemed wrong to do, but sometimes rules *did* need to be bent. An officer doing 700 MPH in a patrol craft to get home from their shift faster was wrong in any case. Cutting corners on regs to investigate a potentially suspicious apartment? Maybe not so bad. Still a possible invasion of privacy.

Jun phased back into the hallway. "There's a dead body in there."

"Shit," whispered Kirsten.

"Uh oh." Nevi whistled. "What happened? If you're using bad language, it must be serious."

"I'm not one of those people who gets all upset over harsh words." Kirsten tapped her forearm guard to access the terminal. "I just try to be professional. There's a dead body in this apartment."

Nevi whistled. "Wow. You're a regular ghost radar. This guy here, too?"

Jun shook his head.

"No. Just remains." Kirsten accessed the building's network and used the police override on the lock.

The door slid to the left with a faint *shht* noise. Fog hung low to the carpet in the room beyond, another multifunction area presently configured with a sofa and large holo-bar for movies.

"Damn," muttered Nevi. "It's twenty-nine degrees in there. I didn't think these environmental control units could swing that."

"Meat in a freezer," said Kirsten, her voice more sigh than anything.

She steeled herself for the cold and walked into the shin-high fog. Unlike Jun's apartment, this one was luxurious with *three* rooms. Two interior doors in the back left and back right corner led to a combination kitchen/bathroom and a small bedroom. From one step inside the door, Kirsten had a clear line of sight on the form of a dead body slumped on the floor beside a desk in the bedroom.

"What are the odds of another guy shot at his terminal?" Nevi shifted her jaw side to side. "You are lucky I care about my reputation."

"Why's that?" Kirsten glanced briefly at her before gazing down at the holo-panel floating over her left arm. She pulled up the apartment's record.

"Because. Half the detectives in my unit would've said 'you found it, you deal with it' and walked out. Unless you tell me this is some psionic shit, it's probably my jurisdiction."

Kirsten smiled, tapping at the electronic menu. "I'm not going to stick you with it and bail."

The system named the present registered occupant of the apartment as Novar Kell, male, age twenty-seven. She cross-checked his PID with the NPF system to bring up his records. The face of a young man with bright violet hair, ice blue eyes, and a light brown complexion appeared in the top left corner of the holo-panel. According to the police database, Novar Kell had a *long* list of criminal charges for GlobeNet trespass. Nothing looked to be more serious than 'slap on the wrist' fines and access restrictions ranging from three to six months. Seems the guy liked exploring parts of cyberspace he didn't belong in, but either had no intention to steal anything valuable or cause damage—or lacked the ability to do so before being caught.

A small sub-window opened showing an active wanted warrant for him in regard to illegal network activities associated to the persona 'DemonCore.'

Kirsten looked up from her holo-panel at the dead guy.

Violet hair.

"I think this is the guy who rents this apartment."

Nevi glanced at the holo-panel, then the corpse. "Don't be so sure. If this guy is trying to fake his own death or someone else is trying to 'make him disappear,' we could be looking at a convincing double. Grab some random patsy, Reinventions them into the fugitive, then blam."

Kirsten blinked. "Are you serious? People do that?"

"Yeah. Though... unless this guy was involved in some serious shit we never found out about, it wouldn't make sense for him to do anything that elaborate." Nevi approached the bedroom, pulling on another pair of sterile gloves. "His record doesn't look bad enough for the 'forces of evil' to spend that much money on making him vanish."

"Yeah." Kirsten paged over the dead man's police records. "All minor things... but so many."

"Oh, ick. This guy..." Nevi leaned over the corpse, evidently studying the face. "This poor bastard should have gone for a ride on the TDC."

"The what?" Kirsten approached the doorway between multifunction room and the bedroom, peering in at an area about the size of an average prison cell, barely large enough to contain a single-person bed, a tiny desk, and a half-size wardrobe cabinet. "Did you say TDC?"

"Not much of a nethead I guess." Nevi laughed. "Of course not. You don't have a jack. TDC is what we call the 'Technicolor Death Coaster.'"

"I don't know what that means." Kirsten decided the bedroom had no obvious clues and walked back over to the detective.

Nevi picked up a thin black cable from the desk, tracing her fingers along it to a metal plug embedded in the dead man's skin behind his left ear. "You are aware that the M3 jack allows for a high-speed data link between devices like decks and the human neural system. It's basically like you are really in another world."

"Yeah. I know the theory, but I've only ever used helmets."

"Right. Well, *really* going online is pretty much impossible to tell apart from reality. There's a fairly specific logout process people need to follow to allow their brain enough time to adequately adjust to changing worlds. If someone rips the wire out of your head before you're ready for it, it's like you're flying face-first down the puke-o-tron 9000. It's a rainbow-colored spiral tunnel of terror and disorientation."

"It can kill?" Kirsten gasped, involuntarily clamping a hand on her head where a jack would be.

"In some cases. Not usually, but it's been known to happen." Nevi pointed. "I said this guy *should* have taken the death coaster. He didn't yank the wire. It's still plugged in. Look at the burns. Someone killed him."

Kirsten leaned closer. Blackened burn marks traced a Lichtenberg pattern on the side of his neck, spreading outward from his ear. Dried blood pooled under his face, evidently having streamed out of his nostrils. Spatter patterns on the desk surface suggested some manner of explosive discharge of bloody phlegm.

"Damn, girl. Do you just sense dead people?" Nevi exhaled. "Hope not. You're in the damn wrong city for an ability like that."

"Sometimes, I do but…" She peered back over her shoulder at Jun. The spirit waited by the door out of the apartment, arms folded, tapping his foot. "This man's ghost isn't here. But… I think he wanted to be found. Or… something wanted me to find him."

Nevi examined the body for a few minutes before standing and taking a step back. "My guess is he's been here like this for a week or two. This apartment's basically a freezer. He probably got into a bigger dick contest in cyberspace and lost. Whoever fried his brain got into the apartment and set the environmental controls to ice planet."

Kirsten nodded. "Wanted time before anyone found the guy."

"Lucky day for you, lieutenant. You're off the hook for this one."

"I'm with you for another three hours." Kirsten held her arms up to either side, then let them fall. "I'll help as much as I can."

3

SELF-SORTING PROBLEMS

S oft thrumming and the rhythmic clicking of dishes jostling around came from a sleek, black cabinet under the kitchen counter. Kirsten found herself mesmerized by the sound, staring at the silver block-letter TMC logo in the upper right corner of the machine. She'd often thought of the dishwasher as a metaphor. Inside, a violent storm of hypersonic waves, detergent, thrashing water, and heat. Outside, a barely audible electronic noise and complete calm.

The dishwasher represented society.

We're all living our own chaotic messes and pretending it's all just fine. On an individual level, everyone panicked almost all the time. Outwardly, society appeared to be in control.

She gazed down past her plain white shirt and sweat pants at her bare toes, not quite able to believe the moment. So normal. Doing dishes after dinner in a real home with a real family. Kirsten found herself thinking back to the first week she'd known Nicole Logan. They'd met in the dorms roughly nine months after Kirsten had been picked up off the street. Most of that time tended to blur in her memory. She couldn't recall if they'd been twelve or thirteen then. Likely thirteen. All she remembered for sure was they'd been the same age. Nicole's birthday followed Kirsten's by two months. September fourth for Kirsten, December eleventh for Nicole.

When they met, Kirsten hadn't even known people celebrated birthdays.

Staring down at her toes reminded her of Nicole teaching her about nail coloring. Nine years later, Kirsten still mostly thought of it as pointless. She questioned if it meant something in her brain was broken. Nail polish, earrings, perfume, fancy hair styles… none of it stirred the least bit of interest. Nicole loved it, so Kirsten had put up with it. She'd tolerate her friend painting her nails and doing stuff to her hair, but she'd not bother to do it herself.

Her thoughts drifted to Evan and his friends from school. Willow, the pyrokinetic girl, had gotten a hold of a Nanochroma wand. All the kids spent the rest of the day sporting wild nail colors. Kirsten still didn't quite understand why her father's ghost thought it so strange for the boys to wear nail coloration. Considering some people out there got cybernetic cat ears and tails, then walked around naked… a boy with blue fingernails hardly seemed shocking.

The dishwasher noise intensified. Its hypersonic system made the hairs on the back of her neck stand up. She couldn't consciously perceive the sound as an audible tone, more of a presence in the room. Out of habit, she looked around expecting to see a ghost. Being six feet away from the dishwasher when it cycled felt rather like having a spirit sneak up behind her.

"Gotcha, stupid goblin!" yelled Evan from the living room before cracking up into laughter.

His voice made her smile. Hearing him happy, safe and enamored with the Monwyn video game made her life thus far all worth it. Everything she'd been through molded her into the person she'd become and the path she'd taken. It did no good to think about where she'd have gone if her awful mother hadn't been insane or if her parents had simply abandoned her like so many parents of psionic children do. That would still have ended up with her part of Division 0, only without the years of abuse and living on the street. What if her parents hadn't cared at all about the psionic stuff and took it in stride?

Kirsten closed her eyes. *No. Stop. Don't fantasize about a happy family that wasn't. I have one now.*

She let the sadness flow out of her, then leaned on the counter to gaze out the small window over the sink at the endless expanse of near-identical century towers. Being on the 41st floor didn't give her much to look at. The seemingly endless grid of plastisteel monoliths blocked most of the world from view, making her feel like a flea clinging midway down the bristle of a hairbrush.

Spots of glowing light in every shade whizzed back and forth, a cloud of busy flying robots stretching from ground level up to the hundredth-and-past story. If she let her eyes lose focus, the frenetic machines blurred to a spectacle like fairy dust twinkling around gargantuan silver obelisks. Humanity surrounded itself with buzzing, blinking, relentless chaos.

Are we suffocating ourselves?

The room's energy shifted again, a sensation as though she didn't stand there alone weighed on her consciousness. Kirsten dismissed it as coming from the hypersonic emitter in the dishwasher and continued watching bots float around.

Evan laughed again at something in the video game.

Why am I just standing here?

Smiling at the thought of spending time with him, Kirsten turned to leave the kitchen... and jumped back with a yelp at the sight of a partially decapitated man standing next to her. She almost landed seated on the countertop, clutching her chest. Two breaths later, she scowled off to one side at being startled. She had, in fact, sensed the spirit manifesting—but mistook it for the weird vibes coming from the TMC-210.

Stupid dishwasher.

The man *had* to be a ghost. Even though to her, he looked perfectly solid and real, people didn't continue to move around as if alive with a significant portion of their head missing. It appeared as if he'd been shot below the left eye by a weapon powerful enough to blow out the back of his skull. A few wobbly lumps of brain matter remained, clearly visible as if set in a bowl, though the vast majority had disintegrated. His already somewhat dark skin appeared nearly charcoal black over most of his face, no doubt burned by the muzzle flare of a near point blank shot. Brittle bone and skin around the right eye somehow managed to stand like a wall in front of the emptiness behind it. A patch of semi-curly black hair attached to a bit of scalp dangled beside his head like a dislodged toupee.

Kirsten grimaced mentally. *At least he didn't feel anything.*

He flailed his arms at her like a castaway attempting to signal a passing aircraft.

"Yes, I can see you. Try to calm down. If you talk, I can hear you as well."

He gurgled.

"Don't think about your injury. Just try to talk as if nothing happened."

The man jab-pointed emphatically at the wall.

"Hey, Mom, I think there's... ack!" Evan stopped short in the doorway connecting the kitchen to the hall. The boy's eyes both glowed bright blue-white, so bright they looked like mini tactical flashlights. He made a face of horrified disgust at the ghost, though appeared to handle the gory sight with far more poise than most would expect from a ten-year-old. After a few seconds, he averted his stare off to one side.

"Ev?" asked Kirsten.

"I felt a ghost in here. But... you found him."

The spirit appeared to be wearing a fairly expensive black suit. Thin strands of glowing teal highlighted the lapels, sleeve ends, and buttons. Another bullet hole in the man's chest appeared roughly large enough for her thumb to fit inside.

He hasn't figured out how to talk yet. Must be quite new.

"Yes, I will help you. Just... try to calm down and talk." Kirsten stepped closer to the spirit, peering up at him. For once, being short proved useful. Since the top of her head barely came up to his chin, she couldn't see into his open brain cavity at this distance. His frantic emotional state might simply be from the shock of death, though she suspected something more urgent than simply bringing killers to justice drove him. "Did you die recently?"

He nodded, still jabbing his finger at the wall.

"There is someone else in danger?"

Relief spread over his features.

"His kids," blurted Evan.

Kirsten glanced at the boy.

"I feel it. He's not dangerous." Evan, still not looking up at the man's face, scurried over to stand beside her. "He's freaking out because he thinks the people who killed him are going to get his kids, too."

Kirsten's heart sank. "Dammit. Okay." She ran out of the kitchen to her bedroom.

Despite Evan and the spirit following, she didn't hesitate to change into her uniform, the only thought on her mind some kids out there somewhere might have minutes left to live.

"Riani. Theo," said the ghost.

Kirsten swung her utility belt around her waist and secured it. "Your kids?"

The ghost nodded. "Talking. Strange it works."

"You are a spirit now. The rules are different." Kirsten jumped into her boots and secured the fasteners. "Where are your kids? What happened?"

"Driving. I was… hovercar." The ghost pointed at the wall. "Shot us. Crash-landed. Bad place. Off map."

Kirsten looked up from her boots at him. "You were flying with kids in the car near a black zone?"

"I…" He let out a long, slow sigh. "Yes."

Evan hooked his thumbs in the waistband of his pajama pants. "You're gonna want me to stay here and not go with you."

"Absolutely." Kirsten pulled him into a brief, but firm hug. "Need you to stay safe."

"I'll go to Shani's." Evan jogged out of the room.

"Six," said the ghost. "Nine. Five, five."

"What?" Kirsten blinked.

"Sector."

She waved for the spirit to follow and rushed to the living room.

Evan stood beside the couch, fiddling at his NetMini. Behind him, the screen remained paused in the midst of a battle in the Monwyn game. The boy looked up at her. "I don't think they're home."

Where would Nila go at this hour? It's almost nine. Well, okay, that's not too late. "Umm...." She bit her lip. Neither leaving him here alone nor bringing him along to a black zone seemed at all smart. However, trusting the boy alone for a short while would be significantly safer than taking him anywhere near a disavowed sector. The thought of two innocent—and likely sheltered—children stuck in such a place got her shaking with anxiety. Their father had an expensive suit and owned a hovercar. Good chance the kids had a relatively easy life up until tonight.

Kirsten's father materialized beside the sofa. "Dear, I could keep an eye on him if you need to rush out."

"Oh, cool." Evan smiled up at 'grandpa.'

"Umm." Kirsten rubbed a hand down her face. "I trust you both, but... Dad, you're a ghost. Legally, he'd still be alone."

"Dear, people leave boys his age home with AIs these days." Her father stuffed his hands in his pants pockets. "Is that much different from a spirit? As long as the boy listens to me, we'll be fine."

"Swear." Evan raised his hand as if in court. "I don't want Mom to get in trouble."

"Raj," said the ghost.

"What?" blurted Evan and Kirsten simultaneously.

"My name is Raj."

"Oof." Dad cringed. "That headache looks a bit too intense for a Narcoderm."

Kirsten stared at her father, shocked and appalled he'd make a joke like that. "There isn't enough time to debate this." She squeeze-hugged Evan. "Listen to Dad until I get back. If anything happens, call."

"Okay." Evan nodded. "Love you."

"I love you too." She ruffled his hair. *I am totally screwing up this mom thing, aren't I?* She glanced at Raj. "Come on. Lead me to your kids."

The ghost began to zoom toward the outer wall.

"No," yelled Kirsten. "I can't fly without a car. Follow me to the roof."

Evan clamped a hand over his mouth to stop himself from laughing.

"Oh. Yes." Raj zipped back to her. "Forgive me. I am worried. My children are in great danger."

Kirsten rushed out of the apartment and down the hall to the elevator. The doors closed a second before Raj reached it, though he phased through them.

"What the hell were you doing near Sector 6955 with kids?"

"I didn't bring them there deliberately." Raj kneaded his hands. "They were with me at the office today."

"You routinely drive past a dangerous sector on your way home from work?" She gawked. "No one in their right mind operates a hovercar within five miles of disavowed sectors."

"No, not usually." The ghost looked away.

The elevator reached the roof parking area.

Kirsten fast-walked toward her patrol craft, obvious in its armored bulk among the civilian vehicles. "You realize you're dead, right?"

"Yes. I have noticed." Raj jogged to keep up with her.

"If you were doing something illegal, it doesn't matter now. It's not like you're going to be arrested for it."

Dorian manifested beside the PC when she grabbed the door handle, giving her a quizzical look. "How bad?"

"Bad." Kirsten jumped in and began the power-up sequence. "Hopefully, it won't be extremely bad."

Raj glanced at Dorian, blinked his one remaining eye in bewilderment, then phased through the hull of the patrol craft into the back seat. "You are right. I should have refused or rescheduled. The boss was demanding."

Kirsten hit the button for emergency activation, forcing the hovercar to go from a powered-down state to flight ready in mere seconds compared to the usual thirty. It lurched into the air in a moderately controlled climb. Being rough on the ion thrusters would shorten their operational lifespan, but car parts could be replaced. Kids, not so much.

"Fill me in on the details." Dorian shifted in the passenger seat to look at both Raj and Kirsten.

"I was sent to meet some thugs. The company wished to hire them to cause problems for a rival company."

She shook her head. "I don't advocate corporate violence, but it sounds like your place was trying to skimp and go cheap... hiring thugs from a black zone?"

"At least have the class to work with *professional* mercenaries." Dorian rolled his eyes, feigning disgust.

"Essentially," muttered Raj. "It developed last minute. I was told to make contact with them, drop off payment, and leave. It should only have taken a minute. They promised our liaison would be safe."

"Right." Dorian shook his head.

"They did not do this. As you might have guessed by most of my head missing, they were not concerned with my safety." Raj pointed ahead to the right. "That way."

"Yeah. I'm aiming to fly around the spot." Kirsten pointed at the Navcon screen. Sector 6955 formed the northwestern corner of a roughly three-sector large disavowed area. "I don't want to pass over six miles of disavowed area to get there. This thing is armored, but a lucky hit could still take out a thruster."

"Oh. That is wise." Raj looked down. "Please hurry. I do not hear them screaming anymore."

Kirsten accelerated without even thinking about it. New spirits could often hear the sounds of the environment around their corpse for several hours after death.

"Hear who screaming?" asked Dorian.

"My son and daughter." Raj struggled to avoid breaking down in sobs. "They were calling for me, but they are not making noise anymore."

Soon, Kirsten swerved into a hard right turn, passing over the grey zones surrounding the disavowed area. She cruised in over Sector 7007, which sat directly north of 6955. It never ceased to mystify her how the city personified the term 'grey zone' or 'black zone.' Something about the blight associated with abandoned areas made them appear scorched and black from the air. Adjacent areas darkened to a dull grey compared to the shiny plastisteel silver of well-maintained sectors. Despite the term 'black zone' originating from the Navcon system, reality often took it literally.

From 400 feet off the ground, the area below resembled the charred ruins left in the wake of a long-ago war. Twisted, crumbling building frames clawed at the sky. Heaps of debris and rubble filled streets impassable to ground vehicles. Here and there, fires burned wherever off-gridders dared to settle amid the ruin. It worked out to be almost paradoxical. Violent gangs, wanted criminals, and psychopaths often flocked to the black zones thinking it would keep them safe from the police and prison. Yet, life in those areas could be much worse than prison... and those inside them would fight to the death to stay there.

They've become their own jailors.

Kirsten swooped in low, flying only twenty feet over the road surface. This deep in a grey area, few operational cars moved around, the streets carried only people and debris. A mixture of gang members, fringers, and those without the resources to flee a declining area milled around, all clad in grungy clothing as well as desperation. Most paused to watch her go by. Those directly beneath either shielded their eyes or scurried out of the ionic downblast. A light peppering of small arms fire bounced off the armor plates. Locals either amused themselves with target practice or showed their contempt for the police. They got away with it mostly because no lone patrol unit would dare stop and get out to chase them down.

She followed the path of the street as Raj pointed, scanning for any signs of a crashed hovercar. It wouldn't be too close. She'd likely have to cross into the actual black zone before reaching the wreck. This, of course, meant they would start taking more intense incoming fire at some point—worse than handguns wholly incapable of damaging the armor. Almost everyone who willingly dwelled in these places thought nothing of shooting at random people, especially the police. They regarded the presence of any flying object as a dare to hit it, regardless of whether or not it happened to be a car with live people inside, a delivery bot, or an advert orb.

The patrol craft's systems picked up a signal originating from 1.4 miles ahead.

"I think we're getting an automated distress beacon," said Kirsten. "Wow. I didn't think civilian hovercars had those."

"They don't... at least not stock." Dorian stuck his hand into the console, staring into nowhere for a few seconds. "It isn't a distress signal. However, I do believe it's the car we're looking for."

"What is it?" Anxious almost to the point of nausea over two children being in mortal danger, Kirsten clutched the control sticks tighter, keeping her attention glues to the plastisteel canyon walls on either side as well as the rubble piles in the road she might crash into. More and more windows appeared to be missing from the high-rises the closer they got to the border of Sector 6955.

"The car is attempting to notify the insurance provider of the crash." Dorian glanced back at Raj. "It's still transmitting, so it likely hasn't established a connection."

"Bastards," muttered Raj. "I'd get a notice about my premiums going up before the Medvan arrived."

Dorian faced forward in his seat. "Medvans won't go to where you crashed. Not even police will unless they mobilize an entire Division 6 strike team."

"But..." Raj pointed at Kirsten.

"She's special." Dorian pursed his lips. "And she's extremely protective of kids."

Kirsten let go of the right-hand stick long enough to tap the screen and set a navigation point for the origin of the transmission. "I'm not leaving children out here. Cops are afraid of two things in black zones: giant cyborgs and psychos with more guns than sense. I can deal with borgs and I have an advantage they don't when it comes to the other thing."

"Oh?" Dorian glanced at her. "Which advantage is that? Cuteness doesn't work out here."

She smirked at him. "Unlike Div 1, I'm not too proud to hide and sneak around. I'm also not planning to stay here long. Just in and out quick."

Dorian snickered.

"Dare I ask what you find funny about this?" She narrowed her eyes.

"A quick in and out usually leads to children," muttered Dorian.

"You are awful." She shook her head.

The number of people in the street rapidly thinned out over several blocks. Soon, it felt as though she cruised into the site of an ancient apocalyptic war. Beyond simple missing windows, the buildings here existed in various states of destruction. Some had collapsed to skeletons of plastisteel girders. Occasional shadows near the ground darted off, no doubt crazed locals spotting a hovercar and running to hide or grab a bigger weapon.

Forty seconds later, the surprisingly intact wreck of a Halcyon-Ormyr Excelsior came into view. The vehicle lay partially embedded in a pile of debris near the corner of an intersection. While expensive, the civilian hovercar did not have any armor plating. Its ground tires remained tucked up into the wheel wells. The left-rear thruster produced a column of dense, black smoke. Dozens of bullet holes riddled the driver's side from front to back. Both doors hung open, revealing an empty interior. Raj's physical remains lay on his back in the middle of the road about twenty feet away. A massive gory bloom stretching upward and outward from his head made it look as if a giant stomped on his head.

No sign of anyone in the area, neither gang thugs nor children.

Kirsten extended the patrol craft's wheels and set down on the closest patch of flat road surface to the wreck.

Raj phased through the door and began shouting, "Riani! Theo!"

"They can't hear you." Kirsten shoved the door upward and hopped out, drawing her E-90. As much as the idea of killing people made her squirm, two children's lives depended on her ability not to hesitate. If she had to end the life of a murderous psychopath to protect an innocent, so be it.

Within seconds of her getting out of the car, faces began appearing in the shadowy gaps of ruined buildings. The few she could see with any clarity past the darkness, grime, or tattered hoods seemed apprehensive. For the moment, none did more than observe her from a distance. No doubt they'd seen a single, smallish woman and become interested… yet they only watched.

"Strange," she whispered. "Not expecting them to just sit there."

"They're confused." Dorian turned in place, surveying the area. "Can't tell if they should be afraid of you for being Div 0, want to attack you for being a cop, want to attack you for being a woman... or they're trying to figure out if you're a kid."

She winced at the memory of something a Division 1 officer said months ago in response to her naïve assumption that gang members wouldn't harm children. The guy, who'd obviously been as cynical as it gets, commented to the effect of 'black zone gangers love kids. Small targets are worth bonus points.'

"Raj, can you feel where they are?" asked Kirsten.

"I..." The spirit whirled around. "No... there is a wall of... something surrounding the intersection. Fog? Smoke?"

"You shouldn't stay here much longer." Dorian nudged him. "It's easy for us to end up being trapped at the scene of our death. I spent years basically tethered to my car. Took a lot of work to break out of that. You're surrendering to futility and guilt. Unless you want to spend the rest of eternity wandering around this intersection, you need to slam shift your mental state."

Kirsten decided to scan the surface thoughts of anyone close enough. For the most part, they recognized her as 'one of those psionic cops' thanks to the black car and black uniform... and didn't dare start shit with her. Normally, people being mindlessly afraid of psionics due to ignorance would have bothered her, but here, she welcomed it. If it stopped her from having to shoot them, it didn't matter what they thought of her.

In one man's thoughts, she picked up on a recent memory of watching a pack of augs chase two children away from the wreck down the street to the right. She dropped her mental link and spun to face that direction. The instant she recognized the street from what she saw in his memory, she sprinted.

"Grr."

"What's wrong?" asked Dorian, easily keeping pace beside her. "Besides the obvious."

"Just angry all over again that the government allows disavowed sectors to exist."

Dorian nodded. "They consider the gangs a self-fixing problem.

Just mix in a whole bunch of weapons and the undesirables get rid of each other."

"Innocent people get caught up in it." She growled again.

"Population control," deadpanned Dorian. "As long as no one wealthy or important gets hurt, they don't care."

She gawked at him.

"I'm not agreeing with it. That's how the senators think. West City is crammed past capacity. There are too many people living in too little space." Dorian frowned. "A small percentage of productive, law-abiding citizens happening to lose their lives in the process of the unwanted getting rid of each other is an acceptable degree of collateral damage to them."

"It can't be that bad. How can anyone be so cruel?"

Dorian opened his mouth, but closed it without speaking.

She grumbled. "I know. You don't have to say it. Look at my mother."

He bit his lip.

"Gonna rip your heads off!" shouted a bass voice, fringed with electronic modulation.

Two children screamed in fear.

The yelling came from the blown-out lobby level of a collapsing century tower up ahead on the left.

Dammit! Kirsten sprinted toward the building. A gunshot went off inside, followed by a much deeper *boom*. She skidded to a halt beside the remains of a doorway, shoulder to the filthy plastisteel wall. Whimpering echoed in the cavernous space beyond. A deep human growl, distorted in a digitized-electronic warp followed. Other voices muttered a mixture of swears, threats, and incoherent babble.

One... two...

Kirsten gripped her E-90 in both hands, then swiveled around the wall, aiming into the building.

The ground floor consisted of one huge open space, the interior walls once dividing it into multiple rooms having crumbled to debris years ago. Thick thermacrete support columns stood in a grid throughout the area, covered in graffiti, bullet gouges, bloodstains, and unidentifiable muck. Trash and rubble gathered in dune piles around old furniture and appliances. Here and there, dark electrical cables hung from the decrepit ceiling.

Her attention went straight to a massive humanoid figure standing by the corner on the far end of the room. He hunched forward, seemingly in order to avoid ramming his head into what remained of the ceiling. Arms far too large to be real extended out from beneath curved metal shoulder plates that made him look like an up-sized version of a pro Gee-ball player. Kirsten couldn't tell if he wore olive drab military style armor over the rest of him or if the armor plating *was* his body. Considering his size, she likely found herself staring at either a combat android or a human brain in an otherwise mechanical beast. His face consisted of an almost-human visage, but lacked a lower jaw. Reddish, scabbed, decaying skin gave him the look of a zombie, made worse by glowing red eyes.

Behind him, two children cowered in the corner against bare grey thermacrete. A girl about Evan's age clung protectively to a boy a few years younger than her. Both had black hair and dark faces, like Raj.

Closer to Kirsten, facing the huge cyberganger, stood five other men fanned out in an arc. All sported multiple cybernetic implants in a haphazard fashion, as if they gradually replaced pieces lost to continuous fighting. Unlike the big guy, none of them had opted for grotesquely inhuman modifications. A sixth guy—now little more than a torso and legs, lay dead on the ground. From the stomach up, his body ceased to exist. The cause of such a detonation appeared to be mounted to the giant's right forearm: a weapon barrel significantly larger than a class 6—the largest available—combat rifles.

Shit, that's gotta be a 35-mil cannon.

The huge metal monster seemed to be putting himself between the cybergangers and the children in much the same manner as a lion defending its kill from other predators.

"Wow. That guy looks fun," said Dorian.

"Ugh."

"I'm being serious." Dorian smiled. "He's full of electricity. Shouldn't be too difficult for me to take control of his body... or at least hold him still."

Kirsten didn't see a way to effectively sneak past the imminent fight to whisk the kids away while the monstrosity had his hands full fighting the normal-sized gangers. The beast penned the children into the corner in such a way as no one could get close to them without being easily within reach of his enormous mechanical arms. The relief of finding the kids still alive drowned in a sea of apprehension. If she shot the big guy, the other cybergangers would be a major problem. Even if she survived a five-on-one fight, she wouldn't be able to stop one of them if he grabbed the kids and ran while she still had four other idiots trying to kill—or capture—her. If she opened fire on the normal-sized thugs, the big guy might use the distraction she offered to finish off what he wanted to do to the children.

Dorian's idea had merit too—*if* he could figure out how to take control of the electronics fast enough before the situation got out of control. She knew he could scramble the electronics, but having a thousand-pound cyborg involuntarily slam dancing so close to kids would not be wise. More reliably, she could disable the big guy with a Suggestion or a Mind Blast so he didn't appear obviously dead. That might distract the smaller gangers enough to give the kids a reasonable chance of walking away from this moment intact. Of course, this plan required the big guy to have a living brain. If she faced an AI-driven combat unit, she'd be in serious trouble if Dorian couldn't power him down or take over.

Raj ran to his kids, yelling their names and trying to shield them with his noncorporeal body. Neither the children nor any of the gang members reacted to his presence.

Kirsten stared at the huge borg, searching telepathically for the presence of a living mind. When she found one, the surface thoughts swirling around in it caught her off guard: he wanted to *protect* the kids. Every other thought in immediate view cavorted about in a chaotic tangle of insanity. In his mind, the gang members appeared to be bizarre creatures somewhere between aliens and demons. Even the ruined city around him warped into a scene far removed from anything possible on Earth. Rather than buildings, his vision filled with twisted spires of onyx shrouded in dark emerald-hued flames. The bizarre sights might have come from bad information fed to his brain from the digital processor between artificial eyes and biological tissue or simply have been hallucinations borne of insanity.

Somehow, he recognized Riani and Theo as innocent children. Aside from seeing them both wearing small e-suits as if they'd gone exploring a hostile planet unsuitable for colonization, they appeared normal to him. This out-of-his mind borg wanted to keep the monsters (cybergangers) from hurting the kids. The gunshot she'd heard earlier came from the splat mark on the floor trying to kill the borg. He'd spent a shot from his 'big gun,' a weapon he only had seven more rounds for. The man inside the monster decided to use one of the precious shells in hopes of intimidating the other 'creatures' to run away so a gunfight didn't erupt around the children, even if it meant he wouldn't have enough weaponry left to fight off 'the big darkness'.

She hoped 'the big darkness' this guy feared came entirely from his insanity and didn't represent any real thing roaming around this sector.

A series of faint chirps came from the gangers, error tones from the electronics in their weapons.

"Guns down," said Dorian. "Want me to see what I can do about the big guy?"

"I don't think he's going to be as much of a problem as he looks." Kirsten stepped into the room, E-90 still poised. "He's no longer part of reality, but… he's trying to protect the kids."

"Wow." Dorian blinked.

The borg shifted his gaze to her. A little remaining humanity in his face gave off a sense of worry. He saw her as another shadowy, alien-demon creature. Her E-90, to him, had become an enormous glowing doom cannon, a distortion created from perceived threat—a weapon he knew could hurt him.

You're guarding the children, said Kirsten telepathically. *I'm not here to harm you. The kids don't belong here. I need to take them home.* She had to break through his paranoia fast. *What is your name?*

The borg said nothing, though the word 'Ohm' drifted across his mind.

Hello, Ohm. I'm Kirsten. You see me as a demonic creature, but something is lying to you. I'm just a person. Since he saw the kids in e-suits and likely believed he had been stranded on some alien planet, she ran with his delusions and concentrated on a mental image of herself wearing an e-suit matching the style of the one he imagined on the children, and sent it into his mind. Her alien figure burst open down the middle, a cocoon of churning black material, partly mist, partly shards of glimmering obsidian breaking apart to reveal another 'lost explorer'.

"You… take. You help?" asked Ohm.

"Yes. That's why I'm out here."

The remaining gangers spun at the sound of her voice. Two attempted to shoot at her, though their de-charged weapons did nothing. One grinned, baring teeth filed into points.

"Then take. I scare small ones. The shadows will hurt small ones. I will hurt the shadows." The borg gave a great bellow of a war cry and hurled himself at the cybergangers.

All five forgot about Kirsten in an instant. Two ran. One stood there attempting to shoot the borg with a dead gun. Ohm swatted him aside like a toy, his great metal arm breaking the man's entire ribcage as well as spine. The body burst open from the force of the strike, spraying gore around in a death spiral before collapsing in a crumpled heap of limbs thirty feet away.

At this, the other four gave up any pretense of toughness and sprinted as fast as they could move, all screaming. Ohm chased after them, not looking back.

"That was much easier than I expected." Dorian headed for the exit. "I'll go get the PC. Best we not remain here."

"Good idea." Kirsten holstered her E-90 and ran to the children, who clung to each other in the corner, eyes closed. "Riani? Theo?"

The kids looked up at her, both shaking, crying, and speechless. They resembled Raj enough for her to assume she'd found the right kids—not that she expected there to be too many children around here anyway.

"Come on. We need to get out of here." She took them each by the hand and pulled them to their feet. "Don't look. There's bad stuff on the ground here. Just follow me."

Theo gazed around. "The monster's gone."

"That man was really scary," said Kirsten in as comforting a tone as she could come up with in the moment. "But he was trying to keep you safe."

"They killed Daddy," whispered Riani.

Kirsten jogged with the kids across the ruins to the opening by the street. "Yes. I'm sorry."

Raj trailed after them, muttering a continuous stream of apologies to the kids in between cursing himself for being such a spineless idiot who couldn't say no to his boss.

The patrol craft glided over and landed nearby. Kirsten rushed to it, practically throwing the children into the back seat before jumping in and lifting off. She swung the vehicle around to face north and accelerated at maximum rate while climbing at a forty-five-degree angle. Speed and altitude would make them more difficult targets… and they had only about a mile to go before leaving the disavowed sector. Hopefully, the locals wouldn't waste ammo shooting at a military hovercar moving at double the speed of civilian ones.

Both children screamed as if on a scary ride at an amusement park, pinned to the seat by the heavy acceleration. Kirsten clenched her jaw, tensing her entire body in an effort to keep her dinner from spewing back up.

Twelve arduous seconds later, her speed reached 604 MPH.

She eased back on the acceleration and leveled out of the climb at 5,000 feet.

"Slightly overdid that." Dorian chuckled. "We're not exactly running away from surface-to-air missile batteries. Pretty sure we're clear now."

"Yeah." Kirsten exhaled. "Sorry, on edge."

"Not a problem. Being overly careful is better than being reckless. Though, you might wish to drop down out of the flight lanes before the military starts asking us what's going on."

"Right." Kirsten nudged the PC into a relaxed descent, steering around to the southwest on course for the Police Administrative Center out of habit.

Riani and Theo sat quietly in the back, still clamped onto each other. They appeared in good condition, if a little dirty and a lot shell shocked. Raj sat beside them, alternating between trying to talk to them and sobbing.

"Raj?" asked Kirsten.

He wiped his remaining eye and looked up at her. "Thank you for getting my children out of there safely. I can never repay you enough for this."

"Don't worry about it." She concentrated, turning her astral abilities inward to make herself solid to spirits, then took his hand. "I'm just glad I got there fast enough to matter. Do they have any family left or... am I taking them to child services?"

The kids blinked at her.

"Who are you talking to?" asked Riani.

"Oh, boy," muttered Dorian.

"Your father. His spirit is here, sitting beside you." Kirsten gestured at him. "He led me right to you."

Riani broke down in sobs. "I don't want Daddy to be a ghost!"

"My wife, Chara, is at home," said Raj. "Please, can you bring them there? She does not know what has happened to us yet."

Kirsten nodded to him. "Yes, of course."

A beep came from the NavCon.

"Kids still have their NetMini's on them," said Dorian. "Got the address locked in."

Another holo-panel opened showing a missing person notification for Raj, Riani, and Theo, since one happened to be active in the police system when she accessed the record for their home address. Kirsten let the patrol craft's computer take over driving, then closed her eyes for a moment to compose herself before calling it in that she'd found the kids. She expected to spend the next few hours at their house playing medium so Raj could talk to his family and say his farewells. Already, the daughter's heavy sobs made it near impossible for Kirsten to keep her eyes dry.

She had to be strong for them.

All *her* crying could happen later once she got home.

4

IMMINENT

The weekend made up for not getting home Thursday night until after Evan went to sleep.

Kirsten had gone to Raj's residence expecting an emotionally grueling process, but mostly acted as a translator while his wife yelled at him for being so stupid. Not only had he gone to one of *those* sectors, he did so while the children were in his care. People dealt with grief in many ways. It seemed Chara Bakshi had to go through a strong denial phase first and distracted herself from grief with anger.

Raj didn't transcend before Kirsten left. He may or may not haunt his family for a time, so she left them with a note to contact her if they needed her to return to help him communicate any more important things to his family.

Friday had the courtesy of being quite slow. Kirsten spent the whole day in the squad room, not that she minded the break. From the time she left at end-of-shift to Sunday night, she spent time with Evan and Sam. Saturday added some of his school friends plus Shani and Nila as they went to a Funzone for most of the afternoon. In the hours after the kids went to sleep, Kirsten had Sam all to herself.

Sex still came with some emotional baggage, though she'd learned to carry it well.

She couldn't really blame her mother for it, at least not beyond ending up on the street. At the time Mother had been an issue, Kirsten was too young for the woman to berate her about any sort of sexual desires. Given what she'd since learned about religious crazies, she had no doubt her mother wouldn't have hesitated shaming her for simply being female past a certain age... an age she never would have reached had she not run away.

The ick of her first experience haunted her still. She no longer blamed herself, and Sam could take her mind entirely off the past once they started kissing. Awkwardness and shame still hounded her during the few minutes leading up to climbing onto the bed with him, but it didn't take long before she could let go of the past and revel in the chance to be with a man who truly cared for her.

MONDAY MORNING, KIRSTEN SAT AT THE KITCHEN TABLE WATCHING EVAN shake Monwyn Stars into synmilk. The crystals falling from the canister like rainbow sugar rapidly soaked up the liquid and expanded into star-shaped cereal bits in multiple colors.

The boy remained on the thin side, though didn't appear *too* thin anymore. Children with the psionic ability of Accelerated Healing tended to be scrawny and undersized since the power hogged energy reserves otherwise used for growth and weight gain. The effect became less pronounced if the child didn't experience frequent injury or sickness. The year or so his drug-addicted bio mother's boyfriend beat on him almost daily, coupled with not being given much food, had done some damage. He'd likely always be scrawny. Yet, somehow, he'd put his awful past behind him. Whenever he smiled at her now, it seemed as if he'd forgotten entirely about having any other life.

Kids are resilient. She let a silent sigh out her nostrils. As a ten-year-old, she decided to trust an outside world she'd never set foot in before to her home, and survived two years in the Beneath. *I guess I'm kinda resilient, too.* She took a long sip of coffee. *Why is it every time I start to feel happy and normal, I dwell on the past?*

Evan rambled about stuff he expected to do at school today,

seeming excited. His joy proved contagious, lifting her out of her odd mood.

After breakfast, they headed up to the roof, hopped in the patrol craft, and began the ride to the PAC.

Evan swigged from a small coffee, gazing off to the side out the electronic window making an unintentional 'ugh, it's Monday. Here we go again' face. He looked so much like a tiny version of a jaded detective—detective due to his not wearing a uniform—Kirsten got a case of the giggles.

Around the time they came within a quarter mile from the PAC, Captain Eze's holographic head appeared, floating over the middle of the console.

"Good morning, lieutenant." He smiled.

"Captain," said Kirsten.

Evan saluted him.

Captain Eze smiled at the boy, then at her. "I'd like you to bring Evan with you to the squad room today for a moment before you drop him off at the school."

Umm. What the heck? "Yes, sir."

Evan cut his gaze to her, both eyebrows up as he whispered telepathically, *What did I do?*

"Wonderful. See you soon." He nodded once and ended the comm.

"I don't know." Kirsten pursed her lips. "Pretty sure you didn't *do* anything. He probably just wants to give you something. Ugh, I hope it's not a badge."

"Umm." Evan scrunched his nose. "It would be kinda cool to go active, but I'm too small. And you'd be too scared."

She chuckled. "Right on both."

"How old do I gotta be before you won't be scared if I get activated?"

"Seventy-five," muttered Kirsten. "Since I'll probably be gone by then."

He laughed.

"I'll always be worried about you, Ev." She sighed. "But if you really want to do this when you're older, I guess eighteen."

"Okay." He sipped coffee.

Kirsten hoped he'd simply become enamored with the idea of being a cop like many children his age did. He might grow out of it. He might not. The boy *did* have a fairly strong urge to help people. After all, he insisted on absorbing Shani's share of 'citizenship points' when they got in trouble for trying to 'help' Abernathy. His being an astral sensitive all but guaranteed Command would try their hardest to convince him to go active, either I-Ops or Tactical. Thankfully, the ability to interact with ghosts didn't lend itself to tactical operations much.

Whatever path he took didn't present an immediate worry for her. They had at least six, hopefully more, years before anyone would seriously consider sending Evan out into the world as a Division 0 officer. Sure, they activated Kirsten at age sixteen, but at the time, they had no one else with Astral Sense. She'd do her best to insist they let him finish school and proper training before he went running around with an E-90 and a sword.

Kirsten sighed mentally at the idea of her son having to cut himself to astrally bind a blade so it could hurt spirits, demons, or other strange beings. The boy did not have Mind Blast, which meant he did not have the ability to use Astral Lash. She didn't understand the mechanism of it, but somehow, having both abilities allowed her to produce a tendril of psionic energy capable of inflicting immense damage to spirits. As far as she knew, no one else could do it. Both abilities tended to be rare, Mind Blast even more so than Astral Sense. To have both at once amounted to winning the genetic lottery—or losing it. At least the boy would never be shunned or feared by fellow psionics.

Much about her abilities remained a mystery. She still didn't understand how spirits like Raj could just find her. Somehow, they knew she existed and sought her out for help, even when she'd been little. Perhaps what pulled her to Novar Kell's apartment had been the same effect in reverse?

By the time she landed at the PAC, she'd stopped wondering why Captain Eze wanted to see Evan, her mind too preoccupied with being annoyed at idiots who believed all the superstitious nonsense about Mind Blast. Sure, so she hammered a man into a permanent vegetative state until he died to some infection or whatever months later. Mind Blast essentially destroyed his higher brain functions… but it *had* been Mick, the wretch who'd beat Evan every day for over a year. And he *had* been trying to kill her at the time. Not like she hunted him down and scrambled his brain on purpose. How is what she did to him worse than a pyrokinetic burning someone alive or an electrokinetic giving someone a heart attack?

Many psionic abilities had the capacity to kill, yet for some stupid reason, only Mind Blast engendered an almost superstitious fear. It had to come from the ability to permanently erase memories, or even someone's personality. Any telepath could temporarily erase memories by overwriting them with a fake one, but the process could be reversed. Mind Blast actually erased memories for good. Kirsten didn't have a strong enough rating in the power to do anything like that. Also, Wipe—as the Division 0 database called the technique—wasn't something anyone could do in the heat of the moment. It took time on the order of fifteen to twenty minutes of intense concentration. No one could roam around casually wiping out people's thoughts or personalities. The recipient of a Wipe would either have to be willing or unconscious. Officially, the process was used to deal with unrepentant psionic criminals likely to abuse their powers as often as they could—to make them forget having their ability. Wipe could effectively destroy all knowledge of almost any skill or practiced aptitude. Perhaps psionics feared Mind Blasters so much because of this… the idea of losing their powers. They didn't lose the power itself, merely the knowledge of how to use it. Effectively, it amounted to the same thing.

When has irrational fear ever obeyed logic?

She dismissed it as 'people are weird' on the way into the PAC. Ever since she'd been upgraded to lieutenant, she got random salutes from enlisted-grade personnel who happened to notice her insignia. Black on black did make it somewhat difficult to perceive from a distance. Also, unlike most brand-new lieutenants, she didn't take herself seriously. Sergeants definitely appeared to appreciate her attitude of quietly deferring to their greater experience rather than pull the 'I'm a lieutenant, so you have to listen to me' thing.

Whenever someone saluted her, she returned it. She also didn't care if people walked by without doing it. Nothing could get someone pranked faster than earning a reputation for giving people grief over failing to salute a 2LT.

The reason Captain Eze requested she bring Evan to the squad room became obvious the instant they walked in: a conspicuous 'Happy Birthday, Kirsten' banner hung on the wall. Nicole squealed in delight and zoomed over to give her a strawberry-mocha latte. Sam got up from the chair at her desk and sauntered up to her, smiling broadly. He definitely looked out of place here in his blue Div 2 jumpsuit.

Kirsten reflexively took the cup from Nicole, then stared in disbelief at everyone grinning. Sam put his arm around her. Even Morelli appeared to be in a good mood. Between the spooky ghost stuff as well as the Mind Blast paranoia, he often avoided being around her. In all fairness, it probably had less to do with Mind Blast and more to do with his bad experiences trying to drive the 'cursed' patrol craft. Dorian and Morelli didn't see eye to eye on many things.

A brick of a cake, plain shiny black with a silver band around it (Division 0 colors) sat on a folding table by the giant window to Captain Eze's office. Twenty-three holographic candles shimmered atop it.

Captain Eze patted her on the back. "Happy birthday, Kirsten. Figured the boy might want a bit of cake."

"You figured correctly," said Evan. "Cake is amazing."

"Sorry it's not fancy. Military issue cake. It came from the mess." Captain Eze chuckled.

"It's not a mess," said Nicole in an airy-ditzy voice.

Despite everyone being fully aware the woman knew exactly what a mess hall was, they laughed.

Kirsten had similar cakes before on other birthdays. Honestly, it tasted fine, merely lacked in fanciness, being a brick-shaped loaf covered in black fondant. Division 1, 2, 5, and 6 got blue cakes. No one really knew if Division 9 did the cake thing for its operators' birthdays, but jokes went around about how a Div 9 cake would kill anyone not authorized to eat it.

"You look stunned," whispered Sam.

She peered up at him. "I honestly forgot. Just don't really think about it. Too much else to worry about."

He kissed her. "It's fine to spend a little time thinking about yourself, you know."

"C'mon," said Morelli. "Make a wish and blow out the candles so we can have some darn cake."

Most everyone in the room clapped.

Kirsten choked up a little at feeling so wanted and welcome. Her team felt more like an extended family in that moment than they ever had. She approached the cake, gazing into the mesmerizing haze of pink light and orange faux flames. She'd been thirteen before having anything even close to a birthday event. Perhaps her parents celebrated her birthdays prior to age six before her powers manifested, but she had no memories of it. By the time she'd ended up in the Beneath, she'd forgotten what birthdays even were, much less the date of hers. The dorm staff pulled her records during her intake processing. She'd been delivered at a hospital all officially and so forth, unlike Evan whose bio mom probably didn't even get up off her sofa. No official record of his birth existed in the system until she found him. Neither he nor she knew his actual birth date, hence why he'd asked the judge to declare his legal birthday the day Kirsten found him.

Rather than get sad, the memory filled her with joy—as did everyone standing around her smiling.

"Old lady of twenty-three," said Nicole.

"This is you in two months." Kirsten grinned at her, then focused on the candles. *Wish, huh? Please let me be able to give Evan a happy life.*

She 'blew' out the hologram candles.

The tiny emitter stuck on a peg into the top of the cake created fake smoke for a few seconds before shutting off. Kirsten plucked it out of the cake, then proceeded to cut everyone a piece.

THE BEST MONDAY IN THE HISTORY OF MONDAYS—AT LEAST IN KIRSTEN'S lifetime—eventually ended.

Not only did seemingly everyone in the PAC know about her birthday and smile at her, the Forces of Evil™ decided to go easy on her. She once again got to spend the whole day in the squad room. Today, however, she made no pretense of doing anything productive. Even the tactical teams had a fairly quiet day. Nicole only needed to run out twice. She and Forrester picked up a telekinetic shoplifter Div 1 already detained on one call. The other turned out to be bogus. A paranoid woman who operated a beauty salon had become convinced one of her clients was telepathic and invading her mind. No psionics were involved, merely a loose grip on reality and possibly some weak hallucinogens.

She, Sam, and Evan returned to her apartment, had dinner, and spent a few hours playing the Monwyn video game. Once the boy went off to bed, she cuddled with Sam on the sofa in the dimly lit living room. A comment about being happy led to an unexpected conversation about the idea of him moving in with them. She couldn't even tell who brought up the idea first, but found it compelling. Sam officially moving in excited and made her nervous in equal parts. Her only experience in regard to a couple living together came from spotty memories of her parents. Dad was a rather passive sort of man who some might have called cowardly. Her mother, perhaps due to her increasing craziness, became more domineering and authoritarian, especially when she hit the synthetic vodka.

Kirsten didn't worry at all she'd ever turn into that type of person, so she discarded her parents as any sort of rational example of how to coexist in the same living space with a man. He had an apartment to himself, far enough from here for the trip to be mildly annoying, even in a hovercar. His place reminded her of the apartment she first got after leaving the dorms—tiny. Where she lived now had six times the space, plenty for both of them, plus Evan… or even two more kids. Dare she think about having actual children of her own?

Dorian often teased her about wanting to collect every abandoned kid she found. Perhaps if she lived long enough to get too old for field work, she'd transfer to Admin and help out at the dorms.

Somehow, talk of living with Sam made for a rather quick migration from sofa to bedroom. Upon realizing the idea of having sex with him put her straight to excited without the usual shame/dread phase first, she practically dragged him down the hall.

Holding each other became kissing and pawing. Soon, they shed their clothes and sprawled on the bed. Sam never rushed. He adored taking his time caressing and kissing her all over, getting her quite well wound up before using more than his hands and lips. She adored being with him, loved that he'd been able to shift sex from something scary and shameful to amazing and wonderful.

Alas, tonight, he'd only just started to kiss his way down her front before an unexpected interruption ruined the mood. With his lips a few inches north of her bellybutton and going south, Kirsten opened her eyes to find a woman staring down at them.

"Gah!" She jumped, clamping her arms and legs around Sam.

"Mmph!" mumbled Sam into her stomach.

The woman, who seemed to be around thirty, appeared more or less ordinary—except for standing thigh-deep in the giant Comforgel bed. A glimmering border of glowing white-blue energy swirled around the point where her legs disappeared into the solid bed, though her body showed no obvious signs of a violent death.

Kirsten squeezed herself around Sam tighter while staring aghast at the spirit for barging in on them in such a moment.

"Mmm?" mumbled Sam.

"You're the one who can see us!" The woman tried to grab her arm and pull, though managed only a barely noticeable tug. "Please! You have to help me."

Ugh. Bad timing. She let her head loll back into the pillow and relaxed her grip enough for Sam to slide up to eye level.

"What's wrong?" he whispered.

"We have a visitor." She flicked her gaze at the spirit as if to point at her, despite knowing Sam couldn't see her.

"My son is about to die." The woman tried to grab Kirsten's hand again, still lacking physical substance. Her touch passed with only a faint chill. "He's only twelve and he's about to do something extremely stupid."

Kirsten's arousal plummeted into a pit of anxiety. "Shit. Okay."

"What?" asked Sam.

"The spirit's telling me her son is going to get himself killed tonight. Soon."

Sam rolled off her to lay on his side. "Didn't you just have a ghost show up the other night asking you to save their kids?"

"Yeah. Ghosts showing up asking me for help happens all the time, at least once a month, ever since I was little. Spirits needing help to protect their kids isn't quite as common. Still get about five a year." Kirsten sat up. Guilt landed heavily on her shoulders, not only for needing to leave Sam in the middle of what would have been a wonderful evening, but for all the time as a child she'd been unable to help wandering spirits. People had undoubtedly died or been injured because Mother refused to let her use psionics. "Sorry…"

"I understand. Spirits seek you out because no one else can help them." He kissed her. "You need to help. It's who you are. I don't mind. We'll just have to work ourselves back into the mood when we can."

The acceptance in his eyes and voice overwhelmed her. Having someone in her life totally at ease with the craziness that followed her brought her almost to tears.

"Please, hurry." The ghost again tried to grab her hand.

Kirsten looked over at the woman. She didn't radiate a strong aura of power. Her light brown skin and features matched ninety percent of the West City population. When she tried to grab hold of a living arm, she'd manifested a noticeable—if weak—physical touch. This all combined to mean she couldn't have been a spirit for *too* long. It wouldn't be likely for her to have learned how to modify her appearance to hide grisly wounds. The woman's plain top and pants hinted at life in the lower end of middle class. Perhaps she'd been sick and didn't notice, or lacked the finances to seek treatment. Free medical care from the government stopped at age eighteen unless one joined the military. The spirit didn't throw off any tangible sense of sadness, making suicide seem unlikely.

"He's going to die in minutes!" yelled the ghost. "Please!"

Shit. Kirsten scrambled off the bed, grabbed her uniform, boots, and utility belt from the top of the waist-high wardrobe cabinet she kept them on top of, then streaked across the apartment, running naked down the hall to the elevator with the ghost sprinting after her. She rushed into her uniform on the ride up to the parking deck, clipping the utility belt around her waist mere seconds before the door opened to the roof. She ran, carrying her boots, across the parking area to the patrol craft. Cold plastisteel under her bare feet shocked the last vestiges of bedroom mood out of her.

Dorian phased into being in the passenger seat as she jumped in and hit the emergency power-on button. He peered quizzically at her until the mother ghost blurred through the hull into the back seat. "Another one?"

"Yeah." Kirsten pulled back on the stick to lift off. "Where is he?"

The ghost stared at the Navcon screen. It beeped, displaying a coordinate plot.

Kirsten swung the PC around to point toward the destination marker, then let auto-drive take over long enough to get her boots on. "Okay, I'm on the way. Tell me what's happening."

"Tobin is trying to impress the wrong kind of people." The woman clung to the back of Dorian's seat, staring desperately at Kirsten. "He's hacked a delivery bot and he's going to try riding it like a hoverbike. It's some stupid game where the longer he rides it, the higher his score. If he gets on that bot, he's going to die."

A barrage of hand grenades detonated in her memory. It hadn't been that long ago she'd taken a dive out of an eleventh-story parking deck before landing on an advert bot... not one of her fonder memories. Kirsten shuddered.

"What drives kids to do stupid things like that?" Dorian shook his head.

"He doesn't realize how reckless it is." Kirsten activated the roof bar lights. Rapid pulses of bright azure made the silvery plastisteel walls of high-rises on either side of the street glow in alternating left-right flickers.

"Heck of a birthday night for you," said Dorian.

She clenched her jaw, overcome by sudden dread. If she didn't get there fast enough or screwed this up… a boy's death would forever make her birthday into a tragedy she'd want to avoid.

Kirsten pushed the patrol craft up to 700 MPH.

5

LIMITED OPTIONS

The Navcon point led to the fifty-fourth floor of a residence tower a hair over sixty miles away.

Kirsten opened the airbrake flaps and yanked back hard on the left stick, dragging the patrol craft from near supersonic to a lazy drift beside the building in six seconds. Before she could decide between heading inside to look for the boy or pulling his NetMini up in the system to track it—Dorian pointed.

"There."

She followed his finger to an open window. Three boys leaned out, all staring to their left. Kirsten pushed a button on the door, causing the armor panel pretending to be her side window to lower amid the labored whine of servos. A chaotic wind invaded the cabin, whipping her hair about as she slide-slid the patrol craft over to the boys. All three lost interest in whatever they'd been staring at to gawk at the large, black Division 0 patrol craft. The kids ranged in age from about ten to fourteen.

"Tobin?" asked Kirsten.

"None of them," said the ghost from the backseat. "Those are his friends. The guys he's trying to impress."

The boys all got the 'oh shit' expressions of kids who'd been caught doing something bad.

"No," said the oldest.

Kirsten didn't care to waste precious time attempting to extract the truth from teenagers focused on not getting in trouble in the traditional manner. The boy's surface thoughts told her right away their friend Tobin had just climbed onto a delivery bot and flown off down the street. All three of them stared in stunned silence, unable to explain how the police showed up so fast.

She growled in frustration and worry. "Get back inside before you fall."

Without waiting for a response, Kirsten shoved the left control stick forward, hurtling the PC down the street. The boys leaned outside far enough to watch her.

"He's already on the damn bot," muttered Kirsten. *Crap. This is gonna be close.*

His mother gave a whine of anxiety.

"Damn." Dorian leaned forward, poking at the console.

"What are you doing?" blurted Kirsten.

"Scanning all bots in our vicinity for abnormal flight tracking. Also, seeing if I can pick up anything on thermal."

The ghostly woman leaned into the front seat. "I can't tell if he's still alive or not. Why can't I?"

"I'm sorry." Kirsten stared out the forward windscreen, her attention jumping from one faint amber targeting reticle to another. Each time the sensor suite detected a bot, it marked it with a virtual square. "I have no idea how spirits know things like their kid is about to die. They just do."

Dorian shrugged. "I'm a ghost, too, and I can't even tell you how it works. Course... I never had kids. For what it's worth, if you don't know for a fact he's dead, he's probably not."

Kirsten squeezed the control sticks tighter.

Beep.

"Got him," said Dorian. "284 meters ahead, high. Left side of the street."

All but one of the targeting boxes disappeared. The remaining amber box outlined a faint speck in the distance following an unstable flight path, part corkscrew, part wave.

"Oh, no!" cried the woman. "It's trying to make him fall!"

"Doubt it." Dorian shook his head. "That would have taken effort to program. It doesn't expect to be carrying any cargo at the moment, so its flight computer is trying to maximize efficiency so it can run longer between charge cycles. Since your son weighs more than nothing, the bot starts to fall out of the sky due to insufficient thrust energy. When it detects it's crashing, it compensates and levels off. As soon as it reaches the programmed flight altitude, it again goes for efficiency and starts the process over again. It's a bouncy ride, but it isn't *trying* to make him fall."

Kirsten sent a brief comm back to Command to report she had a juvenile stuck on a moving delivery bot at 500 feet. Odds were low anyone else would get there in time to make much of a difference, but she'd appreciate any help that tried. Delivery bots tended to fly between 150 to 200 miles per hour depending on size when returning to their distribution hubs, somewhat slower when transporting delicate or expensive cargo. This one carried cargo, both precious and delicate, but didn't know it.

The patrol craft's combat computer calculated its velocity at 180 MPH.

Some people could ride hoverbikes at similar speeds, though they wore helmets and suits capable of withstanding the chill. Tobin didn't have those, merely an ordinary shirt, pants, and sneakers. He did, however, appear to be having the time of his life, waving one hand around over his head and whooping in excitement.

Kirsten sped up, easily overtaking the burdened delivery bot. As expected, the bot ignored her attempt to transmit an emergency 'land immediately' order. In theory, all bots operating within the boundaries of West City were supposed to be receptive to police overrides. In practice, very few ever did. Companies running the bots always blamed software errors or hardware damage, though the unspoken truth was they couldn't be bothered to lose the productivity time. They'd rather risk fines, hoping the tedium of processing the paperwork would dissuade any consequences.

When she pulled up alongside the bot, Tobin glanced over at her. For an instant, the boy looked surprised, as if he couldn't believe his eyes. It didn't take long for his expression to go defiant.

He gave her the finger. "Can't catch me! Stupid cops!"

She glared back at him. Rather than try shouting over the rushing wind and high-pitched scream of ion thrusters, she used telepathy. *Tobin, listen to me. Your mother is here. Your life is in danger.*

"Yeah right," yelled the kid. "My mom's dead. Nice try, cop."

A few seconds later, the realization he'd heard her voice inside his mind clicked. Tobin's cocky grin melted to an expression of unnerved confusion.

I'm not trying to trick you, kiddo. You're going to die tonight if you don't get off that thing right now.

"Oh yeah? How?" he yelled.

"I don't know exactly how it's going to happen," said his ghostly mother. "Just that he's going to die. Tell him Pickles will be heartbroken if anything happens to him."

Kirsten edged the patrol craft closer to the bot, almost enough to reach out and grab the boy's arm. *Your mother says Pickles will be heartbroken if you get hurt.*

Tobin swung his right arm down and grabbed hold of the bot. In an instant, he went from reveling in the thrill of a dangerous ride to seeming on the verge of a freakout. His surface thoughts exploded into a mix of shock, sorrow, heartbreak, and embarrassment. Pickles, evidently, was a stuffed animal he *still* took to bed and didn't want any of his friends to find out about. He stared at Kirsten, astonished at how she could've known about him.

"M... Mom?"

"Yes," yelled Kirsten. "Her spirit is here. Look, just make that thing put you down and I'll explain everything. You are not in trouble... yet."

Tobin appeared close to crying, but didn't. After a few seconds to summon the courage to let go with one hand, he fished a small electronic device out of his flapping faux-denim jacket and fiddled at it. "Oh, shit. It's not listening to me. They killed my connection."

Kirsten frowned. *Comtec would gladly let a child die to save a tenth of a percent of revenue.* She eyed the mini-holo-panel inside the patrol craft showing the registration for the delivery bot, noted its ID, then leaned out the window. "Bot, C-24BFA0, by order of the National Police Force, you are to come to a complete stop."

"Unable to comply," said a generic male voice.

"Bot, if you don't stop right now so I can get that kid off your back, so help me, I will shoot you down."

"You will not proceed with that course of action," replied the bot in a voice devoid of emotion. "If my flight process is interrupted, the juvenile will experience a life malfunction."

Furious, Kirsten screamed, "He's going to die anyway if you don't stop. If I have to pluck that kid off a moving bot, your metal ass is going to end up as a fireball."

"Unit C-24BFA0 is valued at ₵214,000. You will be liable to Comtec International for the replacement cost of this unit if you damage it."

"I'd say 'unbelievable,'" muttered Dorian, "but I'm not shocked."

"Please, do something!" yelled the mother.

Dorian looked at her. "Ma'am, calm down. We'll get your son off that thing."

"Hadley," said the ghost. "My name is Hadley."

"Wow." Tobin stared down at the bot. "These guys are serious assholes."

A streak of silver and bright orange neon shot by—a smaller bot going in the other direction. Tobin reeled backward from the windblast of it passing so close, almost lying down flat on his back. Only his legs squeezing around the bot frame kept him from flying off. Two seconds later, he screamed—as did Hadley.

Flailing, the boy flung himself upright and kept going forward until he bent over the bot like a hoverbike racer flattening himself as much as possible to the chassis. All bravado and defiance had evaporated. "Help! This isn't fun anymore!"

"Bot!" shrieked Kirsten. "Stop immediately or you're going down in flames."

"You will not pursue that course of action as it will injure the juvenile," said the overly calm bot voice. "There is no reason you cannot retrieve the juvenile after I complete my return to DC9442.

LIMITED OPTIONS | 65

There will be a 14.82 second window during which time I will be motionless as the next shipment is loaded."

"He's not gonna fit through the hatches you fly through!" shouted Kirsten.

"Comtec International Corporation is not responsible for the juvenile's lack of foresight."

Kirsten scowled. *Another few like this and I may begin to lose my faith in the inherent goodness of humanity.*

"Incoming." Dorian pointed.

Gasping, she twisted to peer forward, squinting into the 180-MPH wind blasting her in the face. Another, much larger, advert bot trundled down the hover lane in their direction. While it didn't appear to be on a direct collision course with C-24BFA0, the AI plotting the flight paths did not take riders into consideration. With so many bots in the city, their flight control computers plotted paths that often brought them within inches of each other. The giant bot would skim so close over the zooming delivery unit, Tobin would be scraped off as a semiliquid paste.

The boy evidently saw the huge bot coming, too.

He screamed.

6

ACCEPTABLE LOSSES

Kirsten shoved the patrol craft forward, spinning it into a side-slide directly in front of C-24BFA0, drifting high enough to force the big advert bot to change course.

C-24BFA0 dipped down, attempting to go under her. She followed its bobbing motion to stay ahead of it and force it to slow down somewhat. The huge advert bot roared overhead, blue ionic downblast from its thrusters fluttering the boy's long, black hair and sending little lightning-bolt sparks dancing over the hull of the bot. He screamed again in a stuttering manner as if suffering repeated jolts from underpowered stunners.

Jousting with a delivery bot is not what she expected to be doing on the evening of her birthday, but she kept on it, staying a little bit ahead of the bot each time it tried to jink around her. Little by little, her maneuvering forced it to bleed away speed and altitude. Hopefully, she could force it down out of the traffic lane to reduce the odds of another collision.

"Do something quick!" yelled Hadley. "I feel it coming! He's only got seconds."

Fuck it. Kirsten smacked the button to deploy her seat's impact-restraint harness. Six Nylcron straps sprouted out from the seatback, pinning her torso in place. She pushed the gull wing door open, then rolled the car toward the bot, moving herself as close as possible to the boy. "Dorian, take over!"

She let go of the sticks and reached for the kid.

Tobin seized up staring at her. His eyes said he wanted to jump to her but couldn't make himself let go. An instant before Kirsten used Suggestion to force him to move, something caught his eye. With a startled yelp, he leapt into her arms right as Dorian made the PC lurch upward two feet. The second his chest crashed into hers, a dull *thud* rocked the patrol craft. Faint clattering of small metal parts bouncing over the armor plates followed. Several bits of smoking debris shot into Kirsten's field of view from behind, falling like fiery comets toward the street 500 feet down.

Hadley screamed. "Aaah! What happened?"

"A small delivery bot coming the other way just collided with us. It broke apart," said Dorian, calm as anything. He rolled the PC level and used an abrupt slide to the left to finish tossing Tobin into the cabin.

Kirsten clung to the trembling boy, refusing to loosen her grip even a little until her door closed with a soft hiss. As soon as he could no longer fall out, she let him crawl past her into the passenger seat. Dorian obligingly melted down into the car, yielding the seat to a living person.

"You sound so calm," said Hadley. "It hit us."

That oncoming bot would have killed this kid. Kirsten swallowed hard. *Dorian swerved at the last second to block it with the PC.*

"Nothing to worry about," replied Dorian's voice from a speaker. "The car is armored. Bots are not."

Kirsten opened her side window again, drew her E-90, and took aim at C-24BFA0.

"Whoa," muttered Tobin in awe. "What are you doing?"

She narrowed her eyes. "The only way these idiots will learn is if it costs them more to be assholes than to do the right thing."

"Wait," said Dorian. "Let me. If you shoot it, the wreckage is going to hurt someone on the ground… and Comtec will try to sue you. I'd love to see them try to sue me."

She exhaled. The idea of Comtec legitimately trying to sue a ghost hit her funny enough that she calmed down and didn't fire. Also, he had a point. Shooting bots down could easily hurt or kill people on the ground. "Eep. Yeah… you're right." She holstered the weapon.

Dorian appeared as a blur of spectral energy rushing past her out the window. Seconds later, the bot made an abrupt diving turn.

"Where's it going?" asked Tobin.

Kirsten watched it fly off. It didn't appear to be on its way to crash, rather heading off to somewhere specific. "If I know Dorian, that thing is going to end up parked on the Comtec CEO's desk… via the window."

7

TIMEBOMB

"Dispatch, this is 1815-0I4," said Kirsten over comms while bringing the patrol craft to a stop at a hover 210 feet off the ground. "Be advised, I've gotten the juvenile safely off the bot. It's, umm... experiencing an unusual flight malfunction. No idea where it's going."

Hadley phased into the passenger seat, futilely attempting to wrap her son in a hug.

"Copy, 1815-0I4," replied a nondescript female voice. "You say the delivery unit is damaged?"

"It doesn't look damaged. The thing just turned and dove before zooming off. I think someone might have hacked it."

"Understood. Do you require additional units at this time?"

"No. I'm good. Under control."

"Copy. Nice work, lieutenant. Does the juvenile require medical attention?"

Maybe clean underwear... "He seems okay. Tobin, are you hurt?"

"Nah." He wrapped his arms around himself, still shaking. "Just scared."

Kirsten released the harness, and allowed herself a moment to breathe. "He looks okay. Don't need a medical team now. Thanks, Ops."

"Copy," said the voice.

Tobin shivered while gazing around at the inside of the patrol craft. "Wow. This thing is awesome."

"Don't touch anything, please," muttered Kirsten, still staring at the roof.

"Am I arrested?"

"Not yet." Kirsten lifted her head from the seatback and looked at him. "If you swear to me you will never do anything like that again, I'll forget to ask how you ended up on that bot in the first place."

He shivered harder. "Swear. I thought it was gonna be fun, but once I couldn't control the stupid thing anymore it was scary as hell. Wow, you're kinda cool for a cop. Sorry about what I said before."

"It's okay. I'm not Div 1."

"Yeah. I figured that out when you spoke inside my head." He shifted his gaze to the back seat. "Is my mother still here? Or did you just say that?"

Kirsten reached over and took his hand. "She's still here."

Tobin gave her an odd look.

A moment's concentration on her astral abilities aligned her physical body with the astral realm, making it solid to spirits. Further effort pushed some of the solidity into the boy. The instant he slipped part-way between worlds, he made a face as if he'd sat on something cold and squishy. Hadley gave a startled gasp, then, realizing she could mostly feel her son in her arms, squeezed him harder.

"What's happening?" asked Tobin. "I'm all cold and like... slimy. It's getting hard to breathe."

Kirsten smiled. "It only feels like slime. It's a ghost. Your mother is hugging you."

"Mom?" whispered Tobin. Seconds later, he broke down sobbing, and tried to tug his hand away from her.

"If you want her to continue to be able to hug you, you can't let go of me. I'm concentrating on aligning you as much as I can with the astral realm."

He stopped pulling at his hand, doing his best to return his mother's embrace with one arm.

As Kirsten so often did with spirits in their last moments with family, she played translator as they talked for the first time in three years. Tobin tearfully told her about how the place where she used to work still hadn't gotten in any trouble for killing her, even though Dad kept hiring lawyers. Evidently, she and several other employees got trapped in a CPU room when the fire suppression system activated for mysterious reasons, suffocating them. The way she died and the subsequent absolute lack of any accountability is what drove Tobin to get into the hacking community. Tonight's misadventure had been his attempt to prove himself 'serious' about it in hopes of being accepted.

She didn't mind giving voice to Hadley's motherly scolding of the 'don't you ever do anything so reckless and dangerous again' variety. She knew the worry well from some of the things Evan got himself wrapped up in, though her son didn't purposefully do reckless things to show off. He simply failed to appreciate the danger while being too focused on helping someone.

Eventually, she flew back to the boy's building and landed on the roof.

He hopped out. "Thanks for saving me."

"Not so fast, kid." Kirsten also got out. "Need to talk to your father."

"Ugh." Tobin hung his head. "Do you have to?"

"It's that or I bring you to the station and let him pick you up there."

Tobin gulped. "No thanks. You can talk to him here."

She squeezed his shoulder. "Relax. I just need to make sure I'm leaving you with your actual parent in a safe environment. It's not because I want to get you in trouble."

He led her across the roof parking area to the door, Hadley trailing after them both. A short elevator ride and another corridor later, Tobin waved his NetMini at a silver square on the wall, opening the door of a residence.

"Dad?" called Tobin while walking in. "I'm back."

Kirsten stepped into a living room where the three boys she'd seen earlier lounged around on the floor, all wearing senshelmets.

A fortyish man panic-stumbled out of a hallway on the left and zoomed over to grab Tobin by the shoulders, staring into his eyes. "What the hell happened? They said you went out the damn window."

"Uhh…" Tobin scratched the back of his head. "I kinda did. But I was riding on a delivery bot."

The man closed his eyes, shuddered, and mutely hugged the boy.

"Sorry. I messed up," said Tobin.

Hadley's ghost paced around the room, muttering to herself. Her presence caused a grey tabby cat to trot around in circles, following her while meowing repeatedly.

"Hang on, son. We'll deal with this." The father looked over at Kirsten, clenching his jaw in a defensive manner.

She held up a hand. "Easy. I'm not here to initiate an inquest in regard to your son's cyberspace trespassing. I do, however, have to create a record of tonight's events. Due to his age, it'll disappear entirely if he doesn't get in any more trouble before he turns eighteen." She shifted her gaze to Tobin. "If you do get caught again before you're eighteen, they're likely to slap you with charges for what you did tonight."

"How severe are the charges?" asked the father. "And, you are?"

"She saved my life, Dad. It was awesome… pulled me into her hovercar while it was going sideways."

"Lieutenant Kirsten Wren, Division 0." She offered a hand.

"Xander Reece." He shook her hand. "Thank you for saving my son's life… I…"

She waited until he got his emotions reined in. "Any possible trouble wouldn't be *too* bad from what I've seen so far. He basically got into the Comtec system and took control of one of their delivery bots for a little while. No damages or loss involved, he didn't compromise any sensitive data, so it falls under fourth-degree cyberspace trespass. About as bad as a traffic citation."

Both Tobin and Xander slouched with audible sighs of relief.

"There could also be charges related to reckless endangerment from us having to chase down the bot with a patrol craft and pluck him off it… but I don't think that's necessary." Kirsten smiled. "He appears to understand why joyriding on bots is a horrible idea."

"Yeah." Tobin ground his sneaker into the rug. "Almost got pasted twice."

His father swooned to one side and fell seated on the couch. "Boy, you're going to make my heart explode before I'm forty-five."

"Sorry, Dad. But…" Tobin flailed. "Those assholes… Mom. They still haven't gotten in *any* trouble."

Hadley drifted over to sit beside her husband.

"I know, son. I know." Tobin put an arm around the boy and pulled him close. "It will catch up to them eventually. Don't do anything stupid. I'd rather they get away with what they did than lose you, too."

Tobin stared down. "Yeah. Sorry. That was really dumb of me."

"Whoa…" The oldest boy removed his senshelmet. He had the same light brown complexion as most of the population, but clearly did not appear related to Tobin. "Another one just like DemonCore."

"Damn," muttered Tobin. "Really?"

"Yeah," said the older kid.

The other two boys pulled their helmets off, blinking and twitching as their senses adjusted back to the real world. Up close, the smallest looked younger than ten, likely eight or nine. He sported an orb of frizzy ice-blue hair that made him look like a cartoon snowball with eyes. Their other friend seemed around the same age as Tobin and looked normal—no bizarre hair colors, plain black.

"DemonCore?" Kirsten raised an eyebrow. "What do you know about him?"

"Another what?" asked Xander.

Tobin fidgeted. "Some people would kick my ass if they knew I talked to a cop about it, but you're kinda different since you're one of the psionic ones. You guys don't care too much about hacking stuff."

"How do you know about DemonCore?" asked the other twelve-year-old, eyeing her suspiciously. "Careful, Tob. She's a cop."

She gave him a flat look. "I know about DemonCore because I found his body."

The boys all gasped in reverent awe.

"Don't care, Nazim." Tobin exhaled hard. "She saved my ass. I almost died. She won't make trouble for us."

"No way," whispered the little one. "For real? You saw the body?"

"I did." Kirsten glanced back and forth among the boys. "What do you mean by 'another?'"

"Umm, it's kinda going around the scene," said Tobin.

"The scene?" She raised an eyebrow.

"The hacking scene," said Nazim.

"What did the body look like?" asked the little one.

"Stop asking creepy shit, Meep," said the oldest boy.

"Shut up, Kezan!" The small one shoved at his friend, then looked back up at her. "I wanna know."

Kirsten tilted her head. "Your name is Meep?"

The small boy with snowball hair nodded eagerly. "Yep."

"Meep, she's a cop, you can't lie." Tobin rolled his eyes. "We call him Meep. It's his online name. I think his real name's Billy."

Meep stuck out his tongue.

"You think?" asked Kirsten.

"He never uses it." Kezan, the oldest, laughed. "We started calling him Meep because he's easy to scare. Makes this noise like '*meep*' every time we get him."

The small boy growled playfully.

"He's not our son," said Hadley out of nowhere. "Meep's parents are both dead. Xander lets him stay here, basically adopted him. He's a good kid. Bit high strung, though. Terrified of getting in trouble all the time."

Kirsten nodded at the spirit, then looked back at Tobin. "What about DemonCore is going around the hacker community?"

"Black ICE." Tobin grimaced. "There's like a whole bunch of people getting killed by it now."

"Six or seven, I think, with DemonCore." Kezan grabbed his NetMini off the floor and tapped at the screen. "But it's crazy."

Xander wiped both hands down his face. "Crazier than people being killed in the GlobeNet and dying for real?"

"Yeah." Kezan swiped at the screen. Glowing patterns of light from the holographic text painted his face green and blue in spots. "The people gettin' their brains cooked aren't like big time hackers with a rep for going into crazy places. Only the baddest, blackest sites use killer DPs."

"DPs?" Kirsten blinked.

"Defense progs," said all four boys at once.

Nazim whistled. "Yeah. The super serious networks use crap that can kill people. Whenever someone eats black ICE, word gets out there. Most of us try to retaliate… if it ain't the government. Any company using that killer shit is basically begging us to wreck them."

Listening to a bunch of adolescent boys talk like badass 'avenging' hackers would've been adorable if not for the real chance it could get them hurt or killed.

"Truth." Kezan nodded. "Black ICE is no bueno. We hate it. Any company that uses it has forfeited its right to exist. We try to take them down. So far, no one's found any proof of any company being involved. It's like their decks just decided to nuke them for no reason."

Kirsten opened her terminal window and began taking notes. "What exactly do you mean by that?"

"Well…" Kezan stretched. "When we sneak into a network and set off a defense prog, there are traces in the neural memory. A good enough operator can get into a network, see the logs, and know exactly what happened. If these guys got into a dark node somewhere loaded with a black ICE prog and it killed them, there'd be traces of the kill transmission buried in every memory buffer between the origin hardware and the user's deck The GlobeNet feels like reality, but there's thousands of processing units—physical machines—involved in the connection. The killer prog might mask the contents of the transmission, but the link would be visible. Hell, even Meep can find it. Those traces aren't exactly difficult."

"Bite me," muttered Meep. "I might be small, but I don't suck."

Nazim slapped the senshelmet on the rug beside him. "We all suck, Meep. We're kids so we're stuck using these stupid slow-ass helmets until we're eighteen."

"Basically, you can tell where someone went when they got their brain cooked." Kezan held up his NetMini, showing a screen of black with red letters—not that Kirsten could read it from where she stood.

"The guys who got killed, no one's been able to trace it back to any specific connection."

"Gotta be a timebomb." Tobin folded his arms.

"Timebomb..." Kirsten peered at him. "You're not talking about a literal bomb, are you?"

"Nope. Software that sneaks onto someone's deck and randomly goes off later once they're offline." Nazim pantomimed being electrocuted, then fell flat on his back.

Kirsten shivered. *Ugh. I'm so glad I deal with ghosts.*

PATTERNS

The mood never quite returned upon Kirsten's arrival back home.

She spent the remainder of her birthday on the sofa, snuggling with Sam. He stayed the night, which turned into a rushed scramble in the morning for them both to get ready. Kirsten's body decided to remind her she happened to be in her early twenties with a blast of hormones as they attempted to share the autoshower to save time.

A few hours after arriving at her desk in the squad room, she still couldn't look anyone in the eye, certain they'd *just know* what she did. Not that she expected to get in any trouble for it—after all, they worked in entirely different areas. She might have been an officer, but the NPF tended to be quite a bit more relaxed than the military, insofar as its fraternization policy went. As long as no direct command/subordinate relationship existed, no one cared. Especially in Division 0, which seemed to always have a somewhat different set of rules from everything else.

For the first hour or so, she sat there staring into space while sipping coffee, reliving those glorious eighteen minutes. It all kind of happened on a whim. Doing it with Sam inside an autoshower tube felt so... *rebellious* somehow. Stories went around the PAC all the time of new recruits and even some of the older teenage cadets getting caught attempting similar activities. Command tended to frown on that due to the lack of privacy in the shared locker rooms. Anyone could walk in at any time.

Her private bathroom at home had no such risk, barring a wandering ghost.

Eventually, she wrangled her giddy anxiety into an overall warm glow and pulled herself out of the daydream to do some actual work, namely typing up the necessary reports in regard to Tobin's joyride. Anywhere else but Division 0, a report claiming the spirit of a boy's deceased mother came out of nowhere to beg for help would have gotten the officer filing it sent for a psych evaluation. She didn't include much detail about *how* the boy ended up on a delivery bot beyond mentioning observing him attempting to unsuccessfully use an unidentified electronic device to control it.

Alas, people trying to joyride delivery bots happened somewhat often. The only anomaly about this case was her managing to intercept him in time to save his life. According to the system, the survival rate for those who pulled similar stunts stood at around twenty-seven percent. Kirsten tapped some related file links out of random curiosity, losing about half an hour to reading case reports about delivery bots and people doing strange or ghastly things. Due to the tendency of companies to cut corners, the millions of cargo-ferrying devices in West City seldom took the time to evaluate *what* they carried and rarely refused to transport unexpected cargo. Consequently, they'd been used by murderers to discard body parts, by horrible people to abandon pets, by drug-crazed parents to ship their unwanted small children to the authorities or wherever the bot happened to be going, and so on. The list of bizarre, tragic, horrifying, and occasionally funny 'alternative' uses for delivery bots seemed endless.

About the only cargo Comtec consistently rejected was bombs. Kirsten imagined Dorian commenting about how they only scanned for explosives because, if a bomb went off, it would destroy the bot and cost the company money. Of course, this didn't stop hackers from overriding them on occasion and turning them into weapons... hence why she and/or Nicole always had to walk to the garage doors to receive their coffee. NPF policy banned any civilian bot from entering the PAC due to the potential threat of 'spicy' cargo.

A faint change in the room's energy announced the arrival of a spirit. Given the manifestation occurred one desk behind her and had a familiar air about it, she smiled.

"There you are."

"Good morning," replied Dorian.

"Do I want to know what you did with that bot?"

"You already do."

She spun in her chair to peer at him. "I do?"

Dorian reclined in the chair, feet up on the desk, a NetMini holo-panel—or a ghostly version of one—floating in front of him. He smiled, then peered over the transparent screen at her. "You should. You suggested it."

"I did." She blinked. "Wait... you heard me? You put it on the CEO's desk?"

"It was a good idea." He swiped a finger at the holo-panel to turn the page of whatever he read. "I hadn't gotten far enough away from the PC to weaken my connection by the time you said that. Don't get worked up. He wasn't sitting there at the time."

Kirsten buried her face in both hands. "Ugh."

"His personal assistant might still be screaming," mumbled Dorian.

She snapped her head up to stare at him. "Unbelievable. You know Comtec is going to go after that boy."

"Unlikely." Dorian waved dismissively. "There's nothing they'll be able to find in any systems showing he regained control of the bot. The boy never truly had *control* of it. He merely put it on pause, forcing it to wait at the window long enough to climb on top of it. Besides, if Comtec publicly accuses a juvenile of successfully breaching their network, it'll be open season."

"What?" Kirsten blinked.

"If the company admits to the world that a child using a helmet can walk right into their network, it's basically saying real hackers with direct M3 connections could do whatever they want." Dorian swiped a hand at his faux NetMini, changing the page. "Senshelmets are okay for gaming, but they are absolute crap for hacking. Imagine trying to play that Monwyn game you like when your character was stuck moving at forty-percent speed."

She winced. "Oof. Okay. Still… if they can link him to any cyber-trespassing related to that bot, they'll try."

"This is generally why hackers use false names on the GlobeNet." Dorian wagged his eyebrows. "Those boys aren't using real hardware. Just helmets and the equivalent of toys. Corporations who go after kids like them will only set off a negative PR storm."

She spun to face her terminal again. "Hmm. False names. Weird coincidence they mentioned DemonCore."

"You're expecting demons?" Dorian chuckled.

"Argh. I hope not." She gazed at the ceiling, then felt stupid for doing it.

The ceiling never answered her mother when the woman asked it why she'd been cursed with a daughter who loved 'The Devil'. It wouldn't answer Kirsten about demons, either. She glared at the holo-panel in front of her, losing several minutes attempting to figure out if staring upward in exasperation happened to be a normal human reflex, it came from watching her mother do it so often, or if she had a genetic predisposition to expect answers from above.

I should go to Reinventions to erase her from my DNA. She stuck her tongue out at nothing in particular and made a soft raspberry. *Not worth the couple million credits. She wasn't schizophrenic… just hateful, stupid, and totally convinced into believing lies.*

Kirsten protectively stuffed her hands under her arms, shuddering at the long-buried memory of Mother burning her on the kitchen stove. She still somewhat wanted to find the person or people who invented stimpaks and kick them. Sure, the tiny portable medical devices were wonderful to have as a cop in the field, but they also allowed people like Mother to cause repeated injuries to the innocent and defenseless while keeping it covered up. Anyone could buy them. No one ever investigated why an office clerk and a technical sales agent went through twenty stimpaks a month.

I never even realized Mother had a job. Thought she watched religious nonsense on the helmet.

While Mother did spend much of her time listening to crazy cult stuff, she'd also apparently worked as an office clerk. It didn't seem so strange in hindsight. More people worked out of their homes than had to physically go to offices, after all. Even her father *could* have done all his business travel virtually—but that would've defeated the purpose of him running away from the paranormal spectacle in his home... and his raging, crazy wife.

As a ghost, he'd repeatedly apologized for being too cowardly to stand up to Mother and protect her. Kirsten forgave him already, even if she hadn't spoken the words to him out of fear his ghost would transcend and she'd never see him again. The woman *had* been terrifying. She completely understood how he could be afraid of her. It wouldn't have been unreasonable for him to fear she'd have snapped and gone after him with a knife, a gun, or poison if she even slightly suspected he'd been affected by 'The Devil.'

The past is the past. Kirsten stretched, then did a few tai-chi inspired calming motions Dr. Loring showed her. Envisioning herself physically pushing bad thoughts away really did help her stop thinking about them.

As a distraction, she ran a search for DemonCore. Along with several articles from the historic archives about an early experiment with nuclear weapons, the system provided links to multiple Division 2 cybercrimes investigations associated to a hacker using the name as well as Detective Nevi Arun's inquest into the man's death.

DemonCore, real name Novar Kell, had been a twenty-seven-year-old West City native. Up until his death, he worked as a junior software developer for NinTek West. No obvious connections linked his public life with crime. His records for electronic trespass generally involved minor incursions lacking a profit motive. Some of the more recent ones had signs of him having taken on a tone of anticorporate activism.

Kirsten leaned back in her chair, sipping coffee while reading over those notes for a while. "Hmm. That could be a motive."

"What's that?" Dorian looked up from his NetMini.

"That DemonCore guy. He'd been trying to infiltrate corporate

GlobeNet sites to obtain evidence he could use to expose them for hurting people."

Dorian laughed.

"What about that is funny?" She pushed off the desk, sending her chair into a slow spin. Once she faced him, she stopped herself with a boot to the corner of his desk.

"That's like saying he went outside in search of air." Dorian wiped a hand down his face. "Sneaking into 'employee only' files in hopes of finding something he could use to make the company look bad to the public isn't exactly difficult."

She sighed. "You're being cynical."

"Comtec wouldn't slow a delivery bot down for one minute so you could take a child off it before he got killed." Dorian shifted his jaw side to side. "They openly told you that. What do you think they do when no one is watching?"

"That's one company." She thrust her arms out to either side. "And Comtec has a reputation for being horrible."

"My sweet, innocent, Kirsten." He smiled. "Even the most outwardly upright corporations would not hesitate to take actions likely to cause harm to people if they felt they could both conceal it and to do so would provide some net benefit to the corporation."

She grumbled.

"Ask your friend over in Nine about the medical testing lab she found."

"Uhh." Kirsten bit her lip. "Do I want to know?"

"Probably not since it involved children."

She squirmed. "Okay. Now I have to know. Please don't be horrible."

"Relax. She found them before anyone suffered permanent injury. A pharma corporation purchased several orphans from the ACC, children of executed rebels and 'traitors' their government had no use for."

"Purchased?" She scowled.

"Our government made it illegal to perform medical experimentation and testing on chimpanzees or live animals. Non-citizen human children enjoy no such specific legislation."

She stared at him, horrified.

"Nina killed most of the people in charge of that operation. The rest are still awaiting their trial dates. Whole company got dissolved for it."

"Good." Kirsten scowled to one side. "I… don't think I could have handled seeing that."

"You're tougher than you look. You'd have handled it just fine."

"Thanks," she whispered.

"You'd have been a sobbing wreck afterward, but…"

Kirsten threw a foam stress ball through his face.

He chuckled.

Trying to stop thinking about the depraved things some corporations could do, she rotated back to the terminal and continued reading inquest files related to the hacker DemonCore. For no reason she could understand, something about him struck her as significant. She couldn't recall ever experiencing such a gnawing curiosity about a random person, even a dead one. Only once in her life, thus far, had she been gripped by an inexplicable need to do something without an obvious cause.

Hours after the man took advantage of her in exchange for clean food years ago, she found herself racing to the surface to escape the Beneath, convinced she had to get out of there fast without understanding why.

Thinking back on it now, it would make sense she'd have been terrified of that man finding her again, but her memory of squeezing up through the drainage pipes didn't come with the pervasive panic and terror as if she'd fled a monster. It had been almost like she had an appointment she couldn't allow herself to be late for. After she'd run from the man, she'd climbed up into a tiny compartment within the city plates and cried herself to sleep. Hours later when she awoke, sore, ashamed, scared, and guilty, her dread fear that Mother would find her the instant she set foot above the city plates evaporated. Out of nowhere, the need to get to the surface as fast as possible gripped her.

Half a day after seeing the sun for the first time in two years, the police picked her up as they tended to do with any suspected street kid. Someone must have seen her rummaging trash for something to eat and called it in. The UCF government might have been a military state, perhaps even a teeny bit fascist in parts, but it did go out of its way to treat children well—as long as they lived on Earth. Mars had much less media attention as well as money.

Going topside allowed her to be found and end up in the Division 0 dorms.

She couldn't really say it saved her life. Plenty of nice spirits down there looked after her for almost two years. It seemed as though the universe had simply decided she'd spent enough of her life in hiding. Perhaps one of the Seraphim intervened. One had likely given her a little nudge the time she jumped off the parking garage, ensuring she crashed onto an advert bot instead of the ground. Or maybe the urge came from within. She didn't fear the man would come after her, hold her down, and do it again. She feared she would seek him out the next time she got really hungry—and she didn't want to.

I don't understand…

Harbingers showed up all the time to claim ghosts with serious stains on their souls. All energy tended to have its opposite, and the Harbingers were no different. The Seraphim, however, didn't pop in to visit often at all. In fact, she'd only seen them once. Harbingers, on the other hand, she essentially had in her contact list. The ability to summon them didn't ping on the psi scan, or appear to be part of her Astral Sense. Granted, she'd never demonstrated it here in the testing facility. It felt too disrespectful somehow, like a child calling real cops to demonstrate to some friends that their NetMini worked.

Her odd curiosity led her from DemonCore's inquest records via 'possibly related' tangent links to a series of reported deaths attributed to black ICE. The stalled inquests for those investigations more or less corroborated what Tobin and his friends told her: weird crap going on in the 'hacker community.'

Medical examiner reports of the seven other victims all indicated signs consistent with electrocution via the M3 interface jack as the cause of death. Varying amounts of electrical power had been shot into their brains. Problem being, the Division 2 investigators couldn't determine the origin of the kill signal.

From there, she decided to check the law database for black ICE.

Much to her horrified surprise, fatal countermeasure software did not appear to be illegal when employed as a 'passive defense mechanism' in a non-publicly accessible area of cyberspace. It would be illegal to have active black ICE sitting somewhere any user could stumble across it. All a corporation would have to show during an inquest is the dead person had gained unauthorized access to a secure part of their network containing the fatal code, and it got ruled legal.

"This is unbelievably crazy," she muttered to no one in particular.

"Watching a documentary about the Dead Ballerinas, are we?" asked Dorian. "I am still unable to explain how they became famous."

She grumbled. "No. I can't believe black ICE is legal. It sounds actually difficult to get in trouble for having it. Someone suing a company over it would have to prove whatever GlobeNet site they'd invaded did not provide enough warning to the hacker before the fatal exchange."

"When in the history of GlobeNet piracy has any hacker ever stopped at a warning sign?" Dorian rolled his eyes. "Turn back or die may as well be a dare written as 'if you can't beat this next challenge, you are a loser.'"

She twisted around to stare at him. "Are people really that stupid?"

"P23990221F1," said Dorian, not looking up.

Other than starting with a letter, that sounds like an inquest number. She spun back to her terminal and looked it up. The criminal case had been filed by an NBPS security officer working in New Boston Private Sector in East City against a dead man for the crime of 'being dead in public' as well as littering. Further fines were added at three separate five-minute intervals for 'failure to comply' when the corpse did not remove itself from the street.

Kirsten's jaw hung open. "This is a prank."

"Sorry. Nope."

"What kind of idiots join the NPF in the east?"

Dorian chuckled. "Not NPF. Those private sector cops are basically a personal security force for the association running the private sectors. They effectively have police powers, but only in their territory. They step one foot outside their gated communities and they're ordinary civilians. Real cops love giving them the business."

Kirsten sighed. She had learned a little about the concept of private sectors. Thankfully, they didn't exist here. East City had a handful of them, each one roughly about the same size as the pre-war city they'd been named for, all full of snooty rich people and the unfortunate bastards who worked for them.

"Okay, this is *really* damn stupid." Kirsten shook her head at the screens. "But... an idiot with a fake badge isn't the same thing as sneaking into a network and seeing a sign that says if you go past this point, you're going to die... and still going forward."

"That's the magic of being online." Dorian grinned. "People get stupid, reckless, and brave. Though, if you're talking about lethal countermeasure programs... the average idiot isn't ever going to run into that stuff. You only find it in the deepest, darkest, most secure areas of the wealthiest megacorp networks as well as government facilities."

"We use it?" She went wide eyed.

"If, by *we*, you mean Division 0? No. The government does, though." Dorian casually flipped a page on his NetMini holo-panel. "There is probably a room somewhere with a bunch of C-Branch agents watching logs and laughing every time their 'bug zapper' goes off."

That one, she decided to dismiss as his cynicism. C-Branch people didn't have senses of humor. They wouldn't laugh if an idiot tried to hack into a secret government network node and fried themselves... they'd swarm out the door like a kicked wasp nest and detain everyone that person communicated with over the past twenty-four months.

"Even if someone did prove a company didn't provide adequate warning," said Kirsten, "the only precedent in the system is fines. People died and a company got slapped with a tiny fine."

Dorian shrugged in a 'what can ya do' manner. "Do I think it's overkill? Sure. Black ICE is like using proximity mines to kill burglars because the store happens to contain extremely valuable items."

"Not even the exclusive stores would be allowed to use bombs as a theft deterrent," she deadpanned. "Why do they let places kill people who are essentially burglars just because it's in cyberspace?"

Dorian pondered. "Perhaps because bombs pose a risk to innocent bystanders. Generally, those defense programs only kill the miscreant who went where they don't belong."

"Still doesn't seem right." She slouched over her desk, staring into the blurry line of glow the holo-panel cast on the shiny, black surface. *Looks like a nebula in deep space.*

A few minutes passed in silence.

Kirsten started to feel like the kid who got in trouble and had to stay late in class, being the only living person in the squad room.

"Why the sudden interest in the GlobeNet?" asked Dorian.

She sat up. "I don't know."

"You don't know?"

"Unexplained urge. Those kids mentioned DemonCore when I took the boy home." She twisted her chair around to face him again. "It's been gnawing at me like something I shouldn't be ignoring. Think it means something?"

"Suppose." He gestured at her. "You might have an undetected bit of latent clairvoyance. It's not unheard of for psionics to have tangential abilities too weak to show up on a normal scan."

"I don't really think so." She frowned. "If I had even a tiny bit of clairvoyance, that bitch would not have been able to sneak up on me as often as she did and catch me talking to ghosts."

Dorian's expression turned comforting. "You always have been a brave, compassionate person, risking yourself to help total strangers, even as a child."

"I'm not getting sad again. Just saying. Emotions are known to make psionic abilities more intense for brief periods. If my mother wasn't enough to scare clairvoyance out of me, nothing will be." She swung the chair around and resumed browsing inquest records.

Chirps came from the terminal behind her. The lack of Morelli shrieking at a desk unit powering itself on—since he couldn't see Dorian—reminded her of being alone in here. Everyone else assigned to this squad room happened to be away, either on patrol or investigations. Her stomach growled. The random thought to pull Evan out of school for lunch made her happy for all of four seconds. Too late. His lunch period already passed. Grumbling, she resigned herself to grabbing something at the PAC cafeteria. No food there would win any awards, but thanks to the NPF essentially being part of the military, it happened to be free for all personnel.

"It is a bit strange," said Dorian.

"What is?" Kirsten locked her terminal and stood.

"The cases you're looking at. They're associated with low-end corporations or innocuous GlobeNet sites that wouldn't have the financial means nor any reason to install such defenses—barring highly illegal activities they wished to conceal. Yet, the detectives pursuing these cases weren't able to find killware on those networks, and all the companies denied having it."

She shifted her weight onto one leg. "Hmm. Maybe they deleted it as soon as it went off so they could deny it?"

"Perhaps." He leaned back in his chair, lips pursed. "Plausible for a one-off, but seven deaths in nine months. Different GlobeNet sites, not one of which had the means or motive for such drastic countermeasure software. Something else might be going on here."

"Think it's another hacker, like a cyberspace serial killer?" She shifted her weight onto her other leg.

"Going somewhere?"

"Cafeteria."

He rose from his chair as the holo-panel in front of him flickered out of existence. "Don't let me keep you away from lunch."

She waited for him to move around the edge of his desk, then headed for the blindingly white hallway. A scattering of other Division 0 personnel dressed in black broke up the monotony of the architecture. Higher ranking officers walked with purpose in their stride. Tactical staff meandered or jogged about. Admin people walked like they had nowhere specific to be and all day to get there. Several cadets—tweens—raced by.

Shouldn't they be in class now? Must be delivering an important message or something.

Dorian fell in step beside her. "Two deck jockeys in cyberspace *can* get into a fight with the potential to kill each other for real in a manner similar to how black ICE works. But... there are almost always traces of the exchange. All that data has to move through neural memory networks scattered around dozens of server rooms and processing centers. The odds of nine separate attacks all avoiding detection are incredibly low. Unless..."

"Unless what?" She stopped by the elevator.

"Unless it's someone from C-Branch doing it. Their hardware doesn't leave any trace of its access on any system in UCF territory."

The elevator door opened, revealing four people inside. She waited for them to exit. Dorian didn't, making the lieutenant colonel he phased through shiver. Kirsten fought the urge to smile at the face the senior officer made.

"I am, of course, teasing." Dorian stuck his finger deep into the button for the ground level. "No one in government intelligence would really care about a bunch of amateur network pirates. Assuming, of course, they aren't all spies or double agents."

She gave him side eye.

Dorian smiled, raising his hands in a gesture of surrender. "All I'm saying is, if it's coming from that high up—or that far down depending on how you want to look at it—no one is finding evidence because *they* don't want the evidence found."

"Grr."

"Doesn't explain your strange fascination with DemonCore." Dorian whistled innocently to himself. "Perhaps there is something of a paranormal nature going on here."

Ideas stormed around her head while she fast-walked to the cafeteria, got in line, picked up a chicken Caesar wrap plus a green tea, then plopped down to sit at a tiny table. People from the various other divisions, mostly 1, 5, and 6, sat in social groups across the vast, shiny silver room. The aromas of a thousand different foods formed a not-unpleasant milieu in the air. Hundreds of conversations blended together in an indecipherable maelstrom of sound.

While munching on her wrap, she pulled out her NetMini and called Sam.

He appeared as a hologram head, smiling at her. "Hey. Oh, lunch. Cool. Be right there."

Kirsten sighed playfully. "I can see the empty box behind you on the desk. You already ate. It's fine. Got caught up with something and lost track of time. Can you do me a little favor if you have some spare time?"

"Sure." He grinned. "Official stuff or personal stuff?"

"Umm. Kinda both." She bit her lip. "It's about inquests but, not any I'm actively assigned to. Following a strange hunch. I guess you could call it official since there's nothing here I'm going to benefit from personally."

"Fair enough. What's the target?" He winked.

"I'm going to email you a list of inquest IDs. Seven supposed hackers have been killed over the past nine months by fatal intrusion countermeasure software. But… it doesn't make sense. Dorian's telling me the places they went into shouldn't really have that sort of thing. Can you poke around and see what you can find? No rush."

"Yeah. I can do that. Easy enough." He grinned.

The memory of having sex with him hours ago in the autoshower tube returned, warming her face and chest. Her thumb had brushed over the tiny metal socket behind his left ear. At the time, it didn't bother her. The *thought* of cybernetic implants usually made her squirm. Touching Sam's M3 port didn't. He had no reason not to get one, or any of the other stuff he had—all tied to his computer work. Her lunch contained more psionic power than Samuel Chang's brain. Electronic implants made him far more effective—and safer—at his job.

She needed a pro to check on this stuff. No way could she ever keep up in the GlobeNet using a senshelmet.

For the remainder of her lunch, she chatted with Sam about whatever came to mind. They got cute enough for someone nearby to mutter 'get a room.' Blushing, Kirsten decided to go somewhere else. It didn't occur to her that Dorian had given them privacy until she ended the call with Sam and her ghostly partner reappeared in the seat facing her, grinning.

She blushed more.

"It's good to see you so happy." Dorian patted her on the shoulder, leaving a cold spot.

"It's good to be happy, even if I'm faking it."

"You're faking it?" He blinked.

"Umm." She fidgeted. "Not exactly. I *am* happy. Just don't trust it'll last. I'm full of dread and hiding it. Makes me feel like I'm only faking it, being normal-ish."

He folded his arms. "Welcome to society. Life is a constant process of dread management broken up by brief periods of genuine happiness and heavy sorrow."

Unsure whether he meant to be comforting or cynical, she sighed, got up, and approached the nearest trash bin, tossing the empty plastic clamshell in it. The nagging desire to pursue DemonCore needled at her. She turned away from the bin to peer over at Dorian. "Those deaths might be connected somehow. Do you think I'm trying to see patterns where there aren't any?"

"Not at all." He followed her to the dark grey strip of rubbery traction coating that formed a 'carpet' leading to the cafeteria exit. "There's no harm in searching for patterns. The bad stuff happens when people start inventing patterns when they can't find them."

"Right." She snapped her fingers. "I'm not going to do that."

OUTSIDE CHANCE

Another hour of reading over inquest notes got Kirsten nowhere closer to understanding potential connections between the victims.

If anything linked the seven dead GlobeNet pirates, finding it would require doing full background checks on them. Thankfully, the NPF had AIs capable of doing such cross checking and analyzing. Problem being, she couldn't just send off a request to have it done without an active, official inquest in her name. Somewhere between resource management and judicial warrants to go rooting around in citizens' past, she'd at least need the superficial pretext of having an ongoing case.

Merely looking at other detectives' work didn't quite make the cut.

She sat there staring at the empty squad room for a while. It didn't really bother her to be idle as it meant no one had been hurt, terrified, or attacked by anything paranormal. The day might come when Command started sending her out on normal psionic investigations, but for now, they preferred she be available and ready right away should something weird happen. Her present inactivity didn't create a burden on any other part of Division 0. Tactical could keep up with things for the most part. Spikes happened. Ebbs happened.

Not long ago, she found herself scrambling to cope with an explosion of paranormal events. A little downtime was welcome.

Hmm.

A stray idea swirled around her head, growing stronger each time she read a comment from another investigator or a tech who could not offer up any explanation for what prompted seven different cyberspace interface decks to fry their users. Notes from multiple detectives, three medical examiners, and eight different forensic technologists spanned the inquest files. They'd already ruled out manufacturing defects with the hardware. No two victims had the same devices. While none had serious top-of-the-line rigs, they also hadn't been using junk.

Since Kirsten didn't know too much about the online world, she kept a chat window open with Sam, peppering him with questions. Two of the dead net pirates had been using custom decks they'd likely put together themselves, 'Frankensteined' as Sam put it, from different makers' parts. Those two appeared to be the most likely to have strayed into a network badass enough to contain black ICE. Sam explained how 'real' hackers rarely used off-the-shelf decks since they wouldn't trust them not to contain manufacturer backdoors, vulnerabilities, or hidden traceable e-signatures. Among the hacking community, people who just bought a deck and ran it 'factory standard' were considered casuals and not taken seriously. Five of the dead with cooked brains had been using largely unmodified net decks. Three hadn't even been active in the 'hacking scene.' The Nishihama Avatar IV deck belonging to one victim had enough power to support high-end hacking, but its owner appeared to have used it primarily for gaming, lacking any record or even suspicion of cyberspace trespass.

Sam thought the guy might've been good enough not to get caught, especially using a deck worth almost half a million credits. Still, the tech investigators couldn't find any route trace for where the black ICE came from. Having the actual deck in their lab would have made it a veritable certainty they'd have been able to tell exactly where the user had been at the time of the fatal shock. Everything they mined out of the unit's neural memory put him in the middle of a virtual XSB match at the time.

XSB, or 'extreme speedball,' amounted to a video game version of Gee-ball with guns, missiles, and land mines. Sam briefly floated the idea that an angry opposing player might have attacked him using illegal software disguised as an in-game weapon, but dismissed it himself due to the techs not finding any traces.

Seven instances of raw voltage going down the M3 jack into the user's brains from seven entirely different decks ruled out hardware defects. That not one investigator could find any trace of a connection path in the GlobeNet systems should have also ruled out the use of black ICE, yet somehow, it remained the official cause of death.

Kirsten's suspicions deepened. *They're only blaming ICE because they have no other ideas.*

Her weird preoccupation with DemonCore almost made sense. Maybe she'd picked up on something in the apartment unconsciously. Being around Dorian so long taught her how easily spirits could manipulate electronic devices. Ghosts were, after all, primarily made up of electromagnetic energy. They could affect electronic fields, mess with digital technology, even essentially 'feed' on sources of electrical power. Just the other day, she'd watched Dorian jump *into* a delivery bot and take it over.

She swung around in her chair to look at him again.

Dorian continued reading something on his NetMini for a few seconds before shifting his gaze up to peer over the floating holo-panel at her, then smiled. "Something on your mind?"

"Lots. But… specific question."

"Yes. I believe now would be an excellent time for coffee."

She fake growled. "Dammit. Now I want coffee."

He smiled to himself. "It appears you are not the only suggestive in the room."

"Oh, sure. Getting me to want coffee isn't exactly hard." Kirsten rolled her eyes. "Good timing. I think I'm about to take a ride. Question though."

"Hmm?" He shut off his ghostly NetMini and stood.

She sent Sam a text thanking him for his help and letting him know she needed to go on a field trip, then got up. "How possible would it be for a spirit to kill someone who is jacked in via M3 port to a cyberspace deck?"

"Good question. I've never really messed around with those." He tapped a finger to his chin. "On a simplistic level, it would require only bridging a current path between a source of sufficient voltage and the physical lead out to the cable. Ground enough juice directly into their heads, and poof. Doesn't really take that much voltage when it's wired right into the brain. All the components embedded in the skull overheat, catch fire, maybe even burst apart, sending shrapnel bouncing around inside."

"Ick." Kirsten grimaced, then fast-walked out of the squad room. Another reason never to allow anyone to put metal in her head. Even if it didn't cause problems for psionic abilities, it sounded too scary. "So it's possible."

Dorian glided up alongside her. "I'd have to go find a deck and play around. No idea what they look like inside."

"There are seven of them in the evidence storage facility at the RTC."

"At least seven. Probably hundreds." Dorian stopped following her. "I'll catch up."

"Okay."

"Beacon for me if you get into trouble."

She grinned at the swath of ghostly essence vanishing into the wall behind her. "Just going to a dead guy's apartment. I shouldn't get in trouble... which means I'm going to."

A pair of new tactical officers in the elevator snapped to attention and saluted her as she entered the capsule. Both wore rank insignia for Tactical Officer I, enlisted grade three. Kirsten returned their salute, then smiled. The men remained standing rigid. She gave them a quizzical eyebrow lift for a few seconds until it hit her. *Oh, they really are as new as they look.*

"At ease," she said. "Also, we aren't a combat unit. You can save the formality for official events and anyone over the rank of captain."

The guys relaxed, then chuckled.

"Wow, umm... how'd you make LT so young?" asked the one on the left. He didn't seem to be much older than eighteen, if even that.

His partner's expression said 'she's probably the daughter of a colonel or something' though he lacked the nerve to say it out loud.

Twenty-two (at the time of her promotion) wasn't really too young for anyone to be a lieutenant. Most of the 2LTs in the combat units happened to be around that age, coming in straight from university. Young age and lack of experience largely contributed to the preconception of LTs being Napoleonic incompetents drunk on power.

He thinks I'm sixteen or younger.

"Astral," replied Kirsten in an even tone of voice. "I am also not a minor. Yes, I know I look it."

Both men tensed up. The one who made the age comment went red-faced. Not being a telempath, Kirsten had no idea if he'd embarrassed himself or feared reprisal. Before she could tell him not to worry about it, the elevator stopped and they hurried out into another stark white corridor.

Weird. Command loves the color black for everything except the building. It's so damn *white.* She chuckled to herself. *If the hallways were black, too, we'd all be crashing into each other.* The elevator resumed going down to the motor pool. *Backward. Everywhere else in this entire city, hovercraft park on the roof. We keep them in the basement.*

The doors opened again with a chime, revealing the cavernous subterranean chamber holding the majority of Division 0's vehicular assets. Several hundred nearly identical patrol craft parked in long rows, along with a handful of larger units like the big, boxy A3HV transports. Despite the sameness of it all, she had little trouble navigating to her assigned space. The superstition about her PC had become so strong, no one even wanted to park next to it. What most of her team thought a cursed car really came from Dorian having been angry over his death as well as not wanting to ride with idiots.

Kirsten got in, pulled the door closed, and powered the systems on.

Hopefully, without the distraction of having a Div 2 detective hovering over her, she might be able to pick up on latent energy she'd missed before.

TWO THIRDS OF HER BERRY-MOCHA-LATTE REMAINED BY THE TIME KIRSTEN landed on the roof of the residence tower.

Leaving it in the car would allow it to get cold before she returned. Taking it with her all but guaranteed something crazy would happen, forcing her to drop and waste it. In all fairness, any time she got a nice coffee, it felt like daring fate to mess with her. It had, however, been a while since an emergency call interrupted a meal. She decided to sit in the patrol craft for long enough to savor three more unhurried sips before getting out.

If I take it with me, I might still be able to enjoy it warm… and if bringing it ups the odds of finding what I'm looking for, even better. She paused to sigh at the cup. As tragic as it would be to waste such awesomeness by spilling it, obtaining a replacement wouldn't be impossible, or even difficult.

On the walk across the roof parking area, it occurred to her she had no idea if either one of her parents liked coffee. She drowned the maudlin thought under a long, slow sip of chocolate-strawberry. As if sensing her consume sugary caffeine, a large advert bot drifting overhead showed two nude models, a man and a woman, striking poses under text pushing 'Simplefit weight control.' The somewhat expensive pills contained nanobots that promised to 'eliminate unsightly fat, restructure key cosmetic muscles, and keep your skin healthy.'

Ugh. People… I do it the old-fashioned way… running for my life a few times a month.

She walked under the obnoxiously massive advertisement and entered via a pair of silent sliding doors. After an uneventful elevator ride, she headed down the hall without really thinking about where she went. Once again, she found DemonCore's old apartment as easily as if she lived there herself despite the confusing mazelike halls lined with dozens of identical doors.

Yeah… something definitely wants me to find this place.

Upon accessing the building's network via the holo-terminal in her armguard, she discovered the apartment marked vacant and available. Already, six different people had visits scheduled to check the place out, starting tomorrow. Nothing caught her eye as noteworthy about the prospective tenants.

Wonder if any of them know a man died in here? She smirked to herself. *It's probably a hundred times more difficult to find a place where someone has never died.* At least she knew for a fact her apartment wasn't haunted. Whether or not anyone ever died there, she couldn't say. Surely, she'd have noticed a restless spirit by now.

Kirsten glanced to either side as if afraid of being caught, then activated a police override to open the door. *Gah. When did I turn into my son? Sneaking into places I probably shouldn't be going with good intentions.* She hurried into the apartment and let the door close behind her.

The lack of freezing cold compared to her last visit here struck her first. Air inside the apartment felt slightly warmer than out in the corridor. The apartment lay mostly bare, dim and tomblike. A scarce amount of light leaked in from the two smaller rooms at the opposite end, revealing all of Novar Kell's personal items had been removed. The larger multifunction space had no exterior windows, sandwiched between other apartments on either side and the two smaller rooms opposite the entrance.

Only the apartment's modular components remained. Anything not built into the walls or floor had been taken, except for a scattering of loose plastic clips, a few empty Cyberburger clamshells, and a dirty filter cartridge from a vacuum bot. An eerie silence saturated the place so heavily it almost became a presence unto itself. The fragrance of various cleaning products and carpet shampoo made each breath taste like a plastic pine tree.

She stood in place, half a step from the door, listening. After a moment, she took a breath and reached out using Astral Sense, searching for the presence of spirits nearby.

Sudden repetitive clicking and whirring went off at the far end of the room.

"Gah!" she jumped despite expecting—and hoping—for some sign of a ghost.

At the sound of her voice, the lights came on. Since the apartment did not presently have a registered tenant, the system didn't care who entered and would activate for anyone.

The noise stopped.

"Hello? Is someone here? I want to help."

Silence.

"Hello?" she called a little louder.

A labored whirr like a power drill accompanied rapid plastic clicking and thudding. This time, she perceived the sound as coming from the left door in the back, the one leading to the bathroom/kitchen combo. While it made some degree of sense given the need to run water lines to only one spot, the idea of preparing food so close to the toilet turned her stomach. She didn't care said toilet collapsed into the floor to make room for the stove extending from the wall.

Eyebrows furrowed, Kirsten crossed the mostly empty large room to the door on the left, and peered in. Twitching motion drew her attention to the back right corner. A round disc bot struggled to move, stuck half in its 'mouse hole,' unable to put itself away due to the hatch door over the filter compartment jamming into the wall.

"Oh, hi there, you." She set her coffee on the sink, then crouched over the round, flat plastic bot with the mirror finish. "Got yourself stuck."

The bot ceased attempting to ram itself into the wall slot.

Someone had replaced the filter cartridge, but failed to close the hatch all the way. Kirsten pulled the bot out of the wall, reseated the filter, and shut the hatch. The instant she put it back down, it zipped out of sight into the twelve-by-two-inch slot. Seconds later, having rotated around, it edged into view, peering out at the world via two tiny amber-glowing 'eyes'. They flashed in a slow rhythm, indicating charging in progress.

"Aww. That's better." She smiled at it. "Someone was hungry. From the smell of this place, you've been working all darn night."

She stood and grabbed her coffee. *Aaaand I'm talking to a floor-cleaning bot like it's a puppy.*

Shaking her head, Kirsten returned to the multifunction room and went over to where the workstation desk had been. As if catching a whiff of food from a block away outside, the fleeting trace of a spectral presence teased at her senses.

"Deactivate lights," said Kirsten.

The room went dark, save for the feeble bit of daylight coming from the bedroom and micro-kitchen. A faint luminous glow became noticeable on the floor in the general shape of the body she'd discovered the other day. Several footprint-sized spots of similar light dotted the carpet about where a spirit might have been standing beside the chair. They didn't feel the same as the dead guy, nor did it seem likely they'd come from Jun. Residue came from emotion, and Jun had about as much reaction to finding Novar Kell's remains as if someone dropped an empty Cyberburger clamshell on the floor.

Kirsten crouched to trace her fingertips over one spot. Unfortunately, the residue proved too weak to discern much from it other than a general feel for the presence. She did, however, confirm the footprint residue where a ghost had been standing differed from the body outline. A ghost other than Novar Kell had been there, and experienced an emotional response to the death strong enough to 'mark' the area. This, in and of itself, didn't necessarily prove something bad. It could have been a previously deceased friend or relative come to help him through the silver doorway.

Eyes closed, Kirsten focused on the image of the violet-haired man she found dead in this room and channeled psionic energy out into the world, calling for him. The people in lab coats referred to what she did as Beacon. They loved giving names to different uses of psionic abilities, even if it made no real sense. For example, if her friend Nicole used telekinesis to yank a weapon away from a suspect, the lab-coat people would call it 'Telekinetic Disarm' even though the power was functionally identical to her shoving a desk out of her way or picking up any object.

Beacon amounted to standing somewhere high and calling a ghost's name, hoping they'd hear and come visit. As far as she knew, Astral Sense lacked the ability to tell for certain if a particular ghost existed. Novar Kell had not been a synthetic, which meant he definitely had a spirit. However, not all spirits stuck around in the normal world after death. The vast majority went through what she called 'the silver door' within minutes or hours. Some had unhappy meetings with Harbingers. Though rare, complete obliteration remained a possibility even if she couldn't think of any ways for it to happen other than her Astral Lash ability.

Further complicating matters, even if Novar Kell's ghost haunted the mortal world, Beacon would not compel him to appear. She stood there trying it for a while, alternatively attempting to call for DemonCore by his hacker name in case being killed while online caused a mental block similar to the phenomenon of 'latent self-image.' A ghost tended to be stuck looking like they did at the exact moment of death, regardless of what—if anything—they'd been wearing when they died. The more traumatic the death, the more deeply a ghost's latent self-image burned into them. Any spirit could be coached into changing their outward appearance given enough time.

Dorian phased through the door, cringing. "You don't need to shout so much."

"Sorry." She sighed. "He's not answering."

"Figured as much considering you were screaming."

She twisted to look at him. "It really sounds like shouting?"

"Not exactly." He tilted his hand in a so-so gesture. "Not words. Energy, a sense of a name and identity, but it blares like I'm right next to someone who is screaming. Ehh, not exactly 'screaming,' more like speaking at a normal volume over an obnoxiously loud PA system."

"That is kind of the point." She raised her cup to drink. Finding the fluid now tepid, she glugged a mouthful rather than sipped. "Any idea if this guy might be stuck in his avatar?"

"Not sure I follow your meaning." Dorian tilted his head.

She gestured at the empty space where the desk used to be. "He died while online. Looked like black ICE. But, if he hadn't been going somewhere likely to be dangerous, death might have been so traumatic it left him stuck thinking he was whatever avatar he used online."

"Ahh. I see. Yes, he likely found his death quite the shock."

Kirsten stared at him. "That's not helping."

"My guess is he didn't hang out, since you're not having any luck summoning him." Dorian frowned at the empty apartment. "Murder victims usually jump at the chance to talk to someone who can hear them."

"Or he's ignoring me." She folded her arms. "Beacon isn't *summoning*. It's asking."

He chuckled. "Asking like you using a bullhorn in Evan's face telling him to clean his room."

"I don't do that!" She frowned. "I barely raise my voice at him."

"Metaphorically, shouting at someone six inches away with a bullhorn is what it feels like as a spirit when you are using that ability."

"Oh." She slouched. "Sorry."

Dorian wandered about the room, gazing at the floor. "Wow, they cleaned the place out fast."

"Hopefully, his relatives did it." She sighed, not putting it past the building management company to bulk sell the contents of the apartment as fast as possible so they could get a new tenant in and stop 'losing credits' on unrented space.

"Kirsten," chimed the overly cheerful voice of Suri, her NetMini AI. "Incoming vid call from Dr. Loring. I know you're like officially on duty and stuff, but it's her."

"Thanks. Yeah, answer it, please." Kirsten slid the small device out of its belt clip and held it out in front of her.

Dr. Loring's head (and some of her shoulders) appeared in a miniature holographic bust. "Good afternoon, Kirsten."

"Hi, doctor. I didn't forget about an appointment, did I?"

"No." Dr. Loring smiled. "I wanted to ask if you might be able to help a colleague of mine with one of his patients."

She blinked. "I'm not a psychologist, but I guess the amount of time I've spent talking to them counts for something. What can I do?"

Dorian snickered.

"Apologies for the short notice. Dr. Maz Vonn and I met in university. We are dear friends and somewhat regularly meet for lunch. I spoke to them this afternoon, and they've got a rather young patient with a distressing situation that sounds like something you might be able to defuse."

"Oh no..."

"It's not as bad as I just made it sound." Dr. Loring sighed. "I am likely skirting the boundaries of confidentiality here, but if you agree to help, you will technically count as care staff so I can talk about the case with you."

Dorian leaned into the call. "You mentioned a child. Of course she's going to want to help."

Kirsten nodded. "Yes. Absolutely." She gave Dorian side eye. "If there's anything I can do, just tell me what."

"The patient is five years old. She claims to have seen a ghost attempting to harm her mother."

Relief spread over Kirsten's body. "Oh, whew. Nothing horrible happened to the girl? I'm guessing her parents just don't believe she saw a ghost?"

"That's more or less correct, yes." Dr. Loring smiled. "I was hoping you might be able to speak with the girl, perhaps even check on their residence to see if there really is a ghost involved. From what Maz tells me, the child seems legitimately convinced what they saw was real. I'm hoping it was and isn't schizophrenic hallucinations."

"Yeah. No problem." Kirsten scratched her head. "Umm. A kid talking about ghosts is a little much to rush straight to a therapy session, isn't it?"

Dr. Loring grimaced. "There is a little more to it. The girl's mother was working online at the time. The child says she 'just knew' the ghost wanted to hurt her mother because she got a 'really bad feeling.' Before anything could happen—if anything would have happened—the child yanked her mother's uplink cable out."

Dorian squirmed. "Oof."

Kirsten rubbed behind her ear where a plug *wasn't*. Like most people not isolated from modern society, she'd heard stories about how unpleasant an abrupt disconnection could be, but had never experienced it. Suddenly going from one perceived reality to another couldn't be *that* bad, could it?

"The girl's parents were concerned about the girl doing that to her mother and blaming ghosts, which they don't consider to be real," said Dr. Loring. "The child has also screamed and gone into panic attacks every time her mother attempted to log back in to work, as if she's

afraid the woman will die the moment the wire is connected. So...
therapy."

"What does your friend think?"

Dr. Loring raised both eyebrows. "They think the girl is being
honest. This is why I'm calling you. Maz probably would've diagnosed
the poor child with hallucinations if not for spending the past year
hearing me talk about working with you."

Kirsten nibbled on her lower lip. "I'm famous."

"Up until I call them back once we're off the line, Maz doesn't
know your name. I've always referred to you as a patient of mine. If
you're going to meet them—I'll call ahead. They're with the family
now. We are having a consultation while the parents and child wait."

"Oh, ack. Umm. Okay." Kirsten cast a quick glance around the
empty apartment—still no sign of any ghosts—then hurried for the
door. "I'm on the way. Send me a Nav point please."

"Excellent. Thank you, Kirsten." Dr. Loring grinned. "I'll let Maz
know you're on the way."

SPIRITED DENIAL

A family stuck in a waiting room didn't quite rise to the level of urgency requiring emergency mode.

Kirsten still flew a little faster than normal traffic. The Nav point led her to a dagger-shaped silver high-rise in a commercial district packed with office buildings. Due to the artistic pyramid of scalloped arches lit with multicolored holographic swaths at the top of the structure, parking for hovercars occupied four enormous seashell-shaped platforms, one on each side of the building at the forty-fifth floor level, five stories below traffic lanes.

Ugh. I hate merging upward. So scary.

She landed on the northern platform among a mixture of high-end Halcyon-Ormyr cars and upper-mid-grade Timmons Orben luxury models. Luminous neon-green strips in the traction-coated plastisteel defined walkways leading to a façade of bronze and glass containing eight automatic doors. Silent actuators moved an inch-thick slab of glass out of her way. Faux marble gargoyles perched on the walls stared at her while she scurried under them to the elevator.

People in expensive business clothing all paused where they stood, conversations stopping in an instant, to stare at her. Expressions ranged from worry to annoyance that the police would be there. Only one man seemed fearful. Out of reflex, she scanned his surface thoughts. People who acted afraid of the police usually had reason to be. Alas, in this man's case, he simply recognized the meaning of the all-black uniform and had a mild phobia of psionics.

She disregarded his existence and hurried to the elevator.

Moments later, she entered the office of Dr. Maz Vonn.

Two women sat in the waiting area, reading glowing text on plasfilm e-magazines, essentially a cheap disposable datapad consisting of one thin display screen. Both gave her a casual glance upon noticing someone enter the room… and kept staring at her far longer than a simple processing of a new person arriving. Nothing new. People always stared at cops.

She approached the reception desk where a woman around her age with bright pink hair gazed vacantly into space. The receptionist sat beside a holo-terminal, though the screen displayed nothing. A silvery wire draped down off her shoulder, connecting her head directly to the machine. Seconds after Kirsten stepped close enough to seem obviously interested in conversation, the woman's eyes fluttered and she shook off her apparent mental fog.

"Hello. Welcome to Dr. Vonn's office," said the woman. "Can I help you?"

"Hi. I'm Lieutenant Wren. The doctor is expecting me. I'm here to help them with an issue."

The woman perked up, then pointed at one of three doors on the left side of the room. "Oh! Yes. You got here fast. Go on in. Third door on the right."

"Thanks."

Kirsten nodded at her, then crossed the waiting room to a door marked 'employees only'. *Hope I'm not walking in on the patients without seeing the doctor first.* She made her way down a sedate corridor of grey, silver, and black to the indicated door, finding it open. Inside, a person sat behind a modest desk, evidently reading something on a huge holo-panel screen.

They seemed to be in their later thirties, slim, with a pale face, rounded cheeks, and neat, short jet-black hair. Dr. Vonn's slate-grey eyes appeared ever so slightly too large for their face, which gave off an ephemeral, almost elven beauty. The doctor wore a grey business suit with a shiny black necktie that devoured their slight body like a teenager putting on their father's clothes.

"Is that a woman in an oversized suit or a scrawny man?" whispered Dorian.

"Doesn't matter," muttered Kirsten before approaching the desk and smiling. "Dr. Vonn? I'm Lieutenant Wren, but please... call me Kirsten."

"Not judging." Dorian smiled. "Just saying... pick a suit that fits. It's too big for them."

Kirsten wanted to say something about the 'oversized clothing' look being a fashion trend done on purpose, but couldn't possibly say it without the doctor hearing, so... didn't. She vaguely recalled some British music personality starting the look about four years ago.

"Hello," said the doctor in a voice about perfect for a male elf from the Monwyn universe. Slightly low for a woman, slightly high for a man. "Thank you so much for dropping everything and racing over here."

"It's no problem at all. How can I help?"

"Please, sit." Dr. Vonn gestured at one of the three chairs facing the desk. "The patient's name is Emi Mons. She's five and quite certain she saw a... ghost. I understand you work with them and ghosts are actually real?"

Kirsten nodded once. "Yes. Not everything unexplainable can be blamed on spirits, but they are real."

"Interesting." Dr. Vonn shifted their jaw side to side. "Emi tells me she saw a bad ghost trying to hurt her mother. She unplugged the woman's M3 cable abruptly when the ghost got too close to the terminal."

"I understand. Dr. Loring let me know. She's also having anxiety over the idea of her mother logging in again?"

"Correct. That's mostly why they're here. It's unorthodox to involve someone like you in a situation like this. And by that I mean someone who is not a mental health professional. But, I'm told you're an expert... and as best I'm able to tell, the girl doesn't seem to be making up stories. Her version of events is remarkably consistent and at her age, it's rather unlikely for her to imagine everything she's saying."

"I'd be happy to speak with her."

Dr. Vonn exhaled. "My initial thoughts were that the girl is experiencing schizophrenic hallucinations, which are very much real to her. I don't like at all how she's showing no other signs of clinical mental illness. As unbelievable as it is for me to say this, my inclination is to believe she really did see what she claims to have seen. It's fortunate Emma told me in passing about having a client who worked with spirits. Never would've even considered the idea the child might have actually observed a genuine ghost otherwise. Before I start her on medication, I'd really like to know for sure. I've already mentioned you in passing to the parents and they are open to the idea of your help."

Emma? Who is...? Oh! Dr. Loring must be Emma. Kirsten sat up a little straighter, caught happily off guard by this news. "Oh? Wow. Okay."

"Hmm." Dorian glanced at her.

"Don't start," whispered Kirsten.

He waved dismissively at Dr. Vonn. "I couldn't care less what they've got under the hood. Just teasing you. What I'm thinking about... this kid saw a ghost going near her mother's terminal and somehow got convinced their mother's life was in danger. Sounds rather damn familiar, doesn't it?"

"It does," said Kirsten.

"What does?" asked Dr. Vonn. "And what shouldn't I start?"

Kirsten cringed. "Sorry. My partner is with me. He's a ghost. We're looking into a series of unexplained deaths that sound rather similar to what this child thinks almost happened to her mother. I said it does sound familiar."

"Oh." Dr. Vonn's already white face seemed to grow even paler. "There's a ghost in here now?"

"Yes. No need to worry. He's with Division 0 as well."

"Still? After death?" Dr. Vonn blinked.

"Unofficially. He loved the job so much he couldn't give it up." Kirsten winked at Dorian.

"Truth." He held his arms out in a 'you got me' manner. "If this girl did see a spirit attempting to do something to her mother's terminal, it might explain the bizarre deaths."

Kirsten looked at him. "Did you find anything at the RTC?"

"Nothing conclusive regarding whether or not any specific spirit affected the victims' hardware. However, I figured out it wouldn't be too difficult for a spirit to effectively simulate what happens when a user is hit with black ICE."

"It's not complicated?"

Dr. Vonn raised an eyebrow. "Are you asking me or your ghost?"

Kirsten nodded toward him. "Talking to my partner."

"No," said Dorian. "Like I guessed, basic contacts. All the fancy programming for defense countermeasures is necessary to force the operating system to do something it's designed to avoid doing at all costs. There are multiple safety interlocks that need to be disabled, for example. The hardware, as you might imagine, is not designed to be capable of delivering a lethal shock to the user, so black ICE requires overloading components to force that amount of voltage down the wire to the brain. The components on the path between power source and M3 plug can't handle the level of power required and usually burn out. As far as a ghost is concerned, we're basically touching a piece of scrap metal to two contacts and giving the current a fast way out through the jack port into someone's brain. The decks involved in those seven deaths don't have the telltale component scorch path on their mainboards. All show signs that electricity jumped from the power source directly to the M3 port."

"Eek." Kirsten shivered.

"Is something wrong?" asked Dr. Vonn.

"Something is wrong, yes, but not with me. Every day it seems I learn there's a new way the unknown can put our lives in danger. Technology is everywhere." She repetitively rubbed her hands down her legs. The smooth, clingy fabric of her uniform didn't even rumple. "Suppose it's not really much different than the odds of a software glitch knocking a bot out of the air."

Dorian laughed. "The odds of a software glitch committing murder by ineptitude are far, far greater than a spirit learning how to tweak electronics just right. Dare I say that the majority of ghosts wouldn't even think to try. Especially the angry ones. Black ICE isn't as scary or horrifying as the online culture makes it out to be. Plug the other end of an M3 cable into an e-mag and you'll get a much worse result. Hackers talk about this stuff like it's ancient black magic. They're as bad as sailors or starship personnel for superstition."

"Ready to meet the patient and her family? They've been waiting for some time now." Dr. Vonn stood.

"Oh. Yes. Of course."

"Great, well… let me introduce you." Dr. Vonn gestured at the door. "This way. Due to the patient's age, the parents are in the room with her."

Kirsten nodded.

Dr. Vonn exited the office.

"Hmm. Roughly six inches taller than you," said Dorian, rubbing his chin.

Kirsten refused to bite on his troll bait and followed the doctor down the hall and into a therapy room. Unlike the majority of the place in austere black, silver, and grey, this therapy room exploded in vibrant colors and cartoon figures on the walls. If Kirsten considered Dr. Vonn pale, the therapist had nothing on the woman sitting on the neon green sofa, whose skin was the exact color of snow. She sat next to a man with an Eastern European look to his features. Unlike her, he appeared to be an Earth native. The woman almost certainly had been born on Mars. Both of them appeared to be in their later thirties.

A little girl in a purple dress sprawled on the rug in front of them, playing with stuffed animals. She'd inherited her mother's unnaturally white hue, the so-called Marsborn genetic modification being rather strong in that regard.

As Dr. Vonn led Kirsten into the room, the family all looked up at once. The man gave off a sense of relief at a long wait being over. The woman's visible nervousness intensified. Emi, the five-year-old, grinned and waved at Kirsten, then sent a bewildered glance toward where Dorian stood.

He waved at her.

The child didn't return it, suggesting she couldn't really see him as much as perhaps sensed a presence.

Kirsten smiled in greeting at the parents, then sat on the floor next to the child. "Hi there. I'm Kirsten."

"You're a police," said Emi.

"I am."

"Police can't 'rest ghosties," said the girl, busily making two stuffed animals dance with each other.

"You're right. We can't arrest spirits. I can stop the bad ones. I'm a special kind of police." She winked.

The girl peered up, seemed to drink in her presence over the next few seconds, then went wide-eyed. "You're a pasonic?"

"That's right." Kirsten smiled.

Mrs. Mons leaned back, seeming afraid.

"Oh, thank you," said the husband, a noticeable German accent in his voice. "Calm yourself, Tara. That crap you heard back home is nonsense. This woman can tell for sure what happened. She can look right into Emi's head and make sure our daughter isn't crazy."

"I'm not crazy," said Emi. "I saw a bad ghost. Am I pasonic?"

Kirsten flashed a conspiratorial grin at the kid. "I don't know yet, but I can find out if you want."

"You can read her mind, see what's really going on in there?" asked Dr. Vonn.

"I can." Kirsten poked a stuffed giraffe lying on the rug beside her.

"What's involved?" Tara bit her lip. "Will it hurt her?"

Kirsten shook her head. "Not at all. She won't feel anything except maybe a little light-headed for a few seconds. All I need to do is look into her eyes."

"If it will let Mommy believe I didn't make it up, you can look inside my head." Emi stared up at her, widening her eyes as much as she could.

The father nodded. Tara clung to his arm, giving Kirsten an 'okay fine, just get it over with' expression. Emi beamed.

"Okay, kiddo." Kirsten set the giraffe plush atop her head. "Smile at Mr. Giraffe."

Emi giggled.

TECHNICOLOR DEATH COASTER

As soon as Kirsten established a telepathic link to the little girl's mind, the idea presently dominating the child's surface thoughts bled over. She hadn't been trying to read the child's thoughts—merely measure any potential psionic ability—but the strength of the imagery made it impossible *not* to see.

Memories did not always encompass an accurate view of reality, especially in a moment of high emotion. Small details unimportant to the major event could blur, change, or disappear entirely. The scene playing out in the girl's head appeared to be floating in a hazy void. Barely visible scraps of furniture hovered at the edges of a circular area of high detail, like an artistic photograph taken with a 'frosted glass oval' filter on. At the center, a woman—presumably the mother—sat with her back facing the child's point of view, slumped over a desk on a pillow as if having a nap.

Beside her hovered a warped apparition of shadow giving a vague suggestion of a human form. The child sensed malice. No specific cue or psionic ability told her the thing she saw meant to harm her mother, yet the girl was convinced of it. The instant a shadowy tendril stretched toward the terminal as if the spirit attempted to touch it, the scene changed in an instant to Tara Mons flopping around on the floor in the manner of a dying fish, foam coming out of her mouth.

Somewhere back in her basic police training, they'd gone over 'Neuralink Abend,' the official term for the unexpected, sudden disconnect of a user's consciousness from simulated reality. Detective Nevi Arun called it 'riding the technicolor death coaster,' a term Kirsten hadn't heard before. It almost always resulted in seizures as well as an often highly unpleasant cascade of random sights, sounds, and feelings. Stray electrical charges in the interface jack could be interpreted by a person's NIU into various things the same way incoming electrical signals from the deck translated into sights, smells, and sounds of a virtual world… only without control.

In most cases, the barrage ended in a minute or two without permanent physical harm. Rarely, people could suffer complications such as stroke, heart attack, seizure, or prolonged coma.

This kid didn't understand the danger exactly, but she did know it could seriously hurt her mother to yank out the wire… and she was so much more afraid of the shadow person, she still did it.

Kirsten scanned the girl's mind for evidence of psionic powers, though she already suspected none. The distorted shadow figure the kid observed matched the way non-psionic people had been describing ghost sightings for hundreds of years. For reasons still not fully understood even by Division 0, non-psionic children frequently sensed or saw spirits, though typically only when said spirit wanted to be seen. The prevailing theory claimed the amount of effort needed by the spirit for a normal person to become aware of them was far lower in the case of children. In those cases, kids often spoke of seeing actual people and/or talking to them. This spirit likely did not want to be seen, but their use of power—seemingly to affect the mother's terminal —resulted in a manifestation strong enough for the girl to perceive as a shadow figure.

"Are you all right?" asked the father.

Kirsten shifted her gaze off the girl to him. "Yes. Why?"

"The two of you have been staring at each other for a while. I've never seen Emi so quiet for so long." He smiled.

"The police lady saw the ghost, too," muttered the girl.

Tara Mons squirmed. "You're saying she really did see what she says she did?"

"I believe so, yes." Kirsten nodded.

"Emi is not psionic," said the father in a neutral tone.

"Relax Gerhardt," whispered Tara. "It's not illegal here."

He glanced at his wife. "I am aware of that, dear. I'm merely stating a fact."

"What did you see?" asked Kirsten.

"Mommy was doing work. Alla sudden I got scared, an' looked up. The bad ghost was gonna hurt Mommy." Emi dropped a stuffed elephant so she could hug the rabbit in both arms. "It touched the term'nal. Mommy didn't see it 'cause she was in the work, like asleep. I hadda wake her up before the ghost hurt her."

"Officer," said Tara. "If our daughter isn't psionic, how could she possibly have seen a ghost? Are you absolutely sure she's not maybe imagining this?"

Kirsten didn't bother to correct the woman for calling her 'officer' instead of 'lieutenant.' Most civilians referred to any member of the NPF as 'officer' as a holdover from prewar days. "Ordinary people can occasionally see spirits. It's much more common with children. The younger they are, the more easily they notice them. The primary difference between an astral sensitive like myself and ordinary children is, I see ghosts exactly as they were in life, often so solid and real they aren't immediately apparent as spirits. I've lost track of how often I'm talking to someone, not even realizing they're dead. Non-psionic people see clouds of mist, shadow figures, light orbs, or sometimes transparent apparitions—like low quality holograms."

"Oh." Tara shrank in on herself. "So, you're telling me this is real? Not her imagination?"

"Well…" Kirsten took the giraffe off her head and tried to amuse Emi by making it 'walk' around. "The imprint of the memory in your daughter's mind is quite strong. I'm no psychologist, but my experience tells me she did have a genuine paranormal experience. I can't, however, absolutely rule out the possibility she imagined it based on looking into her thoughts alone. Memories as potent as the one she has are generally impossible to create intentionally via imagination. However, in order to declare it an absolute fact you had a dangerous spirit in your home, I would need to go there and detect a lingering trace of paranormal energy."

"Sounds like you're convinced, lieutenant." Gerhardt put an arm around Tara. "Go on. Tell her."

Dr. Vonn raised both eyebrows. "Tell her what?"

"Umm." Tara fidgeted. "It's a bit too much to believe. I needed Emi to be imagining this."

"I'm sorry, Mommy." Emi crawled up into her mother's lap. "I didn't 'magine it."

"It's fine, my love. The lieutenant won't call you crazy." Gerhardt took his wife's hand.

Tara kissed Emi on the head, then looked at Kirsten. "When my daughter told me she saw *something* try to stick its hand in my terminal and somehow just knew it wanted to hurt me, I tried to dismiss it because I couldn't cope with the idea of what might have been happening."

"That's perfectly natural," said Dr. Vonn. "Most rational people would not immediately accept the existence of spirits."

"What is it you think might've been happening?" asked Kirsten.

Emi abruptly looked up, staring across the room at the back corner where Dorian made silly faces at her. She appeared frightened for a few seconds, then confused.

"This is not easy for me to think about." Tara squeezed her daughter. "If it's real, then I almost died."

"No," whimpered Emi, before burying her face against her mother's shoulder.

"Over the past seventeen months, eleven people from my company have been killed at their terminals," said Tara. "Management considers it an act of corporate espionage, hostile operators breaching our network and attacking our people with kill programs. Our security team hasn't been able to find them or even tell what region the attacks came from. Hardware upgrades and additional defense measures haven't helped."

"Eleven?" Kirsten activated the terminal in her arm guard. "Which company do you work for?"

"Atmos." Tara swiped her hair off her face.

Kirsten searched the NPF database, the closest match being a company registered as Atmos Industries. A few finger taps to the holo-panel lifted Tara's PID from her NetMini and compared it to the company. She popped up as a match, employed as an electrical engineer on the design team. Now certain she had the correct company looked up, Kirsten did a little digging around their records. It didn't take her long to find *fourteen* reports of employees being killed while on company time. Their management notified the authorities of suspected inter-corporate espionage. All had been logged into their virtual workspaces via the GlobeNet at the time of death, but not one of them matched any of the names from the other inquests. Atmos Industries' dead employees didn't have any known connections to the 'hacker scene,' thus word of their deaths hadn't travelled among the same circles.

This is getting serious.

"Pardon me saying, lieutenant, but you don't seem happy." Gerhardt Mons gave his wife's hand a squeeze. "Is something wrong?"

Kirsten closed her terminal screen. "Yes, but not with Emi. I'm starting to think there's a spirit running around killing people."

The five-year-old made a 'duh, no kidding' face at her.

Tara stared. "Are you seriously saying that ghosts exist and are doing this?"

"I am. Though, I can only comment with any degree of confidence about what happened to you at the moment."

"Told you," muttered Emi. "Bad ghost wanted to hurt Mommy."

Gerhardt exhaled a long, slow breath. "How could something like a ghost possibly harm people?"

Dorian chuckled.

"I'm sure you don't want a long explanation." Kirsten grimaced. "Depends mostly on the age of the spirit. The longer they've been around after death, the more they're capable of. In this case, having an electrical device essentially plugged right into your brain stem makes it easy on them. It could take decades for a spirit to gather enough strength to be able to shove someone down the stairs, for example. But... ghosts are essentially a gathering of electromagnetic energy.

Manipulating electrical current is easy for them. The amount of power needed to kill someone through an M3 connection is honestly quite small. Beyond simple electrocution, the neural interface unit that's grafted into brain tissue heats up, may catch fire."

Tara shuddered. "So ghosts can just kill anyone with headware whenever they want?"

"No," said Dorian. "Most people don't have a power source strong enough inside their bodies. They'd only be vulnerable with an active connection."

Emi glanced in his general direction. "I hear whispers."

"It's back?" Tara clutched the girl defensively to her chest.

"That's my partner, Dorian. He's a ghost." Kirsten nodded toward him.

Dr. Vonn regarded her with an expression as if to say 'wow, you really do believe in ghosts'.

"A person would only be at risk if connected to a device." Kirsten set the plush giraffe down on the rug. "Internal parts don't contain enough power to be a threat."

Dorian pushed a fake plant off the coffee table.

Tara screamed. Gerhardt jumped. Dr. Vonn gasped, covering their mouth with both hands. Emi giggled.

"Really?" Kirsten peered up at him. "Was that necessary?"

"It seemed as if the good doctor doubted you and wondered if you might have lost your grip on reality." He smiled. "I merely felt the need to validate you. The plant seemed a better idea than manifestation. Though... we *are* in a therapist's office already, so perhaps if I had shown myself to them it would've been equivalent to suffering a heart attack while already at a medical center."

He is so bad. She fought the urge to smile.

"I'm also mildly annoyed this woman didn't believe her child and dragged her to therapy as an excuse to ignore the truth." Dorian frowned. "This girl saved her mother's life and she gets treated like she's got mental issues."

Kirsten twitched. A mother having a bad reaction to their child interacting with the paranormal hit a bit close to home for comfort. However, Tara didn't respond with anger and hatred, merely concern something might be wrong. Now, the woman appeared to have done a complete reversal in attitude.

"What happened?" Gerhardt picked the plant up from the floor and put it back on the table.

"My partner wanted to offer some evidence as to the reality of spirits." Kirsten smiled at the doctor, then looked at the parents. "I'd like to take a look around your residence where this happened if you don't mind."

Tara offered a hesitant nod. "I don't have a problem with that, but… will it help?"

"It may allow me to identify or locate the spirit responsible and stop it before it hurts anyone else."

Gerhardt leaned back, seemingly relieved. "Later tonight would be fine. We'll need to finish up here and have an errand or two to deal with after. Is there a way for us to protect ourselves?"

"Senshelmets." Kirsten tapped her head. "The risk comes from having the direct connection to your headware."

Tara appeared to relax a little. "Ugh, those things are so slow, but I can cope."

Dr. Vonn smiled at Kirsten. "Thank you so much for helping here."

"Happy to." Kirsten got up. *Well, I've got some work to do now.* She gave the family her departmental contact information. "Let me know when would be a good time to stop by."

"Any time after, oh, about seven should be fine," said Gerhardt.

"All right." Kirsten smiled at Emi. "I'll let myself out then. Hope the rest of your day is good."

"Should be." Dorian followed her out of the therapy room. "They know their kid isn't crazy."

"Yes, but," whispered Kirsten once she closed the door, "now, that woman realizes she came within inches of death. I don't think her daughter is going to have to beg too hard to keep her offline."

"No doubt." Dorian whistled.

ETHICAL GREY ZONE

The increasing likelihood a spirit was responsible for the deaths presently blamed on black ICE drove Kirsten up to a fast walk.

A different set of detectives worked on the Atmos employees than the dead hackers, taking two different approaches. In the case of the fourteen employees, investigators tried to find an unknown outside party responsible for murdering them—after eliminating hardware failure. Detectives assigned to the hackers' deaths tried to figure out what part of cyberspace the victims went to in order to blow themselves up. Predictably, the 'murdered employees' got more effort from the police than 'hackers who probably got what they deserved.'

Kirsten's mental grumbling paused two corridors away from the therapy room when she heard someone crying. Concern as well as curiosity drew her to a doorway beside a small silver sign marked 'staff lounge.' She paused, listening for a few seconds to what sounded like a man sobbing quietly to himself before peeking inside.

A late-forties man stood by the window, staring blankly at passing hovercar traffic. He had a professional look to his outfit, perhaps another doctor, therapist, or counselor of some form. His demeanor fit a man who'd just learned of a close relative's death. The scene didn't appear to require her intervention. Nonetheless, she hesitated, debating between asking if he was okay or slipping away before he noticed her.

Upon noticing her reflection in the window, he peered back.

"Oh. Sorry." She offered a weak smile and started to back up. "Didn't mean to intrude."

He stared at her.

She took another step back.

"Wait." The man raised a hand, beckoning her. "You're psionic, aren't you?"

"Uniform gave it away, didn't it?" Kirsten attempted a weak smile, hoping this guy might not turn hostile if she admitted it without hesitation, as if it really wasn't a big deal.

"Wonderful." He wiped tears from his eyes. "Is there any possibility you can help?"

She blinked, not expecting such a warm reaction. Still a bit guarded, she advanced into the small break area, stopping on the opposite side of a small table. The man wore an ID on a lanyard around his neck identifying him as Dr. Gig Larson.

"What kind of help do you need?" asked Kirsten.

Dr. Larson glanced out the window again. "I'm running out of ideas to help a young patient, afraid it's at the point where I'm going to have to insist she be involuntarily committed until someone can figure out what's driving the depths of her depression and self-destructive behavior. If I let her family take her home today, I don't think she'll live through the night."

Kirsten pressed a hand to her chest over her heart. "You think she'll commit suicide?"

"Possibly... but." Dr. Larson shook his head. "This poor kid might just die of pure sadness if that's even a thing. You caught me trying to compose myself before going back in there to talk to her and her father. I'm at my wits' end and don't know what to possibly do to help this girl."

She winced.

"Hey..." He made eye contact. "This isn't exactly ethical in the strictest sense of the regulations, but if it saves this kid's life, I don't care. Is there any chance you could maybe read her mind and see if there's anything in there going on in her life she refuses to tell me about that's driving her into such a state of depression?"

Kirsten buried her face in both hands. "It's not ethical."

"I know." Dr. Larson sighed. "I had to ask though."

"It's not ethical." Kirsten lowered her hands and bit her lip. "But… I can look. However." She held up a finger. "If this girl is not an immediate danger to herself or others, I won't be able to tell you what I see in her thoughts."

He managed a wan smile. "That is fair. I'm all out of ideas for how to help this poor girl. It's going to haunt me for the rest of my life if she dies and there's nothing I could've done."

"Barging in on them might not be the best idea." Kirsten glanced down at herself as if to call attention to her uniform. "She might think I'm there to arrest her."

"What would work best? Can you observe her from some distance or would you rather I ask them if it's okay?"

"Definitely more ethical to get consent," said Dorian. "But if they say no and you do it anyway…"

Kirsten fidgeted. *It's for her own good. Only a breach of ethics if I act on knowledge I shouldn't have from invading her privacy.* "I can take a quick look from the doorway then say 'oops, wrong room' or something."

"Ahh, rules. There to be bent." Dorian smiled at the ceiling. "Or ignored."

She shot him side eye.

"Thank you. If there's nothing you can tell me or any way you can point me in the right direction to help this kid, feel free to do the 'wrong room' act and leave. But I do appreciate whatever assistance you can offer. Is there anything specific I should do or not do while you're looking?"

"If you ask her if she knows why she feels the way she feels while I'm there, it should pull the cause to the tip of her brain… assuming she subconsciously or consciously understands it. If there's no causative behavior or event in her life—like a brain chemistry situation —she won't know why she's sad all the time. I will let you know if it's nothing I can tell you or nothing I can find."

"Great. Thank you." Dr. Larson took her hand in both of his, squeezed, then let go. "This way, please."

She hurried after him down the hall to another consultation room, then waited ten seconds after he entered before nudging the door open an inch and taking a step in, pretending to stop short as if she'd made a mistake.

A slim girl on the younger end of teenage reclined on a therapist's couch, clutching a big teddy bear in her arms. Pink flip-flops lay abandoned on the carpet nearby. Her wide, almond-shaped eyes brimmed with sadness, red around the edges as if the poor kid had been crying the entire time the doctor left the room. Not far from the girl sat a man in his late thirties, murmuring quietly to himself in Spanish. His unfocused gaze suggested he was on a headware call, reflexively speaking aloud along with whatever he said to the person on the other end.

Dr. Larson spoke in a quiet, calming tone, addressing the girl as Allie and asking her if she could describe the things that make her feel so sad.

Less than a second after Kirsten started to peer into the child's thoughts, the girl shifted her gaze off the doctor to make eye contact. Three things hit Kirsten all at once. One: the girl was psionic. Two: she had no idea why she kept getting so sad her body nearly shut down. Three: she felt Kirsten's telepathy the instant it started, but didn't understand the meaning of the sensation.

"Someone's watching us," said Allie.

The girl sensed a spike of anxiety from the doctor, like a kid caught stealing cookies. It rapidly drowned in an otherwise overpowering sense of concern for her. Allie seemed to know the doctor *really* wanted to help her and cared a great deal, and felt even worse about her situation since being sad made him sad. Complicating matters, each time she came to visit him, he became more and more distraught, which made her think she did something wrong.

Kirsten stepped into the room. "Excuse me... I believe I can help."

Dr. Larson looked back at her, hope and surprise etched on his face.

This girl is psionic, said Kirsten telepathically to the doctor. *I'm pretty sure she is a telempath. She knows you are concerned about her... and probably knows I am, too. That weird look she's giving me now is because I'm excited.*

He blinked, wondering why she'd become excited when faced with a depressed thirteen-year-old.

Because. Kirsten smiled at him. *She's psionic. There is a good chance she isn't actually depressed.*

The father's eyes fluttered. "Oh. Umm. Sorry. Who are you? What are the police doing here?"

"I happened to be in the building and ran into Dr. Larson. He's so worried about Allie that he asked me to see if there happened to be anything I could do to help." Kirsten glanced back and forth between the girl and her father.

"That's..." He stared at her.

"Ethically questionable, yes." Kirsten nodded. "But, when a child's life is at risk, I'm willing to lean across lines if not step over them. The good news is, I don't think your daughter is mentally ill."

Allie scrunched her nose. "Are you serious? I can't even get out of bed. I cry all the time. I just want to stop existing. That's not normal."

Her father choked up.

"No, you're right. It's not normal." Kirsten sat on the end of the couch by the girl's feet. "If you weren't ill, if it was something else going on, you'd want to know, right?"

Allie shrugged, staring down. "Yeah, I guess."

That's the sadness talking. "Give me a moment to check something?"

"Whatever." Allie picked at the sofa. "You're the cops. You can do anything you want and we can't stop you."

Kirsten squeezed her hands into fists. She couldn't say the child was wrong, but didn't have to like hearing that. "There are some things we can't just do. I'm here to help."

"I believe you." Allie summoned the weakest smile she'd ever seen.

"Just relax and go with the flow of whatever you feel natural, okay?"

"What are you going to do?" asked the father.

"Your daughter is psionic." Kirsten glanced at him. "Telempathic to be exact. She can read the emotions of other people as well as change them if she wanted to. I don't think she's aware of her abilities. She sensed me looking into her thoughts, but didn't understand what she felt."

"Me? Psionic?" Allie's demeanor shifted in an instant to awestruck. She sat up and squish-hugged the bear. "No way."

Kirsten stared into the girl's eyes, telepathically probing her mind in the usual evaluation process. Anyone with a psionic skill could use it to oppose another person with the same skill. A telepath could resist mind reading for example, if they could overpower the person trying to read their mind. The scanning process involved lightly 'poking' the target brain with each ability and looking for a subconscious reaction. A person's brain would not respond at all to a power they did not have. In most cases, a psionic doing the scan wouldn't be able to detect low levels of powers they didn't have. Kirsten sensed weak telepathy and strong telempathy.

Given that Kirsten did not possess any telempathic ability, for her to detect it meant Allie had a significant gift.

Allie. Can you hear my voice in your mind?

The girl squeezed the bear. *Yeah.*

This is called telepathy. You can speak in other people's minds, too. Kirsten thought about the use of telepathy—basic tasks like talking, listening, and scanning surface thoughts—then sent those concepts into the girl's awareness.

Allie swooned as if dizzy. *So weird.*

Relax your mind. I'm still looking around. Won't be long. Kirsten pinged mentally, focusing on sadness and what caused it. Allie didn't appear to lack the will to live as much as she wanted to die to escape the interminable, constant, sorrow haunting her all the time. It appeared to be at its worst when she was at home. Here, visiting the doctor, it eased off to tolerable levels. Visiting her mother and maternal grandparents also made her sad, but not as severely as being at home with her father. The emotions didn't correlate directly to her father, mother, or even family, but appeared to originate from the physical location.

"Oh, I think I see what's happening. You aren't mentally ill, Allie." Kirsten let go of the telepathic link. "Mr...?"

Dr. Larson sat up, his expression relieved. "Do explain. Please."

"Karo," said the man. "Karo Dez."

"I'm not crazy?" Allie sniffled.

"No, sweetie. You're what we call a telempath. You can feel emotions from other people. I think you're very strong at it because I am not a telempath and I'm able to sense that you are. Mr. Dez, where do you two live?"

"Sector 1148," said Mr. Dez with an air of pride. "Amanita Tower. Eighty-fifth floor. We've got a wonderful view, not hemmed in by the surrounding buildings."

"Not cheap," said Dorian. "This guy's got money… and he's proud of it. It's true what they say. Money can't buy happiness."

Kirsten pulled the Navmap up on her armband terminal. "Sector 1148. That tracks."

"Pardon?" asked Mr. Dez.

"Sector 1148 is in the top fifteen percent of the most densely-populated areas of the city. You're also about thirty miles away from a huge grey zone around a dead area. If I had to guess, I'd say that the majority of people living within a reasonable radius of your home are highly stressed out and, well, not happy. Your daughter is picking up on ambient emotions of everyone in her area. All their discontent, anxiety, sadness, anger… everything negative is flowing into her mind and she thinks it's her own emotions."

Allie burst into tears.

Mr. Dez leapt from his chair to sit on the edge of the therapist couch, pulling his daughter into a hug. "You are being serious here?"

"I am. If I wasn't certain of her psionic abilities, I wouldn't be ethically able to discuss what I discovered in her thoughts. The instant I confirmed she is psionic, I had full jurisdiction to intervene if needed."

Dr. Larson practically melted back into his seat. "This is wonderful news. And it completely explains why I haven't been able to help her cope with her feelings. They're not *her* feelings."

Kirsten waited for the girl to calm somewhat, then explained how it seemed she suffered the most at home, less while visiting her mother, even less here.

"What can we do?" Mr. Dez appeared shocked at the revelation of his daughter being psionic, though not disgusted, hostile, or terrified.

Kirsten scanned his surface thoughts—an act she deemed fully within her purview as a Division 0 officer making first contact with a psionic. She needed to verify what, if any, threat a parent posed to a psionic child when they previously had no idea their kid possessed psionic abilities. Far too commonly, parents could abandon them or turn abusive. Fortunately, Mr. Dez had no real opinion about psionics. His thoughts appeared to fixate entirely on the hope his daughter might not be suicidal and mentally ill.

"A few things." Kirsten smiled at them. "The best fix would be for Allie to learn how to control her abilities. It will be possible with some training for her to tune out the 'noise' of her environment. However, until she learns how to do that, the wisest thing for her would be to live in a place that doesn't have tons of angry, miserable people in close proximity."

"They're not going to want to leave Earth," muttered Dorian.

"Way north or way south," said Mr. Dez. "Off the elevated part of the city."

"That's an option." Kirsten nodded. "North is cold and you get the occasional critter from the Badlands wandering into town. South is hot, but dry... and much closer a ride if you're interested in having Allie visit us for help learning how to use and control her abilities."

"I'm not crazy?" Allie sniffled. "Really? It's *other people* making me sad?"

"Yes." Kirsten reached over and took her hand. "Look at me and tell me how I am feeling."

Allie stared at her for a moment. "You're happy... and you're kind of like 'ugh' the same way I feel at school when I get a lot of homework."

"Heh." Kirsten chuckled. "That's not from you. I've got a difficult case to solve hanging over me. But, see? You are reading my emotional state."

Allie looked at her father. "My dad's trying not to cry. Umm. How can someone be so happy they cry?"

Mr. Dez's lip quivered.

"I understand now." Allie rested her head on her father's shoulder. "He's why I'm still alive. Whenever Daddy is with me, I just knew he loved me so much I couldn't even think of doing anything to myself. I'm sorry for thinking about stuff like that. Promise I won't hurt myself."

Mr. Dez broke down and wept.

Kirsten couldn't hold back tears, either.

Dorian found the opposite corner of the room suddenly rather interesting.

After a long, heavy, emotional moment. Mr. Dez tearfully thanked Kirsten.

"It's lucky you were here," said Dr. Larson.

"Agreed." Mr. Dez sniffled, then cleared his throat. "So, how can I get her into training so she can protect herself? I mean, if she wants."

"I want, Dad. I definitely want." Allie wiped her eyes.

"Whenever you are ready, just stop by the PAC."

"PAC?" asked Mr. Dez.

"Police Administrative Center. It's a giant building in Sector 2147. Can't miss it."

He stared at nothing for a few seconds, likely reading a virtual screen in his headware. "We could go now… once we're done with Dr. Larson."

"I can wait and follow you in, get the process started." Kirsten stood.

"Great. Yes, let's do it now. Allie?"

The girl grinned. "Yeah. I'm tired of being sad all the time. Umm, do I have to become a cop?"

"Not at all. You can, but you don't *have* to do anything. That thing about Division 0 *making* people join is anti-psionic propaganda," said Kirsten.

"Oh, they do lean on people pretty hard." Dorian examined his fingernails. "But she's only an empath so they probably won't bother."

Kirsten fought the urge to laugh. Telempaths being 'weak' happened to be a running joke despite its falsehood. Empaths could be dangerous. The present head of Division 0 being a telempath only made it funnier as obvious sarcasm.

"People are going to hate me now." Allie frowned.

"Possibly, but the ones that do... it comes from jealousy." Kirsten patted her on the arm. "No matter who you are, what you can do, or what you think, there's always going to be someone out there who hates you for it. I call it a 'them' problem. Not a 'me' problem."

Allie smiled.

"All right. I'll wait outside for you guys to finish with the therapy session and we can go get her started in the system." Kirsten headed for the door.

Guess I know what I'll be doing for the rest of the day.

COST FACTORS

The strange sensation of a squidgy gelatinous mass compressing Kirsten's entire head woke her up.

Some invisible force lifted her head away from her desk in the squad room, gently guiding her into an upright-seated position. It felt as though an invisible man with huge hands clutched her head in between his palms. She tried—and failed—to look to her left when something black moved closer to her.

"You seriously need this." Nicole leaned into view, holding a coffee cup in front of her face. "Sleepyhead."

The telekinetic grip released. Kirsten flopped back in her seat. "Ugh. Thanks."

"Bad case?" Nicole sat on the corner of the desk.

"Nah. Stupidity. Stayed up too late doing research on a case I'm not even officially assigned to."

"Wow. Why would you do that?" Nicole rolled her eyes, sipped coffee, then laughed. "Had a store full of chickens yesterday. *That* was fun."

Kirsten took her time on the first sip. Straight mocha this time, no berry. "Chickens? Like… the birds? Real ones or synthetic?"

Nicole sputtered coffee foam—possibly whipped cream—laughing.

"Not actual chickens. People. Suggestive went on a bender. Made everyone in the place cluck."

"I shouldn't laugh, but..." Kirsten covered her mouth to hold it in.

"You didn't say what kept you up late."

As soon as Kirsten could breathe again, she said, "Filing reports for a new psionic, and looking into—"

"Toddler, too. Poor little guy didn't even know what he was doing." Nicole gazed at the ceiling.

"Huh?" Kirsten blinked.

"The suggestive. Not quite three years old. Kid *really* likes chickens." She sipped coffee. "Ooh, you found a new psionic?"

"Yeah. Thirteen-year-old named Allie Dez. Serious empath. Poor kid."

"Neat. Did you know 'Dez' is the fourth most common family name in the UCF?" Nicole sipped coffee. "Couple hundred years ago, it used to be spelled H-e-r-n-a-n-d-e-z. Gah. So many extra letters for such a short sound."

Dorian cracked up laughing.

Kirsten shook her head, barely keeping a straight face. "I didn't know that."

"Oh wow. You're getting better." Nicole snickered. "Didn't fall for it?"

"I know you're not that much of an airhead. You don't honestly believe all those letters used to be silent."

"It's true though," said Nicole. "The name used to be much longer. Not sure why it got shortened so much."

"People are lazy as hell." Dorian reclined in his chair, lacing his fingers behind his head.

Nicole scrunched her nose in thought. "Wasn't that right around the time all citizens had to wear ID badges?"

Kirsten stared over her coffee at Nicole. "What? When did that happen?"

"Oh." Nicole biffed herself in the forehead. "Sorry. I keep forgetting you missed a lot of school. It's like... third or fourth grade history. Real soon after the UCF formed, they were like *suuuper* strict with security. Everyone had to have ID displayed at all times."

Dorian chuckled. "Did you forget there was a war going on back then? Wartime rules are a little different."

"Bet they shortened it to fit on the badges." Nicole made a shrinking gesture with her thumb and index finger. "Three letters is a lot easier to fit on a nametag."

"Ugh. Glad they stopped doing that." Kirsten inhaled the scent of her coffee, trying to wake up from the caffeine fumes while savoring the wonderful aroma.

Dorian summoned a spectral coffee in his hand. "Don't be fooled. Everyone still wears badges all the time. They're just not visible. Nowadays, we call them PIDs."

Being too tired to get into a back and forth about whether or not the UCF government happened to be benevolent or suffocating, Kirsten simply stretched, yawned, and stared at her terminal screen until the graphics came into focus.

"Are you going to tell me what kept you up?" asked Nicole.

Kirsten narrowed her eyes. "Are you going to keep changing topics before I can answer?"

"Umm." Nicole shrugged one shoulder. "Probably. My brain moves faster than my mouth can keep up."

"I find that difficult to believe," muttered Dorian.

"Spent the rest of my shift yesterday downstairs helping this girl get used to being here and settled." Kirsten yawned, then drank roughly a quarter of her mocha latte in one gulp.

"Dormer?" Nicole made 'aww' face.

"No. Her father's amazing. She's just going to stay in the dorms for a week or two until he finalizes plans to move. Her present home is... dangerous for her."

Nicole stared.

"This kid tested at a startlingly high rating in telempathy for someone who didn't even know she had abilities. Grade 7."

"Wow," whispered Nicole. "That's huge. Even Director Carter's supposedly only a six."

Kirsten put her feet up on the desk, leaning back. "Might be an abnormal reading since she's uncontrolled." She explained how the girl, without knowing she did so, constantly read the emotional state of everyone within a six-ish mile radius around her. "The overwhelmingly negative energy almost drove her to suicide to escape it."

"Oh wow. Poor thing." Nicole tossed her empty cup in the bin. "So that kept you up?"

"No, that consumed the rest of my time here before I went home. After Evan went to bed, I made the mistake of starting to look into some inquest records that might be related to other inquest records I've been preoccupied with."

Nicole slid off the desk to her feet. "That interdivision cooperation exercise get you addicted to Div 2 cases?"

"No. For some reason, I couldn't stop thinking about the guy we found dead."

"Ick?" Nicole grimaced.

"Not like that. Like... something wanted me to investigate the death and not just accept he was a hacker who got himself killed."

Nicole flopped into her seat. "Oh. Yeah. Div 2 detectives call that feeling a 'hunch.' For us, it's actually real."

"Some of them might be psionic, too, and not realize it." Kirsten drained the last of her coffee into her mouth.

In between bits of random conversation with Nicole, she proceeded to dig into the records of Atmos Industries. The company primarily manufactured e-suits used by people working off-Earth in unbreathable (or no) atmospheres. They also made airlock systems, habitat modules for scientific survey expeditions to uninhabited planets, air scrubbers for starships, and a few different types of survival systems installed on large starships to help protect crew in the event of catastrophic depressurization.

Though stable and successful, Atmos didn't exactly top the charts of the most valuable or profitable companies in the world. They also didn't appear to be involved in any technology likely to be worth stealing and selling.

The information Sam sent her in regard to the seven dead hackers backed up her thinking. He felt confident in declaring that not one of them had been killed by high-end defense programs. Even military intelligence wouldn't have been able to kill them without leaving at least *some* evidence of a kill command being sent into their net deck. Where it came from would be impossible to find without C-Branch hardware, but the existence of the signal couldn't be perfectly concealed. Since no such signal trace existed, Sam suggested three possibilities. One, someone got direct access to the decks and installed a kill program locally. Two, a serious defect in the hardware resulted in a fatal malfunction. Three, something paranormal happened. Since all seven victims used different makes and models of net deck, Sam declared option three a thousand times more likely than option two— especially when she explained what Dorian found regarding the lack of a 'burn path' on the mainboard.

Initially, Kirsten couldn't find anything to connect the seven victims to each other for establishing the motive of someone trying to kill them —until now. While researching the fourteen dead Atmos employees, she chanced upon an adjacent record for Haan Markus, one of the dead hackers. At the time of his death, he'd been an off-gridder. However, up until three months prior, the man worked for Atmos.

One by one, Kirsten compared the dead hacker list to the employee records for Atmos.

Four names matched. DemonCore, a.k.a. Novar Kell wasn't one of them.

"Grr."

She sent an email to Sam with the four outliers, asking if he could find any connection between these individuals and Atmos Industries. While waiting for him to reply, she resumed poring over the employee records of the fourteen dead. Internal memos from the company's investigators tended to write them off as 'well, they obviously poked their noses into places it didn't belong.' The four hackers who previously worked for Atmos had all been fired for 'business needs' reasons.

"The heck does that mean?" Kirsten scowled at the holo-panel.

"Your query requires more information to process," said Dorian.

"Hmm?" Nicole shoved off her desk, rolling her chair over to collide with Kirsten's.

Kirsten pointed at her screen. "Fired for business needs."

"Means the company wanted more money, so they made one

person do the work of two and fired one of them." Nicole rolled her eyes.

"Valid." Dorian peered over his ghostly NetMini screen at her. "It could also be a generic reason, because they didn't want to list the actual one. If they caught the employee doing something they didn't want them doing, and didn't want to call attention to that, they'd put a generic reason in for the termination. Maybe they didn't even tell the person why they let them go other than 'business needs.'"

Kirsten stared at the floating text in front of her. "All four of them had criminal records for cyber trespass. If they got caught doing illegal things on the net while at work, wouldn't the company fire them for that specific reason?"

"You'd think," said Dorian.

"Yeah. Probably." Nicole shrugged. "But companies are weird. They'll always lie if they think it will make more money."

She glanced at her red-haired friend. "How does catching someone breaking the law and then lying about it make them money?"

"Because, a company wouldn't necessarily go through the hassle of firing someone for breaking the law in a way that doesn't directly involve the company. Getting a new employee and training them up to speed costs money. If these guys did illegal stuff on the GlobeNet, they'd only be fired if their activity was a threat to Atmos. Like, these guys might have been trying to steal data from the company's own network." Nicole wagged her eyebrows and shoved off Kirsten's desk, rolling her chair back to her spot. "Or hunting for dirt that management really wants to keep hidden."

"Ugh." Kirsten let her elbows thud onto her desk, then grabbed her head. A cascade of pale blonde hair fell over her face, hiding her from the world. "This doesn't make any sense. Atmos looks so bland. They make e-suits, air scrubbers, and stuff. Their products aren't even considered expensive. Tons of companies manufacture the same sort of stuff. What could they possibly have on their network valuable enough to use killer software to safeguard?"

"Lots of competition." Nicole gestured at her in a 'there's your motive' manner. "They gotta save all the money they can everywhere they can."

"Never underestimate the capacity for a corporation to be shitty," said Dorian. "Sometimes, it's the most outwardly upright ones with the dirtiest laundry."

Kirsten slumped forward, head down upon her folded arms. "This place isn't even 'upright.' It's just boring and bland."

"What are you thinking?" asked Dorian.

"I'm thinking there's a ghost out there who is targeting employees of this place and killing them by frying their brains while they're plugged in. He's killing hackers with overclocked net decks as well as ordinary people using ordinary terminals."

Nicole yawned. "Damn. Stop that. It's contagious."

"I didn't yawn. I just thought about being tired." Kirsten yawned. "You made *me* yawn. Stop eavesdropping."

"You sure it's a guy?" Dorian also yawned, then blinked in confusion. "Good grief, it's true. They really are contagious."

Kirsten pushed herself up off the desk, swiping her hair back over her head. "That little girl called the spirit she saw 'he' even though it looked like a shadowy blob."

"Shadowy blob?" Dorian blinked. "She saw Morelli in uniform?"

Sputtering coffee, Kirsten tried not to laugh-spray mocha all over her desk. Once she could breathe again, she stared back at him. "Morelli's not fat."

"He's not exactly in the upper ninety percent on the fitness index either." Dorian snickered. "And don't look at me like that. You still laughed."

"What did I miss?" Nicole started laughing before Kirsten could answer.

Kirsten tried to ignore both of them, enjoying her coffee.

Predictably, Nicole burst into giggles a few seconds later.

"You could start checking Atmos records for all employees who died within the past fifty years under suspicious circumstances." Dorian tapped his thumbs on his phantom NetMini. "Figure at least thirty years for this guy to figure out how to do the electrocution thing. Not too long, though. Someone angry enough to kill wouldn't be patient. As soon as they had the ability to get their revenge, they'd take it."

"Right." Kirsten attacked her terminal, searching the Atmos Industries company records for employee deaths.

To her surprise, the list didn't have many names. A handful of 'test pilots' died to various accidents fifty-three years ago during prototype testing of the company's first-generation e-suits on Mars. Evidently, Cydonian crabs found the color of the suits particularly attractive. Whether or not the 600-pound armored crustaceans had been horny or hungry didn't make much difference to the end result. Other than those early fatalities while evaluating the company's product for use on the Martian surface, the only other fatalities employees suffered on the job sounded like obvious accidents the company couldn't be responsible for. A hovercar-on-fire crashing into the building, two employees on their way to give a technical sales presentation getting plowed down by a PubTran taxi, and so on.

Considering Dorian parked a delivery bot on the desk of the Comtec International CEO, she didn't necessarily dismiss the idea an angry ghost might have been responsible for vehicular mishaps, but it did seem like a stretch. The only thing she truly regretted about Dorian smashing some asshole executive's office is the man had no damn idea *why* it happened… and she couldn't tell him without creating a legal mess for Division 0 *or* Tobin. She'd have to hope the CEO made certain assumptions if, in fact, he even learned about the bot refusing to stop.

I am going to file an official complaint about the bot refusing to acknowledge an override command. She frowned. *They're going to use the out of control flight and crash as evidence the bot was compromised, but dammit. I am going to make them deal with the paperwork.*

Kirsten's department-issued NetMini rang with an incoming vid call. She glanced at the tiny physical screen only long enough to see "Chang, S" before grinning like an idiot and yanking the device from its belt clip. Sam's face appeared in hologram as she balanced the small black slab on her outstretched palm.

"Ooh," chimed Nicole. "Naughty. He's calling you on department hardware."

Sam rotated to look at her. "It's an official call… this time."

"Uh huh." She grinned, then blinked. "Oh wow. You're not kidding."

"He's not kidding." Kirsten rolled her eyes. *One of these days, you're going to eavesdrop on someone's mind and regret it.*

"Doubtful," singsonged Nicole.

"The four PIDs you sent… it took a bit of alchemy, but I am reasonably certain there is a connection to Atmos." Sam pursed his lips. "One is a guess. For three of them, I was able to compare hardware-level identifiers in the deceased individuals' decks to border routers at the edge of Atmos Industries' GlobeNet real estate."

Kirsten bit her lip. "That means they hacked into the company?"

"It might. It definitely means someone using that deck at least entered the public areas of the Atmos GlobeNet site." Sam glanced to the side as if reading something. "This is just a few minutes of casual checking. I didn't go into the site to check the hardware for restricted nodes. It's possible they only visited the public areas."

"It's also possible I'm going to spontaneously regenerate a new body." Dorian laughed.

"Yeah. People with a list of citations for cyberspace trespass would surely confine themselves to public network areas." Kirsten leaned back in her chair far enough to stare up at the ceiling. "Are you assuming the fourth person did too?"

"Yes." Sam lowered his voice. "I'm assuming because I can't check. The Nishihama Avatar IV deck is, uhh"—he coughed—"*missing* from evidence."

Nicole and Kirsten gasped at the same time.

"Someone stole it?" blurted Kirsten.

"Or it sprouted legs and walked away." Nicole smirked at her.

"As expensive as that thing is…" Sam chuckled. "It wouldn't shock me if it had retractable legs. I'm not going to outright say it's been stolen. Most likely, one of the techs over there took it home to play for a while. If it doesn't come back in a few more days, it probably won't. Then we can call it stolen."

Nicole tilted her head. "Think this guy's mad someone took his deck?"

"No. There's no way the owner of that deck could have figured out how to 'ghost' properly in, at most, fourteen months, to be able to kill people yet." Kirsten drummed her fingers on her desk. "So, everyone who appears to have been black ICEd is in some way connected to this company."

"And one person who was *almost* zapped." Dorian held up a finger.

"Yeah." She frowned.

"Anything else I can help with from down here?" Sam raised both eyebrows.

Kirsten huffed. "Umm. Nothing I can think of right this second. Will definitely let you know if I do need help. Thank you."

"Of course, hon." Sam blew her a kiss before they hung up.

"He's really cute." Nicole rested her chin on her interlaced fingers. "You guys are great together."

Kirsten smiled, allowing herself a moment of happiness. "Thanks. You and Jaden are cute together, too."

"We're going to Mars again soon. This hotel is *so* romantic." Nicole fanned herself. "I can't wait."

After the brief respite from anxiety thinking nice thoughts about Sam—and taking the half hour or so to file the citation against Comtec—she dug back into the records of Atmos Industries. The company filed hundreds of complaints against 'network trespassers.' A few even involved minor children using senshelmets who essentially 'tugged on a locked door' in cyberspace before walking away, not knowing they technically attempted entry to a nonpublic area. Of course, a prosecutor would have to work extremely hard to prove a seven-year-old tried to intentionally invade a corporate network with hardware only designed to play video games or edu-tainment software. Needless to say, those inquests were dropped. A judge even slapped Atmos with a frivolous complaint fine.

Hmm. They're super sensitive about people trying to get in. What could they be hiding?

The more she read, the more she suspected Atmos of having some stains on its metaphorical laundry. It remained possible they might simply be guarding some new secret technology that would revolutionize the e-suit industry... but that sounded roughly as exciting as Cyberburger coming out with a reformulated OmniSoy cheeseburger that never melted back into beige goop no matter how long it sat uneaten. Far from society-shaking.

Gotta be a ghost looking for revenge against Atmos for… something. Why target hackers, though? They'd be antagonistic to the company. Maybe a crazed network defense person? Hacker killed him and he's pissed?

She swiped at the holo-terminal, pulling up the ID photos of all twenty-one dead people, arranged in neat rows. "Hmm. Wonder if Emi Mons could identify the spirit."

"Didn't you say the kid saw a shadowy figure?" Dorian looked up from whatever he'd been reading.

"She did. But… maybe one of these images will 'feel' like the ghost to her." Kirsten let her head fall back into the headrest of her chair. "Yep. I'm reaching. But what else do I do? Wait for the next attack?"

"If this spirit is targeting employees, you're looking at a pool of around 5,000 potential victims. Closer to 2700 if you limit it to staff present on Earth." Dorian pointed at her terminal screens. "It's functionally impossible to predict where this guy will strike next."

Kirsten swung her chair around to face him. "Think he'll go back for Tara?"

"Hmm." Dorian tapped his foot. "I suppose he might—unless he figures the daughter will interfere again. Any patterns to the dead?"

"Hackers and employees."

"Any pattern among the employees?"

Kirsten twirled her hair around one finger. "All worked for Atmos."

"Obviously. Anything deeper?"

"Nine were part of their network defense group."

Dorian pointed at her. "That's significant."

"They'd be the most likely to spend all day plugged in."

"If it's merely the convenience of being plugged in, you'd need to consider all of their employees who work off site." Dorian blurred out of his chair to reappear standing beside her desk. A sub window opened by itself on her holo-panel, full of stats. "Sixty-five ish percent of their staff work virtually. That's a big number. It's significant that nine out of fourteen dead are part of the network security team. More than half."

Kirsten exhaled. "Yeah. You're right. So, this spirit could be targeting their cybersecurity people. Why? Former employee or are we looking at an angry hacker who got himself killed trying to break into Atmos?"

"There's nothing about that place valuable enough to defend with black ICE." Dorian scratched at his eyebrow. "You think a company would kill someone trying to steal an 'innovative new concept' for an e-suit with a built-in snack bar?"

She shrugged. "Maybe they came up with a design for women's clothing that has real pockets."

"That might do it." Dorian pointed at her. "You know the Corporate War is really a propaganda piece to cover up the fact that they gave women pockets in 2094 and the resulting unrest led to nuclear war and carnivorous mutant bio weapons."

Nicole cackled. "Yeah, and the whole Neko fad is a protest. You don't want us to have pockets? Fine, we won't wear anything at all."

Kirsten blushed.

"Tell her there are plenty of guys into that, too." Dorian held his fingers to his head, simulating cat ears.

"You can tell her yourself." Kirsten shuddered.

"Hah." He grinned.

"Yeah, I know guys are into it too." Nicole yawned, stretched, then yawned again. "But that ruins my pocket protest joke. Did you know 'the community' refers to guy Nekos as 'twin tails'?"

Kirsten scrunched her nose. "They get two?"

Dorian whistled innocently.

"No, Kiki…" Nicole shook her head. "They already had one dangly thing before they had a tail grafted to their spine. Wow you are almost too innocent to believe."

Eyes closed, Kirsten wished a hole would open up beneath her so she could fall in and disappear for a few months. It embarrassed her enough to think about people who could parade around in public wearing only cat-themed cyberware. To walk right into Nicole's joke— she *hoped* her friend just spontaneously made that up to tease her— only worsened her embarrassment. Of course, people into the 'Neko fad' were hardly the only ones to push the boundaries of 'high fashion' by attempting to elevate streaking into socially acceptable attire. In addition to the extremely poor, dosers, prostitutes, and entertainment shock personalities, the ultra-wealthy occasionally did bizarre things. A few years back, one model got paid an exorbitant amount of credits to gallivant around wearing something that looked like a plastic bowl over her left breast, a few decorative swooshes of glowing fiberoptics, and nothing else. The 'outfit' supposedly cost forty thousand credits because a famous designer came up with the idea.

Kirsten thought the woman looked utterly ridiculous and couldn't believe they showed her in advertisements all over the city.

"Dorian, did you know Kiki thought neko was street speak for naked?" Nicole giggled. "She didn't know it's Japanese for cat."

"Okay. Okay. Okay." Kirsten raised both hands, still not opening her eyes. "Nekos have nothing to do with my case. Can we please focus?"

"Focus away. It's your case." Nicole's chair creaked. A second later, she hugged Kirsten. "Be right back. We both need more coffee."

Kirsten looked at her. "Why are you yawning?"

"Standoff last night went until two-thirty in the morning." Nicole scowled, all playfulness evaporating from her face. "Call came in about a psionic in a rage, killing people. They'd gotten into an apartment and were making demands or they'd kill the family inside."

"Ugh." Kirsten cringed.

"It was a total lie. Some guy found out his kids were psionic and tried to kill them. Kids managed to fight him off to a stalemate. Wall gave out. Neighbors got dragged into it."

Kirsten gawked. "Oh no... son of a bitch."

"Both kids are going to be okay, at least physically. Their dad, not so much. Crazy bastard, uhh, raised a knife at me. Had to put him down."

You didn't... Kirsten stared at her friend.

Nicole examined her fingernails. *I might have telekinetically spun him around to face me. It's possible he originally raised the knife to finish off his nine-year-old daughter.*

Oh. Well. Umm. Are you okay?

"Bit rattled. Didn't sleep much last night, but the bastard deserved it. He almost killed his oldest son. If I didn't get tired of waiting for the negotiator, he *would* have killed that little girl. We were too late to save the mother. Asshole blamed her for giving him psionic kids. Called her evil."

Kirsten scowled. *Please tell me the Harbingers got that twisted shithead.*

"How should I know?" Nicole raised an eyebrow. "Or were you asking in general?"

"More wishing. And yeah. Coffee is a good idea." Kirsten yawned.

Dorian clenched his jaw.

Nicole breezed off out of the squad room.

Dorian yawned. "Dammit."

"Why are you yawning?" Kirsten blinked at him. "You don't need air."

"Exactly why it's infuriating." He fake growled.

"Was that true about guys and the cat thing?" whispered Kirsten.

"They exist. If you go to the sort of clubs they tend to prefer, you'll see tons of them." Dorian returned to his desk. "They don't show them in the media very often."

"Huh. Wonder why."

"Certain swinging bits are evidently less aesthetically pleasing to the public consciousness, I suppose," said Dorian in a blasé tone. "Look at all the giant advert bots showing barely dressed women models. Imagine all the traffic accidents a twenty-foot dick floating down the street would cause."

She rolled her eyes. "So, this ghost is hunting their network people. Just a theory here. It's a long shot, but I can try something."

"What are you thinking of? Beaconing? You have no idea who this spirit is."

Kirsten poked one of the images on her screen, making it expand. "That's Jace Tomlin."

"Should I recognize his name?"

"Ehh, probably not. He wasn't famous. His mother is Ryn Tomlin, CEO of Atmos. She's *still* trying to sue Matsushita for her son's death. What are the odds I can convince her to help me figure out what's going on?"

"Matsushita?" Dorian furrowed his brow. "Was the guy using one of their decks? And he's on the list of hackers, not employees."

"Yeah. Suspicious the one deck that went missing happens to be the

Masushita. Our investigation failed to show any evidence a flaw in the device caused the death, but she's still suing them. I might be able to get her to help if she believes my investigation might help her legal action."

He idly scratched at his chest while thinking. "Hmm. Depends."

"On?"

"On how much it will cost the company in bad PR."

She stared at him. "Wow, you're more jaded than I realized."

"No, merely realistic."

Kirsten sighed. "It shouldn't cost them anything. Ryn Tomlin isn't going to want to bring anything involving ghosts or psionics into a hearing and no judge would want to hear it either."

"Okay." He gestured toward the door. "Let's go talk to her."

"Not yet." Kirsten folded her arms. "Nikki's getting coffee."

ATMOS

While the patrol craft auto-drove, Kirsten studied a holographic model of the Atmos Industries facility. She didn't expect the sort of unfriendly welcome that involved large angry people with guns, but on the off chance something went wrong, better to have at least some idea of the layout so she could get out of there fast if necessary.

The company's headquarters occupied a one-mile-square lot in Sector 7866, a touch north of the center of a swath of industrial properties stretching a little over a hundred miles, twenty sectors, north-to-south and three sectors wide. Clouds of various unknown vapors rose here and there from pipes and tanks littered about the landscape below. Hundreds of glimmering lights in red, orange, and blue perched atop tall scaffolds, pipes, satellite dish towers, flashing a warning to any flying vehicle.

Few buildings in the industrial district passed—or even neared—the fifty-story mark, resulting in 'naked' hovercar traffic lanes uncontained by walls of plastisteel and glass. Division 1 loved to cruise around here hoping to catch reckless drivers who took manual control and chanced risky shortcuts outside approved flight paths. The distant, boxy monoliths of air scrubbers loomed over the bustling manufacturing area as if standing in disapproving judgment of all the chemical mess being ejected into the sky. Each one had to be twenty stories tall and as big as a warehouse, likely intended originally for off-Earth terraforming. Those machines proved too small to be effective on Mars, so the government put them to work here on Earth in hopes of making sure an already breathable atmosphere didn't become toxic.

"Paradoxes are everywhere," said Dorian.

She looked over at him. "Random."

"You're staring at the air processing units." Dorian gestured at one. "They originally decided to use them as CO_2 scrubbers because of how the war and the elevated city design killed off so many trees. Now they eat more industrial pollution than CO_2."

"How is that a paradox?"

"That part isn't." He smiled. "The more, and bigger, scrubbers they used, the more various companies stopped caring about pollution control, figuring the machines would just scrub it. Let the taxpayers cover the cost of cleanup."

Kirsten let out a long, sad sigh. "Sometimes, it really does feel like humanity is trying to kill itself off."

"At least you're ready for it."

"I am not."

He laughed. "You work with the dead. When civilization finally collapses entirely, *you* will still have purpose. Marketing weasels and lawyers will be out of luck."

"Umm." Kirsten stared at him. "Are you suggesting the collapse of civilization is going to happen in my lifetime?"

"Not really. Just saying if something unforeseen happened to speed things up, you'll have a useful talent."

She looked down. Roaming the Beneath as a child with no possessions other than a plastic tarp poncho held on by a power cable belt seemed like training for how to live in a post-apocalyptic society.

I never would have survived without all those spirits helping me find food, avoid bad stuff... be there for me.

In a way, she'd been the child of an entire village with fifty parents. If only she'd listened to the ones urging her to go back to the surface before that man found her. Then again, perhaps he hadn't done as much mental damage as her mother. How much difference to her life would avoiding him really have made compared to if her mother hadn't been a cruel monster?

Kirsten didn't know, nor did she want to think about something so depressing and pointless. So, she stopped staring out the front viewscreen and resumed studying the holo-map of the Atmos facility. A relatively small office tower—merely thirty stories—occupied the southwest corner of the company property. Three elevated walkways connected it to a pair of manufacturing buildings as well as a storage warehouse. Tanks in various sizes and shapes from sphere to oval to cylinder took up most of the north and northeast area. A spaghetti pile of pipes carried the contents of the tanks to the two factories. Close to the east edge of the property, a delivery bot the size of a small shuttle sat on a landing pad. It appeared idle, neither loading nor unloading cargo.

What she needed to do here wouldn't involve visiting anywhere but the offices, so she gave only a cursory look to the outlying areas around the main tower before zooming in on it. The interior layout appeared quite ordinary as corporate offices go. Some of the lower floors contained smaller scale production labs and clean rooms, cafeteria, and a day care. The majority of the structure consisted of offices, cube farms, break areas, and conference rooms. Unlike some massive companies, the CEO had an office in the same suite as other executives.

That's a good sign.

Whenever a CEO monopolized an entire floor all to themselves like some kind of Japanese warlord emperor, she expected them to be arrogant, condescending, and confrontational. Executives of any level tended to act above everyone else. UCF society teetered on the edge between legitimately treating them like a higher social caste and claiming all citizens were 'equal' under the law.

Were that true, we wouldn't need Division 9.

Executives, rich people, and celebrities who continually thumbed their noses at the law and evaded legal consequences would eventually end up on the wrong end of an operative's sniper rifle. Rumor had it a cadre of billionaires tried to get rid of Division 9...

until several senators died under mysterious circumstances. Whether or not Nine killed those senators remained one of the great urban legend-slash-mysteries of the world. However it really happened, Nine enjoyed almost total autonomy from the government. Dorian had been rather vocal about his fear of such an arrangement, claiming it only gave Nine the opportunity to become as corrupt and power drunk as the billionaires and politicians it existed to protect society from. Worse, nowhere did Division 9 openly say 'keep exploiting legal technicalities to get away with your crimes and we're going to blow your brains out.' On paper, they existed as an anti-espionage unit to defend against foreign (mostly ACC) agents operating inside UCF territory.

Kirsten knew for a fact Div 9 hunted down and executed anyone who killed or tried to kill cops. She'd been on the receiving end of corporate assassins already. Though she hadn't looked into it, the unspoken aftermath of the attempt on her life involved Div 9 sending five or six people to Miami. It took her a little while to understand the meaning of the phrase. Miami, a pre-war city, no longer existed, having long since been covered by the elevated plates of East City. The phrase was a cute way to say they killed someone. Of all the ancient pre-war cities in North America, she had no idea why they chose Miami as a euphemism for assassination.

Her thoughts ceased circling aimlessly at an alert beep from the console. She'd flown within range of the Atmos Industries office tower and needed to take over manual control. Dorian chuckled. The alert noise always made him laugh, or at least smile. While auto-drive certainly had the capability to maneuver a hovercar into a mid-building parking garage and choose an open space to land, almost every manufacturer disabled the feature out of fear of lawsuits. If the car struck anything or caused damage while a person operated the controls, no one would sue the manufacturer of the car, they'd sue the driver.

Dorian laughed because even corporations like StarPoint that made vehicles for the military did it.

As far as Kirsten thought, the government vehicles disabled auto drive for landing not out of fear of lawsuits but to ensure the personnel operating them paid attention to their surroundings. Her rationalization didn't stop Dorian from finding it hilarious.

A large opening in the west-facing side at the fifteenth story led to the hovercar parking area. Ground cars gathered in a sizable lot in the southeast corner of the property, almost a mile walk from the office tower. The distance looked annoying, even with little shuttles going back and forth. She descended to match altitude with the opening, slowed to fifteen MPH, and guided the patrol craft inside, squinting somewhat at the bright white ceiling and walls.

After locating an available parking spot reasonably close to the enclosed elevator chamber at the center of the building, she landed, and shut down the drive system. Within seconds of her opening the patrol craft door, the garage assaulted with the smell and flavor of cold metal plus a vast array of unfamiliar—and unpleasant—chemicals. She recognized only the acrid, nose-stabbing reek of Cryomil fumes among them.

Coughing, she briefly considered pulling the door closed, but the stink had already gotten into the car. No doubt the bulk of the stench came from outside. The air quality at the approximate center of a massive swath of industrial properties stank—literally.

No wonder the terraformer units choke on the air here. Gah.

She opened a case on the right rear side of her belt, pulled out a rebreather, and put it in her mouth. Almost miraculously, she no longer smelled—or tasted—any awfulness. The six-inch cylindrical device with small filter orbs on each end had been designed for emergency survival in places like the Moon or Mars during an atmospheric depressurization. They also worked underwater. Using it here might have been overkill, but she'd rather look silly than have her lungs melt or grow a dozen tumors in five years.

No overly chipper Mitsu style mascot doll appeared to greet her as she jogged across the parking area. In the absence of a faux teenage marketing intern to show her around, Kirsten headed toward the only visible entrance: a square bank of elevators at the center of the area. Each face had eight elevator doors. As with the majority of high-rises in West City, the elevators ran along a central shaft containing most of the plumbing and cabling for the building while also serving as the primary conduit for the HVAC system to move air between floors.

A wall of clear panels surrounded the elevators, creating a 'moat' of lobby—with grey carpet, fake plants, and benches—between them and the parking area. A test sniff confirmed the air inside the enclosure to be much more tolerable. It still smelled off, but no longer had the flavor of cancer.

Kirsten collapsed the rebreather and put it back in its belt compartment, then called the elevator. Deciding to start off polite, she went to the ground floor lobby.

Her uniform, badge, smile, and pleasant demeanor got her past two layers of receptionists, then a building manager, and finally a PR executive over the course of twenty-two minutes. Finally, she found herself on the way up to meet with the CEO. Dorian wandered around, often out of sight, scoping the place out for any signs of paranormal wonkiness.

Right as she stepped off the elevator on the 29th floor, Dorian reappeared and smiled at her.

"What?" she whispered, hoping Dax, the PR rep, didn't think her nuts.

"I can't go on letting Nicole get one over on you," said Dorian. "Men who embrace the Neko trend aren't called 'twin tails.' They're called Toms. Sometimes Tomishonen."

She coughed.

"It's a portmanteau of Tom with Bishonen, which means—"

"I know what it means," she rasped. "Good grief, I shared a room with Nicole for five years."

"Guys who do the cat thing are usually pretty-boys." Dorian examined his nails.

Kirsten shook in place while mortification got into a fistfight with frustration. Less than a minute from meeting Ryn Tomlin, CEO of Atmos Industries, and Dorian *had* to make her think of gallivanting nudists with cat ears. Her face had to be as red as a fire suppression bot. She narrowed her eyes at him, certain he'd waited for this exact moment to spring that on her. *Classic Dorian. He teases me like a big brother.* She grumbled to herself, scrambling to shove thoughts of such things out of her mind. It backfired. She abruptly pictured Sam Chang wearing only cat ears... and couldn't tell if she found it cute or hilarious.

Dax swiped his company ID at a dark burgundy door, one of the few deviations from beige in this place. Everything about the Atmos Industries office gave off the sense of safety. They didn't even take risks with the décor. A flicker came from one of two light sconces flanking the door. Squared bands of decreasing size formed an upside-down stepped cone, light leaking out from between each semicircular piece. A faltering LED didn't always mean spiritual activity, but it could. She stared at the eye-level fixture while walking through the doorway, hoping to see it react again. Alas, it didn't.

The outer office, also overwhelmingly beige, contained a personal assistant at a desk, a small table with a cookie printer, coffee dispenser, and multiple comfy chairs. Dax waved at the woman behind the desk, saying nothing as he led Kirsten across the room to another door.

Also beige.

Ryn's office, though nice, didn't reek of wealth or ego. It didn't look significantly larger than the office she'd met Dax—vice president of public relations—in. An almost-one-year-old boy crawled around on the floor, trapped in the distant left corner by a collapsible playpen wall.

The CEO didn't react to the two of them walking in, deeply engrossed in the contents of her terminal screen. She embodied a balanced mix of poise, confidence, and 'I should not have done that'. Long, straight black hair framed a face of intense concentration. The woman appeared to be in her early thirties, though according to the citizen registration Kirsten reviewed the other day, she should be forty-seven. Not an extreme shock. Many people with the financial means to do so often visited Reinventions to shave a few years off. Other than her unusual youth, the woman didn't stand out as remarkable in any way, neither pretty nor ugly, neither heavy nor thin, with dark hair and a light brown complexion like most citizens who didn't or couldn't pay for custom genetic tweaking.

Dax approached the desk, waiting in silence.

A moment or two later, Ryn looked up from her screen. She opened her mouth, but noticed Kirsten before saying anything... and ended up merely staring at her. The woman's expression said 'why are the police here' strongly enough that Kirsten decided not to invade her thoughts yet.

"Good morning, Mrs. Tomlin." She offered a hand. "I'm Lieutenant Kirsten Wren with the National Police Force, Division 0. I was hoping you might spare a few minutes of your day to assist me with an investigation."

"One moment," said Ryn, before leaning toward her terminal. "Fiona Montgomery. Urgent."

The holographic head of a somewhat older woman—middle fifties—appeared above the terminal a few seconds later. She had the same sort of permanent disapproving expression as Mother on one of her 'happy' days. "Yes? What's on your mind?"

"I'm about to speak with the police." Ryn indicated Kirsten with a nod. "I needed you to be part of this conversation."

"Oh." The hologram head rotated to face her. "Good morning... officer?"

"Lieutenant," said Kirsten, trying not to snap. The woman's relatively pleasant tone of voice didn't match her annoyed expression. "It's all right. Black on black is difficult to see."

"Apologies. Good morning, lieutenant. I'm Fiona, chief legal counsel for Atmos Industries. Is this meeting official on the record?"

"Ahh, corporates." Dorian whistled. "They can't even go to the bathroom without having their lawyers present."

Kirsten tilted her hand in a so-so manner. "I haven't yet opened an official inquest into my line of investigation, as I am still collecting evidence to support my theory of certain events. My visit is official in the sense that I'm investigating in accordance with my department and specialty."

"Division 0, correct?" asked Fiona. "Do you suspect unauthorized activities of a psionic nature?"

"Yes and no." *Might as well get them thinking I'm nuts right away.* "Do you believe in the existence of spirits, ghosts and such?"

"Yes," said Ryn, without hesitation.

Fiona gave her side eye. "If you're going to ask me to be here for this meeting, you can at least wait for my cues on if or how you should answer."

"I'm aware of that." Ryn smirked. "There is no possible way my opinion on the supernatural is going to present liability for the company."

Dorian whistled. "At least they're honest about potentially lying to you if the lawyer says no."

Wow. Really. Kirsten blinked. "You did answer that quite fast. Have you had an experience with ghosts?"

"I'd like to think so." Ryn smiled over at the baby, then looked at Kirsten. "What is this about?"

The office door opened again, admitting a group of executives all in black suits. A sixty-something Chinese man with hints of grey in his hair led the group, walking too fast for the comfort of those following him, almost like a small boy dragging his parents around a Funzone. He stared at Kirsten in an unsettling, and decidedly unhappy manner that reminded her of the way the clerk at the Nippy-Nom convenience store looked at her the day she surfaced from the Beneath. Rather than help a scrawny, filthy twelve-year-old in a plastic tarp, the man immediately assumed she planned to shoplift and chased her out of his store.

She half expected this guy to do the same here and now.

He didn't, though, merely stopped about five paces away, as if to stand there and observe her conversation. The other six people with him, four men and two women who ranged in age from late thirties to late seventies, gave off little in the sense of emotion or interest in her. They all appeared to simply be following the one man. One or two looked as if they didn't understand why they'd been hustled in here.

Kirsten locked stares with the older man for a few seconds. An almost instinctive dislike for him welled up inside her. Most excessively wealthy, arrogant people had the same effect on her, so she didn't pay it enough attention to bother scanning his thoughts. Nothing about his body language suggested he posed an immediate threat to her, nor even regarded her in a lewd manner. The man radiated pure irritation at her presence and not the slightest hint of any interest in her.

I wouldn't trust that man to ask him what time it was in a room full of clocks.

She returned her attention to the CEO. "As I'm sure you are aware, fourteen employees of your company have, over the past two years, died under mysterious circumstances in a manner consistent with lethal GlobeNet countermeasure software."

A flicker of rage danced across Ryn's eyes. "I am aware. Unfortunately, the investigation into the agent responsible for these attacks hasn't seen much progress. Whoever they are, they're good enough to hide all traces of their presence."

Fiona cringed. "Be careful, Ryn. Even if you mean well, things you say can be taken the wrong way."

"It's a little unusual to share internal information, but I don't see the harm in it here." Kirsten smiled. "I happened upon some similar cases of people being killed by their network interface decks without apparent explanation. Turns out, all of them had connections to Atmos —either former employees or people who attempted to illegally access your network. Did you realize that nine out of the fourteen dead employees all worked in your GlobeNet security team?"

The scowl coming from the older Chinese man bored into the back of Kirsten's head.

Ryn glanced at Fiona, who gave a slight nod. "Yes. This is why our belief is an outside rival has been attacking us, attempting to harm Atmos."

"What does this have to do with any belief in the theoretical existence of ghosts?" asked Fiona.

"I've got twenty-one dead people with cooked brains and no technical or scientific explanation for how that happened. Analysis of the hardware is inconsistent with the mechanism of death when lethal countermeasure software is employed. The expected burn path left by the overcharge current isn't there. It's as though the electricity simply leapt from the power capacitors directly to the M3 outbound port, which should not be possible." Kirsten set her hands on her hips. "As you noticed, I'm with Div 0. Specifically, I'm an astral sensitive. I deal with paranormal issues. Ghosts are a real phenomenon, and occasionally, they gather enough strength and enough anger to pose a threat to the living. A situation like having your brain plugged into a power source makes it easier on them if they want to cause harm."

A collective, but soft, gasp came from the people in suits behind her. Ryn furrowed her brow in contemplation. Fiona appeared to be fighting the urge to roll her eyes.

"My working theory, as of right now, is there's a spirit out there who is targeting Atmos employees or people he thinks might be Atmos employees." Kirsten paused to let everyone process that. "The non-employee victims were all present on your network. Considering their criminal history, most likely to infiltrate it. This points to a connection. I think the spirit could be operating at a simplistic level. Perhaps his mind sustained damage in a similar manner to the victims, so his capacity for rational thought is lacking. He may be targeting any victim he finds within the Atmos network, unaware of their actual status as an employee."

The older man laughed.

"You're saying a ghost killed my son?" Ryn stared at her. "And the others?"

"It is somewhat too early to say that definitively, but it's my theory, yes." Kirsten let her hands slide off her hips, arms dangling at her sides. "Forgive me for asking, but did you see your son's ghost?"

Ryn seemed inches from yelling, but reined her emotions in, standing in silence for a moment before giving a sigh. "See? No. More felt. It was like Jace followed me around for days after they found him, trying to tell me something I just couldn't hear. I suppose it's why..." She glanced again at the baby.

"Oh... wow." Dorian whistled. "Is that Jace?"

Kirsten observed the almost-toddler playing with a clattering toy. "Jace?"

"Yes. I... couldn't let go." Ryn looked down. "Familyperfect Corporation was able to help my husband and I recreate him. Jace is going to grow up to look exactly like Jace. Part of me hopes his spirit came back. We're not expecting him to be exactly the same person, even though he will look like it." She gave a half-hearted chuckle. "I must have been out of my mind with grief. Who has a baby at forty-seven?"

"People who can afford to turn back the clock," muttered Dorian. "The woman's biologically around thirty-four, give or take two years. Must be nice to have a few million credits sitting around to blow on stuff like that."

"So, what are you asking me for?" Ryn looked up, once again seeming confident and powerful.

"I was hoping you might be willing to help me track down the entity responsible for killing those people, including your son, Jace." Kirsten smiled.

"How could I possibly do that? The police haven't been able to find anything yet." Ryn folded her arms.

"They haven't been able to find a suspect because they are searching for a living person," said Kirsten.

The older man laughed again.

Kirsten ignored him. Lots of people refused to believe in ghosts. A surprising percentage of people still considered psionics to be fake, too. "This spirit is killing people by causing a short-circuit within whatever device they are using to access the GlobeNet. I'd like for you to instruct your employees to all use senshelmets."

"You are asking us to leave ourselves vulnerable," blurted the older man. "Miscreants will run rings around our people if they're using helmets."

Ryn narrowed her eyes at him. "I was not about to order our network team to rely on helmets."

"What proof do you have this nonsense is actual?" The old man scowled.

"One of your employees, Tara Mons, almost became the next victim. Her little daughter noticed the spirit in time to yank the cable out before he could electrocute her." Kirsten fired off her best 'be quiet and stay out of this' stare at the old man, though he didn't appear the least bit intimidated by her. Grumbling mentally, she turned back to face Ryn. "If he'd let me finish, I was about to say, I'd like you to have your employees using helmets except for your network defense people who work physically out of this building."

"Can you elaborate on the reasons for your request?" Fiona tilted her holographic head.

"The mechanism by which this spirit attacks is ineffective on people using senshelmets. It requires a direct current path into the brain, and the associated internal electronics which can overheat and do damage. If the only vulnerable targets are here, all in one place, it allows me to know where the next attack will occur, so I can be present and stop him."

The old guy laughed again.

Frustration slipped past professionalism. Kirsten pointed her thumb back over her shoulder. "Who is this guy?"

A mild note of amusement teased a partial smile out of Ryn. "That is Mr. Chaoxiang Liu, the founder of Atmos, first CEO, and presently the head of our board of directors."

"Oh," said Kirsten, acting as unimpressed as possible. *That explains his attitude.* "If only your security people are susceptible to the spirit's attack via their M3 connections, I can predict where he'll go. If I'm in the room when he shows up, I can put a stop to this for good, thus sparing any future Atmos employees from death... and getting some measure of justice for those who already died."

"Nice," said Dorian. "Work that in there. Get the grieving mother to take your side."

Ryn pursed her lips in contemplation.

Mr. Liu burst into laughter. "So, not only are you asking us to believe ghosts are real, you plan to arrest one?"

"No," said Kirsten in a flat tone without looking back at him. "I am going to order him to stop under threat of permanent destruction."

Dorian raised a hand to his mouth as if whispering to Mr. Liu. "She'll most likely end up talking to him, feeling bad for him, and helping solve whatever situation is driving him to kill."

Sigh.

"I'm not sure this is a productive conversation." Ryn gestured at Mr. Liu. "I should be using this time for the board meeting."

"Do you want to really know what happened to Jace?"

"Matsushita's shoddy electronics killed him." Ryn gazed at her desk, her softened tone suggesting she tried to convince herself as well as everyone listening to her.

"There have been twenty-one fatalities in basically identical circumstances." Kirsten opened the holo-screen above her left arm. "None of the individuals used the same hardware. Only two had Matsushita made decks, and not the same model. The rest involved everything from Nintek to Teradyne. There's no commonality, and like I said, the burn marks on the mainboards are inconsistent with the mechanism of operation for lethal countermeasure software. The reason your legal actions against Matsushita keep stalling is there's no credible evidence indicating *how* the electronics failed. Neither our forensic techs, nor Matsushita's people, nor the private firm you hired have been able to prove the existence of a manufacturing defect responsible for the electrical discharge. The same failure occurred in all twenty-one cases, including several who used off-the-shelf terminals, not even decks. I'm sure Matsushita's lawyers will love hearing a ghost story."

Mr. Liu shook his head. "Ghost stories will get laughed out of a courtroom."

"Mrs. Tomlin's suit against Matsushita is not a criminal inquest. All it takes is doubt." Kirsten leaned on the desk, staring at the CEO. "Look, I'm trying to help you here. My only goal is to prevent anyone else from dying. I'm Div 0. I really don't care that much about corporate stuff. What I'm asking won't cost you a single credit, merely inconvenience some people for a few days. Even if you don't really believe me about ghosts, if it's a chance to understand why Jace is dead and maybe get some revenge on the thing that killed him, isn't it worth it? I understand your anger. But… Matsushita is not the right target."

Ryn rubbed her forehead.

"Dooooo," called the baby.

Ryn jumped, then stared at her new son. "Did he just…?"

"Baby noises," muttered Mr. Liu. "Meaningless coincidence."

The baby appeared to hold up a middle finger at the old man.

Dorian howled with laughter.

No way… Kirsten scanned the baby's surface thoughts. The child's mental state appeared to be a chaotic blur, reminiscent of a drunk person staggering out of a bar then being hit in the head a few times. One second, he seemed adult, another infantile. Language couldn't form properly. She couldn't discern clearly if the child actually wanted his mother to follow the plan or had merely babbled 'doooo' randomly at the exactly right moment. The middle finger took a bit more mental gymnastics to explain, though could still have been the unintentional flailings of a not-yet-one-year-old baby. While she hadn't exactly attempted to use telepathy on many children so young, intermittent glimpses of frustration at being unable to speak, remember things, or even stand up did not seem normal for a baby his age.

She shifted her gaze to Ryn. *Mrs. Tomlin, don't panic. I'm speaking to you with telepathy. I am not reading your mind, only sending my voice into it. I think your son's spirit might really be inside your new baby. He doesn't seem to remember much of his previous life. He is frustrated because he can't figure out how to speak. That makes me think something in there* used *to know how to speak. But I think he really tried to say 'do it.'*

The CEO gawked at Kirsten for a long, uncomfortable moment. People tended to react to unexpected telepathy in a myriad of ways from awe to terror to violence. Certainly, had Kirsten ever dared to try speaking telepathically to Mother, the end result would have either been the woman dropping dead where she stood to a heart attack or delivering a severe beating.

In the seconds before Kirsten dropped her telepathic link, a strong surface thought unintentionally slipped across. Ryn appeared to be stuck in decision paralysis with Mr. Liu right there, as if she worried how he would react. She suspected her role as CEO might be more ceremonial than she'd been led to believe, but in the moment, her emotions over the death of her son won out.

"All right." Ryn tapped her fingers on the desk for a few seconds, lost in thought. "I'll ask the staff outside the network security team to refrain from direct connections for a few days. However, I am not going to penalize any who don't comply. It will be a request, not a directive."

"Thank you." Kirsten nodded once.

"Assuming you are correct about there being a spirit involved..." Ryn conspicuously avoided looking in Mr. Liu's direction. "When would you expect the next attack?"

Kirsten skimmed the case notes on her armband terminal. "The deaths have occurred approximately twice a month. Considering the recent attack on Tara Mons that failed, it's likely another attempt could happen at any minute. As soon as you have your off-site employees using helmets instead of direct connections, I'd like to arrange with your network security team to spend the night in their work area."

"Very well." Ryn reached for a wire, then seemingly thinking better of it, stretched out her arms and began to type on a holographic keyboard. "I'll send a note down to Lam Orben. He's our director of network security. It shouldn't be a problem for you to shadow his team at your convenience. Do know that it might take a day or two for the memo to make its way around and people to switch over to helmets. To avoid stirring panic, I'm going to make it sound like a necessary diagnostic procedure related to system maintenance."

Mr. Liu stepped closer to the desk. "You're going to let her roam around the security room? She could be up to anything. Are you sure this kid is even a genuine officer?"

"Feel free to call the NPF public relations line and request an identity check." Kirsten forced herself to smile at him. "Also, I don't have an M3 plug. No cybernetic implants at all. I am not even capable of attempting to sneak onto your network when no one is looking."

Fiona, Dax, and Ryn all went wide eyed.

"Nothing? Not even a plug?" Dax whistled. "Seriously? How do you survive?"

Dorian stuck his hand into Mr. Liu's back. Seconds later, the chairman's stomach gave a gurgling noise and his expression became urgent. He cleared his throat, shot an annoyed look at Ryn, then fast-walked out of the room.

Kirsten gave Dorian side eye.

"Didn't hurt him." Dorian pantomimed wiping his hand off on Dax's sleeve. "Merely created the false sensation that he's seconds from having a serious unburdening. He's rushing to the bathroom where he will proceed to sit for a while wondering why nothing is happening. This meeting will be much smoother without him in the room."

She exhaled. "Thanks."

Ryn nodded, as if she'd been talking to her.

"Might as well go visit your security team now," said Kirsten. "Just to introduce myself. I'll come back later tonight."

"Dax?" Ryn flicked her gaze to Kirsten. "Would you mind introducing her to Lam?"

"No problem." Dax started for the door, waving at her to follow. "Back to the elevator we go. This way."

Baby Jace rolled onto his back and emitted a pleased coo.

Kirsten trailed after him, her gaze lingering on the kid. *So eerie.*

SECRETS

Kirsten followed Dax out of the executive offices, down a beige corridor decorated with various corporate milestone achievement placards as well as multiple emitters projecting holographic photos of current and former CEOs posing with various groups. An image blinked on showing a much younger Mr. Liu shaking hands with a military general. The caption said something about official thanks from the UCF for the company's contribution to 'making the Moon ours.'

They stepped into an elevator capsule—also beige.

Kirsten raised an eyebrow when Dax hit the button to go to the -1ˢᵗ floor. Given the vast majority of West City had been built on a uniform deck suspended an average of fifty meters above the natural ground, no structure had an actual basement. An interlocked grid of 'plates' twenty-five meters thick formed the bed upon which the city rested. Much like starships, they contained interior hallways divided into two stories sandwiched between thick outer hulls. The hollow spaces underground held almost all of the city's plumbing, power cables, data lines, and storm drainage.

The building having a 'basement level' meant the Atmos Tower's property descended roughly ten feet into the plate beneath it, not an unheard of thing. Companies and some residence towers saved money by placing their computer equipment 'underground' where it had easier access to the data mains. Good chance Atmos had their servers down there, so decided to put the security team as close to them as possible.

She didn't fear the Beneath the way most citizens did. Kirsten also didn't exactly like going there, as it brought back bad memories. She'd only been ten years old when she ran away from home in the middle of the night at the urging of Ritchie, a ghost who warned her mother would kill her that night if she didn't flee. Fearful Mother would find her if she stayed on the surface, little Kirsten followed him into the Beneath.

Her nightgown lasted a few months. Her underpants held on a little longer before the chemical muck and harsh terrain ate them. It took a while for her to become desperate enough to suffer the disgust of making a tunic out of sticky old plastic tarp material. She likely could've stolen actual clothing from one of the random off-gridder settlements, but she'd been too terrified of adults back then, convinced everyone would be like Mother. As soon as they realized she had psionic powers, they'd try to kill her. Considering she used Astral Seeing and Darksight near constantly back then, her eyes always glowed white like Evan's did now when he wanted to see ghosts. She'd used Astral Seeing so damn often as a kid, she no longer needed to consciously activate it to see spirits, and her eyes no longer glowed —unless she turned on Darksight. But back then, she had tiny flashlights for eyes all the time. Anyone who saw her would've known immediately she was either psionic or mistook her for a child-sized android.

Being extremely superstitious, the people down there would likely have tried to destroy her—or they'd have ended up worshiping her as some form of goddess. Had she risked approaching one of those settlements as a child, she'd *still* be down there today, either dead or as the queen of primitives. On the elevator ride to the Atmos basement, she wondered if she secretly *envied* the cat nutballs for their 'freedom' of not giving a crap what anyone thought of them, the same freedom she briefly enjoyed before she'd been mature enough to handle it.

There I go with the what-if crap again. She closed her eyes and thought of Evan smiling at her. *Happy. I am happy now. Stop thinking about the past or what might have happened.*

This trip didn't go into the Beneath, merely ten feet down into the plate. As if sinking into a bath of paranormal energy, tingles spread up her body the instant the elevator sank below 'ground level.' So many ghosts gathered in the depths where the living didn't go, West City basically floated on a sea of ectoplasm.

Being inside the plate definitely increased the chances a wandering spirit might enter the room.

The door opened with a soft hiss, allowing them to step into another beige hallway.

"At least they're consistent," said Dorian. "Every corridor looks the same. Did you know most of the e-suits made by Atmos are also beige?"

She stifled a laugh.

Dax led her past a few offices belonging to the physical security team, maintenance group, and a storage closet before they reached an airlock-style set of two doors, both requiring badge swipe access. Past the second door, they entered a hallway with grey carpeting and white walls.

"Wow. Not beige." Dorian whistled. "They splurged."

Kirsten smiled.

"Straight ahead is our data center." Dax pointed. "There usually isn't anyone in there unless something needs attention. Break area on the left here…" He badge-swiped a door open on the right. "And here is our network room."

Kirsten stepped past him, expecting something like the control center at a military base. Most corporate network rooms waved high technology in visitors' faces. This one, however, momentarily confused her. If she hadn't been escorted here, she'd have assumed she made a wrong turn and ended up in accounting or sales.

A medium-sized space held a cluster of cubicles. Three doors on the far wall opposite the entry door appeared to lead to a small office, a conference room, and a storage closet. Of twenty cube workstations, only eight presently contained an employee: five women and three men.

Except for one woman with whitish-pink hair and a guy sporting a royal-blue spike-do, the remainder of the staff looked as boring and bland as accountants. The two dressed like street gang punks also appeared to be the youngest in the room, neither of them past their mid-twenties.

All eight seemed partially comatose, gazing into nowhere, a strong indication their consciousness presently wandered around the GlobeNet.

A man poked his head out from the office at the rear of the room. He wore a fairly standard business casual polo (beige) and dark grey slacks, though had hair more like a ganger. It stood straight up on end, about ten inches high in the manner of a paintbrush. His dark complexion made the snow white of his hair seem to glow. The man appeared simultaneously older and not so old, somewhere between thirty and fifty, depending on how the light hit his face.

"Lam." Dax waved him over.

Dorian cackled with laughter. "I had an affair with a shaving brush in college. I think he's my son."

Kirsten smirked.

The man she presumed to be Lam Orben, director of network security, approached. "Dax? What the heck is this? I'd ask who sent the stripper, but this can't be a stripper. This kid's like thirteen. Why's she dressed up like that? You know kids aren't allowed in here."

Dorian's laughter died in an instant to a grim stare.

"She's not a child, Lam. This is Lieutenant Wren. Ryn emailed you about her."

"Oh…" He paused, looking her over again.

It didn't help he happened to be on the tall side. Standing next to him *did* make Kirsten feel like a kid. Thanks to Mother practically starving her and a couple hard years on her own, she'd always been on the small side. Dad, too, wasn't the biggest guy. Kirsten likely wouldn't have been too much taller if she'd gotten proper nutrition. Worse, she'd met a few thirteen- and fourteen-year-olds at the dorms who stood eye level with her. Some even taller.

"You must be Lam Orben." She offered a hand. "Lieutenant Kirsten Wren, Division 0."

"Must be true." He shook her hand. "They really do send kids out there."

"Not that it's any of your concern, but I'm twenty-three."

Lam raised both snow white eyebrows. Surprisingly, he appeared genuinely embarrassed. Most people tended to either not believe her or pretend they hadn't mistaken her age. "Sorry. You look kinda…"

"Yes, I know." She let a sigh out her nose.

Dorian again snickered.

She shot him a mild glare.

He pointed.

Kirsten followed his gesture to a 'sexy e-suit calendar' hanging on the wall… which happened not to be sexy at all. A person—she couldn't even tell gender—posed in a pinup posture while wearing a full-body e-suit plus helmet with opaque gold-screened visor. Rather than the name of the model, the text beside the figure read: Atmos H14 – Light Hazardous Environment Protection. Clearly, the 'sexy' part of the calendar had been intended as a joke.

She didn't laugh, but ceased being annoyed at the guy mistaking her for a child.

"So, what's this about a ghost? Are you serious?" asked Lam.

"I am." Kirsten went over a basic explanation of the deaths and her suspicion that a spirit caused them. "There is some connection between this and Atmos. I'm still trying to determine what it is. The most reasonable idea I've come up with so far is between twenty and forty years ago, someone attempting to break into your network fried themselves and now they're back for revenge."

Lam chuckled. "I really doubt it. Look at this room even. Atmos is not what you'd call a glamorous high-tech shop. It's seriously unlikely any hackers would be interested in us."

"Can't argue that, which makes it all the more baffling." Kirsten gazed around at the eight employees slumped in their chairs or over their desks. All had wires connecting their heads to identical dark steel-blue network interface decks as big as portable electronic piano keyboards. Big didn't necessarily mean powerful. It could be cheap. *So creepy. They all look dead.* "Do you use black ICE?"

Lam stiffened. "It's illegal for you to read my mind without a warrant."

Whoa. Seriously? Kirsten gawked up at him. "I didn't, but... I don't have to since you basically just admitted it. You getting immediately defensive is a big giveaway."

The security director stared slack-jawed at her for a few seconds before closing his mouth and giving off angry vibes. He appeared to be annoyed with himself for blurting.

"Okay. If this place is so boring and routine, what's it need black ICE for?"

Lam's expression fell.

"Now there's an 'I'm screwed' face if ever there was one," said Dorian.

"Lam?" asked Dax. "Is she right? Do we really have killer D-progs on our network?"

The director paced, shifting his jaw side to side.

"It's not necessarily illegal for companies to use killer defense software." Kirsten folded her arms. "Assuming you have the proper permits and there are sufficient warnings in the virtual world. Why are you acting like you just admitted to something that's going to result in a long prison term?"

Lam whirled to face her, eyes widening. "It's not like that. Look, I haven't been in this role *that* long. Only six years. I don't have any idea where it came from or what it's protecting. Our network has an empty data storage node guarded by the kill soft. It looks like an ancient treasure chest made of infinite darkness sitting on a table in an empty room. The defense program is a winged snake flying around it in circles. It also looks so black it's basically a hole in reality. Any hacker who's been at the game more than two weeks is going to recognize what it is."

"Why? Because it looks like a snake?" asked Kirsten.

"No. The total blackness. It's a convention." Lam shrugged. "Any free-running program capable of killing people in the real world appears to be made out of pure void. It's illegal to disguise kill-softs like real objects, animals, or people. They *have* to be made of void."

"Huh. Learn something new every day." Dorian whistled. "And I just thought they were trying to be edgy and cool with overwhelming amounts of black... like Division 0."

I should submit a report to Div 2. Atmos has black ICE on their network without a permit or registration. Probably a fine. Not my jurisdiction. "It's nothing to come unglued over, but I will have to note the presence of lethal intrusion countermeasure electronics here in my reports."

Lam stopped pacing and stared at her, one eye twitching.

She tilted her head. "Is there something you aren't telling me? Your reaction is a bit extreme."

"Maybe this forgotten countermeasure soft has been roaming the network killing randomly?" Dorian pursed his lips. "Can they do that? Go rogue? It might explain why only people who have connected to the Atmos network are dead. But... it wouldn't explain why no one can find an incoming kill trace."

"I didn't put it there." Lam shook his head.

"You didn't remove it either." Kirsten pretended to meander a few steps casually, while purposefully putting some distance between her and Lam in case he lashed out. She let her right arm drop at her side, close enough to grab her E-90 if needed. "Technical things aren't my expertise. Could this black ICE program have gone roaming around your network attacking people on its own?"

"No." Lam seemed to snap out of his panic. "Absolutely not. The software is not autonomous. It's not even close to an AI. Think of it as a spiked door that only stabs people who try to open it."

She nodded. "Okay. So if you are certain it's just been sitting there idle for years, why are you so nervous?"

"Just read his mind already." Dorian gazed at the ceiling.

"No one has touched it." Lam exhaled. "I'm sure. At least... not since I've been here."

Kirsten stared at him. The man thought mostly about getting fired for the police poking around the network. Mr. Liu had personally told him not to give any information about anything to anyone not employed by the company. He seemed convinced as soon as the chairman learned it was his fault the police discovered the quasi-legal software in their network, he'd be terminated. His anxiety did not, however, rise to the level of wanting to kill her to keep her quiet, though he did ponder bribing her—just hadn't summoned the courage yet.

"That's good." She smiled at him. "There's no need for you to be so anxious. If anyone even bothers to care about my report, the worst thing to happen will be you having to fill out a permit application and maybe a small fine. Assuming you even want to keep the program."

A strong paranormal energy welled up on the far side of the cubicle farm, near the storage room. Nothing visible manifested, but the intensity—and darkness—of the presence caused her to jump back into a defensive stance.

Lam peered quizzically at her.

"Oh, crap," whispered Kirsten. "He's here."

"Lucky." Dorian cracked his knuckles. "That didn't take long. Guess you're off the hook."

Kirsten stared fixedly at the place the negative energy gathered, still not seeing anything. "This does not feel like I'm off the hook. He's gonna be a nasty one."

"I meant off the hook in the sense you won't need to have Evan camp out at Nila's apartment all week while you sleep here."

"What's going on?" asked Lam.

She stepped around him, closer to the energy. "You might want to back up."

"Lieutenant?" asked Dax.

"The spirit. He's here." She flexed her fingers, ready to summon the Astral Lash at any second. Doing it too early could spook the ghost into running. They could sense the energy in the lash. Even new ghosts instinctively knew it could destroy them, almost like waving a flamethrower in a person's face. Better to lure him in with a false sense of safety.

"He's going to try to kill someone?" asked Dax.

"Pretty sure he's not here to sell chocolates to raise money for the company amateur Gee-ball team." She swallowed dry. *Come on, that's it. Eight people sitting here all plugged in and ready for you. Hope I'm fast enough.*

ASTRAL RECKONING

The apparition of a man exuded through the storage room door, mostly in silhouette.

Whoa. He really is a shadow. Kirsten clenched her fists. Wraiths didn't usually take on such a human outline. They tended to ignore legs and float around like a cloud with arms. This, she hadn't run into before. Unsure what, exactly, she faced, Kirsten remained still, watching.

Soon after the last vestiges of black vapor peeled away from the storage room door, the silhouette quality of the figure brightened. Except for his head, which had been warped beyond all recognition like a giant hunk of taffy twisted around and around, the rest of him now appeared no different from a normal, living person to her. The man was effectively shirtless in a see-through fishnet mesh tank top, Mars-camo military BDU pants, and beat-up sneakers. A small, silver crescent moon dangled from a nipple piercing on the right side of his chest. Curiously, he held an ornate gold-and-silver dagger in his left hand. The curved, notched blade came to a triangular point, matching the style of the elven weapons from the Monwyn universe.

Hackers like fantasy stuff. Bet he was holding a prop knife when he died.

"Ouch," muttered Dorian. "I have no idea what happened to him but it looks painful."

Not even the smallest remaining bit of facial features remained, only a 'dough spiral' of fleshy substance with bits of long black hair sticking out between the twists. Human heads did not cartoonishly squish into ropes like unbaked soft pretzels, so she figured this appearance came from his subconscious reaction to whatever killed him.

Black ICE… gotta be.

"You going to try talking to this guy?" Dorian raised an eyebrow. "He doesn't have a mouth."

The spirit rushed forward, heading for the nearest employee, a woman in her later forties.

Kirsten ran for the cubicle, jumping over the grey fabric wall three seconds before the spirit stuck his hand into the huge cyberspace deck. "Hey! Stop!"

"Mrrgh!" roared the spirit, voice muffled as if he had tape over his mouth. He kept reaching for the deck.

It took Kirsten a second to focus on her power enough to latch onto his presence and mentally shove him away. The woman twitched as the spirit's hand flew out of her deck amid a small cloud of sparks. He staggered through the cube wall, caught his balance, then pivoted and rushed toward the guy in the next cube. Dorian jumped in front of the spirit, which caused him to swerve across the aisle and go for the pink-haired woman.

"I said stop!" shouted Kirsten.

Mumbling in rage, the spirit kept charging at his intended victim. The sense of hate and malice saturating him—and the entire room— left no doubt in her mind what he would do. *Dammit.* Kirsten ran after him, unfurling the Astral Lash. Dorian rushed him from the opposite side.

At the appearance of a long, glowing tendril of brilliant blue-white energy extending from her hand, Lam screamed incoherent non-words. Dax simply stared at her in mute awe.

Dorian gee-ball tackled the spirit, knocking him to the floor. Flailing, the angry ghost attempted to scream in rage, his muffled, anguished cries sounded like a soul being electro-tortured in the bowels of a corrupt mental asylum. The 'dough twist' he had for a head flapped about in the manner of an octopus tentacle trying to grab onto something.

They untangled in mere seconds, the raging phantom momentarily dissipating into a wispy swirl of black vapors before coalescing back into his normal ghost self, standing upright. His mangled head continued flopping around while he attempted—with limited success—to scream in blind rage. Dorian, still on the ground, rolled over and entangled the spirit's legs.

"I think black ICE cooked his brain." Kirsten skidded to a stop nearby, hesitating to swing the lash while her partner grappled the dangerous spirit. "Any idea if this guy's intelligent or is this basically a creature of pure ID?"

"How should I know?" rasped Dorian between grunts as he pulled the other spirt back to the floor. "Bastard's pretty strong for a skinny guy."

They rolled over each other a few times before the warped spirit ended up on top. The ghost raised the 'elven' knife. Dorian grabbed his wrist in both hands.

Kirsten flung her arm out to the side, willing the lash to unfurl. Any second now, her partner would throw the ghost off, giving her a chance to strike. "If a person with severe brain damage dies, are their ghosts stuck forever in the same state?"

"No," said Dorian. "I've met several dead politicians who can still talk."

She sighed.

"No, the spirit remains intact. It's just stuck piloting a meat robot that doesn't work right." Dorian shifted in preparation to throw the hostile spirit. "Remember Raj? He was completely lucid after having his entire head blown off. That guy had less brains left than an entire room of media executives who decide which shows get cancelled and which ones run for twenty seasons."

"You have such a way with words." Kirsten nodded. "Ready."

Dorian hurled the dark spirit off to his right. The ghost crashed partially into the floor, struggling to keep himself in the building. He began to rise to his feet, already moving toward another Atmos security person, reaching forward to plunge his hand into the man's deck.

Kirsten lost hope this specter could be reasoned with. She lunged, swinging the lash as much by arm power as by mentally commanding the energy tendril to move. The last three or so feet of the whip tore through the spirit's torso, encountering a squidginess similar to walloping a Comforgel mattress with a club. Impact flung the spirit off his feet onto his chest. He lapsed into a convulsing, flailing fit, screaming and gurgling.

The instant her lash made contact with the ghost, the ceiling lights faltered. All eight security employees promptly flung themselves out of their chairs to the floor in the throes of twitching seizures.

Dorian glided to his feet, overacting a grimace at the dark spirit. "The last time I heard a person make noises like that, they had a stunrod shoved... never mind."

He didn't say it as if joking. Kirsten did *not* want to know.

Five or so of the security staff began scream-gurgling.

"What the fuck is going on?" called Lam from behind a desk.

"I believe your staff was effectively all unplugged at the same time." Dorian grimaced.

Sounds of vomiting came from the pink-haired woman's cubicle.

The deranged ghost stopped convulsing and crawled forward.

Kirsten stalked up behind him. *Shit. I hate the ones I have no choice but to destroy.* "Sorry, but you're a threat to people."

"Wait..." said the ghost.

She hesitated. "You *can* talk."

He collapsed over onto his back, staring up at her past defensively crossed arms—his head no longer twisted into an unrecognizable lump. It occurred to her that a significant amount of darkness had faded from his presence. He still threw off tons of anger but didn't radiate such pure malice as he did mere seconds ago. His intact face put his age in his late twenties. Aside from his having silver metal eyes with glowing green markings—miniature rune circles—forming the irises, his appearance reverted to being quite ordinary.

Kirsten lowered her arm, letting the lash coil around her boots. "All right. I'm waiting. Are you in control now?"

"Who are you talking to?" whispered Dax.

"Probably the ghost." Lam shivered. "She's staring at empty floor."

"Ugh. Oh man… I shit myself," moaned a guy from one of the cubes.

"Why am I on the floor in a puddle of puke? Ugh?" the young pink-haired woman gagged, then threw up again.

"Yes! TDC!" shouted another, deeper male voice, sounding sarcastic. "Awesome. This migraine is going to last for hours. Woo!"

"Comm – Ops," said Kirsten. "Request medical unit to my location. I have eight adults here who experienced Neuralink Abend."

"Copy, lieutenant," replied a female voice in her earpiece.

Dorian walked up to stand near Kirsten—on her left side away from the lash. "I thought the phrase 'slap sense into someone' was metaphorical."

Zombie-like groaning arose from the stunned employees. Lam cautiously emerged out of the empty cubicle where he'd taken refuge and began checking on his staff.

The ghost sat up—and his eyes disappeared, leaving the mildly disturbing sight of empty sockets staring at her. "Yes. I can talk. What did you do to me?"

"Call it an attitude adjustment," said Dorian. "Play nice or she'll adjust it again."

"Why are you killing people?" Kirsten coiled the lash around her boots in the other direction, making it appear to be a restless snake.

"It's all a big wad of fuzz. Crazy with rage, not thinking." His silver-and-green eyes reappeared. "Just… angry. Hey, wait a minute." The ghost got to his feet, staring at her. "You're alive."

Kirsten glanced down at herself. "Last time I checked."

"How can you talk to me?" He stepped closer, studying her like a normal person seeing a ghost for the first time.

"It's a long story."

He stopped short when his foot came within a few inches of the scintillating blue-white energy tendril floating above the floor. "Help me."

"Glad to." Kirsten stared into his once again empty eye sockets. "If you stop killing people."

"I will. Unless it happens to me again." He twitched. "If it does, just do whatever you have to do. Maybe it'll fix me again. Maybe it'll destroy me. Either way… don't care."

"Just a little damage there," whispered Dorian.

Seriously. "All right. What made you angry?"

He looked off to one side. Again, his eyes vanished. "If I tell you here, you will be in danger."

"From what?" She set her left hand on her hip.

"If they hear you say the wrong thing." He rubbed both hands down his face. "Let's go somewhere else. I'll tell you whatever. Just not here."

"What's your name?" Kirsten considered releasing the lash to enter notes in her armband terminal, but didn't quite trust him enough yet.

"H1ghb0rne," said the ghost. "A one for the I, a zero for the o, and an e on the end."

"No way do I think your parents gave you that name." Kirsten chuckled.

"Explains the costume Monwyn dagger." Dorian rolled his eyes.

"It's the only name I really cared about for the last six years of my life. It's my identity. My meatspace name is Avor Marles."

Kirsten watched him. He didn't radiate significant amounts of malice at the moment, at least no more than any other ghost upset about their death did. Earlier, he'd felt almost like a true wraith. Perhaps he'd been on his way to becoming one. Still wary, she released her concentration on the lash and activated her armband terminal.

Two men and a woman in white jumpsuits rushed in carrying suitcase-sized medical units.

"Need a moment," whispered Kirsten to the spirit before raising her voice to the medics. "Thanks for being fast. The whole team got yanked out of cyberspace simultaneously. I think their interface decks either shut down or restarted at the same time."

One of the employees gave off a continuous, low gurgling noise. The rest had gone quiet except for deep breathing.

While the medics got to checking on the workers, Kirsten searched the NPF database for the name Avor Marles—after confirming with him how to spell it. A record came up of his body being found twenty-four years ago in a grey zone apartment. His death had been ruled a justifiable homicide by means of anti-intrusion countermeasure software. The inquest report didn't identify the company or network location he'd unsuccessfully attempted to access, merely wrote him off as a criminal hacker who deleted himself from the gene pool. The ID photo of him in life matched the spirit visage in front of her now. He looked considerably less pretty in the crime scene images. Evidently, his cybernetic eyes had either exploded or caught fire when he died, burning off most of the top of his head. Instead of a brain, a fist-sized wad of charcoal sat inside the skull amid a fray of wires.

"That's... excessive," muttered Dorian. "Ouch. Poor son of a bitch. I've seen some horrible things in my day, but nothing quite this gruesome."

"Ugh." Kirsten grimaced and closed the holo-panel. "Sorry that happened to you."

"It is what it is. I don't believe I felt anything." He leaned his head left, then right, cracking a neck he no longer had. "The fire inside my skull started after I died."

You probably felt something, just don't remember it... which is good. Kirsten figured the twisty, misshapen head must have come from his subconscious memory of extreme pain in the nanoseconds before death. "If you can't talk about it here, then hang out until I can leave. Once the medics finish up, we're out."

"You found him?" asked Lam.

"Seems that way." Kirsten faced the network security director. "To be safe, I'd suggest continuing the helmet thing for a day or two. I'll let you know once I've solidified my conclusions."

"All right." Lam resumed helping the employees clean themselves up.

All but one appeared to be mostly okay now. A mid-forties guy had lost consciousness, bloody drool sliding down his cheek. Predictably, he got the medics' attention first.

Might as well get this over with now. Kirsten opened her terminal again and began typing in notes for the scene report she'd eventually have to write about what happened here.

17

DOOM PIT

Two medics stayed behind to check on the other seven security staff while one went with the unconscious man for transport to the nearest med center. He'd evidently suffered a seizure severe enough to leave him in a coma.

Kirsten mostly kept it together, managing the scene for the twenty minutes or so it took the medtechs to clear the other people who'd been abruptly punted out of cyberspace. When no one happened to be looking at her, she fidgeted in worry and guilt. Her psionic ability colliding with a spirit's energy had likely created an electromagnetic pulse powerful enough to temporarily shut down every bit of electronic technology nearby. This included all eight Titan Corporation 'Gold' cyberspace decks.

She'd learned a whole bunch of things she never cared about before, like how off-the-shelf interface decks had four common quality levels: Silver, Gold, Platinum, and Ultra. They also came in multiple other custom configurations that cost even more, such as the 'alchemist' series that had more memory for programs or a 'bersker' model optimized for virtual combat. Atmos essentially gave their security people mass produced hardware at one level above 'doesn't suck.' She also learned the spontaneous shutdown—which baffled the medics as those devices aren't supposed to be able to instantly power off—is marginally safer than yanking a person's wire out while they're live in cyberspace since there's no chance of a small spark jumping from contact to plug causing a voltage surge into the headware.

The man who'd lost consciousness likely had an innate susceptibility to complications from a Neuralink Abend, or an 'abnormal end' to an active connection to virtual reality. The perpetually smiling medic, Kim Park, said the poor guy risked a seizure any time he logged in or out and probably shouldn't be working a job that required him to use the GlobeNet at all.

This helped Kirsten not feel quite so stupid and foolish for getting into a fight with a spirit while surrounded by delicate technology. Fortunately, the minor EMP surge of one lash strike didn't cause permanent damage. The machines simply shut off for a few seconds. Had she obliterated him, all the electronics likely would have been fried for good.

Once certain everyone else would be okay and the scene was under control, Kirsten thanked Lam for his time, assured him everything would work out just fine, left her contact information, and made her way back to the parking area.

H1ghb0rne kept quiet, patiently waiting nearby. He followed her and Dorian, bouncing with restless energy all the way to the patrol craft. "Oh, whoa. Check this thing out. Pretty hardcore."

"So they say." Kirsten opened the door. "Hop in."

"What kinda weapons you got on this thing?" H1ghb0rne slid into the back seat.

"None. Only patrol division gets the cannon." She started poking buttons to bring the drive system online.

Dorian laughed. "If they even think about activating it, there's about forty pages of forms to fill out. If they *use* it, make it about a thousand."

"Crazy." H1ghb0rne whistled.

"That eye thing is unnerving." Dorian glanced back at him. "Any chance you could knock that off?"

"What eye thing?" asked the ghost, seeming genuine in his confusion.

Kirsten grabbed the control sticks and lifted off, steering for the exit. "He had artificial eyes. They must have been fairly new at the time you died."

"Yeah. Wow." H1ghb0rne scratched his head. "How'd you know that? Got them like a month before."

"Even I'm impressed." Dorian raised an eyebrow at her. "Did you sense that?"

"No. Educated guess. The eyes aren't firmly embedded in his latent self-image. When he thinks about having them, they appear. If he concentrates on anything else enough to lose track of being consciously aware of his own appearance, they disappear because they're not part of his actual body."

"Oh, shit." H1ghb0rne leaned into the front seat. "They're disappearing? Sorry. That's gotta look creepy as hell."

"No more strange than you carrying a knife around all the time." Dorian chuckled.

"Uhh, sorry. I can't put it down. I always held onto it while infiltrating. Was kinda my thing, yanno. Died with it in my hand, so it's like part of my ghost avatar."

"Ghost avatar?" Kirsten smiled. "It kinda works. Easier to say than 'latent self-image.'"

The patrol craft zoomed out through the giant opening in the wall. Kirsten accelerated, pulling up into the nearest traffic lane at the fiftieth story level without too much care for which way she happened to be flying.

"Safe to talk now?" asked Dorian. "Why would talking back there be dangerous for her?"

"Because, if someone heard her talking about what I'm gonna say, they'd try to get rid of her." H1ghb0rne leaned back, stretching his arms out across the top of the rear seat. "This is nice. Like a limo. Lots of room."

Kirsten flipped on the auto drive, then twisted to peer at him. "Okay. We're out. Like I said, I will help you as long as you stop killing people. Tell me what's going on."

"Atmos has a doom pit. Lots of us tried to get in there. I'm the only one who made it." H1ghb0rne grinned.

"You have a strange definition of making it." Dorian blinked.

"I got in. So maybe I didn't live... but I got in. Counts to me." H1ghb0rne examined his fingernails.

Kirsten couldn't think of any meaning to the term. "What's a doom pit? Gotta be some kind of hacker stuff, right?"

"Yeah. It's a room—or storage object—in the GlobeNet that's really damn difficult to get into... and even harder to get out of. Case in point." H1ghb0rne gestured at himself. "I is ded. Spelled d-e-d."

"Right." She sighed. "What's the point of these doom pits? Just to trap and kill people?"

"They can be used for that. Not this one, though. It had data in it. I got the data out... but bastard snake got me before I could bail out. Doom pits block the logout command, forcing you to physically run out of the area so you can't just 'disappear.' That's how the bastard program got me."

Dorian flicked a bit of lint off his sleeve. "I don't mean to sound unduly harsh here, but you illegally broke into a company network and basically fried yourself trying to steal their data."

"Accurate." H1ghb0rne nodded, flashing a goofy smile.

"You realize your death is not their fault, right?" Dorian tilted his head.

"Oh, yeah. I know. I'm not pissed off at them for that."

Weird way to show it... Kirsten cringed mentally when she remembered his warped apparition. *Okay, he was out of his mind.* "What is it you need help with?"

"The data. I need to get it back."

Kirsten and Dorian exchanged a stare.

"You know you're dead, right?" Kirsten blinked. "Data isn't any use to you."

H1ghb0rne raised his hands. "Hey, I know. I might be dead, but I'm not stupid. Well, not *too* stupid." He laughed. "Hit the cortical booster chems a bit hard. Rumor has it they make you dumb after a few years but, I haven't noticed any change yet. Anyway... the data I nabbed isn't any shit I was gonna sell for profit. I don't know the full details since I never got the chance to actually look at the data before my brain melted, but, squeaky-ass-clean Atmos is responsible for something like twenty thousand deaths and they covered it up."

Her unease being around this particular spirit lessened. "You died trying to get data that would've proven Atmos responsible for killing people?"

"Yeah. Not sure 'killing' is the right word. The data will explain what happened exactly. My guess is they had a design flaw or something in their e-suits, knew about it, and didn't fix it because it cost too much. A whole bunch of poor bastards suffocated to death or got exposed to toxic environments thanks to shitty suits."

"If they knew about the flaw and ignored it, I think 'killing' is the right word to use." Kirsten squeezed the control sticks tighter.

Dorian narrowed his eyes in suspicion. "If they killed that many people, you'd think their offices would be full of angry spirits. Not just this one guy."

"Depends on where these poor people were when they died. It's not easy for ghosts to travel between planets." Kirsten nudged Dorian. "Remember when you went to the Moon?"

"Not fondly." He frowned.

"Yep." H1ghb0rne exhaled hard. "Almost all of the fatalities occurred on Mars, in Mars orbit, out on distant colony worlds, or way off in the middle of deep space while people had to go outside their ships to do stuff. Blowing an ion emitter on a hovercar doesn't suck near as bad as crap going wrong on a starship at the ass end of nowhere."

"So…" Kirsten shifted her gaze to him. "You want me to get this data."

"Yes. I really don't know why I was randomly frying people. It ain't their fault. I…" He leaned forward, grabbing his face in both hands. "That fuckin' black ICE scrambled my brains. All I could see was lightning. I had to share the lightning with everyone. Somehow, I blamed Atmos and… I guess it just led me to follow link traces in the system to people I could vent on. Really sorry. Feel like shit now."

Dorian's expression gave away no indication of his opinion. Blank.

"Not really my job to judge." Kirsten squeezed and relaxed her grip on the control sticks. "If he's sincere, the fluffies won't bother him."

"Wow." Dorian whistled. "I don't think Harbingers would appreciate being called fluffies."

"Oh, they're cute. In a dark, morbid, existentially terrifying sort of way." She twirled a lock of hair around her finger.

H1ghb0rne grimaced. "I do not wish to know what these harbinger things are. Data. I really need you to get the data and make it public. All I ever wanted to do with it was blast it as wide and far as possible."

"Seriously?" Dorian raised an eyebrow.

"Yeah, man. Not every net pirate is out there to make money. Some of us are crusaders for the greater good." H1ghb0rne saluted him with his 'elven' dagger. "If the data's legit, as soon as it goes public, it could take down the whole company, or at least leave them exposed to a shitpile of lawsuits. It'd make other companies think twice about brushing known defects aside."

"That's the hope." Dorian chuckled. "Never underestimate a company's ability to screw people over for a profit."

H1ghb0rne stared at Kirsten until his eyes reappeared. "Will you help me expose the truth?"

"If you're being honest with me now, yes. I will." She offered a hand.

He grasped it, chilling her fingers. "I am. Find the data and you'll know for sure."

"All right. Where is it?"

"My deck is a custom job. Put it together myself. Started with the guts of a Nishihama Oracle, grafted on the memory and I/O module from a Starpoint Galaxian, along with its compression accelerator co-processor. Added the supercharger from a NinTek Gladiator on a hot-swap toggle. That way I get the added punch when I need it but my defenses aren't paper thin all the time. I hand-made the case myself."

Kirsten blinked rapidly. "I don't understand a word of what you just said. Is any of that telling me where to find it?"

"No, he's bragging." Dorian smiled. "You know how tech heads get with their gear. Sounds impressive."

"Oh, it was a thing of beauty." He gazed into space, his cybernetic eyes fading in and out. "I called it Alondrien."

Kirsten raised both eyebrows. "The capital city of the high elves?"

"Exactly!" H1ghb0rne pointed at her. "You're a fan? Didn't think many people knew about it."

"Yeah. My kid's super into Monwyn. Guess I am getting there, too." Kirsten removed her hair clip, re-tucked her blonde mess back into place, and clipped it. "You died before I was even born. Monwyn... might not have been as big back then as it is now. It's everywhere."

"Oh, wow. Really?" The ghost laughed. "I remember it being this like niche thing with a small group of super hardcore fans. Most people were into the space stuff. Aliens and crap. Explosions."

Kirsten poked the auto-drive, setting a course for the PAC. She still had forty-two minutes before Evan got out of school. Retrieving an old network deck from wherever it ended up sounded neither difficult nor incredibly urgent. She wouldn't dawdle, but felt no need to rush.

"Do you know where your rig is?" asked Dorian.

"Yes. I can sense it. The only time I remember feeling kinda peaceful since I died is near it."

"If you'd like her to get it for you, the odds of her finding it are greatly improved by you telling her where to go." Dorian gestured both hands at Kirsten while flashing a 'stop being an idiot' smile at the other ghost.

"It's in the basement of a club, B0rderland. Dude named Nebula is using it now." H1ghb0rne cracked his neck again. "He hasn't found the Atmos data since I stuffed it into an unlisted neural memory bank. Won't even show up on diagnostic scans. Gotta attempt to access it directly by address."

"Umm. I *think* that makes sense." Kirsten smiled.

"Think of it like a hidden compartment on a smuggler's space ship. If you know where to look, it's easy to find." H1ghb0rne tapped a finger to his temple. "I obviously don't need the deck anymore. You don't need to steal the physical thing, just get to it with a portable neural memory stick. Plug it in and download the data. I can walk you through how to access the hidden memory."

"She doesn't have a plug." Dorian smirked.

"Oh. That might be a problem." H1ghb0rne chuckled. "We'll have to figure something out then. She might be able to access it via link cable from a NetMini. Be a pain in the ass to navigate but not impossible."

"B0rderland, huh?" Kirsten stared out the viewscreen at the endless stream of hovercars in front of her. She knew almost nothing about nightclubs. But… how difficult could it be to sneak into a room, plug in a mem stick, then leave? It had to be much easier than attempting to steal a giant box of electronics. "Okay. Might take me a bit to plan this out, but I will do it."

"Thank you." H1ghb0rne brought his hands together beneath his chin and bowed in the same manner the elves in the Monwyn movies and video games did.

Kirsten leaned back in her seat.

Wow. This case went in a direction I was not expecting.

18

UNOFFICIAL ASSISTANCE

Her investigation had become official.

It didn't matter to Kirsten that some of the Div 2 detectives seemed amused or even laughed when she submitted a request to take ownership of inquests they'd filed. Once back at the squad room, she'd created a master inquest record, then associated the twenty-one Division 2 inquests—one for each victim— as subordinate records. Few people in the NPF outside of Division 0 took claims of ghostly activity seriously. However, their disbelief didn't prevent them from happily dumping 'garbage unsolvable cases' on her.

She found it distasteful how an alarming number of detectives over in Div 2 treated their job as a game, questing for 'high scores.' Some investigated crimes based on the motivation to solve more cases than their peers rather than out of any sense of finding justice for victims. She resigned herself to ignore it. As long as they didn't cut corners and blame innocent people, justice eventually happened even if it hadn't been the investigator's motivating force.

Captain Eze seemed proud of her initiative. If not for her digging into old, stalled cases, the deaths might have remained unsolved for years while an out-of-control spirit continued killing. The captain did, however, offer a few words of caution about possibly opening the door to Division 2 getting in the habit of trying to chuck their cold cases across the hallway. The 'if I can't explain it, must be a ghost' rationale could both overwhelm Kirsten as well as cause some less-than-thorough detectives to rush unwanted cases to a point they could ditch them.

For now, she didn't worry too much about that happening. In order for Div 2 to punt a case to her (as opposed to her requesting it from them) they'd have to admit they took spirits and paranormal things seriously. Most wouldn't since it opened them to ridicule from other Division 2 staff.

Dorian called it fear. He thought people didn't so much have a strong desire not to believe spirits could be real as they truly *did* believe in them—and didn't like it. As he said, few things scared people more than the mere idea of death. It's one of the strongest, most primitive fears humanity had, second only to speaking in public... or the dread of being unexpectedly summoned to the captain's office.

H1ghb0rne made a complete reversal since she first encountered him. His quiet, calm patience surprised her. It seemed almost unbelievable for one swipe of her Astral Lash to turn him from a mindless killer to an unusually friendly spirit. She knew ghosts didn't all follow the same rules. Some degenerated into personality fragments that barely counted as sentient—e.g. poltergeists. Others could get trapped in the area where they died, thoughtlessly reenacting the moment of their death over and over. She'd run into ghosts who couldn't see the world as it existed, instead occupying a delusion of the past. One spirit she'd met had even regressed to childhood, despite having lived into her sixties. The neighborhood she saw around her as a ghost matched where she'd grown up, proving some spirits could willfully occupy a different perceived reality.

Somehow, a network interface deck pumping raw voltage into his head scrambled his sentience. The more she thought about it, the more sense it made. Ghosts came from whatever remained of a person after the biological parts ceased to be. A spirit encapsulated the personality, thoughts, and memories of the individual they'd been in life... and they were made up entirely of electromagnetic energy. A sudden blast of electricity directly into the brain might be capable of damaging the ghost. While she couldn't explain how she slapped him back to rights, Kirsten much preferred not having to destroy him. By the time she finished entering all the details of the case in the master inquest, she decided to trust him enough to go home.

Kirsten flopped on her sofa with Evan and Sam, all wearing senshelmets to enter the world of Monwyn the Magnificent. Their 'party' had a fourth member: H1ghb0rne. He'd essentially possessed the Yume Koujou game system the same way Dorian took over hovercars or delivery bots. Predictably, he selected a high elf tracker. Within the virtual reality world, his character appeared as genuine as any character controlled by a living person.

Having died before the Monwyn franchise went mainstream, he found the vast game fascinating. The thirty-year-old man raced about exploring with the exuberance of a boy. In fact, if Kirsten didn't know better, she'd have thought one of Evan's friends from school joined them. The man took things to the next level, speaking entirely in character and behaving as if the fantasy world around them happened to be reality.

He even knew minutiae of trivia Evan didn't, having been introduced to the setting via novels over forty years ago when he'd been a teenager. Most people tended to consume entertainment in the form of movies and video games, though literature hadn't entirely died out. Kirsten rarely read anything in text form other than training materials and school books—stuff she'd been ordered to read. She also hadn't really bothered with video games (or movies) much prior to having Evan around. According to Mother, everything not associated with her religious mythology was 'evil,' hence, banned. As a child, Kirsten hadn't been allowed to watch any holo vids, play any video games, or even know about the existence of entertainment ebooks.

Hard to have fun while spending twelve hours a day locked in a closet.

She also didn't bother trying to speak with Mother's wizard in the sky to ask him to 'save' her. Even as a seven-year-old capable of seeing ghosts, Kirsten thought the story nonsensical. Her mother believed a being of supreme and total power existed and somehow humans could do things he didn't want them to. The first time she asked her mother *how* it could be possible for weak humans to overpower this god of hers and do something he truly didn't want them doing had been the first time Mother became so enraged she burned Kirsten's hand on the kitchen stove.

Kirsten stopped asking questions… not that it helped.

What started off as a random idea to 'show the ghost the new Monwyn stuff' turned into two hours of rather entertaining fun. She almost forgot one member of their group died before she'd been born. Twenty-four years didn't amount to much in terms of ghosts. Few spirits could gain the power necessary to manifest, even as mere light orbs, in so little time, much less kill the living. However, he did have an abnormally potent level of rage and relied on a fairly unique way to attack people. Perhaps the mechanism of black ICE coupled with the manic desperation he must have felt while being unable to log out to escape a demonic-looking void cobra resulted in him being stuck in what would otherwise have been a fleetingly brief emotional state.

Sitting near him now, he gave off energy like any other fairly recent ghost, seeming innocuous and incapable of causing serious damage. The oddity of having a killer ghost playing a video game in her home with her ten-year-old son (who showed no signs of fear toward the spirit) distracted her from the game. Evan was over the moon, having a ghost interact with the Yume Koujou and play video games with him. The boy'd been grinning nonstop since they'd gotten home.

Wow. It's almost been three hours. Where the heck did the time go?

Similar to the way her combination of Mind Blast and Astral Sense produced the ability to use Lash, Evan's mix of Clairvoyance, Precognition, and Astral Sense somehow combined to give him the ability to look at a ghost and know with a high degree of accuracy in seconds how dangerous the apparition was. Since he acted completely at ease around H1ghb0rne, she tried to stop feeling as though she'd made a mistake bringing him home.

While Sam and Evan's characters debated the best way to proceed down a likely trapped dungeon corridor, Kirsten—in her avatar as an elven archer—waited a short distance away, keeping an eye on the passage behind them in case the game sent an ambush. H1ghb0rne, also a high elf, stood beside her. His tracker had many of the same skills as her, though favored swords to bows.

"Tell me about this B0rderland place," said Kirsten.

"I know not of this B0rderland." He raised an imperious eyebrow.

She sighed. "Out of character."

He seemed reluctant, staring at her for a few seconds before slouching in defeat. "All right. It's a hangout for a group of low-rate hackers and data pirates. They don't claim to be part of a gang but basically are. This guy Nebula runs the GlobeNet side of things and calls the shots. The place is not exclusive to his crew, though. Any lowlife can walk in off the street and get messed up. Last time I went there, it was trendy and expensive. Now, it's a shithole in a grey zone."

"Wonderful," she muttered. "How bad is it? Is this a 'grab a couple Tac officers for backup' bad or 'bring Division 6' bad?"

The entrancingly handsome elf winced. "You cannot storm into the place the way the police tend to steamroll everything. If you show up there with an army, they're going to hit a kill switch and wipe all the data they have in an instant."

"Isn't your data in an unassigned memory module?" She nocked an arrow and shot a small, grey goblin like creature trying to sneak up behind Evan's wizard without really even looking at it. "A wipe program wouldn't be able to access it."

H1ghb0rne rubbed his chin. "You are correct. However, I am concerned Nebula would not rely only on software deletion. An EMP device or perhaps even an incendiary charge would wipe everything out. Hardware *and* software. Nothing would be salvageable. The law wouldn't be able to reconstitute any information from puddles of smoking plastic. Simply erasing files is not secure. Data can be reconstructed with the kind of equipment the cops have."

"So, they see police outside and they'd just blow all their stuff up right away?" She whistled. "Seems excessive." Kirsten shot another goblin creature.

"You have to understand what goes on there. It's almost all GlobeNet related. People meet there to sell illegally obtained data. They buy softs, stims, chems, and rumors." H1ghb0rne leaned to his right and stabbed a cave goblin attempting to backstab her.

"Gah!" She spun, startled by the tiny death wail so close.

A blast of heat and orange light came from Evan tossing fireballs at a larger group of cave goblins in front of him. Kirsten started shooting arrows as fast as she could offload them at a horde of the creatures approaching from the distant end of the underground corridor.

"I do believe you got the rune sequence wrong," said Sam, raising his shield. "Conjuration trap summoning more of these guys."

"Oops," deadpanned Evan, not sounding overly concerned. "Ugh. More math homework."

"Math homework?" asked Sam.

"Yeah." Evan waved his arms around. "What is thirty-two goblins plus one fireball?"

Sam laughed. "Zero goblins."

"Exactly." Evan hurled a flaming orb down the hallway into the cluster of little grey creatures. It burst into a billowing torrent of flames that threw tiny screaming bodies in all directions.

H1ghb0rne took a defensive position in front of Kirsten, slicing down any goblin coming from the rear that managed to make it past her barrage of arrows. "*One* cop walking in the door might not make them go for the death button right away. If you made it downstairs into Nebula's throne room, they'd totally blow the thing. If you swoop in there with an entire assault squad, they'll push the button as soon as they see you outside."

"Throne room? Are you back in character or does this guy have a literal throne room?"

"It's just what he calls it. Desk. Big chair, eight decks around him like an overachieving keyboardist." Having run out of cave goblins to kill, he pulled his sword between two fingers to clear it of grey slime.

"Just like hackers," called Sam. "They're always getting into a bigger deck contest."

H1ghb0rne laughed.

Kirsten blushed.

Evan peered up at Sam. "Deck size doesn't make that much difference. Sometimes the small ones are surprisingly powerful."

Sam laughed too hard to effectively fight goblins for a moment— thankfully, all the ones on his side of the hall died to a fireball.

The boy doesn't realize what he just said. Kirsten got stuck between wanting to laugh and being mortified. "You're right, Ev. The little ones can surprise you sometimes." *Oh gah! Why did I say that?*

Sam collapsed into the wall, almost unable to stay on his feet due to how hard he laughed.

"I meant..." Kirsten sighed. "Size isn't an accurate measure of power."

Sam fell over.

Oh for... grr.

H1ghb0rne cackled. "Keep trying."

"Why is everyone acting like dorks?" asked Evan. "Network decks aren't really that funny."

"Stress, child." H1ghb0rne's elven tracker bowed to him. "Occasionally things which are not considered humorous make people laugh as a way to cope with stress."

"Oh." The boy—who looked like an adult wizard inside the game—cracked his knuckles and faced the rune trap again. "Sorry about the goblins. Let me try this again."

Kirsten slouched, relieved the ambush ended—but more relieved the off-color joke had finally run its course without her having to explain the meaning to her kid. "You're saying I'll need to go in there basically undercover."

"That would be ideal." He smiled. "You don't need to worry about talking to anyone. Just find my old deck. Plug the memory fob in and get the data. Should take about forty-three seconds."

Ugh. Kirsten pressed a hand to her stomach to hold down the butterflies. Alas, her elf character in the video game didn't care one way or the other about going to a dodgy hangout spot full of low-grade criminals, gang punks, hackers, chem dealers, and whoever else frequented such areas. The uneasy feeling remained squarely in Kirsten's real stomach, creating a sense of dissonance between two perceived realities. Perhaps if she had an M3 port and plugged in, sensations would combine so she felt as if she'd *truly* been transported into the body of an elf.

It's not as bad as it sounds. A woman like her wouldn't be safe there, and not so much for her age and size. B0rderland likely had plenty of

young women, even teenage girls, hanging out without an issue—
because they fit into the 'scene.' Kirsten most certainly did not. Any of
the locals would take one look at her and smell outsider or easy prey.

*I have two advantages. They'll never think I'm a cop... and I have
Suggestion.*

A command to 'go away' worked far better than physical violence,
took a mere second, and wouldn't make anywhere near as much of a
scene as pulling out a gun. Ironically, she had better odds of making it
into the place and back out unhurt than some hardass augmented
Division 6 meatball of a woman who'd try to rip the arms off any guy
trying to grope her.

She swallowed a little saliva that gathered in the back of her mouth.
This 'mission' as she thought of it, would probably require she tolerate
some unwanted touching, if only long enough to make eye contact
with the person doing it to send them on their way. Undercover
Division 2 detectives often had to do far worse. Some took drugs or
committed crimes ranging from burglary to assault, and occasionally
even murder. Others had to fake their way into relationships with VIP
suspects, even having sex with them to gain trust.

Thankfully, she wouldn't need to do any of that, merely find a piece
of electronic hardware and connect a mini neural memory fob to it...
then leave. The most difficult part would be figuring out how to access
the hidden memory location and initiate the transfer. She'd never once
in her life touched an interface deck. Having H1ghb0rne's spirit
standing beside her to walk her through the steps made it possible, but
far from easy... especially while nervous and trying to hurry.

*Doable. Don't overthink it. People would freak out more at the idea of a
child going alone into the Beneath than a twenty-three-year-old hitting a
night club in a sketchy sector.* She didn't feel the least bit confident in her
ability to act like a street rat, despite literally having been one for two
years. It didn't really feel like that back then, though. She'd been a kid
guided by friendly spirits, exploring an old, forgotten world full of as
much wonder as it held danger. Perhaps her memory applied a rose-
colored filter, but except for that one horrible man, her time in the
Beneath felt like an adventure. Not exactly the same situation as kids
dodging gang fights and chem dealers.

"All right. This may take a little more planning then. Mind if I go after the data tomorrow night?"

"Not at all." He smiled. "I'm dead. Got all the time in the world. Atmos has been hiding this stuff for almost forty years. Another day won't matter. Besides... it gives me more time to enjoy this game."

Kirsten gazed at the moss-covered corridor ceiling. *He's as bad as Ev. Could play Monwyn all damn day. Wait. He'll be worse. No need to take bathroom or food breaks.*

As far as Kirsten could tell, H1ghb0rne spent the entire night inside the game system.

After dropping Evan off at the school the next morning, she headed up to the squad room. Once the group briefing ended, she returned to her desk and updated all the inquest notes and reports she needed to fill out. The distraction of her planned visit to B0rderland later that night made it difficult to concentrate.

"You seem nervous," said Dorian.

Kirsten spun her chair around. "Little bit."

"Want to talk about it?"

"Yeah." She leaned on his desk—which remained officially unassigned for some reason despite desks being in such demand a few people from Tactical (like Nicole and her partner, Forrester) used this squad room, too. Perhaps Captain Eze considered it *Dorian's* desk, since it should belong to her partner. It might also be Command not assigning her a living partner due to the lack of Astral Sensitives or other personnel being too wary of anyone who could Mind Blast. "The data he needs is in this club, B0rderland..."

Dorian listened as she explained the situation. "You're right. Those people would sniff you out right away."

"I don't look like a cop *that* much, do I?"

He smiled. "Only when you've got the uniform on. I mean, you'd look like a girl who quite obviously went into the wrong place. Someone would either try to get the 'innocent kid' out of there before she got hurt... or try to take advantage of you."

"Yeah. I don't know how to blend in among that crowd. I don't even have an M3."

"Easily fixed."

"Eep." She covered her neck.

"Get a fake stick-on one."

Kirsten stared at him. "They have those?"

"Oh, yeah. They have all sorts of fake costume cybernetics."

"Why?"

He shrugged. "The same reason humanity makes countless inexplicably pointless products: we can."

"It's going to take more than gluing a little plastic bit to my head to get me in there."

"Quite." He chuckled. "If you go in the door and bee-line for the stairs, you're going to look like the shy, unpopular girl at the house party who just can't wait to get out of there."

"So? I really am trying to get out of there as fast as possible." She laughed into a sigh. "If they didn't have a kill switch, I'd totally bring an entire Tactical unit."

"You're not going in there alone." Dorian gave her his 'big brother' stare.

"Great. Thank you." She exhaled. "But... you don't exactly fit in among that crowd either. What I'm really anxious about is trying to get the data off that old deck. I've never even touched one before. Those things don't have screens. They're just oblong loafs of technology with ports. It would take seconds if I had an M3 jack, but..." She blinked. "Ooh. Idea."

"Uh oh. What's on your mind?" He overacted cringing.

"Sam can speak their language, but he's too clean cut. They'll peg him as a cop right away." Kirsten plucked her personal NetMini from its belt clip. "I need an expert. Someone who's part of the scene and who I can trust."

He raised an eyebrow.

"Hope she's up for it." Kirsten scrolled down her list of contacts.

"Who? That Adrienne girl?"

Kirsten smiled to herself that Dorian spoke of her as a woman. Honestly, no question remained. She might have started off life with a male body, but the girl could get pregnant now. She'd also gone from twenty-one to about sixteen for a 'do over' of her worst years. Hopefully, in the grand scheme of things, Kirsten turning a blind eye to a psionic person manipulating electronics to generate credits out of thin air to pay for gene surgery wouldn't be considered wrong. Reinventions did amazing work.

"No…. I was thinking Skittles."

"That crazy cat girl?" Dorian whistled. "Are you sure?"

"She's not crazy." Kirsten poked the contact entry to open a vid call. "She's got a cheap language chip. The woman doesn't speak English. She's French."

"Oh, yeah." He snapped his fingers. "But most Nekos don't literally behave like cats. Purring, curling up on tables, that sort of thing. This girl's got some damage."

"She's also got… that stuff."

"Stuff? Ears? Tail? Complete disregard for societal norms?" Dorian raised both eyebrows.

"That too, but it's not important. I mean the…" Kirsten snapped her fingers a few times. "The cyberware that makes her really fast and whatever. Remember when she shredded those Diablos?"

"Speedware?" Dorian folded his arms. "Most wired-up assassins charge about fifty thousand credits for a job like what you're going to ask her to do."

Kirsten grinned. "Good for me she's not an assassin."

"You're sure about her?" He winced. "That woman is not exactly 'law abiding' if you know what I mean. And something about her story doesn't quite add up."

"How so?" Kirsten stared at her NetMini's holo-panel. Skittles' young, innocent face smiled up at her, surrounded by a halo of abnormally fluffy charcoal grey hair and two prominent cat ears.

Dorian paused for a few seconds, as if thinking. "Her story about being grabbed off the street at seventeen and waking up with cat parts sounds a little embellished for sympathy, if you ask me. Not saying the upper class over there couldn't be that depraved, but rich eccentric perverts don't usually put a million credits worth of combat speedware into their pets."

"Yeah. I know." Kirsten traced her fingertip around the contract entry. "She's not lying. It's a partial truth. Started off being abducted, but after pretending to be loyal long enough, she got promoted to bodyguard or something."

"You mean assassin." Dorian folded his arms. "The rich guy let her off her leash long enough to kill people he didn't like."

"The man didn't keep her on a literal leash." Kirsten frowned. "Things are so desperate over there that reliable food and a comfortable place to sleep kept her far more effectively than any chain."

Dorian's expression said 'things aren't so different here.' He sighed. "You trust her?"

"Well, she wasn't perfectly loyal to him. Don't forget, she set him up to be executed for treason. And she made her way to the UCF from Europe by herself. She's way more capable than she looks." Kirsten thought back to their first meeting. "You remember what she did to those Diablos, right? She could have killed me at any time and didn't, even though I was a cop. Don't forget I helped her with that bastard of a cyberdoc. She still thinks of me as the reason she isn't in constant, crippling pain."

"True." Dorian tapped his chin. "Hmm. Maybe she got the reflex boosters after arriving over here. A million credits is only a lot of money if you actually earn it. Hackers…"

"Right." Kirsten chuckled. "Problem with our money only being numbers in a computer somewhere. We should go back to gold coins like in Monwyn."

Dorian laughed. "Well, I suppose if you're sure about her, go ahead."

"I am… if she agrees. She's at least as good a hacker as H1ghb0rne was." Kirsten tapped the contact entry to initiate a vid call. "Worst thing that'll happen is she says no."

BEING IN FULL CONTROL OF HER WARDROBE, KIRSTEN DID *NOT* ATTEMPT TO wear high heels.

Even if jinxes weren't really a thing, she didn't want to tease fate. It seemed every time circumstances conspired to force her to wear heels, the night ended in disaster. Besides, fancy shoes wouldn't be appropriate for a club like B0rderland. They also made it difficult to run. If she ended up barefoot tonight, she'd much prefer it happened at home.

Riding in a PubTran car felt slow and tedious. The thin fabric, grey and patterned with tiny teal squares, did nothing to cushion her butt from the hard molded plastic bench seat. No point complaining out loud. The car's AI would only offer to sell her an optional comfort adjustment, a fancy way to refer to spray foam.

Ruin your pants for only ninety credits.

She didn't want anyone in the area to see her get out of a patrol craft. However, she also didn't want to take a PubTran car on a sixty-eight-mile trip. So, she compromised. Her patrol craft sat on the rooftop parking area of a hotel about two miles away from the line separating Sector 6929—the grey area containing B0rderland—and Sector 6877, one grid square south. PubTran Corporation would occasionally allow their cars to go into grey zones, but charged exorbitant trip fees plus forced the passenger to accept liability for the full value of the vehicle if it got destroyed.

Even though the government would likely cover it in this case as she used the automated taxi as part of an official inquest, she didn't want to bother with the paperwork. She'd selected an innocuous cyberware shop near the northern edge of Sector 6877 as her destination, close to where the city declined into grey, but not so close as to earn 'risk fees.' The last mile and change into the official grey zone, she'd cover on foot.

As far as her attempt to look like an off-gridder went, she more or less thought she made a passable go of it. Baggy olive drab pants with a bunch of extraneous pockets and some decorative chain bits gave her room to carry a couple of extra e-mags, her NetMini, a blank neural memory fob, and even a stunner without looking like she had a ton of hardware on her person. The shirt she ended up choosing only barely qualified as a shirt. It consisted of a clingy black fabric band around her chest that covered a little more than a bikini top. The addition of a puffy greyish-silver jacket kept her from feeling overly exposed as well as allowed her to conceal the E-90 in an armpit holster she'd borrowed from Division 2.

For shoes, she'd bought a new pair of TMC Hunters. They seemed to ride the line between athletic shoes and combat boots. Dorian spent a while debating if he should call them snoots or beakers, combining 'sneaker' and 'boots.' He thought the joke far funnier than it was.

Carrying a weapon wouldn't stand out as long as no one got a close look at it. Most adults in the city had a gun on them. An energy weapon, however, would attract attention. She doubted anyone in B0rderland would take it as proof of her being a cop. Only Division 0 routinely used energy weapons on Earth, thanks to the technicality of them being partially effective against ghosts.

Great idea. People trying to shoot shadow figures or light orbs they can barely see with weapons powerful enough to penetrate through four apartments. It made no sense to her. Even among Division 0, most staff didn't take ghosts seriously. In the seven years since she'd been activated to deal with the Wharf Stalker incident, her cases helped increase the percentage of Division 0 personnel who considered spirits real from about 9% to 34%. Using ghosts as a reason to issue energy weapons sounded like a convenient lie. Nine percent of the staff considering ghosts real didn't support using them as a rationale for why Division 0 *needed* lasers. Someone wanted to play with fancy, dangerous toys and found a loophole for it.

Her outfit also included a few cosmetic items stuck to her body. She sported a fake M3 port behind her left ear as well as a one-inch strip of silver with tiny blinking blue lights pasted to her left temple. It resembled the miniature hatch for a skill chip reader. If she needed to spend any significant amount of time trying to blend in among the hacker crowd, she'd probably have taken it farther, adding false tattoos or faux neural wiring lines, maybe even cosmetic contact lenses to create the effect of cybernetic eyes with glowing irises. The vast array of 'fake' cyberware available for purchase stunned her at its seeming purposelessness. That a market for costume augments existed came as a surprise.

All I need to do is look acceptable enough to walk in. It doesn't matter I have no damn idea where I'm going because H1ghb0rne will be there… and I have Dorian.

Her ghostly partner sat on the rear-facing bench seat, arms folded, head tilted slightly to the side like a guy too tall to fit inside the tiny PubTran car. He did not seem pleased with the arrangement, but hadn't yet complained.

The brief—and jerky—ride came to a harsh stop at the designated address. An ordinary Cyberwave outlet shop—the fast food of cyberware sellers—occupied roughly a third of the ground floor beneath a 103-story residence tower. Shiny silver plastisteel framed windows spanned the entirety of the ground floor. Above it, the second story had more holographic advertising panels than windows, but still appeared relatively clean. Higher than that, decades of grime darkened the metal structure to indigo except where long brownish trails of deposited rust browned it. A near perfect repeating grid of rectangular windows stretched upward into the night sky. Somewhere around the sixtieth floor, they became fewer, wider spaced, and larger —the point where the apartments went from economy to standard.

A smell neither pleasant nor foul rode past Kirsten's face on an unnatural wind driven by advert bots and hovercars racing by overhead. Amid the prickling scratch of stray ions lurked the fragrance of seafood, a hint of ocean water, trash, melting plastic… and the murk society had come to regard as the odor of grey zones, itself a mixture of human waste, leaking chemicals, decaying trash, and dead body.

Her nose said someone died nearby, but she didn't see any spirits. The faintness of the odor suggested the dead person had been left in place for some time before being removed. A corpse could haunt the scene of their death in more ways than paranormal. Some smells remained forever. Or… it might simply be the ambiance of the grey zone a mile away to the north carried far afield by the constant stream of flying vehicles.

She visually scanned the pedestrians as a habit borne of training, then regarded the building in front of her. Only the commercial façade showed any effort whatsoever to maintain it. People generally didn't look upward very often. Perhaps the building management decided it a waste of money to clean anything above eye level. This tower couldn't seem to decide if it wanted to fight for civilization or slip quietly into the approaching ruin. Grey zones tended to grow over time. Left long enough, the core would get so bad the government deleted it from maps, making it a black zone.

I don't understand why they just let bad spots fester. Fix them before things go past the point of no return.

In some areas of the city, the first one-to-three floors of every building contained commercial space. Somehow, despite the ubiquity of NetMinis, advert bots, and delivery bots, a significant portion of the population continued to shop in person, especially for items like clothing or expensive electronics they wanted to check out before committing to a purchase.

"Thank you for choosing PubTran Corporation for your transportation needs," said an overly pleasant male voice from the mini car she'd stepped out of, right before the side hatch door practically slammed shut with enough force for the breeze it made to fling her hair forward off her shoulders.

The tiny car's eight-inch wheels squeaked on the plastisteel road from the effort it put into speeding away, worsening the 'melted plastic' portion of the olfactory malaise hanging in the air. That Kirsten could tolerate the odor without a face covering or flinching at all made her feel tough. Grey zones had nothing on the Beneath for stink.

"Damn thing's late for an appointment." Dorian frowned at it.

Kirsten eyed the crowd of pedestrians passing in front of the Cyberwave—and other storefronts in the same building. Most of the traffic collected around the open counter of an Asian noodle kitchen. All twelve barstool type seats were full, the lucky ones who got to eat the food fresh and hot. Everyone else jogged off with take-out packages. To be fair, the aroma of shrimp and whatever else the people inside happened to be cooking almost made her hungry, despite her having already had dinner at home.

She nervously looked at her left jacket pocket, where the NetMini hid. Evan hadn't called. He didn't seem worried about her going on this trip. While it *could* mean she'd be fine, precognition could be fickle. When Evan freaked out, he sensed her walking into a situation so dangerously fatal her best way to survive it would be to avoid it entirely. Something like going into this nightclub could seem benign to him initially, but depending on what she did inside, turn deadly without warning. In that case, the boy wouldn't get a precognitive flash until a deadly chain of events had already been set in motion... which could translate to mere seconds. Not enough time to warn her.

Evan not being afraid tonight only suggested that if she were careful, she'd be fine. It did not mean nothing could go wrong.

I'm going to jump out of my skin if my NetMini rings before this is over.

"Your kitty is late," said Dorian.

Multiple advert bots going overhead saturated the street in the holographic glow of sexiness, mouthwatering food, shiny electronics, fancy cyberware, and vistas of foreign lands still full of trees. Several of them had time displays.

"We're a little early." Kirsten tried to strike the pose of a surly teenager totally unimpressed with the world. "How's this?"

"Are you trying to look like a kid who's worried about what she's going to get in trouble for?"

"No." She scowled. "I'm trying to look rebellious."

"Keep trying." He winked.

She sighed. "This outfit should work."

"The outfit works." He tugged at her jacket. "The problem is your face."

"What's wrong with my face? Did the thing fall off?" She poked at the fake skill chip hatch.

"No, it's still there." He smiled. "There's nothing *wrong* with your face."

"What the heck are you talking about then?" She squeezed her hands into fists.

He appeared to be fighting the urge to smile. "You don't look rebellious. You look like you're lost and homesick."

"Grr." She stared up at the thousands of bots and hovercars whizzing by overhead at varying speeds.

"Just think about a system glitch making you have to rewrite all those reports from a couple months ago when that Marley Santiago girl was driving ghosts crazy."

"Oh, hell no. Don't even joke about that." Kirsten shuddered.

"There you go. That's a perfect 'don't mess with me' face." Dorian snapped his fingers. "Hold that thought."

Another PubTran car rolled to a stop by the curb at the end of the block.

The side door opened a few seconds after the vehicle stopped moving. A slender woman with the waifish figure and innocent face of a fashion model flowed out onto the sidewalk. Her outfit looked remarkably similar to Kirsten's with a few minor differences: form-fitting black tights instead of baggy pants as well as a grungy white T-shirt long enough to serve as a skimpy dress. A pink cartoon rabbit on the front of the shirt stood with its head cocked to one side, pointing some manner of electronic circuit board to its temple in the manner of a gun, tongue lolling out, eyes crossed. She'd also skipped shoes.

Long, straight slate grey hair hung down to her butt, thick and fluffy like fur. Large cat ears protruded from the top of her mane. A feline tail the same color as her hair hovered inches off the plastisteel sidewalk behind her, swishing side to side. Skittles glanced around for a few seconds before spotting her, then proceeded to saunter over in no great hurry.

Kirsten raised both eyebrows. *Wow. She's wearing clothes.* Given the relatively comfortable temperature, she'd honestly expected the woman to show up stark naked.

"That's unexpected." Dorian gestured at the black fabric strip pretending to be Kirsten's shirt. "*You* are showing more skin than a Neko."

"Hah. Yeah, right? Weird."

"Her outfit is probably holographic."

She exhaled. "I will never understand why people who aren't dirt poor willingly run around with nothing on."

"Didn't you first meet her living in an empty cargo transport trailer in an abandoned swath of grey zone?"

"Yeah, but…" Kirsten puffed at a strand of hair draped in front of her face. "Having credits and using them aren't the same. No one with her skills is poor unless they want to be. She's gotta have credits stashed all over the net."

"You're saying her relationship with money is the same as her relationship with apparel?" Dorian chuckled. "Has it, but leaves it littered around not using it."

"Yeah…" Kirsten frowned. "Basically."

"By 'skills,' are you talking about her hacking abilities or her suite of mods perfect for assassination?"

Kirsten blinked. "I meant the GlobeNet stuff, but I suppose both would fit my meaning. She's not an assassin though."

"Everyone who ever had speedware and claws installed says they're not an assassin." He winked. "Even when they're killing people for money."

"She doesn't." Kirsten almost stomped like a ten-year-old. "It's self-defense."

"When you looked up her record, it's clean. Doesn't mean it never happened. Only that she's good enough to not be caught."

Kirsten stared at him. "Consider her personality and… unique habits. Do you really see her being a hired killer? The instant a laser dot appeared, she'd drop the gun and go chasing it."

He howled with laughter. "Good point. That's beyond anything synthetic DNA might have caused. Didn't you say she used to be some rich guy's pet in the ACC? Probably has a behavior modification chip in there somewhere."

"That's illegal." Kirsten gasped. "Immoral."

"Oh, my sweet innocent little partner." He shook his head. "Since when has something being illegal or immoral ever stopped the ACC from doing it." He sighed. "Or our government."

Kirsten stared down. "Do you think it's forcing her to hate clothing?"

"Can't say. There are plenty of fools over here who do that without an illegal bit of headware." Dorian pointed at the pedestrians wandering by. "Extreme fashion. Like that guy passing the noodle bar. Most of the expensive designer stuff is a few scraps of fabric in strategic places. The only reason complete nudity is still a fringe trend and hasn't gone mainstream is the famous designers haven't figured out a way to make money off people for wearing nothing. However, it seems they are trying."

She blurted a chuckle at the ridiculous comment while following his pointing finger toward a man on the older side of his twenties, whose entire outfit consisted of red sneakers and a dark blue cube of unknown material covering his naughty bits, held in place by three metal hoops that curved around his hips about where a belt would be, floating an inch or so above his skin, somehow staying in place despite not touching him. She tried not to gawk.

I really don't want to know where the other end of those metal bands go.

"That guy's 'outfit' probably cost ten grand," muttered Dorian. "And as soon as he looks behind him and sees Skittles, he's going to rip it."

Kirsten blushed at the thought. She couldn't even say 'at least if Skittles had showed up nude no one would pay attention to me' because society had become somewhat jaded to it. Outside of hoity-toity business districts, people—especially the sort of counterculture undercurrent as around here—would barely notice another cat person exhibitionist.

"Ten grand?" She rolled her eyes. "Doubt it. Look where we are. This is not exactly fashion central. We're three blocks from a grey zone."

The man wearing a fabric cube for pants passed by. Despite not wanting to know where the other ends of those metal hoops went, Kirsten couldn't help herself and turned to look. Thankfully, they didn't plug into a body cavity as she feared. They attached to six metal studs embedded in the small of his back. This did, however, leave his backside completely exposed. Getting cybernetic implants purely to serve as attachment points for extreme clothing made Kirsten squirm. The thought of having metal inside her body bothered her far more than nudity.

"Yes, well," said Dorian. "However much his dick box set him back financially, it cost more than what your friend pays to wear nothing."

Kirsten sputtered into laughter at his term for the guy's outfit. "Nah, Skittles is wearing real clothes. Who'd go on a data nab in their birthday suit?"

"A Neko." He gestured at her.

"That would attract way too much attention."

"Like the ears and tail don't?" asked Dorian. "If those leggings aren't holograms, they're painted on."

Skittles walked up to her, smiling wide enough to reveal her small fangs. Amusement gleamed in her eyes, right one gold, the other green. Vertical slit pupils made it seem as if someone had taken the eyes out of an actual cat, enlarged them, and put them in a human face. "Hi, and not really. Lots of people get cat ears. And my leggings are real, not paint."

Dorian winced. "I forgot you can hear me."

"Hello, Kirsten's no-see friend." Skittles looked generally in his direction. "I sometimes do not wear the clothes for the intimidation."

"Umm…" Kirsten fidgeted. "How is being naked even remotely intimidating? Doesn't it make you feel vulnerable?"

"*Non.*" She shook her head. "If walk into a place with nothing on, the people know I am fearless. Not to be messing with."

"Or out of your mind," said Dorian.

"That too." She grinned. "No one do the messing with the out-of-mind girl who has claws."

"… and military-grade speedware." Kirsten chuckled.

"Military-grade only means it cost six times what it's worth." Dorian brushed lint off his uniform sleeve. "Not feeling fearless today?"

"I am feeling the sneaky. Trying to be inconsistent." Skittles made an annoyed face. "No. That is not the word. Silly chip. *Discrète.*"

"Inconspicuous?" asked Kirsten.

"Yes. This." Skittles pointed at her. "I should really buy better English word chip. This portion of feces is so basic. Maybe take learning sim, but too much work. I am lazy."

Dorian snickered. "Are you sure you aren't doing that on purpose to mess with people?"

"I keep bad chip on purpose to make people think I am not smart." Skittles crossed her eyes. "If people think that, they are easy to fool. I wear the clothes for now. You prefer, yes?"

"Yeah." Kirsten whistled. "Thanks. Though, if you had shown up in uhh, 'comfortable attire', I'd probably have been too busy being embarrassed for you to be worried about this mission going bad."

"It will not go bad." Skittles winked, then waved at her to follow. "To B0rderland we go."

Kirsten fell in step on her left, away from the road. Dorian walked on her other side, watching the street for out-of-control PubTran cars or idiots on Mishiro booster skates.

"Honestly?" Skittles glanced over at her. "If you wonder why I am so blasé about clothing, it cooks down to pure laziness. Less time wasted doing laundry. Why generate work if I do not leave my place?"

"Cooks?" asked Dorian.

"Boils down." Kirsten snickered. "The phrase is 'boils down.'"

"Oh. Thank you." Skittles laughed. "This language is so confusing."

"Last time we met, you didn't have a place. You lived in a truck," said Dorian.

"Fair." Skittles examined her fingernails. "But I have place now. Not staying with Incubus and his friends. Too many bullets. Too loud. And kitty is lazy. I much rather would sleep than work."

Kirsten smiled at her. *Just like a cat.* "Well, thanks for being willing to help me out."

"You made the doctor fix." Skittles swung her tail up and tickled Kirsten's nose. "It does not hurt. I must help you much to properly thank you."

Dorian gazed around. "Let's hope your new friend shows up. We're not going to get very far without him."

"H1ghb0rne?" Kirsten stuffed her hands in her jacket pockets. "He's probably waiting for us at the door."

"If he's not still at your place playing video games." Dorian laughed.

"Oof. Yeah." She grinned. "So weird. Watching him and Evan last night… like I had two ten-year-olds. They're both so into the game, though H1ghb0rne takes it way too far."

"Well, of course he takes it too far." Dorian wagged his eyebrows. "He literally gets *into* the game."

"Ugh." Kirsten groaned at the clouds.

"Who is Highborn?" asked Skittles.

Kirsten explained.

"Oh. Another no-see person." She bit her lower lip. "You have many unique friends. Your life must be fun."

Fun is one word for it. Kirsten pushed away all thoughts of the past, focusing entirely on Evan, Sam, and the good she tried to do for the citizens of West City. "Yeah. It's kinda fun."

19

BoRDERLAND

S kittles led the way down the street in a most bizarre scene.

One moment she projected the air of an exclusive fashion model, almost royalty, while simultaneously looking at people going by in a 'please mess with me. It's been weeks since I got to kill someone' manner. Then, out of nowhere, she'd completely shift gears and turn into a creature part frantic feline and part tween with severe ADHD, running after a bit of bouncing trash or swiping her hand at some fluttering plastic hanging from a kiosk wall.

Kirsten couldn't tell if the woman had actual mental problems, or the behavior came from deliberate modification. Surface thought scans confirmed only that she didn't fake it. Every so often, the 'cat' lurking in her mind took over and compelled her to do things. Considering the man who kept her as a pet was dead, it would serve no purpose for her to go digging into Skittles' past. Some rich guy in the ACC sent his goons to grab a random pretty woman of the commoner class off the street—or purchased her from kidnappers. As far as she told Kirsten, she blacked out one day around age seventeen and woke up in a cage with cat ears and a tail.

Though she did say the man never hit her, he had essentially enslaved her as a pet... until she arranged his arrest for treason.

Kirsten had no love for the ACC's government—a disgusting capitalist runaway nightmare that put profits above the value of human life wherever and whenever possible—but she had to smile at what happened to that Montpierre guy. He never knew one of the girls he abducted happened to be a gifted hacker. She'd spent over a year helping the resistance online in the GlobeNet while leaving calculated 'mistakes' for the authorities to use in order to track her down. Only… she made it look as though her 'owner' ran the avatar. The ACC's general contempt for women worked to her favor. No one suspected a scatterbrained 'indentured servant' catgirl who randomly chased dust bunnies to be capable of anything requiring intelligence.

Brief daydreams about rushing over there to 'make a difference' in the lives of the poor ended fast. Not only was it entirely ridiculous to think that one person, even a psionic suggestive, could fix an entire corrupt, greedy, misogynistic society, the ACC considered psionics illegal and often shot them on sight. Division 0's archives contained tons of heartbreaking accounts: children as young as seven being arrested at home like hardened criminals for the crime of being telepathic. They'd be dragged away from their families—who would be shot if they tried to protest. Some of those kids ended up with explosive devices wired to their brains in case they dared to think for themselves, forced to sniff out other psionics and help the people in power control them. The ones they couldn't control didn't survive to adulthood. Some escaped and fled to UCF territory.

So no, going to the ACC would not end well for her.

Vibration in the air snapped her out of her somber mental wandering. Kirsten held back a gasp at the sight of burned-out cars on both sides of the road. Almost half the buildings across the street appeared to be in various stages of collapsing. Nearby on the left, a group of young-looking teens clustered around a trio of e-heaters set atop broken appliances too far damaged to recognize what they used to be.

Just past eighteen… Kirsten frowned to herself. *No more free food or medical care… unless they join the military or go to a colony.*

Pounding music came from the ground floor of a high-rise tower half a block ahead on the left. Holographic text spelled out

'B0rderland' in shimmering orange, pink, and dark blue above the door in three-foot-tall letters, askew to the left, taller toward the end of the word. Most of the buildings on the same side of the street as the club appeared intact. The stark contrast with the facing structures pointed to deliberate acts of destruction, as if those who frequented this club made a habit of shooting randomly across the street or even throwing explosives. All the properties on the right seemed long abandoned and more like the ruins one would find in a black zone.

B0rderland offered an oasis of relative clean and high technology, sandwiched between a drab laundromat and a small gun store—which appeared to be closed after dark. Armored metal plates protected the windows. Two red hologram signs on the weapons shop warned of active automatic defense systems in the building.

Idiotic. "Who puts a gun store right next to a criminal hangout?"

Dorian laughed. "The same people who sell junior explorer club cookies outside recreational chem shops. They know their market."

She frowned. *He's being cynical. The gun store was there first, before the club went underworld.*

Thirty or so gang members milled around outside the place. They didn't seem to be part of a line waiting to get in, merely loitering while drinking, huffing chems, or tinkering with electronic devices. Wisps of smoke rose here and there from a guy attacking an open network deck with a soldering iron.

The majority of the people seemed to be younger than thirty, most on the scrawny side. This gang didn't strike her as the type of criminal group to engage in physical violence very often. Thinking of them as 'militarized tech geeks' eased her anxiety somewhat in the hopes they would be less prone to violence than, say, a gang like the SecSpiders or Angels.

They also didn't get too crazy with their attire, hair, or cosmetics, seeming to favor a 'comfortable grungy' look, which surprisingly worked with Kirsten's attempt to 'dress like a punk.' She'd initially worried not doing anything with her hair other than letting it hang wild would out her as a norm, but... most of these punks did the same. No spikes, no wild colors, no weird styles. They all looked as if they avoided doing anything that might take too much time away from being online—including laundry, personal grooming, bathing... and so on. What Kirsten initially thought to be some sort of post-apocalyptic themed decorative rubble around the base of the club turned out to be millions of discarded Cyberburger (and other take out) clamshells.

Guess they don't even want to waste time cooking.

She scanned the crowd, still not seeing any sign of H1ghb0rne.

Skittles patted her on the arm.

Kirsten looked at her.

The woman tapped her head.

"What?" asked Kirsten.

Head tap.

Confused, she peeked into Skittles' surface thoughts. The loud music—even standing thirty feet from the door—hurt the woman's ears so much she'd dampened them. With her ears set to 'normal human range' sensitivity, she couldn't hear Kirsten's voice apart from the pounding of heavy techno-metal.

Sorry. Yeah, it is kinda loud. I'm definitely going to have a headache by the time we're done.

Quoi? Je ne vous comprends pas.

Kirsten blinked, realizing the woman's English language chip didn't allow her to understand the language... it intercepted and translated. If her ears heard English, her brain would hear French. Directly inserting speech via telepathy bypassed the chip. She held up a wait a minute finger, fished her NetMini out of her pocket, and opened a translation app. It took her a moment to type in an explanation on the crummy little holographic keyboard—almost no one bothered to type rather than speak to the device—about how telepathy skipped over her chip and they wouldn't be able to understand each other.

Skittles read the French text on the screen, then rolled her eyes in an exaggerated, annoyed matter, then thought, *Cet endroit va vraiment me faire apprendre la langue, n'est-ce pas?*

Kirsten blinked. In no possible way could she even imagine how to spell any of those sounds into typed text. Her clueless 'mouse about to be hit by a truck' stare made Skittles burst out laughing.

"Idea," muttered Kirsten to herself before standing up on her toes to put her mouth as close to the woman's large cat ear as possible. "Can you hear me if I do this?"

Grinning, Skittles nodded, then leaned over to put her face by Kirsten's ear. "Yes. The music. It is so loud. What is your plan?"

Before Kirsten could answer, Skittles licked her ear. "Augh!" She squirmed.

Dorian raised an eyebrow.

Kirsten grimaced, shifting her gaze over to the woman. "Why?"

"Sorry. It happened without thinking." Skittles offered an apologetic shrug.

"Did they put actual cat genes in her?" Dorian whistled. "Never heard of a Neko involuntarily acting like an actual cat. When they lick people, it's… usually rather intentional."

Naturally, the phrase 'intentional licking' made Kirsten's thoughts leap to something Sam did a few weeks ago in the bedroom. Her cheeks burned with blush, mostly because she liked it and wanted him to do it again sometime… yet still felt weird talking about it.

After wiping her ear, Kirsten squinted up at Skittles. "Okay. Let's forget that happened."

"What?"

Kirsten grabbed a handful of T-shirt and pulled Skittles down enough to speak into her ear like some sort of triangular furry microphone. "Plan is to find a place the ghost called a 'throne room.' The guy who runs this place has a setup with eight decks. One of those decks used to belong to the ghost. He's hidden the data we need in some kind of hidden memory."

"Oh." Skittles grinned, then put her mouth beside Kirsten's ear again. "It is not so difficult to find. Merely time consuming. Easier to open the unit and look at physical modules. If the diagnostics show less available memory than what looks like it should have, you know there's a prison pocket."

Kirsten cringed again, expecting a lick, but Skittles refrained. "What is a prison pocket?"

"You don't want to know," said Dorian.

"Is slang term for hiding memory." Skittles offered an innocent smile. Too innocent.

He's right. I don't want to know where the term came from. It's probably disgusting.

"Okay. We go." Skittles grabbed Kirsten's hand and started leading her toward the building.

Obviously, acting like a pair of tween sisters wouldn't work here, so the woman must be attempting to imply the two of them were romantically involved. Kirsten had no idea how Skittles felt about women, though she personally had no desire to fool around with a girl. According to Nicole—and several others she dormed with back in the day—'everyone' went through an experimental phase. Nicole freely admitted to having made out with another girl before deciding she didn't really care for it. Kirsten had yet to find such desires. Granted, after her experience in the Beneath, she'd been afraid of sex, so wouldn't have dared think about it.

Kirsten tolerated the handholding, her thoughts drifting into a strange place. Dr. Loring thought Kirsten had an unusually strong level of discomfort with nudity, something more along the lines of how society was before the Corporate War centuries ago. According to her, it used to be illegal to show nudity—even topless women—on broadcast media. As crazy as that idea sounded, she *did* find herself blushing whenever confronted with a floating advert containing nudity.

It's shame. Guess I'm still blaming myself for what that man did. She shook off the distracting thoughts. *Later. I'll talk to Dr. Loring about it next time.*

Waves of sound crashed over them as the door opened, so powerful it seemed to possess physical mass. As if trying to walk into a standing wall of the viscous gel used in medical tanks, Kirsten tucked her shoulder and pressed forward, up against Skittles.

In addition to the punishing music, the interior of B0rderlands contained a much rougher-looking element than the more techno-nerdy crowd outside, likely a mixture of 'locals' as well as members of other gangs who'd come here looking to buy tech or software… or even contract the pros to do jobs in the GlobeNet for them.

She gazed around in disbelief at a scene straight out of an adult-only holovid set in a dark post-apocalyptic nightmare. A man in his later fifties sat in a booth seat, evidently selling chems in little glass ampoules to a pair of gang punks who'd come to 'his booth'. He had a pair of Nekos draped over him, one on either side, a boy and a girl. Both looked slightly underage and wore only collars—his pink with a little blue heart-shaped pendant, hers blue with a matching pink heart. Shocked, Kirsten dove into their heads. The boy looked about sixteen but thought of himself as twenty-one. The girl actually was seventeen but lied about it, claiming to be eighteen. Both appeared to genuinely be fond of the chem seller and willingly worked for him.

Before Kirsten could decide if she ought to intervene in the case of the girl being a technical minor, a man wearing an outfit equal parts transparent plastic and bright pastel neon glow bumped into her from behind and right. She jumped, whipping her gaze away from the dealer and his two 'cats' to this dude attempting to grind against her. She managed to resist going for her stunner long enough to peer into his head. He thought of dancing so close to her as 'asking' if she was interested, evidently a normal thing to do in this place.

Kirsten forced a weak smile at him, then scurried after Skittles. Much to her relief, the guy didn't follow them.

In the back, far corner of the room, a massive tangle of rusty scrap metal formed a bar of sorts. Someone had designed it to resemble a barricade made of ancient cars and other pre-war junk. The man serving drinks had a pair of huge shotguns crossed like swords on his back and wore an outfit similar to a Badlands raider—filthy leather armor and a facemask.

She couldn't understand why anyone would dress up like that when both the Badlands and the raiding gangs out there happened to be real. People cosplaying Monwyn characters made sense. That universe didn't really exist. It could be fun. Why anyone would want to pretend to be *real* bad guys, she couldn't even begin to fathom.

Her heart nearly stopped beating when she noticed a cluster of rusty cages hanging to the right of the bar under a metal sign. Cutout welds in the steel formed letters 'Orphans for sale – no sickos.' Three filthy rag-clad children, two girls and a boy between the ages of seven and ten, sat in the dangling cells, peering out at the room past spikes and rusty chains draped around the outside. She had her hand on the

E-90 under her arm before her brain processed the kids had no surface thoughts.

Not real. Just dolls.

Despite their robotic nature, the artificial children did not seem happy with being used as scenery props to create apocalyptic ambiance.

She stared, torn between needing to save them and being able to think of them as machines used for decoration. WellTech child dolls did not count as sentient. They only ran programs with a limited set of reactions, behaviors, and abilities. Technically, nothing prevented someone from replacing the factory chipset with a real AI, but... none of the 'orphans for sale' looked particularly frightened or upset. If they did happen to be full AIs (and thus legally sentient) they willingly worked as actors or would have been screaming for help and attempting to escape.

Sick. Not funny. Not cute, but... not illegal. She exhaled.

As they moved deeper into the club, Kirsten panned her gaze to the right. It occurred to her that the other half of the room shifted tone to high-tech... or at least as close to high-tech as grey zone scavengers could get. Against the left wall, the place had a Badlands-themed bartender with his shotguns and fake orphans for sale. The opposite side of the club looked like the inside of a starship. Silvery tables with neon glowing trim, comfortable, clean padded booth seats. Random bits of technology formed the wall, panels textured to resemble the interior of science fiction movie spacecraft. Two obvious android waiters made their way around the seats, checking on the club goers. Each side of B0rderland represented an extreme, with a gradual shift from one to the other across the entire room.

No one person stood out as a serious threat. The place didn't appear to have designated security or bouncers. However, everyone in sight had at least one gun on them... except the two cat-modded teens draping themselves over the guy selling chems, who had nowhere to conceal anything—except inside their bodies. They might have claws like Skittles. She proved that looking vulnerable and defenseless meant nothing.

Kirsten again found herself watching them. The way the dealer had his hands all over both Nekos when he wasn't counting tiny chem-filled phials made no secret of their relationship. The two also appeared into each other, pawing and/or kissing whenever the chem dealer attended to a customer. Consent remained a legal grey area if an adult went to Reinventions to de-age themselves below eighteen. She hadn't probed into the male Neko's memory deep enough to know for sure if he'd done that. He *looked* like a teenager but believed himself to be in his early twenties. Hell, people mistook Kirsten for anywhere from thirteen to fifteen, depending on her outfit. Could be the guy simply looked young the same way she did. The girl *was* under eighteen, if only by seven months. She certainly didn't mentally dwell on any traumas in her past life for Kirsten to read anything from a casual poke into her thoughts. The girl also appeared to be on some manner of chem, feeling overheated despite being naked, all her thoughts hazy and random, abnormally mellow and relaxed.

Not that Kirsten possessed vast experience with narcotics, but she didn't get the sense the girl had been drugged against her will. She'd taken something relatively mild to feel good the same way people drank alcohol. She obviously wanted to be here. Seven months from now, no one would care, as if the magical number eighteen made all the difference in the world. She'd gotten cyberware installed, so she obviously had a decent enough fake ID.

I can't save everyone… especially the ones who don't want to be saved. As wrong as it felt not to do anything, making a scene in the middle of this club would probably ruin her chance to get the Atmos data and succeed only in making that girl upset and furious—assuming no one ended up being shot in the ensuing fiasco.

Skittles tugged Kirsten across the room.

She kept staring at the drug dealer and his two companions for a moment longer while thinking about the 20,000 who died to Atmos Industries' carelessness. Whatever mechanism in the universe drove the sense of morality responsible for Harbingers would most likely consider all those deaths a greater wrong than some girl being reckless with her life a few months before crossing some arbitrary legal line in the sand in regard to her age.

She knows what she's doing… not like I did.

Kirsten pulled her gaze away from them after scanning the dealer's thoughts to make sure he didn't traffic in dangerous chems like Lace. Seems he mostly sold cortical boosters and performance enhancers, the kinds of enhancement drugs hackers, try-hard gamers, and corporate spies used to push their cyberspace performance beyond human limitations.

Skittles stopped at the bar.

Kirsten glanced up at a fake boy sitting in a cage, the closest 'orphan for sale' to her while Skittles ordered drinks.

"Robots," said Dorian. "They're not real."

She looked away from the ersatz child, then sighed.

Holo-panels on the wall behind the bar showed scenes from various movies, mostly crazy vehicles made of rust and spikes racing across the desert while leather-clad barbarians shot at each other or fought with spears, the past hundred or so years of post-apocalyptic cinema in montage. Even though humanity had essentially created such a world for real not all that far from here, it remained a popular genre in entertainment. Perhaps it explained why the UCF government left the Badlands alone and didn't put serious effort into reclaiming the land. Society might adore the spectacle of having a giant 'sandbox' of post-apocalyptica to watch.

Division 0's database had all sorts of unsubstantiated stories about the presence of an incredibly powerful paranormal entity out there. Kirsten stumbled across the notes from a Sgt. David Ahmed in Tactical. He'd been assigned to a remote outpost in the Badlands. Most of the details hid under a high level of classification Kirsten lacked the security clearance to see. However, she'd heard rumors involving a psionic child with crazy powerful healing abilities. The parts of the reports she could access mentioned something the child referred to as 'The Sentience,' essentially a demonic entity formed by the twisted, angry souls of everyone who died during the Corporate War. Sgt. Ahmed postulated that this entity was responsible for the failure of all efforts to reclaim the Badlands to civilization.

Having now seen at least two genuine demons, Kirsten took the story at face value. She also had no desire to go anywhere near the Badlands, especially if a demon lived out there. Such a being certainly explained how people could descend into violent depravity when civilization existed elsewhere in the world.

Unless humans are just inherently violent. She smirked back over her shoulder at the frizzy black hair of the male Neko affectionately clinging to the drug dealer. *Crime boss having two pets is different from a Badland raider chief keeping slaves how?* She sighed. *Well, I guess that guy would let his cats leave if they wanted to. They're as into it as he is.*

Skittles handed her a drink.

Kirsten peered down at the smallish glass containing clear, translucent blue, and opaque orange liquids in three distinct layers with a purple blob the size of an egg yolk suspended in the middle layer. "Umm..."

"Sip gently. The top layer is fruit. It won't bother you. If you tilt the cup too far, the other two layers will come up. They'll make you happy. Don't eat the purple goop unless you want to go into outer space." Skittles hovered close, breath from her nostrils puffing into Kirsten's ear. She did not, however, lick again.

She's pretending we're a couple. Act natural. Kirsten waited for the woman to lean away, then took a tentative sip, gingerly tilting the cup so only the upper fluid layer reached her mouth. The overpowering flavor of artificial mango exploded across her tongue. It clearly had *some* alcoholic content but not so much a single sip had her seeing vapor trails. She couldn't help but think of Mother and her fondness for synvod. This in turn led her to remembering her own habit of having a shot or five of synvod herself after a particularly bad day coping with other people's tragedies. Evan got her to break the habit with a single, fearful stare when he'd caught her drinking. His bio-mom's shit of a boyfriend constantly drank himself into a stupor before the beatings. The boy thought alcohol could turn anyone into a raging monster.

Regardless of if she had the mental strength to resist becoming an addict like Mother or not, no sense risking a genetic predisposition.

Skittles sipped from a tall, narrow glass filled with a pearlescent violet liquid.

"Are you two having fun?" asked Dorian.

"Not really. No," muttered Kirsten.

"I was being sarcastic." He chuckled.

"Wait." She glanced over at him. "We can hear each other over the music? Oh, stupid. I'm not thinking straight. I don't hear ghosts with my ears."

He smiled. "Are you okay? You look... troubled."

"That kid over there making out with a guy old enough to be her father... and another boy." Kirsten indicated the chem dealer with a nod. "She's seventeen but..."

"You can't save them all." Dorian observed the trio. "It's uncomfortable to see, but the young lady doesn't appear under duress."

"That kinda makes it worse somehow." Kirsten stopped herself before sipping the drink again. "Like society failed her."

Dorian glanced at the dealer for a moment. "That girl looks older than you."

"Not helping," muttered Kirsten.

He smiled at her. "There you go. Keep making that face and you look like you belong here."

Sigh. He's only trying to help keep me safe, not tease me.

Skittles moved away from the bar, heading toward the middle of the rear wall. Kirsten followed. No longer fixated on staring at any one person, she allowed her gaze to meander around. Anyone who made eye contact got a quick surface thought read. Some regarded her in much the same way as she thought of the teenage catgirl: too young to be here. Others found her attractive, hesitating in approaching her only because they assumed Skittles claimed her already. Almost all of them assumed her an innocent naïve kid brought to a 'real' club for the first time.

At least no one suspects I'm a cop.

"Surveillance cams are all over the place." Dorian pointed out a few, all lurking in dark places near the ceiling. "The older android girl has a directional mic disguised as a broken toy. She—it—is aiming it at people. Someone's keeping tabs on everything that goes on in here."

The more she looked around at the array of people in post-apocalyptic fashion ranging from body armor to strategically placed metal bits held on by leather straps, to punks in similar attire to hers, to the techno-junkies whose outfits, hair, and sometimes even eyes glowed in various shades of pastel neon, the more she wanted to get out of there. She felt like a mouse trying to sneak through a room of sleeping alley cats.

Kirsten glanced left at the fake orphans in the rusted cage. Sure enough, the ten-year-old girl held what looked like an old plastic-headed dolly. Unlike the way any natural child would hold such a toy, she pointed it longways like a gun. Even though the false girl's face displayed no emotion beyond innocence, she seemed suddenly sinister, an active part of this whole criminal enterprise.

Whoever has their hand on the wipe button is probably on the other end of the cameras.

Skittles tugged her forward, pressing her against the wall before leaning against her, nose to nose. "Wow, you're short. I don't have shoes on and you're still tiny."

"Umm." Kirsten stared up at her. "You're only like six inches taller than me. What are you doing?"

"Trust." Skittles leaned close, brushing her lips lightly across Kirsten's cheek on their way to her ear. "Pretend we are making the love. This is the door. Must go in. Hold me up."

With a drink in her right hand, Kirsten had no choice but to wrap her left arm around Skittles and pull her in close. The only way she could support the woman using one arm would be to cling. Thankfully, Skittles had extremely fluffy hair, poofy enough to hide behind. No one in the room could see what, exactly, they did—only that their faces had to be touching. Assumptions would be made.

Skittles lifted a thin, black necklace out from under her shirt, which turned out to be an M3 link cable. After unfurling it, she connected one end to the plug at the tip of her cat tail. The other end went into a socket on the lower portion of a security panel beside a knob-less door covered in apocalyptic graffiti.

In seconds, the woman slumped seemingly unconscious. Her breath reeked of alcoholic grape, though she hadn't shown any signs of inebriation. Kirsten grunted, not quite ready for the sudden load. *Oof. Good thing she's so damn skinny.* It surprised her no drink crashed to the floor. At some point while they'd been crossing the room, Skittles must have finished her drink and set the tall glass down. Kirsten hadn't even noticed.

She's gotta have a tox filter.

Kirsten's struggle not to lose her grip on the woman and let her fall to the floor had to look like making out. She tried to resist touching her anywhere inappropriate but it didn't take long before she had to grab the woman's butt to hold her upright. Dorian 'helped' by lifting Skittles hand to Kirsten's shoulder. Manipulating a physical object took enough effort out of him for fatigue to show in his face.

This girl's barely 110 pounds. How can she feel so damn heavy?

She struggled to stay upright for the better part of five minutes. Finally, dead weight lifted away from her as Skittles returned to consciousness. "All done. When door opens, I will move fast. Be ready. Don't squeak."

"Okay," rasped Kirsten, out of breath.

Three seconds later, reality blurred. A person with speedware grabbing and moving her effectively felt and looked as if she'd teleported from the club to a hallway saturated in dark azure lighting. Metal walls simulated the interior of a starship out of science fiction. The door they'd slipped through had already closed. Somehow, it managed to hold back the oppressive music from the club enough to talk. Despite being much closer to the music, standing in this hallway seemed quieter than twenty feet from the building outside.

A stunned man in a heavy armored trench coat gawked at them, not quite recovered from the speed with which Skittles moved. Certain he would object to them being in this private area of the club, Kirsten held her drink out to him.

"*Chug it.*"

Like an automaton, the man mindlessly grasped the drink and downed it, including the purple glob. His eyelids fluttered, gaze losing focus.

"Why did you do that?" asked Skittles.

"So he doesn't set off an alarm." Kirsten peered at her. "I thought you said the purple thing would throw me into outer space."

Skittles grinned. "It would have. Didn't think you had any tolerance for drinking."

More than you'd have expected but... it has been almost a year since I had any. "Right..."

The man fell over backward like a board.

"Maybe he doesn't either." Skittles tsk'ed. "Poor guy can't hold his drink."

"If you thought her a lightweight, why the heck did you order her a void hammer?" asked Dorian.

"Void hammer?" Kirsten blinked. "That sounds like a magical weapon from Monwyn."

Dorian gave her side eye. "The drink will hammer your brain into the void."

"I told her not to drink it. Is for show." Skittles stepped over the unconscious man and proceeded down the hall. "Top layer is foo foo drink like for girls. Middle one is little stronger. Bottom is the space juice. The danger is the goop."

"Do I even want to know what that is?" Kirsten also stepped over the man.

"It is synthetic fruit. Like plum or something..." Skittles waved her hand around. "Saturated in alcohol for weeks. It probably tastes yummy, but no one ever remembers having it."

Kirsten stared at Dorian. "Why? Why would people make, sell, and buy an expensive drink that messes them up so bad they can't even remember enjoying it?"

"They taste it in the moment." He winked. "Just don't remember when they wake up."

Skittles hurried down the corridor, peering into each doorway they reached. "I am sorry if that was awkward for you pretending the love."

"Just a little. It's fine."

"Is less uncomfortable than shot or stabbed."

Kirsten peered back at the corridor. No one had yet come running after them. "Shot or stabbed? Did you see something? Are we in danger?"

"Not yet. You look totally out of place here." Skittles smiled, then peeked into another door. "Bathrooms. Nope. Not here." She shut the door and moved on.

"I *am* out of place here."

Skittles checked another room on the right. "These losers may think you are cop. Better they believe you are some innocent girl I am corrupting with my sensual ways."

Dorian chuckled. "No one believes she's really a cop. Even when she's in full uniform and stepping out of an official patrol craft."

Smirking, Kirsten made herself solid to spirits so she could thump him on the arm.

He laughed.

H1ghb0rne phased out from the wall beside her. "Greetings, huntress."

Skittles froze in place, her tail fur fluffing out to triple its normal diameter.

Despite having ghosts do that all the time to her, Kirsten still jumped. "There you are."

"It is I." H1ghb0rne bowed. "Forgive my tardiness, for I had matters of great importance to attend."

She shook her head. "Did you finish the quest?"

His haughty elven posture faded to a guilty slouch. "Yeah. Sorry it took longer than I expected. Stupid side quest kept branching. One more thing. Oh, this will only take a minute. I, umm, sensed you getting close to my deck so I zoomed over here."

Enlightenment dawned. She tilted her head at him. "It's your focus, isn't it?"

"My what?"

"You return to your deck to, umm, basically sleep. It's your anchor to this world."

"Oh. Yeah. Right." H1ghb0rne smiled. "Totally. It's also downstairs. You don't have to check every single room here. Just go all the way to the end and down."

"All right." Skittles stood straight. Seeming ever so slightly annoyed, she grabbed her tail and smoothed a hand down it several times, trying to get the fur to de-fluff as she walked.

"Downstairs," whispered Kirsten. "Why does that sound so... foreboding?"

20

NO FREE DATA

The locked door at the end of the hall delayed them for only a moment.

H1ghb0rne and Dorian both started to reach for it, paused, then seemed to do a rock-paper-scissors with a stare before Dorian leaned back and made an 'after you' gesture. Skittles fished her M3 wire out.

"Wow, all three of you can open this?" whispered Kirsten.

H1ghb0rne stuck his hand into the wall. "I got it."

The door clicked open at roughly the same instant Skittles plugged in. Her tail frizzed out again.

"Eep!" She jumped. "Your no-see people like to scare the fornication out of me."

Dorian cackled. "Okay, I'm starting to understand the appeal. It's like adopting a cat you can have a conversation with and who can help out with housework."

Skittles narrowed her eyes in his general direction.

H1ghb0rne phased through the door. Kirsten pushed it open and followed, Skittles and Dorian trailing after. The spirit headed down four sets of switchback stairs, about two stories' worth, which put them at the bottom of the city plate. Only a three-foot-thick layer of metal superstructure stood between them and a long fall to the natural ground. Depending on the terrain below, the gap separating the underside of the plate level from natural Earth varied from almost nothing to over a hundred meters. It averaged out to about fifty. In some places, a person could slip through a hatch and find ground so close they'd have to crawl to fit.

Various areas toward the eastern edge of West City remained exposed natural Earth where the mountainous terrain rose to or past the altitude some ancient planner decided on for the city. Thankfully, they didn't destroy the Earth, opting instead simply not to build plates there. Anywhere a person could still live upon natural ground and still be inside West City tended to be extremely expensive. If normal people wanted to get away from the unnatural metal ground, they had to go far to the north or far to the south, where the legal boundaries of the city extended past the point construction of elevated plates stopped.

The ghost led them down a relatively narrow metal corridor lined with pipes and wire bundles, as close as Kirsten ever got to feeling as if she'd set foot on a military spacecraft. As a kid, she didn't spend too much time inside the plate layer, even though they did contain a scattering of fringers and off-gridders in little colonies. Those who lived close below the city surface generally had to go topside to find, steal, or beg for food... or catch, kill, and eat rats. At ten, Kirsten hadn't been equipped—physically nor mentally—to kill animals for food. Back then, she didn't even realize animals *could* be eaten. 'Meat' came in plastic packaging, not fur.

"I hear servos. Sounds like a robo-gun." Skittles pointed at a left-branching offshoot to the hallway up ahead. "Whoever invented them is an anal sphincter."

Dorian howled, laughing.

Kirsten almost smiled.

H1ghb0rne held up a hand. "Wait here a moment. There's a turret. Let me turn it off."

"Hang on." Kirsten grabbed Skittles by the shoulder. "The ghost is going to disable the gun."

"Good. There is not much room in here for me to avoid bullets." Skittles gazed around at the walls and ceiling.

"Thanks again for helping me."

"Happy to." Skittles stretched. "My spine no longer screams."

A moment later, the whirring of servos ceased.

Skittles went around the corner, but stopped after three steps. She looked back at Kirsten and tapped her head.

Recognizing the cue to rely on telepathy, Kirsten did so.

Rather than think to her in French, Skittles concentrated on the idea she could hear voices, people doing some manner of deal in one of these rooms, while making a 'shh' gesture.

Kirsten nodded.

They crept along. Hatch-style doors on either side led to chambers containing all manner of mechanical systems. Vent fans, water pumps, purification units, as well as electrical relay boxes, fuse clusters, and everything that kept the city above in working order. Some rooms served as storage or simply remained empty for unknown reasons. In one such empty room, a group of people discussed transactions involving hundreds of thousands of credits' worth of weapons, chems, and data.

Div 2 would absolutely lose their minds if they found this place.

H1ghb0rne went straight past the deal room without hesitation, then rounded a rightward corner some forty meters later. Kirsten hurried after him. The next stretch of passage ended at a heavily armored-looking door, which meant they'd reached a join where two city plates met. She didn't understand why the designers felt the need to put such massive hatches on the 'outside' openings. No one ever intended to fire these giant blocks of plastisteel into outer space nor float them on the ocean.

When companies do something that seemingly makes no sense, it probably came down to money somehow.

Best she could tell, they used an already-finished design for starship hulls so they didn't have to pay someone to invent new stuff. Perhaps the plans for what became the city plates had initially been developed for use as artificial islands, which might explain the need to have airtight doors around the outside edges.

H1ghb0rne went most of the way down the passage before stopping and pointing at a doorway on the left. "In here. Be quiet.

Nebula's there. He's in the GlobeNet, so he won't notice you if you stay quiet and don't touch him."

Kirsten crept over and peeked in.

A big, muscular man reclined in an elaborate chair like something taken from the cockpit of a military combat aircraft. He wore a simple white tank top and a ViewPane—a small slab of armor over his eyes shaped like oversized military sunglasses. Light from the screen on the other side glowed out over his eyebrows and on his cheeks. Sweat beaded on his dark brown skin. Veins bulged from his massive shoulders and biceps.

Kirsten paused in the doorway, watching the sleeping giant. Despite facing her—and theoretically being able to see her easily—he didn't move. The soft, steady sound of his breathing mixed with the continuous electronic thrum of technology.

The cable bundle draped from the back of his head resembled a continuation of his long dreadlocks that split apart into eight distinct wires, each one routing to one of an array of network interface decks arranged on two racks, four on either side of the grungy steel desk in front of him.

Two decks looked sleek and futuristic, black with glowing red trim. A bulky olive drab one resembled the sort of case the military might use to carry a small, portable rocket. The second one down from the top on the left had to be H1ghb0rne's deck: the Epoxil faux wood case and glowing green runes made it an anachronism from the Monwyn world, an enchanted artifact rather than a chunk of high tech.

"Wow. I wonder which one is his," deadpanned Dorian. "Good thing he came with us to point it out."

Kirsten removed the empty neural memory fob from her pocket and crept into the room, gaze locked on the 'elven' deck.

"The hell are you?" blurted Nebula.

Eep! Kirsten jumped back. "Oops."

"Wrong answer." Nebula reached for a gun on the desk in front of him.

Before he could pick it up, Skittles blurred into the room and leapt onto the desk, pinning the gun under one bare foot while pressing her claws to the side of his neck. "No. Don't do that."

Nebula held still. "Well, this is it. Nano claws, eh? You don't work cheap, whoever you are. Least I got the pleasure of a beautiful face as my last sight. Before you do it, tell me who sent you."

"I can't afford Nano claws yet, but mine are still sharp enough." Skittles smiled.

"We aren't here to kill you." Kirsten raised her hands in a placating 'calm down' manner.

Skittles pursed her lips. "We would really rather not be shot. It fornicating hurts."

Dorian facepalmed. "This girl needs to hack herself a bunch of credits and get a real chip."

"If you aren't here to kill me, then what you doin' in my throne room?" Nebula remained still. The ViewPane concealed his eyes, making it impossible to tell where he looked or even read his expression.

Kirsten pointed. "One of your decks used to belong to someone I know. He tucked something away inside it I need. Just gonna download it and leave."

"Data huh?" Nebula tilted his head. "What's it worth to you?"

Nervous, Kirsten opened a telepathic link to the 'ruler of B0rderland.' He struggled to understand how people got in here without setting off alarms. A proximity sensor on one of the decks alerted him to people entering his room. That two women managed to make it to him undetected convinced him high-paid assassins had come to take him out. Now, he realized she wanted some 'super valuable' data in one of his decks… and intended to stall her until his people got down here. He hadn't yet decided if he wanted to kill her or simply have his people 'teach her a lesson' before dumping her in a PubTran and sending her to the ass end of nowhere.

Nebula had no intention to let her simply take the data and walk out unless she had a couple million credits to give him. He'd keep her talking while calling for help thanks to being simultaneously wired in to eight network decks. It would take only the speed of a mental impulse to set off all sorts of silent alarms.

"*Stop!*" said Kirsten. A faint flash of white light shone from her eyes.

The suggestion slapped Nebula's thoughts to emptiness. She hadn't specified any specific activity to stop, so he stopped thinking about everything. Such a general command could be powerful, but would not last long.

"*Sit there doing nothing.*" She stabbed the command into his brain, then tossed the memory fob to Skittles. "We got about five minutes before he moves."

"Plenty of time." H1ghb0rne clapped. "Hey, since stealth is ruined... any chance you might grab my deck? Kinda sucks having my home attached to an explosive device."

Kirsten sighed. "Sure. Fine. I'll see what I can do."

21

GANG WARFARE

S kittles leapt down from the desk, her long, fluffy hair trailing after her graceful motion like a cape. She disconnected the wire connecting H1ghb0rne's deck to Nebula's 'dreadlock tentacle', then plugged it in to the end of her tail.

H1ghb0rne shrugged, then disappeared in a blur of light as if drawn into the device.

Nebula continued to stare into space.

Skittles opened her mouth to say something, but paused. Her ears twitched. "Feces. People are coming."

Kirsten looked back and forth between her and the door. "Shit."

"That is what I said!" whisper-shouted Skittles. "Do we fight or hide?"

"I didn't come here to hurt anyone." Kirsten ran around the desk. "If we can sneak out, let's."

"Okay." Skittles grabbed her by the arm and dragged her into the hollow under the desk between Nebula's feet.

A spaghetti nest of thick cables on the plastisteel ground made for a most uncomfortable seat. Kirsten glanced up past the man's crotch at his face, debating the usefulness of giving him another command to tell his people to leave.

Dammit. I'm an idiot. He was plugged in. As soon as he thought about calling for help, he'd already called for help. I stopped him from giving details at least.

Seconds later, the rapid shuffle of footsteps became loud enough for her to hear. Skittles did not fully commit to cyberspace, remaining conscious. Outwardly, she appeared to be doing nothing other than hiding and trying to stay quiet. Kirsten didn't dare make noise enough to ask if she worked on getting the data or waited.

The approaching group stopped moving.

"Six at the door," said Dorian.

A man emitted a confused noise. "Where'd the bitches go? No way outta the throne room."

"Under the desk, you idiot," replied another man, sounding frustrated. "Where else could they have fuckin' gone?"

"Oh. Yeah," said the first guy.

Dorian whistled. "If nothing else, you shouldn't have too much trouble outsmarting them."

"Hey kitty," yelled a woman. "Let us know who sent you so we can send your bodies to the right place."

Kirsten bit her lower lip and eased her E-90 out of its holster.

After a long silence, the same woman yelled, "No point pretending you aren't there. We saw your ass on the security system. Get away from Nebula and we'll make it painless."

"That's not much of an incentive," called Kirsten.

Skittles' ears went back like an annoyed cat. "Stupid illegitimate offspring."

"If she learns the English word, can she say it or would her chip override it with 'proper' words?" asked Dorian.

Skittles shrugged.

"We're hoping you make this take a long time." The frustrated guy sucked in a loud inhale, as if savoring some fragrance. "Been a while since we got into a proper scrap."

"Is it really necessary?" Kirsten squirmed around and peeked out over the top of the desk, pressing her shoulders against the front of Nebula's fancy chair. She doubted anyone would try to shoot her while her head happened to be right in front of their leader's stomach. "What we're doing here has nothing to do with you or your operation."

"Aww," said the only woman among the gang members. Her wild explosion of unnaturally dark scarlet hair shimmered to orange metallic at the tips. "It's just a kid."

Kirsten stared over a scattering of junk atop the desk at the doorway. Clear plastic credit chip 'coins' gleamed in rainbow patterns thanks to embedded holograms. A huge gun, several spare magazines, chem injector ampoules, candy bar wrappers, small electronic bits, and wire scraps covered the desk around the base of four holo-terminal screen emitters. Six gang members crowded into the front of the room, blocking any chance of leaving. None stood out as an immediate greater threat. All had cyberware, but small parts—electronics and headware, mostly. Of course, she couldn't see speedware or concealed claws and had to rely on her hope this operation didn't move the kind of money needed to afford the truly dangerous augments.

An average-looking man in his mid-thirties with a few days of beard staining his face chuckled in the same voice as the frustrated guy. "It's not necessary, but it's fun. That ain't no kid."

"She can't be older than thirteen," said a guy with messy, long hair.

"Sixteen at least." The older guy folded his arms. "Old enough to get herself into trouble, old enough to pay for it."

All six gang members brandished handguns, though appeared somewhat hesitant to point them at Nebula.

"Should I tell them I'm with Div 0?" whispered Kirsten.

"I doubt that would end well." Dorian shook his head.

She scowled mentally. "Pretend to be a kid?"

"Possibly. If they believe it, they might let you off with a beating."

Kirsten cringed. "Better that than dead or having to kill people."

"I said they'd let *you* off with a beating." Dorian frowned. "They'd still kill Skittles."

Skittles looked up, faking an expression of fear. "I am not willing to die. That was not in our agreement."

Grr. Kirsten looked back at the gang members. "Guys. You have the wrong idea. We aren't here to mess with this guy. We don't even know who he is or what you're involved in."

Mr. Frustration gestured his gun at her. "Then what the fuck are you doing under his desk? Nebs ain't into little ones like you. Ain't gonna convince me you're giving him head."

Kirsten fought the urge to blush. "No. That's—"

"And what the hell did you give him?" The dumb guy pointed at Nebula. "He's just sitting there staring into nothin'. Hasn't said a damn word yet."

This appeared to call the other gangers' attention to Nebula's mental state, as if they hadn't noticed how still and quiet he'd been up until that point. While they whispered amongst themselves, trying to figure out what happened to their boss, Kirsten skimmed their surface thoughts.

Everyone but the woman believed she and Skittles were assassins sent by a corporation to take down Nebula and his operation as revenge for something their group did in the GlobeNet—or possibly a rival gang. Their opinion on her age ranged from thirteen to sixteen… and it didn't make much difference to them. Only the woman hesitated at the idea of killing her, but not entirely because she believed Kirsten to be thirteen: she thought her adorable in a stray kitten sense. She'd have had no qualms about killing a thirteen-year-old if she didn't think of them as cute.

Shit. Pretending to be a kid won't help at all.

Two of the male gangers who had not yet spoken wanted to take her and Skittles alive and keep them as toys for a while. Neither had the nerve to say it out loud because they knew Nebula would kick them out of the gang for it. In a crazy sort of twisted moralism, Nebula would think nothing of murdering both of them… but rape crossed a line he refused to touch.

Her skin crawled at the mere thought of what they wanted to do to her. She also gained a sliver of respect for Nebula, even if he did happen to be the leader of a criminal gang. Her hesitation toward violence weakened. She could confuse them with a mass suggestion long enough to probably shoot three of them. The more people she tried to affect with a single psionic command, the less effect and duration it would have. Doing it to six people simultaneously would dilute her power too much for any of them to obey... but it would zone them out for a few seconds.

Alternatively, she could ask Dorian to manifest and scare them away. That could work, or it might backfire into a hail of panic shooting.

"Zap their batteries?" whispered Kirsten.

Dorian smiled. "Already done. Did that as soon as they walked in."

"You are the best."

He examined his fingernails in a sarcastic 'I know' manner.

Kirsten rose to her feet and pointed her E-90 at the gangers. "Okay. Enough of this bullshit. National Police, Division 0. All six of you need to just walk away right now."

Five men all clicked their triggers, though their guns did nothing. The woman aimed at her, then went wide-eyed, evidently recognizing the E-90 as an energy weapon.

Damn morons. She stared at Mr. Frustration. "I said *go away.*"

A flash of white psionic light in her eyes illuminated the front of the dim 'throne room' for two seconds, casting all the gangers in shadow against the dark plastisteel wall. The woman, the dumb guy, and one of the two who wanted to use her as a sex toy all yelled out some variation of 'oh shit' in response to the glow.

Mr. Frustration pulled an abrupt heel turn and fast-walked out of the room.

The other creep didn't seem frightened by her display of paranormal ability. Rather, his intention toward her shifted dramatically from sexual assault to murder with contempt, the way someone might anger-smash a spider after it startled them. He tossed his dead gun aside, pulled a knife, and—promptly died to a bright blue laser beam Kirsten put into his chest. His body collapsed away from his ghostly self. For as long as the spirit remained superimposed over his remains, his visage appeared transparent and bluish. The instant he fully separated from his body, the spirit solidified to her perception, appearing as if alive.

Creep number two and the dumb guy rushed the desk. Dorian intercepted the idiot, managing to summon enough tangibility to redirect his lunge into a face-first collision with the front of the metal desk. A *boom* almost as loud as Ohm's arm cannon firing filled the relatively small chamber. Kirsten tried to shoot the other creep, scoring a superficial wound on his shoulder as he flew over the desk and tackled her. They bounced off Nebula and crashed to the floor, sending the big boss rolling away on his chair, spinning.

The creep's weight knocked the wind out of her.

Nebula zoomed toward the back wall until the seven remaining wires jerked him to an abrupt stop, almost dragging him out of his throne by his hair.

Kirsten struggled to shake off the paralytic stun of a two-hundred-some-odd pound man hammering her into a metal floor. She had to move before he could grab her throat or do worse. Much to her surprise, the man didn't move at all, merely stared vacantly into space. Blood began dripping from the creep's nose. A second copy of him split away from the body and floated up to stand nearby—his ghost.

What the... Kirsten blinked. *How did he die from jumping at me?*

"Fuck this," muttered the woman ganger. "Run, you dipshits. If she's really a cop and you kill her, they're gonna burn this whole goddamn place to the fucking ground."

"Don't be a chickenshi—" A man's voice rose into a shriek of pain.

Having a dead body lying on top of her didn't shock Kirsten nearly as much as the oddity of how he died so fast. Grunting, she shoved the corpse aside and sat up. Skittles attacked the only ganger still on his feet, the man who'd shrieked. Her arms moved as a blur, claws shredding in a seemingly haphazard fashion that sent scraps of fabric and skin flying off him. She'd advanced to the absolute limit of her tail's length, which hung straight out behind her by virtue of still having a wire plugged into the end connecting her to H1ghb0rne's deck.

The woman was gone, no doubt sprinting off down the hallway. Groaning, the idiot who face-planted the desk crawled to his feet and made a swaying, drunken break for the exit, heeding her advice.

Skittles gave him a passing swipe across the ass as he went by, perhaps cat instinct, perhaps as a 'and don't you come back' message. Screaming, the guy bolted out the door. The man she'd been shredding stumbled backward too far for her to reach without unplugging. Skittles didn't disconnect, merely stood there growling at him.

Gasping at his mostly skinless chest, he deliriously staggered out of the throne room.

Kirsten glanced down at the dead man who'd landed on top of her. Four triangular claw holes in the back of his skull dribbled blood onto the floor. "Damn, she's fast. I didn't even see her do anything."

Skittles smiled. "That's what she said."

"What?" Kirsten blinked.

"Oh, *mon cheri*..." Skittles made a pouty face at her. "You are so innocent, aren't you?"

The creep who tackled her—rather his ghost—tried to grab Kirsten. A faint cold tingle spread across her chest where his hand passed right through.

She faced him. "You..."

He proceeded to curse her out in between randomly asking no one in particular what happened to him.

"The lifeguard has ordered you out of the gene pool for being a piece of shit." Kirsten stared at him. "What you thought about doing to me and Skittles... you've probably done it to other women. Don't even start with the guilt thing. I *tried* to end this confrontation without violence. You are the dumbass who pulled a knife and took it too far."

"Fucking psio freak!" shouted the ghost of the first creep she shot.

Kirsten sighed. *Can't read his mind anymore, but I'm sure these two have hurt a lot of girls.* She spared a moment's concentration on pinging a Harbinger with a 'might want to check this guy out' vibe. Merely fantasizing about kidnapping them to use as a sex toy for however long she and Skittles survived wouldn't put them on the Harbinger's list. However, anyone who could give serious consideration to doing that almost certainly had done similar horrible things before. Not her judgment to make. If they wanted him, they'd take him. Kirsten couldn't decide his fate, however, she could arrange the interview.

"Done," chirped Skittles. She disconnected the wire from her tail, then unplugged the memory fob from the deck. "We can go now."

H1ghb0rne's voice came from a speaker on the deck. "I'd appreciate it if you could take me with you. Please remove the two brick-shaped things from the bottom of the deck first. They're bombs."

"On it." Skittles flipped the 'elven' deck over, revealing a pair of three-by-ten-by-one inch silver slabs. Both had cartoon mushroom clouds on them beneath a fancy product logo. She blinked, reading out loud. "Megaton Data Security. Electromagnetic incendiary charge. Do not activate within 100 feet of anyone you do not wish to ruin their day. Guaranteed to secure your private data in an unrecoverable state. Skittles raised both eyebrows. "Do they have pressure triggers? Are they going to go off if I peel them away?"

Unbelievable. Those things are off the shelf? Kirsten lost some faith in society.

"They did, but they are now inoperable," said H1ghb0rne. "Safe to pluck them loose."

Dorian stuck his hand into one of the charges. "Confirmed. No power left in it."

Skittles grunted, struggling for a moment before her efforts pried one charge loose. "Son of female dog they are stuck good."

Dorian chuckled.

"What the absolute fuck is going on?" muttered Nebula, draped halfway out of his chair. Some of his weight hung suspended on the spiderweb of M3 cables coming out of his head. "Why can't I move?"

Kirsten faced him. "Relax. I'm making sure you stay alive. Don't panic. You will be able to move in another minute or two."

"Bullshit on you being a cop." Nebula ground his fingertips into the armrest of his fancy chair. "You some kinda crazy ass kid."

"Sorry. I'm a little older than I look." Kirsten held up the E-90 sideways so he could see it. "Also, Division 0. I'm not here about anything you're doing in the GlobeNet. You probably wouldn't believe me if I told you why I'm here, so I'm not going to waste the time. Best thing for you to do is forget entirely about our visit and go back to doing whatever you do."

Clank.

"Other bomb free." Skittles picked up the 'elven' deck. Her arms became a blur for a few seconds as she rigged a carrying strap out of some cable scraps, and slung the deck over her shoulder. "I make the suggestion that we exit rapidly."

"Listen to Kitty," said Dorian.

22

THE BETTER PART OF VALOR

Kirsten paused at the door, listened to silence for a few seconds, then swung her E-90 around the doorjamb into the corridor, aiming at empty passage.

"Clear," she whispered before advancing out of the room.

Skittles followed, one hand grasping the cable holding H1ghb0rne's deck to her back as casually as if she wandered down the street with a backpack over one shoulder.

Dorian hurried out of Nebula's room, seeming wary… a good sign a Harbinger approached.

The ghostly creep who died on top of Kirsten continued ranting and swearing as if he'd merely lost at a video game and accused the other player of cheating.

"Think we can make it back out through the club?" Kirsten kept her weapon trained down the hall, though snuck a quick glance behind her at the heavy door leading to the adjacent plate.

"Highly doubtful," said Dorian. "Nebula's kind of upset we're stealing his hardware. Already calling down the troops. If you ever find yourself in a situation like this again, it is a good idea to disconnect the power-drunk virtual king from his electronics."

She again looked at the heavy door. "We're not stealing it. I'm confiscating it as evidence for an active inquest. He can fill out the proper forms and get compensation for its value."

Dorian cackled. "Are you serious?"

"Yeah. Why?" She stared at him for a moment, then crept forward to the corner.

"Do you honestly believe a man like Nebula, who is up to his eyeballs in illegality, is going to file an asset forfeiture reimbursement claim on a piece of hardware he probably stole originally?"

She bit her lower lip. "Oh. Well. When you put it like that."

He smiled. "You are adorable."

"Thanks," she deadpanned. "But if he stole it, then he's got some nerve being angry with us."

"Criminals are a lot like the government." Dorian edged up next to her, holding his ghostly E-90 at the ready. "Stealing is only bad when they aren't the ones doing it."

Skittles backed up. "We should not go that way. I hear many people running toward us."

"How can you hear anything over that music?" Kirsten peeked around the corner.

Gang members spilled into the corridor at the other end, too many to count. They didn't look like the harmless techies she'd seen congregating outside B0rderland. She clenched her jaw. Ninety-five percent of the time, announcing herself as a member of the National Police Force would be enough to scare the hell out of people. No one wanted to be on the receiving end of the government's revenge for attacking or killing the police. Of course, the other five percent went in the entirely opposite direction. As soon as they heard the word 'cop,' it set off an almost supernatural bloodlust. Perhaps for underworld bragging rights at taking out such a risky target or as an outlet for generations of repressed societal resentment, some people would just go crazy if they found a cop alone.

Kirsten had the genetic misfortune to be short, thin, and have a nonthreatening appearance. As much as she initially bristled at being called an 'elf,' she couldn't dispute that she did come close to resembling the fantasy race in the Monwyn world. *Tall* elven men stood around five-foot-four. Some referred to this phenomenon as 'easy target.' As the gang raised their weapons, she yelled, "*Shit*," and ducked back around the wall. Several boisterous farts fired off before the guns.

Oops. She grimaced while sprinting toward the heavy bulkhead door. Accidental Suggestion proved she'd become quite a bit more frightened than she consciously admitted to herself. Dorian returned fire from his ghostly simulacrum of a laser pistol. The whitish energy bolts he created fell far short of the lethality of a real E-90, having about the same hitting power as a wad of dense gelatin shot out of a pneumatic cannon. It would definitely bruise, maybe knock someone over, but not kill. He fired a third shot off to the side, rotating to keep facing her as she zoomed by. Bullets pinged all over the distant corner of the passage. Several zinging ricochets whizzed by Kirsten's head.

Skittles let out a worried yowl and bolted after her.

Kirsten sprinted to the end of the hallway. She grabbed the handle of the huge door and pulled, but it didn't budge. Locked... and her ability to invoke a police override on all the security systems in the city required her electronic ID as well as the transmitter in her forearm guard—which she'd left at home.

"Crap!" Shaking, she turned, putting her back to the door, and aimed at the corner. "I can't open this."

The instant someone started coming around the corner, she fired a laser bolt at the motion. A guy screamed, collapsing backward. Howls of agony continued, confirming she hadn't killed him. In time with the corridor lights flickering and a whole mess of guns chirping as if they'd rebooted, a terrified screech came from the ghost in Nebula's room.

"Your friends are here..." Dorian winced, then stuck his hand into the wall.

"I can make the door open." Skittles started unfurling the M3 cable from around her neck.

"No time." Dorian's body shimmered, going from solid, lifelike appearance to blue-hologram-ghost for two seconds. The door emitted a happy electronic chirp. Red lights turned green.

Gangers spilled around the corner. Kirsten fired into the crowd as fast as her E-90 could cycle, a shot every 1.8 seconds. Each laser beam lasted four-tenths of a second, piercing multiple gangers in a pin-straight line from the tip of her weapon's barrel to the wall behind the targets. The punks tripped over themselves to change direction, but the onrushing group behind them continued surging forward, shoving the first ones helplessly into her line of fire.

"No-see man is now see man." Skittles spun to hiss at the gangers.

"I'm going to forget you said that," muttered Dorian.

Kirsten wanted to duck, to look for cover, to do anything other than just stand there like a tool firing a weapon into a crowd. But… only the panic of laser beams slicing through multiple people at once kept the gangers from being able to aim and return accurate fire. Smoke and the stench of burning meat made for quite the distraction. As much as what she did horrified her, if she stopped… she would die.

The big door opened outward with a rubber-on-metal sucking sound. Since she'd been leaning so heavily against it, Kirsten spilled over backward, landing on the floor in the space behind it. Skittles turned into a blur, jumping after her, spinning around, and shoving the massive door more than halfway closed in under a second. Bullets pinged off the armored hatch in a hail of sparks. Skittles grunted from the effort of shoving the thick plastisteel slab.

Clanking from fast-approaching boots echoed down the corridor toward them.

Kirsten scrambled upright and hurled her body against the door. She and Skittles gave a desperate shove, ramming the hatch closed.

Dorian reactivated the lock.

Skittles slumped against the door for a few seconds, trying to catch her breath, then hurried off down the corridor.

Kirsten ran a few steps, then turned, aimed, and shot a dark azure laser beam into the door's security panel, which promptly exploded in a shower of sparks and black smoke.

"What did you do that for?" Dorian stared at her.

"So they can't hack it open." She made a 'well duh' face at him.

"What made you think shooting the control circuitry out would make the door seal?"

She tilted her head. "They always do that."

"In movies." He facepalmed.

The heavy door started to swing open.

"Oh, shit." She bolted, sprinting after Skittles.

"Safety interlocks." Dorian effortlessly jogged alongside her. "One of the few things our government did right. Doors lose power? Anyone can open them. That way, no one gets trapped somewhere and dies."

"Dammit!" shouted Kirsten. "Why do they always have people shooting out door panels to lock them in movies then?"

"Probably because it looks cool."

Skittles came to a stop up ahead at a T intersection. "Which way?"

"Doesn't matter right now," shouted Kirsten. "Just keep going until they stop chasing us!"

The woman darted to the left. Kirsten reached the intersection a few seconds later, running so fast she had to grab onto a pipe to keep from wiping out as she cornered. A few bullets whizzed by, pinging off the walls and gouging rips in the plastisteel grid floor. Dorian stared at the oncoming gangers.

Kirsten almost yelled at him to run, then felt like an idiot.

Inches short of panic, she ran wherever Skittles led without paying any attention to how often they turned or which corridors they followed. The vast majority of the plate interiors looked the same. It would be almost impossible for anyone to remember their way around inside them as tens of thousands of identical modules knit together to form the surface supporting West City. Every plate had been manufactured identically before being put together like some massive child's building block toy. Occasional modifications like extending buildings downward into 'basements' happened long after the initial construction.

It didn't matter where they went. The sameness of the plate design worked to her advantage. She wouldn't have too much trouble locating an access hatch to the surface wherever they ended up. Then, it would only be a matter of summoning a PubTran car... or waiting for Dorian to go get the PC and pick her up.

The gangers chasing them thankfully stank at shooting and running at the same time. Kirsten caught a few splinters of shrapnel from nearby ricochets—painful but not deadly. Alas, what they lacked in marksmanship they made up for in tenacity. Being on the small side did have some benefits. She could get into places most adults couldn't fit. It would have been much more of a help if she could locate a small, concealed spot. Alas, Skittles seemed to have a knack for finding long corridors or large, chambers of industrial equipment. Not having a ton of weight to carry also let her run for a decent amount of time before getting tired.

Skittles also didn't have a lot of weight to carry. Her longer stride and reflex boosts made her crazy fast, even within the narrow maintenance passages. Kirsten could tolerate a brisk jog for a fairly long time, but maintaining the hard sprint necessary to keep up with her feline-augmented friend wore her out alarmingly fast.

They're going to catch up to us. Shit. I really kicked a damn bees' nest this time, didn't I?

Almost as soon as she thought the word 'bees,' a hot sliver of plastisteel stabbed into her back. The tiny sliver ejected from some nearby surface by a ricocheting bullet sank into her skin with the fury of a red-hot needle. It hurt enough to make her stride falter momentarily. Sheer determination to survive kept her on her feet.

Skittles, seemingly at random, stopped short and darted through a hatch door on the right. She'd been zig-zagging constantly as an intelligent person tended to do when running away from people with guns. Kirsten raced after her, pausing only long enough to slam the hatch. This one didn't lock, merely had a wheel with gears meshed to a sliding bar. She gave it a spin before staggering after Skittles.

Halfway down this thirty-meter-long passage, an alcove on the left held a curved bit of wall with a sliding door. Kirsten immediately recognized it as the face of one of the great columns supporting the city.

Elevator...

"Skit!" shouted Kirsten. "Back here! Quick."

The woman stopped and whirled, tilting her head. "What?"

Kirsten rushed to the elevator and mashed the call button. "I'm about to fall over. They're going to keep chasing us until I'm too exhausted to move. No chance they'll follow us down."

"Wow. You are desperate." Skittles whistled. "Are you sure?"

"I don't have enough e-mags on me to kill everyone chasing us. Also, don't wanna do that if I can avoid it."

The elevator capsule opened.

Kirsten jumped in. "C'mon. It's not as bad as the rumors say."

Loud metal slamming and shouting announced the gangers burst through the old submarine-style door. A barrage of gunfire filled the hallway.

Skittles appeared inside the elevator, solidifying out from a ghostly blur. "Okay. I change mind. We do the down."

Kirsten stuck the E-90 out into the hall, firing a few shots blindly to the right as she hit the elevator's only button with her knee, ducking back in as the door closed—and three bullet holes appeared in it.

"Gah!" She curled up in a ball on the floor, hands over her head as if they'd stop a ricocheting bullet from hurting her.

Skittles also got down, but appeared to be trying to shield the deck with her body.

It took mere seconds for the capsule to descend far enough to where no more bullets could find it.

Kirsten blinked at her.

"What?" Skittles cocked her head. "Stimpaks cost less than replacement parts. This is a custom rig."

"Unbelievable," whispered Kirsten. She peered up at the ceiling. "Do you hear them coming down the ladder?"

"What ladder?"

"All of these shafts have ladders in them in case the elevator dies. These things are almost 250 years old or something like that. They fail all the time."

"Eep!" Skittles gawked. "Why didn't you fornicating say that?"

"Didn't really have the time."

The elevator came to a gentle stop.

"Ooh. Nice." Kirsten stood. "We didn't fall."

Skittles' ears went back. She narrowed her eyes, rose to stand, and kept expressing her displeasure via silent staring.

"Sorry. I figured even if this elevator failed, we'd have better chances of walking away from it than our odds if those shitheads caught up to us." Kirsten pushed the button. Nothing happened. "Well, crap."

"Ugh." Skittles sighed at the floor. "In cage again. I do not like this."

"It's not a cage." Kirsten put the E-90 back in its holster and crouched to examine the control panel.

"It is small space made of metal we cannot get out of whenever we want to. That is cage." Skittles frowned.

"I'm sorry that happened to you."

Skittles shrugged. "Is not your fault. Montpierre thought of the commoners as animals already. Giving me cat parts only made it more official."

"Still. I can't believe he kept you in a literal cage. That's disgusting." Kirsten pried the panel open.

"Only for sleeping at night. Not like I had to stay in it all the time."

"Still." Kirsten shivered at the idea of it. The way Mother used to lock her in the closet for hours at a time had been bad enough... but being stuck in a literal cage, with bars, naked, like some kind of zoo animal while the rich elites socialized and looked down their noses at her. Horrid. *What is wrong with people? Seriously.*

Her mood darkened. Keeping a woman from the commoner class as a literal pet was definitely dark and twisted. However, such depravity seemed mild compared to the things the cops here had to deal with. One file she'd come across during the interdepartmental cooperation thing damn near made her approach Commander Ashford and ask him to erase the memory. The Diablos gang had barged into a family's apartment, lined the kids up against the wall, and started shooting, trying to see how close they could get without hitting them... and started betting money with each other over which child would piss themselves first.

The Diablos preferred to cause permanent mental damage, so they'd left the family alive.

Kirsten growled to herself as she yanked a wire bundle out of the capsule wall. "Shit. This is more complicated than I thought."

"What on Earth?" Skittles peered up.

"Hmm?" Kirsten studied the mechanism, looking for a contact she could short to make the door open.

"I hear screaming. Many people shrieking."

"Oh. Dorian probably manifested." Kirsten gasped in delight when she spotted a broken wire. "Aha! There you are... I hope."

"Manifested?"

"Appeared. Scared the shit out of the bastards chasing us." Kirsten gingerly nudged the two broken pieces of wire together. They gave a small spark on contact, and the door opened. "Got it."

Skittles grabbed the opening to hold the door back from closing them in again. "Go."

"Thanks." Kirsten let go of the wire and darted out of the elevator.

Skittles bumped into her back. By the time Kirsten took another step and turned around, the door had closed again.

"Well, here we are." Kirsten gazed around at the darkness of the Beneath.

Weak LED bricks on the underside of the plates above them gave off such little light they resembled stars in an unnatural grid pattern, doing little to allow anyone to see. Occasional bits of light from ground-level sources illuminated a scrap of column here, or an old building there. The air tasted like stale dirt, chemicals, and something faintly fruity-sour.

"It is quite dark down here. No wonder people are afraid," whispered Skittles.

"They're afraid of the dark, the monsters, the mutants, secret government labs that they kill people for discovering, and the wild primitive cannibal tribes," deadpanned Kirsten.

Skittles glanced at her, two faintly glowing eyes floating in darkness, one green, one gold. "You are teasing, yes? Please be teasing."

"Yeah." Kirsten chuckled. "Just saying what the rumors claim. I'm not totally sure about the mutant thing. Never saw one, but it wouldn't surprise me if some corporations dumped their genetic experimentations down here. Stuff like that really does exist out in the Badlands, after all."

"Ick." Skittles' will-o-wisp eyes disappeared for a second as she blinked.

Kirsten concentrated on Darksight. As if standing in a room full of impenetrable black smoke, the darkness retreated from her in a rapidly expanding circle. Her senses reached out into the Astral realm, allowing her to see the old paved road they stood on as well as all the abandoned houses around them.

"Eww." Skittles glanced down. "This road is stickier than the floor inside B0rderlands. Okay, now I kind of want shoes."

"Tell me about it." Kirsten frowned.

"Hmm?" Skittles raised one dark grey fuzzy eyebrow. "You have shoes. Or are those boots?"

Dorian's voice said 'beakers' in her memory, teasing a half smile out of her.

"I don't think the people who made them even know what they are." Kirsten chuckled. "I meant the first time I came down here, I didn't have shoes either. It gets pretty disgusting in places."

"It is not the sticky I am worried about." Skittles turned in place, looking around. "I hear whispers. People are watching us."

Kirsten nodded. "Probably ghosts. There are tons of them since the living don't usually bother coming down here. Nothing to worry about. Most are either nice or don't want to be bothered. I can handle any spirit who wants to make a nuisance of themselves. Maybe it's kinda bizarre, but I'm much less afraid of malevolent spirits than I am of that group of morons with guns."

"All right. I trust. What about the monsters?" Skittles shivered. "I see stories. This is the Beneath they all talk about, isn't it?"

"Yes." Kirsten lifted her arms, then let them flop against her sides. "Like I said, lots of exaggeration. People are always scared of what they don't understand. There are so many ghosts down here that a person doesn't have to be psionic to feel them."

"Oh. Is that what is making me scared?"

"Probably." Kirsten chuckled at the fluffy tail. "Unless someone is psionic, they wouldn't know what they felt, only that they felt weird and uneasy. The sweetest, kindest ghost in the world would make someone feel on edge merely by being near them. So... multiply that by a few thousand ghosts, someone comes down here and they get really scared and freaked out. Since they don't know exactly why they feel that way, they make up stories."

"Mmm." Skittles angled her ears around like little furry satellite dishes searching for a signal. "If you say so."

The area gave off a weak sense of familiarity, making her think she'd been here before. Other than a few brief excursions somewhat recently, she hadn't spent much time in the Beneath for eleven years. During the roughly two years she'd lived down here, learning her way around hadn't been a priority. It didn't matter where she went. One couldn't get lost if one had no home to return to. She slept wherever she could find a hiding spot, not caring if she napped in the same place twice.

Most of her time went toward obtaining food, having fun exploring the ruins, playing with old stuff, and keeping away from the living. She'd waste hours in ancient houses amusing herself with toys, pool tables, dolls, whatever happened to survive almost three centuries of abandonment. Her fondest memories were of discovering an ancient amusement park. Obviously, nothing requiring electricity worked, so she'd basically gone back in time much farther than the 2090s. Still, to a ten-year-old who'd spent her entire life thus far living in terror while banned from doing anything even remotely fun, being down here had been an amazing adventure.

She couldn't say for sure if she'd really been in this particular old neighborhood before, but she did kind of recognize it. Then again, private houses with enough property to have front and back yards had been the norm back then. Multiple old neighborhoods (the local ghosts called them suburbs) tended to look generally the same. Her sense of familiarity might be a mind trick, her brain fooling her.

"I lived down here for about sixteen months as a kid." Kirsten started walking down the street, a sticky peeling noise coming from her shoes with each step. "C'mon. In all that time, I never saw any crazy mutants, aliens, or government labs."

Grimacing, Skittles followed. "Is this muck on the street going to hurt?"

"It might cause a mild rash. It's not as bad on skin as it is on fabric. It ate my nightgown, but I did fall into a pool of the stuff."

"Why did you go down here in a nightgown?" Skittles blinked in disbelief.

"Asks the woman who goes outside naked most of the time."

Skittles laughed. "I think nightgown is much stranger than being natural."

"Maybe." Kirsten exhaled. "I ran away from home at night. My mother was going to kill me… literally."

"Aww." Skittles hugged her. "Sorry. So, the sticky melts clothes?"

"Not the way you're thinking. Our stuff won't disintegrate the instant this slime makes contact. It took a couple months of continuous exposure before the fabric fell apart. I think it's mildly acidic. Getting it on you and washing won't be a big deal."

"You didn't wash your nightgown?"

"Are you teasing me or serious?" Kirsten glanced at her.

"Serious."

"Nothing down here has worked for like 300 years. Doing laundry would've required going up top. I was too scared. Thought Mother would be waiting right there to grab me if I dared try to return to the surface."

Skittles followed her down the street for a while, occasionally gasping at something she heard in the distance or making noises of mild disgust whenever she stepped in squish. "I am glad you are okay, but it seems difficult to believe a child could survive down here alone."

"I wasn't really alone. Had a whole bunch of ghosts taking care of me, leading me to food. Distracting the villagers so I could steal stuff… you know."

"Villagers?"

"There are settlements down here. Off-gridders." Kirsten waved randomly. "They live here and there inside the old buildings or make new ones out of scrap. They are kinda primitive and don't understand too much about the world. Some of them even think they're trapped on a giant spaceship after Earth was destroyed. They climb the columns and tap into the power grid so they can run grow lamps for small farms."

Skittles peered up at the metal sky. "I understand how they might believe it. Shame never to see the sun." She gasped again. "Vampires?"

It took Kirsten a lot of effort not to laugh out loud. "No. As far as I know, those are not real. Just people with cyberware."

They walked for about fifteen minutes, Kirsten doing her best to keep going in a relatively straight line through an old suburban development with tons of mazelike cul-de-sacs, collapsed houses, and debris fields. Sooner or later, they'd reach another support column with a ladder or elevator. All they needed to do was go far enough away from B0rderland to avoid the gang. Maybe not even very far after Dorian went on the offensive. He'd likely been avoiding doing it before out of concern the gangers would freak out and hit Kirsten in the crossfire. Once the two of them took the elevator, he had the gangers all to himself.

Those idiots will probably give up, eventually. A street gang isn't going to bother trying to track me down.

Kirsten continuously looked around as they walked, staying alert for potential problems. The Discarded would probably try to attack them as they tended to become violent toward everyone not part of their group, even the settlers who lived down here. Fortunately, the Discarded happened to be incredibly superstitious. Darksight made her eyes glow brilliant white. As soon as they saw the paranormal light, they'd run away screaming. Settlers, however, stood as much chance of being friendly as they did of trying to kill her for being 'a demon.'

Upon reaching a point where the rubble of an old building much larger than the houses in the area blocked off the road, she decided to climb the enormous mound in order to keep going in a straight line. It had to have been some manner of store. Skittles followed without much difficulty. Her tail swelled up to maximum fluffiness, appearing almost a foot thick.

"Nervous?" asked Kirsten.

"Not really."

"Look at your tail."

Skittles paused to glance behind her. "Ooh. Little traitor. Okay, I am nervous. This place does not feel nice. I would like to leave."

"Leaving is exactly what we're doing." Kirsten stopped at the highest point on the rubble mound, stood to her full height, and scanned the area. "I'm trying to locate the nearest place we can climb up that isn't dangerously close to the people trying to kill us and preferably won't put us in a bad area."

"Can I ask you something?" Skittles edged closer.

"Sure. Let me ask you something, too."

"All right. You first."

Kirsten gestured at the tail. "Do you make it fluff up like that for comic effect or is it really doing that because you're scared?"

"It is real. My tail is a bio-graft. It is not synthetic, at least not the same plastic stuff they make synths out of. It is generated from my DNA. It reacts to my mood like any cat. Scare a cat and their tail goes poof."

Huh… maybe she doesn't have a behavior control chip. "Interesting. You're probably only sensing the massive amount of paranormal energy down here. Try to relax if you can. Okay. What's your question?"

"You do not have cyberware."

"Nope."

"How can you see and make your eyes light up?"

"Psionics." Kirsten resumed moving, carefully making her way down the other side of the rubble mound. "I'm an astral sensitive. There's a spirit world that exists in parallel with our own. Everything we see has a shadow in the astral realm. Even this junk. If something sits in the same place long enough without moving, it'll reflect on the other side. What I'm doing is basically looking into the astral world at the shadow of reality. If you want to get technical about it"—she jumped across a hole in the concrete slab, likely a former window—"I still can't really see the physical world. If you moved an object, I wouldn't be able to see it. Takes a couple of weeks for the astral shadow to update."

"That sounds so creepy." Skittles jumped down off the rubble behind her, lifted one leg, and peeled a scrap of plastic off her sole. "I want a hot shower."

"Lovely idea." Kirsten clapped dirt from her hands. "And really?"

"Yes really."

"You don't hate baths?"

Skittles laughed. "I am part cat, but not that much cat. I do not mind water. Swimming is fun. Hot, relaxing bath even more fun."

"I think I see a way up over there." Kirsten pointed at a distant column. In the hazy, wavering, sepia-toned view of the Astral Realm, it *appeared* to have a ladder on it, but she'd have to get closer to know for sure.

"We are being followed," whispered Skittles. "Two men are trying to be sneaky."

Kirsten looked back.

A pair of human figures wrapped entirely in shrouds of grey and black fabric stopped short amid the debris, roughly sixty feet behind them. Both hid their faces under baggy hoots, old pre-war gas masks, and numerous wraps of gauzy scrap cloth.

They stared at Kirsten for a moment before emitting cries of alarm and sprinting away.

"Just Discarded."

"Discarded?" Skittles scrunched her nose. "Who threw them away?"

"It's what civilization calls them. I don't know that they have a name for themselves." Kirsten scratched her head. "Most people in the city don't know about the settlements down here. They think everyone who lives in the Beneath is like that. The Discarded are... weird. It's almost like they've devolved away from human intelligence. They don't speak in words, just whoops, and moans, and grunting noises."

"Are they dangerous or just bizarre?" Skittles stopped walking to pluck hunks of something off her foot. "It is so foul down here. Everything is sticky. What *is* it?"

"Centuries of industrial pollution, oil, chemicals, rotting bio matter, pee, crap, anything you can think of. Cryomil fumes from hovercars coat everything on the surface and the rainwater gathers it up—as well as all the other nasty junk—and carries it down through the plates."

"That. Is. Disgusting." Skittles stuck out her tongue.

If we get out of here with only a bit of sticky on the bottoms of her feet, we'll be lucky. "The Discarded *are* dangerous, but they're afraid of me.

Well, anyone with glowing eyes would scare them. You should be fine."

"My eyes don't glow."

"They do." Kirsten glanced at her. "Before I activated Darksight, all I saw of you was a green and a gold spot floating in darkness."

"Is reflection." Skittles laughed. "I have low-light seeing. All the stars above us are enough for me to see down here."

"Those aren't stars."

"I know. Being poetic." Skittles whistled. "I would like very much to be poetic in a bath now. Please walk faster."

Kirsten obliged.

23

GUNK

Before too long, the column Kirsten had been focused on came into clearer view.

Darksight could get quite disorienting when staring at distant objects. The world looked like two copies of the same video overlaid but not perfectly lined up while focus wavered back and forth. Thankfully, the column she'd fixated on *did* appear to have a ladder on the side. Designers hadn't paid much attention to safety. None of the ladders had cage enclosures, consisting of bare metal rods bent into squared-off C shapes attached to the side of a massive vertical tube.

For some silly reason, the thought of climbing five or six stories on such an exposed ladder worried her more now than it had when she'd been a child. However, it bothered her less than being stuck in a jammed elevator or ending up trapped in a plummeting capsule. The one situation in which the pervasive stickiness down here came in handy: climbing. All the chemical gunk made it slightly more difficult to slip off and fall.

"They are returning," whispered Skittles. "Where is your no-see friend?"

"Probably still making Nebula's people regret trying to kill me.

He's really protective." Kirsten sighed and spun around to glare at the stupid Discarded.

A small army of rag-clad figures emerged from the remains of collapsing houses. Not two individuals this time, more like sixty, all armed with spears made from traffic signs or scavenged kitchen knives, hammers, swords, or whatever they could get their hands on.

Come on. See the eyes. Run away screaming already. She leaned at them. "Go away!"

One figure near the middle of the formation jabbed his spear into the air while pointing at her and calling out in a string of meaningless gobbledygook. His voice, like a chicken being electrocuted, would have made her laugh if not for the deadly serious meaning behind the insane sounds.

The other Discarded whooped and wailed in response, waving their weapons high over their heads.

"What the hell did he say?" asked Skittles.

"Kill the demon."

"Wow." Skittles gawked. "You speak... whatever the fornication that was?"

"No. Just guessing." Kirsten took a step back. "We should get the fornication out of here. Like... now."

Skittles narrowed her eyes at her. "You tease me. But... that bad?"

Kirsten squeezed her left arm against her side to remind herself she had the E-90. "I suppose I *could* start shooting. But..." She backed up faster. "I don't think enough of them would process what's happening in time to not overwhelm us. We have the advantage."

"You are either very bad at math or talking about something else." Skittles whirled away from the approaching Discarded and broke into a run.

Kirsten sprinted after her. "I don't mean advantage of numbers. They're still basically human. Adapted to darkness, sure, but they can't see very well. They hunt by sound. If we get far enough away and hold still, they will lose us."

It didn't take long for the shortcoming in Darksight to bite Kirsten in the ass—or at least the toes. Her left foot smashed into an unseen, dense object, throwing her into a flying dive. Somehow, she crashed to the ground, somersaulted forward, and bounced back upright before fully processing how much her foot, as well as five or six other spots on her body, hurt.

"Gah!" She gasped, limp-running. "Ow. Ow. Ow."

Despite their flailing, frenetic gait, the Discarded didn't cover ground as fast as it appeared they should. They swung their arms about, their heads back and forth, likely listening for echoes or whatever sound cues they could pick up on to navigate. None of them stumbled over the same object she hit. Whatever she'd tripped over had to be heavy, on the small side, and recently moved. Perhaps a hunk of concrete, or some mechanical part fallen off the 'sky'.

The scariest part of being in the Beneath—other than having an army of Discarded chasing her—was witnessing the disrepair of the city's undercarriage. Knowing neglect occasionally led to various mechanical components corroding to the point they fell from the plates stirred her nightmares about the city collapsing someday. At least running for her life from a mob of crazed primitives kept her mind off worrying about the future.

"This way." Kirsten grabbed Skittles by the hand and veered left, away from pavement across what used to be someone's front lawn. "They go even slower in the ruins. We have to get off the roads."

Skittles said nothing, seeming focused on watching the ground— no doubt so she didn't step barefoot on anything sharp or disgusting.

Sure enough, the rag-clad army slowed to a more cautious 'stalking' pace as it moved among old fences and the decaying remains of houses. Eleven years ago, Kirsten could crawl inside ancient cars, these strange empty metal cabinets ghosts referred to as mailboxes, or large appliances like washing machines and hide successfully from the Discarded. She'd grown too much for that now. They'd see her inside one of the cars, and the rest of the things she couldn't fit in. A hiding place big enough—like a dumpster—would still work if she could find one.

They raced across multiple backyards, front yards, streets, and driveways. Most of these houses looked intentionally abandoned. No cars anywhere in sight, the place gutted of furniture. The people who lived there in the days during the construction wisely picked up and moved before the expanding plastisteel roof blocked out the sky.

Why did they bother building that mess? Just replace houses with towers. On the ground. She sighed. *They didn't need to have a uniform surface. Someone just saw a way to make a ton of money, I bet. Asteroid mine executives, no doubt. All this metal used to be space rocks.*

By now, the Discarded had fallen back at least a hundred meters or more due to their caution... but they would continue pursuing as long as their ears could guide them.

Little bit farther and we're going to—

With a wooden splintering crunch, the ground abruptly gave out under Kirsten's boots. She reflexively tried to catch herself on the edge of the hole opening up to swallow her, but the material broke apart in her hands, plummeting with her.

Glorp.

A few seconds of free fall ended at a soft, squidgy landing. To her increasing horror, Kirsten found herself armpit deep in the viscous gunk she knew all too well. The sickly sweet raspberry-sour-awfulness invaded her nostrils. For the briefest instant, the fragrance offered the nicety of fruitiness, then rapidly melted into a biochemical horror that made her gag. Trapped in a gummy mass with a consistency part way between dried out Comforgel pad and tar, Kirsten could do nothing but hold perfectly still. It would be impossible for her to get out of the muck fast enough to avoid the Discarded. Struggling would only make noise and lead them to her.

She turned her head toward Skittles, who landed right next to her. Despite being taller, the poor woman had fallen in even deeper, up to her neck. She'd managed to get H1ghb0rne's net deck off her back, holding it up in both hands to keep it away from the slime. *Shh. Don't move. Don't speak. Umm.* Upon remembering telepathy spoke English to a brain that only understood French, Kirsten thought of herself making a 'shh' gesture and sent the image across.

Skittles nodded once.

Kirsten held her breath as much as she could, both to avoid the stink of the slimy morass as well as out of fear the Discarded might hear her. Outside on the surface, soft woos and other bird-like noises came from the deranged denizens of the Beneath. The sounds gave off a sense of confusion. With as much of a lead on them as she had, Kirsten doubted any of them could have seen the two of them fall. The Discarded didn't rely much on eyesight. No one really knew if they'd actually evolved to have bad eyes or no eyes. Such drastic evolutionary changes generally took more than three centuries to manifest. However, according to what she learned in history class, back when humans could go blind without the option to get cybernetic eyes, people used to experience heightening of their other senses, especially hearing. As if the body had a finite amount of resources devoted to 'senses,' whatever power it no longer needed to use for eyesight went elsewhere. She figured something similar happened with the Discarded rather than mutations or evolution.

Having nothing else to do but wait and hope, she gazed around at the walls of her enclosure. She'd fallen into a fairly big pit. It had to be at least thirty feet long and twenty feet wide. A little over four feet of blue and white tile wall separated the surface of the gunk from a concrete lip around the top. A rickety-looking metal ladder hung over the edge, way out of reach, suggesting people used to go in this pit for some reason. Far to her left, almost at the opposite end of the rectangular hole, half a patio table stuck up out of the gunk. It seemed strange for a metal object not to have gone completely under, which meant it hit solid ground. One end of the pit clearly had to be significantly deeper than the other. Behind the table on the right, steps in the corner led up to the surface.

Oh, shit. This is a pool. Or was. We're in the deep end.

The various avian calls and wails of the Discarded grew closer. They had to be right above her now. Kirsten gazed up at the hole, surprised to find it so close. In her moment of panic at suddenly having the ground fall out from under her, the drop felt so much worse than four-ish feet. Broken wood, ripped plastic, and three centuries of accumulated junk formed a cap over an old in-ground pool. Low spots frequently collected the slime she hated so much. The last time she'd fallen into a vat of it at the bottom of an old elevator shaft, the substance had been runnier, closer to syrup.

Assuming we aren't glued in place... She focused on the steps at the shallow end of the pool. *We can get out easily enough. It's just going to take a while... and totally suck.*

The Discarded all ceased whooping at once.

Silence lasted for eight seconds.

Screaming filled the air. Sounds of destruction made her picture bodies crunching through old fences and trampling the ancient patio furniture. Horrified wails receded into the distance. All manner of splintering, breaking, crackling, and metal jangling echoed for several minutes until it became quiet once more.

Dorian stuck his head down through the barrier covering the pool. "They're gone."

"Thanks," rasped Kirsten.

"Your no-see friend is back," whispered Skittles. "It is okay to speak now?"

"Yeah. He scared them off."

Skittles struggled and squirmed, seemingly trapped in the ooze. "What is this feces?"

"It's the coalescence of all the negative emotions of West City. Turns into a sludge down here." Kirsten started trying to drag herself forward in the exceedingly sticky mess. She instantly regretted wearing such a skimpy top. The jacket didn't stop the gelatinous horror from adhering to her bare back and stomach, then peeling away over and over.

"Whoa." Skittles whimpered. "That's bad."

"I'm being melodramatic." Kirsten grunted, continuing to drag herself forward inches at a time. She had to stop every few seconds to fight her pants back into position lest she pull herself right out of them. "It's that same industrial crap I mentioned before. The sticky road? That's like a light coating of this same muck. I'm serious. It's literally everywhere down here."

"Eww. Now I really want bath."

"I would not advise licking yourself clean," said Dorian.

Skittles scoffed. "I don't lick for cleaning. I lick for pleasure. And... I cannot lick myself. That is too much flexible for my bones." She peered up, turning the deck in her hands to aim it endways at the opening above her head. A second later, she closed one eye and launched H1ghb0rne's prized possession—and new home—into the air. It passed clean through the opening, landing what sounded like a safe distance away from the pool.

"Careful. Don't break it," whispered Kirsten.

"No break." Now that she had her hands free, Skittles began to pull herself forward. "It is made well. Much pretty, but tougher than looks. Like us."

It took almost a full hour—including rest breaks—for Kirsten to reach the shallow end. Once she got far enough across the pool for her feet to reach the bottom, it became much easier to move forward. She still ended up mostly submerged in the foulness thanks to the covering over the pool giving her only about eight inches of open air above the slime. No sense trying to rip a hole in it until she reached the stairs. The brittle layer concealing this pit of foulness wouldn't support her weight.

At long last, she made it to the corner and pressed a hand against the ceiling, testing it. Felt like heavy vinyl covered in several inches of dirt and scraps. Likely a winter pool covering the former owners of the property put over it before they left.

Skittles slithered up beside her, staring into her eyes with an utterly horrified expression. "It's between my toes. They are stuck together."

"Yeah. Been there. Know the feeling. Hate it." Kirsten squirmed. "It got inside my shoes. It's everywhere."

Skittles sprouted her claws and tore at the covering overhead. "Please tell me this will wash out of hair."

"It does. Eventually. We're both going to need to spend a long time in the tube. You more so than me with all that hair."

After a short while of slicing and ripping, Skittles made an opening large enough to crawl out of. Someone years ago also put plywood sheets over the pool. They'd become brittle after so many years—and exposure to the gunk. Like dilute acid, the chemical morass gradually weakened everything it came into contact with except plastisteel and concrete.

Kirsten climbed out into the former backyard of a large house. Even the fetid air of the Beneath felt like paradise compared to being trapped down in the hole.

"Are these clothes doomed?" Skittles frowned at her huge T-shirt, now plastered to her body. "I liked this one. Cute."

The sight of her stalled Kirsten mute. She looked so bizarre with her fluffy hair all matted down against her head. It made her cat ears seem creepily oversized. "Depends on what they're made out of. My uniform has survived this crap. The slime will dissolve fabric but... it takes a while. Weeks of not cleaning it. Should be fine if you wash it as soon as we get back to the surface."

Skittles grimaced and took a step. "Eww. Everything is stuck to me. I'd take it off right now if it wouldn't rip my skin."

"It won't rip your skin. Might feel like it, but it won't."

"Naked time?" asked Skittles.

Kirsten peered down at herself. Her formerly baggy pants now looked like tights. The ribbon of a skimpy shirt she'd worn to blend in with the gang punks vanished somewhere in the pool, torn away by the adhesive muck. She hadn't even felt it go amid the constant stick-unstick-restick of the slime on her skin. *Ugh. Glad I wore the jacket.* Despite being a little embarrassed, she didn't dare close the molweave zipper before washing it. If she did, it would never open again. A narrow strip of bare skin down her front didn't matter. Not like the wind could move her jacket away from her breasts right now with anything short of tornado force.

To think. Some people pay ten thousand credits for garments that stick to them like this. "Nah. It's almost tempting. But... not yet. It will take too much work to get out of these clothes. I'd rather do that at home."

"Okay." Skittles stood there, waiting.

Kirsten raised an eyebrow. "Not going to ditch your outfit?"

"Not if it makes you uncomfortable."

"Hah. I'm covered in this stupid black-purple-raspberry gunk again." She held her arms out to either side. "It's not possible for me to be *more* uncomfortable than this. If someone gave me a choice between this mess or going naked? I'd streak."

"Wow." Dorian blinked. "You really hate that stuff."

"Sooo much." Kirsten narrowed her eyes. "*Soooo* much. I have nightmares about this smell."

WHERE INNOCENCE DIED

"Which way do we go from here?" Skittles wandered over to the deck, picked it up by the cord (to avoid touching it and getting gunk all over it) then started to walk off randomly, but stopped, realizing she had two broken-off chunks of old plywood stuck to her feet. "Oh. I have shoes now."

Chuckling, Kirsten looked around until she spotted a promising column. Not all of them had ladders or elevators, only one every eight or so. "Think I see a way up." She grimaced at the sensation of being coated in slime, but didn't let the feeling stop her from moving.

She crossed the remainder of the yard toward a hole in the fence.

Skittles plucked the wood off her feet before jogging to catch up. She paused every few steps to remove some other random object from her soles.

Kirsten squeezed through the hole and stepped out onto a street, then followed the deserted road for a little over half a mile before it looped around to the left, heading down to go under an old highway overpass running beside a vast open lot. The area ahead looked as if it had formerly been a giant commercial space like a mall or some such thing—and fallen victim to the Corporate War. Whatever structures stood there in the past had been bombed into a completely flat field of concrete rubble.

Looking at such destruction would have shocked her, but the several-mile-square area of concrete fragments and metal scraps barely registered to her consciousness thanks to one small shack made of scrap metal standing in the shadow of the overpass. The entire world, except for that tiny place, stopped existing.

A chill ran down her spine.

Never in her life would she forget this place. The last time she'd been to this shack, she was twelve years old. Her hands began to shake before she fully processed the sight. Tears gathered in the corners of her eyes. The terror of a child screamed at her to run away before he got her again. The anger of an adult woman demanded revenge.

"K?" asked Dorian in a soothing tone. "What's wrong?"

Kirsten looked down. For an instant, her slime-soaked pants and boots became dirty bare legs under a scrap of plastic tarp material. She remembered untying her electric cord belt and letting it fall to the floor. The man allowed her to eat the beef stew ration first. She'd been afraid he wanted to trick her. Would make her do the 'sex' thing and then not give her food. She hadn't known anything at all about sex other than people got naked first. He told her she'd like it and it would be fun. And he'd let her eat first.

It hadn't been fun.

It hurt.

She'd been too frightened and guilty to move. Simply closed her eyes and waited for it to stop.

He'd seemed disappointed in her 'lack of energy' but not angry. Once he'd finished, she lay there paralyzed for some time until he said she could come back whenever she wanted for more stew. Somehow, his words lit a fire under her. She grabbed her tarp and ran out of there without looking back. Couldn't sleep. Couldn't even stand being in the Beneath anymore. He'd find her. Maybe next time he wouldn't ask.

And now she'd stumbled right back to the crux of her dread, the thing she feared almost as much as Mother.

I'm not a child anymore.

"Kirsten?" Dorian stepped in front of her. "Are you okay?"

"Not really." She peeled the left side of her jacket off her chest, reached under it, and—with some effort to unstick it—drew the E-90 from its holster. "Be right back."

"I don't like that tone." He winced. "Talk to me, K. What's wrong?"

"Beef stew," she muttered, then walked past him toward the shack.

He spun. "Beef stew? What? Oh…." The concern in his face melted to rage. "By all means. Proceed."

As if not fully in control of herself, Kirsten walked across the long swath of parking lot. She no longer even noticed the stickiness everywhere. Squishing came from her hand as she tensed and relaxed her grip on the rubberized handle. She wouldn't even say a single word to him, certain what he did to her, he'd done to countless others. The world would be better off if she got rid of him.

When she reached the shack, she grasped the flimsy corrugated metal sheet serving as a door and pulled it aside. Without ceremony, she raised the E-90 and stepped inside. The shack hadn't changed much at all. On the right lay the dingy, moldy mattress. She couldn't look at the blood stains.

On the left, a tiny blue table sat between two metal chairs—patio furniture. A human skeleton sat slumped on the floor in the corner behind the table, skull tilted to one side. Two ripped-open plastiboard boxes on the floor near the skeleton still bore the hexagonal indentations from the military ration cans they once contained. The last time she'd been in this room, one case had been unopened, the other mostly full.

Kirsten stared at the skeleton. Two unnatural lighter spots on the skull somewhat resembled the holes from a low-energy bullet, only… they hadn't made holes, merely discoloration. The markings as well as the remains—in fact the entire shack—radiated a strong paranormal energy. She'd know it anywhere.

She remembered Ritchie 'shooting' Mother. He'd conjured an apparition of an old pre-war gun. Spectral bullets hadn't truly hurt the woman, only knocked her out. Here… it seemed Ritchie had been so enraged he'd been powerful enough to kill—or so she assumed. The remains had decayed too much to tell if the spectral bullets directly killed him or if they triggered a heart attack.

The paranormal energy saturating this place felt like Ritchie. She'd been around him long enough to recognize the feel of his aura. Yes. He had definitely been here, and he'd been *furious*. Kirsten also sensed guilt. Did he consider himself responsible for what this man did to her? Because he hadn't been with her all the time, hiding out in that old church afraid of Harbingers? Or, did he regret bringing her to the Beneath in the first place?

Kirsten closed her eyes. A latent imprint on the environment conjured images in her mind. The wretched bastard sitting at the table eating. Door flies open. Ritchie manifests. The man screams, raising his arms as he falls off the chair into the corner. Her guardian spirit is an apparition of pure raging vengeance. He says nothing. Raises his old gun. Fires. The monster dies.

"Good, you bastard," whispered Kirsten.

"What's wrong?" asked Skittles.

"It's nothing," rasped Kirsten.

Skittles moved up beside her. "I see girls cry like this only for one reason. Some fornicating illegitimate son has done the sex with them when they don't want it."

Somehow, this woman's botched language made Kirsten burst out laughing despite her emotional state and tears. "He... he had food. I was alone. A runaway. Starving."

Skittles pulled her into a squishy, sticky embrace. "I understand. It is the same where I was young. The citizen men, they go to find commoner girls. Young and pretty. They tempt us with food."

"Thanks. You don't have to say that. I'm—"

"I do. I was a commoner in the ACC. No money. No status. No rights. I had sex with the police for extra food, for nice clothes, for small pleasures—candy, coffee. It is same thing. Someone has power, so they take what they want from those who have no power."

Kirsten shuddered, tears streaming down her face. "Twelve."

"Thirteen," said Skittles in a hollow voice.

"Military beef stew ration," whispered Kirsten. "I still can't stand the smell of it."

"Crepes with strawberries and chocolate sauce." Skittles seemed emotionless, like an android. "I thought the officer was nice and kind."

Kirsten closed her eyes. "I thought the man was nice, too. It really *could* have been so much worse, but..."

"But. Yes." Skittles squeezed her a little closer. "A nice man would just give the food."

Clinging to this woman she barely knew, Kirsten's emotions spiraled from rage to despair to worthlessness to relief... and finally to a sense of kinship that transcended country, language, or family. For years, Dr. Loring had been telling her she wasn't alone. In that moment of sharing their past shame, grief, guilt, and hopelessness, this oddball cat-eared woman suddenly seemed like a sister.

They held each other in silence until emotions settled.

Gradually, the truth sank into Kirsten's mind. The man she'd spent so many years terrified of was dead. Gone. He could never hurt her— or anyone else—again. Odds were, Ritchie killed him quite soon after it happened. Is that why he'd been trying to avoid her when she sought him out last year? Guilt? He feared she'd be angry with him for not protecting her?

I need to go talk to him soon. Tell him it's okay. Thank him for this.

"If we keep clinging, we're going to end up cemented together," said Kirsten.

"I think maybe too late." Skittles chuckled. "I am stuck."

They pushed apart, carefully enough to avoid ripping fabric or tearing hair out.

"Son of a bitch is gone," muttered Dorian. "Dammit. I really want to kick his ass."

Kirsten started out of the shack, but paused in the doorway upon noticing a tiny spot of long-dried blood on the scrap wood floor.

Skittles slipped past her and took a few steps more before spinning around. "Coming?"

"Sec." Kirsten shifted her stare to another blood spot, then a larger one, and numerous others forming a trail back to the filthy mattress. She raised her E-90 and fired, lighting the interior of the shack dark blue for a fraction of a second. Amid a wisp of smoke and a faint crackle, the dried-out bedding caught fire. She watched the flames licking at the hole, then fired a second laser beam into it for good measure.

The fire spread outward from the two points her weapon struck, none-too-slowly devouring its way across the desiccated fabric. She gazed impassively at the burn as it consumed the dirt, the stains, and the blood. Soon, flames licked up the tattered scrap wall behind it.

Kirsten stood there, staring into the growing fire. Hot wind licked at her face, making the stink of the goop soaked into her clothes turn sour and more acrid. Before long, the mattress collapsed into an unrecognizable dark lump surrounded by flames. It—and all the memories associated with it—became toxic smoke set adrift into the ether. Satisfied, she turned away.

Skittles stood about twenty meters off down the road. As soon as they made eye contact, the woman raised a fist into the air and let out a triumphant cheer, almost war cry.

Kirsten took in a deep breath and raised her head. She couldn't quite summon a sound, but raised her fist as well. When she reached Skittles, the woman turned to walk in step with her down the road. The Beneath seemed to slip into a strange silence save for the crackle of flames behind her and the clatter of scraps as the shack fell in on itself.

"K?" Dorian jogged up beside her. "Are you sure you're okay?"

"Yeah." She smiled, sensing an invisible weight she'd been carrying around for years had, at long last, slipped off her shoulders. "I'm fine."

"Fine? You shot a mattress. Twice."

Kirsten glanced at the E-90. "Damn. I'm going to have to clean this thing. It's all gunked up now. And yeah, I shot a mattress. It's weird, but doing it just put that bastard behind me entirely. I don't have to think about him anymore."

No one spoke for the next several minutes as they walked down an old four-lane street to the base of a massive plastisteel column. She glanced in the direction of the shack, happy to see the entire thing fully engulfed in flames. Fire wouldn't be a big deal in the midst of an ocean of concrete rubble. The burn had nowhere to spread and would soon put itself out. She didn't even notice she still had the E-90 in her hand until she tried to grab onto the ladder.

Oops.

She had to pin the weapon between her arm and side in order to peel her hand off the grip. *Damn, I hate this sticky shit.* Kirsten grasped the nearest rung and began the long, treacherous climb.

"Are you fornicating serious?" Skittles gawked at the series of metal rungs going roughly six stories up the side of the massive column to a small hatch in the plastisteel 'ceiling'. "Not taking the elevator?"

"Nope." Kirsten kept climbing. "These elevators are centuries old and not well maintained."

"But…" Skittles bounced on her toes. "We took one down."

"Gangers were shooting at us. I chose the less likely of two ways to die."

"Eek." She muttered to herself in French for a few seconds, then sighed before starting up the rungs behind her. "Fine. Fair enough."

25

DATA CLEANUP

Jets of hot water cascaded down Kirsten's body in the autoshower tube.

For the first three wash cycles, she rubbed her hands all over, trying to help the machine break up the layer of stickiness covering her from shoulder to toe. Now, on the fourth repeat of the wash/rinse phase, she merely stood there enjoying the sensation of being clean.

One stimpak took care of all the little bits of metal shrapnel.

Three runs of the shower system took care of the physical muck.

Two shots from her E-90 took care of the mental muck.

She leaned her head back as the sprayer worked over her hair. For years, she'd felt stupid for not knowing she had Suggestion back then. He'd seemed so nice and friendly. She didn't understand why he'd been peering up under her tunic as she climbed down the ladder, nor did she comprehend what he had in mind. By the time the true meaning of what he wanted in exchange for food sunk in, it had been too late. She'd already eaten it. She'd promised. She feared what he'd do if she tried to run away.

I'd been so isolated. So innocent.

Maybe if she'd known about Suggestion she'd have told him to *stop*, or commanded him to just give her something to eat.

"Maybe it doesn't matter." She let her head hang forward as the sprayer continued down past her waist. "No. It doesn't matter. Over. Done. May I never waste another brain cell thinking about that piece of shit."

The spray ring dispensing jets of soapy hot water reached the floor. She stuck her toes directly into the stream, eager to forget the sensation of having ooze-filled boots. With any luck, the cleaning place would be able to save them. They hadn't been terribly expensive, but she still hated the idea of ruining them the same day she bought them.

A heavy *clonk* shook the tube as the mechanism reversed.

Spraying only water—no soap—the metal ring made its way back up.

Kirsten looked at her hands. Wrinkled fingers told her she'd probably had more than enough showering for now. Despite not wanting to, she thought of the man's bones... and smiled.

Ritchie... She opened her mind to the astral, trying to use Beacon in a different way: not to summon but to send a message. "Ritchie, don't feel guilty for bringing me down there. What he did wasn't your fault. Thank you for what you did to him."

A moment later, a tornado of hot air filled the tube. Kirsten held on to the handrail until the tumult subsided, leaving her dry. Seconds after the wind died down, the safety lock on the tube hatch disengaged. She stepped out and crept to the bathroom door. After a quick peek into her bedroom to confirm it empty, she walked over to her wardrobe cabinet. A pink tank top and sweat pants worked for now, since she had no plans to do anything other than rest for a while.

Kirsten padded down the hall toward the kitchen, the sensation of soft carpet underfoot abnormally wonderful. The shower in the hall bathroom continued running. She cringed, pitying Skittles for having to deal with that muck in such lush, long hair—not to mention her tail. Neither dark charcoal grey color nor a texture like angora fur were natural things for human hair. Both traits had to be a side effect of whatever Montpierre had done to her.

She must not hate it if she hasn't gotten it reversed by now.

Once in the kitchen, Kirsten 'semmed herself a cup of orange herbal tea with a note of honey—something warm and soothing that wouldn't make sleep impossible. She leaned on the counter sipping it, thinking over the oddity of Skittles following her home. Stray cat jokes aside, it seemed simultaneously weird to bring a near total stranger into her home as well as it felt natural, as if she'd become family. Neither of them even talked about it, merely hopped in the same PubTran car and wordlessly went back to Kirsten's apartment.

By now, Dorian would likely have moved the patrol craft to its usual spot on the parking deck. He'd been quite thankful they didn't smear the purple-black goop all over the inside of 'his' car. PubTran Corporation noticed the mess and charged her an extra 200 credits for the cleaning fee. She didn't mind paying it. It beat having to clean the gunk up herself.

She idly daydreamed about speedware and claws. Despite owning all sorts of cat-themed stuff—sneakers, NetMini, clothes, and so on—and finding cats cute, she didn't want to *be* one. The ears, she had no interest in other than perhaps the utility of enhanced hearing. Difficult to argue the ability to eavesdrop on suspects from a hundred meters away wouldn't be nice for a cop. Still, she'd rather be psionic. If she didn't have those abilities and found herself in Skittles' place, she'd probably have kept the cyberware, too. Much better to be dangerous than helpless.

A few minutes later, Skittles wandered into the kitchen, not having bothered to put anything on. Her hair and tail appeared damp, though mostly returned to their former fluffiness. "Ugh. So annoying to get that mess out of my hair. I think it is gone now." She ruffled both hands back and forth through her mane. "Feels clean."

Kirsten froze for a second in awkwardness. Sure, she'd spent plenty of time at the PAC and even the dorms using co-ed shower rooms. No one there really seemed to care about being naked in a room with twenty other people who were also naked for as long as it took to shower and change. The tendency to put efficiency and speed over such trivial things as privacy came from the military. In a technical sense, the National Police Force *was* the military, merely a branch entirely dedicated to law enforcement among the civilian population.

However, spending twenty minutes in a locker room at the PAC with other people all trying to get cleaned up and ready as fast as possible was something altogether different from a visitor in her home casually hanging around in her birthday suit.

Of course, Skittles didn't exactly impose a pushy sense of familiarity with Kirsten's apartment. The woman thought nothing of walking around outside like that. And, to be fair, all the clothing she had with her remained saturated in horrible slime. Even Kirsten would have preferred to remain naked than put that crap back on after a shower.

Bleh. Whatever. It's her life. She decided to ignore the nudity, just like being in the locker room.

"Thanks for letting me clean up here." Skittles smiled.

"No problem at all. Least I can do."

Skittles swished her tail back and forth as if trying to help it dry faster. "Mind if I 'sem something? That tea smells wonderful."

"Go for it." Kirsten sipped her tea. "Make yourself at home... just don't scratch the furniture."

Skittles meandered over to the reassembler and tapped at the controls, giggling to herself.

The worry Evan might walk in and see nudity bothered Kirsten for a few seconds, until she remembered how his bio-mom did the same thing. Only, that woman didn't skip clothing because she found it comfortable or healthy... or even out of laziness to avoid laundry. The woman had been too high on chems to even comprehend the idea of clothing. According to Evan, she'd even sold off most of her possessions—including clothing—to buy more chems. The boy had no doubt seen it all already, probably also including catching his mother and the asshole she lived with having sex.

The woman probably didn't even notice when Mick touched her.

Kirsten stared into her tea, listening to the reassembler hum while making something for Skittles. She'd found Evan locked in his room, battered and near starved. Miette—Skittles—had sex with the sorry excuse the ACC had for police at age thirteen in exchange for food, only to end up being abducted four years later and turned into a pet cat. Kirsten didn't know—and didn't want to know—what, if anything, that Montpierre guy did to her other than decorate his home with cat girls. Skittles said something about how the man regarded her —and all commoners—as animals. She claimed he'd no more have thought about forcing himself on her than a normal person would have romantic thoughts about a housecat. The whole situation made her skin crawl to think about.

Evan's life, Skittles' life, Kirsten's past... between Mother and that creep in the Beneath.

Does anyone *escape childhood without being traumatized? Is this world even worth trying to help anymore?* She swished the orange tea around in her mug. *Yeah. I can't give up because of a few sick bastards. Or a lot of sick bastards. If people like me give up, the bad guys win.*

"Well. We are alive." Skittles faced Kirsten, arms out to either side. "And clean."

"Sorry." Kirsten chuckled. "I wasn't expecting it to be that dangerous. Figured we'd walk in, get the data, and walk out."

"Aww. You are such the idealist." Skittles flailed her tail back and forth. "Darn it. Hurry up and dry the complete already." She huffed, feigning exasperation. "Fur is lush. Takes forever to dry."

"Looks soft."

"It is." Skittles pet her own tail. "Took some time to get used to, but I like now."

The reassembler beeped.

Skittles opened the door, removed a plate in one hand, then used her tail to grab a cup from inside. After closing the reassembler door, she transferred the cup to her free hand, and used her tail to tug one of the chairs away from the table before sitting in it.

Wow. That thing's flexible. Maybe it is useful. Kirsten un-leaned from the counter and sat in another chair, setting her tea on the table. "Speaking of people trying to kill us... the data."

"Is safe. I clean slime off memory module."

"Nice. One second." Kirsten got up and jogged to her bedroom to fetch her NetMini. After returning to the kitchen, she placed an order for another memory storage module. "I'm going to take a copy of the data just in case. And, of course, it will need to be part of my report. However, it wouldn't necessarily be a tragedy if, oh... say, a copy of the data leaked to the NewsNet thanks to someone who is not with the National Police Force."

"Oh, yes, that would be interesting." Skittles fanned at the steam wafting from her tea. "Do you know someone who has this data and is not with the police?"

Kirsten glanced over at her. "Depends on if you are asking in an official or unofficial sense."

"Unofficially." Skittles nibbled on her food. The plate appeared to contain macaroni and cheese with some unrecognizable beige lumps in it.

"What is that?" Kirsten pointed.

"Tuna."

Kirsten blinked. "You put tuna in mac and cheese?"

"It's good. You should try it." Skittles ate a big forkful.

Eek. Well... I mean... I like sushi, how awful could that be? "Maybe sometime later. Unofficially, I was hoping I do know someone who could possibly help get that information to the NewsNet anonymously."

"Officially?" Skittles flashed a cheesy smile.

"Well... I obviously will need to mention B0rderland in my report. When Captain Eze becomes aware that Nebula ordered his gang to try and kill me, even after I identified myself as a cop, he's probably going to get angry. Not sure if it's your kind of place, but you might want to avoid going there for a while. At least until Division 6 finishes giving it a cavity search."

Skittles squirmed. "Do not like."

"Right. Bad place to be." Kirsten made eye contact. "Look, I know you sometimes do stuff that's not quite legal. I'm not going to mention you on my report. As far as Command is going to know, I went in there with two ghosts. Captain Eze is probably going to give me his 'I'm disappointed in you' speech for not requesting backup... but it'll be fine. Backup wouldn't have gotten there in time to matter... and if I rolled in there with an assault team, Nebula would've blown the data to bits before we made it *to* the front door."

"A rival of this company might pay a fortune for the data." Skittles gazed off to the side. "Make Atmos buy it back or they release it public."

H1ghb0rne appeared in the archway separating the kitchen from the hallway, frowning.

She's gotta be teasing me. "True. And I'm sure you're kidding... but once someone tried to sell it, Atmos would come looking for whoever ruined them. A company willing to let tens of thousands of its customers die, not to mention largely ignore so many of its employees dying under mysterious circumstances, would totally retaliate."

"I know." Skittles sighed, deflating over the table in a feline slump, head resting on her arm. "Is fun to talk about, though."

H1ghb0rne exhaled, seeming relieved.

"And... once they knew the company was going down, they wouldn't really care about getting in *more* legal trouble. So..." Kirsten grimace-smiled. "Assassins."

"Ugh." Skittles cringed as if smelling something bad. "Do not like."

"Neither do I." Kirsten drank the last of her tea.

"Yes. Better to be done with it. I will... umm... carelessly leave the data where NewsNet can find." Skittles ate a few more forkfuls of her tuna-mac. "Can I bug you for a ride home?"

"Gonna put anything on?"

"Don't have. My clothes are slime pile."

Kirsten gestured at the window. "You could send them off to be cleaned. I got a few things you could borrow if you wanted."

"I do the laundry." Skittles rolled her eyes as if agreeing to a Sisyphean task of epic proportions. "If I borrow, I have to send back. Clothes in bot either way. What do you want to do with the deck?"

"It should go into evidence, at least until the inquest is officially closed." Kirsten slid the empty mug back and forth between her hands. "After that... well, I doubt Nebula will be claiming it. If he's still alive and not in jail, he wouldn't dare go near anything official with the police. Why? Did you want it?"

"Don't really need. I have a better one." Skittles examined her fingernails.

"Better?" H1ghb0rne gasped. "I hand-built that from top of the line hardware. It's got sixty-four terabytes of memory! How can you have better?"

Skittles' cat ears thwapped a few times, as if in response to the ghost's voice. "How long ago did you die?"

"Twenty-four years," said Kirsten. "According to the record of his body being discovered."

"Yeah." Skittles stared at the archway. "Sixty-four tera back then would've been amazing. Now, it's like entry level to be taken seriously. My primary rig has fifty-two petabytes."

H1ghb0rne's jaw dropped open… and his eyes disappeared.

"Sorry. It's a pretty deck, though. Someone who likes that Monwyn stuff would adore it." She winked at Kirsten.

"I have no use for a cyberspace deck. Sam would think it's the coolest thing. And, well… it's not really stealing, since Nebula had no legal claim to it. Besides, it's a spirit's focus." Kirsten got up to make herself more tea. "It needs to be somewhere safe."

Skittles groaned and pushed herself up to stand. "I will clean the slime off your floor and order laundry bot."

Kirsten gazed at the ceiling. *Evan is going to be back from Nila's any minute now. Do I tell her to get dressed or just hope the bot returns fast enough?* She fidgeted. *Bleh. He could see cat-modders streaking around outside. It just feels different here, though. Am I being a prig or… Argh! I don't know how to handle this.*

The front door hissed open. "Mom? I'm back."

Crap! "Hey, Ev. In the kitchen."

Soft thudding of child footsteps came down the hallway, but stopped before he reached the kitchen. "Oh, hi. I'm Evan."

"Hello," said Skittles.

Shit. Kirsten cringed, close to bonking her head against the 'sem in frustration.

The boy scurried into the kitchen—running right through H1ghb0rne—and hugged her. "Hi, Mom. Did you beat the bad guys?"

"Still working on it." She twisted around to face him and hugged him back. "Got some evidence now that should do the trick."

"Nice." He grinned.

Skittles walked into the kitchen—wearing a bath towel like an off-the-shoulder shift dress and carrying a coagulated lump of fabric dripping with black-purple slime.

Oh, thank you. Kirsten relaxed.

"Guh." Evan gagged, cringing away from the blob as the woman carried it to the window. "You went down there again."

"We had to." She squirmed. "Didn't want to get into a shootout with fifty people. Worked out for the best."

A bot floated up to the window. It almost appeared to shiver in disgust when Skittles reached out to insert the stained clothing. Probably only a buffeting in the wind, though the bots always did seem to convey human-like emotions, sometimes with small gestures.

"I'm gonna go get ready for bed," said Evan. "Nila and Shani say hi."

"Okay." She kissed him on top of the head before he ran out.

Skittles crept up beside her. "Cute kid."

"Thanks."

"Umm..."

Sensing the awkwardness, Kirsten shook her head and smiled. "No. He's not from... that. I didn't have him at twelve. Got a call last year about things going crazy in a cyberware shop. Sounded like a ghost messing around..."

Their conversation migrated to the sofa in the living room. Soon after she finished explaining how she'd come to adopt Evan, the laundry bot returned. Skittles dropped the towel on the kitchen floor and pulled on her still-warm (and clean) clothes.

"I can run you home now." Kirsten picked up the box containing the blank memory unit she ordered. "Mind copying the data first?"

"No problem." Skittles nabbed the memory fob from her. "It will take only a few minutes."

26

NOT EVEN DEMONS

The following day went about as Kirsten expected it to.

Captain Eze did *not* seem happy she'd gone to B0rderland undercover. Off the record, she confided in him she'd brought one non-ghost along to help out. Learning she had someone not only familiar with the hacker scene but also what he called a *tí-zhèn*, eased his nerves. She got off with a 'don't do that again' warning that sounded more like a worried father asking her to be safe rather than a superior officer threatening a reprimand.

She had to look up the term *tí-zhèn* once she got back to her desk. Apparently, it was street slang for someone—typically on the small side and often female—who had speedware and various cybernetic implants that turned them into high-priced corporate assassins. She sincerely doubted Skittles had it in her to kill for money despite Dorian's doubts, but the woman did have the required hardware to fit the term.

As a member of the National Police Force, Kirsten would get in a ton of trouble, possibly even sued, if she were to do anything with the compromising data she recovered about Atmos other than turn it over to Division 0. Odds were, the data—which she *did* attach to her report as well as handing Captain Eze the physical memory fob—would eventually make its way over to the corporate crimes desk in Division 2. It would take years for someone to sort out if Atmos had simply made an error and covered it up (bad, don't do that again) or had deliberately used inferior parts and or processes knowing it would cause fatalities (serious legal and criminal penalties).

H1ghb0rne didn't want to wait that long. Kirsten didn't want him to rage out and get all twisted—literally—up over it again, so she let Skittles keep a copy of the data figuring that if H1ghb0rne got it once, it wouldn't be impossible for another hacker to get it.

Captain Eze also fumed when she'd told him about the gang attempting to kill her even after she identified as a cop. No doubt Division 6 would be stopping by B0rderland for some fun later tonight. It wouldn't matter if they flushed their data the instant the A3Vs rolled up to the door. Unfortunately, since she hadn't been in uniform with all her gear, no video evidence of the events existed. Eze couldn't file charges—or issue execution orders for attempted murder of law enforcement—without that. So... Div 6 wouldn't be able to kick in the door shooting. They would be doing a shakedown instead of a sweep and clear. Assuming no one went for a gun, they'd spend the night detaining everyone in the place while running deep background checks, arresting whoever they could find any excuse to detain.

She spent the remainder of the day typing out reports, practicing at the firing range, and nervously watching the NewsNet for a bomb to drop on Atmos. Surprisingly, none did. She didn't really doubt Skittles would give the data over freely. However, the woman *was* self-admitted lazy as hell. Maybe she'd slept all day so far.

I'll give it another day.

Kirsten awoke that night to Evan screaming.

It had been a while since he had a nightmare, especially one bad enough to punt him awake and shrieking. Ever since she'd obliterated Mick's ghost right in front of him, the boy had become damn near fearless.

Someone mangled probably woke him up. He's screaming at the gore.

Rapid soft thuds came down the hallway.

And now he's running to my room. She sat up, waiting for him to leap into a hug.

Evan zoomed into her bedroom, but rather than bee-line to the bed, he darted over to her desk. He grabbed her E-90, holster and all, then raced over to the bed, holding the weapon out to her. His light brown hair fluffed up in a wild orb. Sweat trickled down over his bare chest. He'd run so fast his pajama pants threatened to slip off his scrawny hips. The boy trembled, seeming unable to speak.

"What's wrong, hon?" She took the weapon from him in one hand, resting her left on his shaking shoulder.

"Mom," he squeaked, throat tight and dry. "Bad guys are gonna break in and kill us in our beds."

Fuck. Kirsten flung the holster off the E-90. *Atmos can't be this stupid, can they? No way this is Nebula.* She tossed the covers aside and jumped out of bed. "Tonight? Now?"

"Yeah," he whispered. "Minutes."

The boy seemed so thoroughly and genuinely terrified he had to have experienced a precognitive flash in his dreams. She ran over to the same desk where all her work gear sat waiting for morning and hit the panic button on her forearm guard. Not for a second did she even entertain the idea the boy might be making it up. It's possible his precognition misfired or he had an ordinary nightmare. However, she'd much rather embarrass herself calling for help when she didn't need it than not have backup while assassins kicked in her door.

"Bathroom. Get down." Kirsten grabbed her earbud, popped it in, then hurried over to the adjoined bathroom, which felt like the most easily defended spot in the entire apartment.

Evan darted inside and scampered around behind the sink cabinet, crawling under the toilet. She partially closed the door, leaving a gap only wide enough to peer out. The entire outer wall of her bedroom was floor-to-ceiling window. An assassin could easily float up outside in a hovercar. They'd have a few minutes before a patrol unit noticed the deviation from traffic lanes and came to check it out. Plenty of time to fill a room with bullets and disappear.

She left the lights off... and waited.

"Lieutenant Wren," said a female voice in her earpiece. "What is your status? We've received an emergency backup call."

"Confirm," whispered Kirsten. "Unknown number of hostile assailants will be trying to kill me in my residence."

"Did you say *will be*?" asked the dispatch doll.

"Yes. They're on the way. Not here yet. I got advanced warning."

"Copy that, lieutenant. Help is already en route, merely confirming for procedure. Good to hear you're still alive."

Gee thanks.

"Wren!" Captain Eze's voice blurred into the comm channel, sounding worried. "What's going on? Got a notification you hit your 'oh shit' button."

The deep bass tenor in his voice sent tingles down her back like a warm, comforting blanket. So what if most cops had an adversarial relationship with their captains. She both trusted and liked hers.

"Evan just woke up out of a deep sleep, freaking out," whispered Kirsten. "Precog dream. Figure I've got seconds to a few minutes before someone's trying to shoot me."

"Is the boy okay?" asked Captain Eze.

"He's scared, but not hurt," whispered Kirsten. "I'm a little less scared, and not hurt." *Yet.* "Wait. Change that. I'm more pissed than scared."

"Good. Keep alert and stay down. Don't go hunting until you know exactly how many of them there are. Don't let them catch you on a blind angle."

"Copy," whispered Kirsten.

Hissht.

Evan twitched.

"Front door just opened," whispered Kirsten.

"Not friendlies. Repeat. *Not* friendlies," said Captain Eze.

Kirsten tightened her grip on the E-90 and Beaconed for Dorian. He'd be in the patrol craft resting. Not far. A ghost could go from the parking deck to her bathroom in seconds.

Nothing threatening appeared outside the window-wall. Faint rattles of tactical gear came from the hallway. *There's someone in the apartment.* She leaned out of the bathroom, raising the E-90 to aim at the door connecting her bedroom to the hallway. The weapon would chirp a ready tone when she touched the trigger, so she let her fingertip hover a millimeter away.

She held her breath.

The tip of a combat rifle poked into view, the person holding it hesitating. They might be scanning the room or have seen the bed empty. Kirsten reached out with Telepathy, sensing a living brain. *Whew. Not a doll or synth.* Her confidence tripled.

A man in light body armor, visor, and helmet stepped in.

Kirsten peered through the blue ring-dot sight of her E-90, lined up perfectly with his head, and let her fingertip make contact with the trigger.

Bwee-oop.

"Fuck." The man froze. He had to know what the sound meant... the ready-to-fire tone from a laser weapon. His light armor wouldn't do a damn thing to help him against it. After a second's pause and her not boiling his brains off, he turned his head to the left.

"Don't move," said Kirsten, the flare of white from her eyes briefly illuminating the room.

He shook in a mild convulsion. "What the hell are you doing with a damn energy weapon?"

"What the hell are you doing in my apartment?" asked Kirsten slightly louder than whispering.

"Move it," rasped another man in the hallway behind the one she could see.

"I can't," snapped the guy. "Target's a damn psionic. She did something to me."

"What the fuck?" blurted the other man. "They didn't tell us that."

Kirsten drilled into his surface thoughts. Mercenaries. This guy had no idea who sourced the contract or that his target was a psionic, much less a cop. He took a job to kill a data thief.

"Now I understand," said Kirsten.

"What's that?" asked the merc in her room.

"How someone could be so stupid as to come here trying to kill me in my sleep. They didn't tell you much about this job. Like exactly who your target is. Lieutenant Kirsten Wren, Division 0."

"Oh shit," blurted the man in the hallway—right before sprinting away.

"Fuck," muttered the paralyzed merc. "We didn't know. Never would've taken the job if they told us you were NPF. Can we call this a mistake?"

"Little late for that. You were going to murder me and my son in our beds."

"Nah, we wouldn't have killed a kid."

Dustblow! said Evan in her mind. *He's lying.*

"No point lying to a telepath." She frowned. A minor lie, but she didn't want to talk about precognition to everyone, especially a mercenary thug. *"Drop the gun."*

His fingers snapped open. The rifle clattered to the rug. His surface thoughts became a continuous detonation of f-bombs. Shouting and the commotion of a scuffle echoed down the corridor.

His friend met my friends.

Kirsten cautiously approached him, keeping the E-90 pointed at his face. She grasped the carry strap of his rifle in her toes and dragged the weapon out of his reach, then relieved him of a handgun, tossing it onto her bed. *"Get down on your front."*

Moving in the manner of a malfunctioning doll, he jerkily lowered himself to the floor, struggling against the compulsion the whole way. She pivoted right, leaning forward enough to aim down the hall while keeping most of her body under cover behind the wall. Four figures in police armor, three blue, one black, advanced into her apartment. For a second, she and the other cops pointed guns at each other. The backup team lowered their weapons.

Thank you, night vision. Kirsten lowered her E-90.

Satisfied the rest of her apartment was clear, she focused her attention on the one merc and cuffed him as her equipment happened to be right there in easy reach.

"Lieutenant?" called a man in the living room.

"Got one in here, in custody," yelled Kirsten. "I'm okay. Good to see you guys. Oh. Lights, please."

The apartment lights came on.

Division 0 Tactical officers and a handful of Div 6 assault troops swarmed in, checking every room. She backed off and let them drag the mercenary out, handed over the pistol she took from him, then sat on the edge of her bed beside Evan, who clung to her. He'd calmed somewhat, no longer trembling. The tightness of his hold on her seemed equal parts protective as it did frightened.

Dorian walked in through the wall. Upon seeing her, his expression shifted from worry to relief.

"There you are." She blinked at him. "Started to get worried."

"I would've been here sooner. Ran into a few more of these idiots outside. Kept them busy." Dorian scowled. "Any idea what the heck this was?"

"Has to be Atmos." She exhaled. "I don't know how, but they seem to be aware I found this data and they're pretty pissed off."

Various calls of 'clear' or 'secure' came from at least ten different Div 0 Tactical or Division 6 officers.

With the scene declared secure, they tried to sort out who happened to be the highest-ranking person here to assume control of the scene. Kirsten was the only commissioned officer present, but a sergeant wasn't sure if she should assume scene management, given the attack targeted her in her own residence.

Kirsten didn't feel too rattled to take on the responsibility of it, but wouldn't necessarily mind not having to deal with it. Also, it did seem a bit inappropriate, like a lawyer representing themselves.

Before the responding officers out in her living room could make up their minds who should assume command, their conversation abruptly ceased. Silence lasted six seconds before one of the women said, "Captain. All secure here."

Kirsten closed her eyes. *Don't get sappy.*

Captain Eze entered the bedroom, attempting to walk unusually fast while trying not to look as though he rushed. "Kirsten…"

"Hello, sir." She stood.

He smirked in a 'don't sir me right now' manner. "You okay?"

"Yeah. Fine. Little shaken up." Kirsten swiped her hair off her face. "Adrenaline now."

Evan saluted him. "Hi, Captain Ezzeh."

He returned the boy's salute. "At ease, cadet."

Evan grinned.

No one—perhaps except for the boy—took the exchange seriously.

"Any idea what happened here?"

"I only made visual contact with one. He's a mercenary on a contract. Didn't know who posted the job and didn't know I was Div 0. Thought he was going after a data thief, which makes me suspect Atmos."

Captain Eze nodded. "Sounds like it. Gonna send this over to Nine. They should be able to figure out where that contract originated."

Kirsten grimaced. "Okay."

"I know you're not always comfortable with their methods, but—"

"They were going to shoot us both, captain." Kirsten squeezed Evan. "I'm comfortable with their methods in this case. Dammit... if he wasn't a precog..."

"Don't think like that." Captain Eze's expression went grim.

"Yeah. What-ifs are bad."

She continued to hold Evan while the rapid response team finished up and left the apartment to return to their normal duties after wishing her well. Her panic button had essentially called in all active units able to respond in under two minutes. Captain Eze managed the scene personally, even talking to the two Division 9 operatives who arrived about fifteen minutes after the tactical squad left.

Her interview with them surprised her both in its brevity and tone. Both guys from Nine acted more like some people she went to school with being annoyed someone picked on their little sister rather than the uptight 'we kill everyone who pisses us off' stereotype of Nine. Their cordiality came off as sinister when they smiled and assured her they'll 'make sure it doesn't happen again.'

Captain Eze remained behind for a little while until he seemed to trust she'd be okay, then went home.

Kirsten sat on the sofa, staring at the wall where the holo-bar usually projected its screen. Evan had calmed enough to stop trying to squeeze her in half. He still sat next to her, squished against her side. From what the tactical guys said, they nabbed five total mercenaries. The guy who tried to haul ass barreled out of her apartment only to find himself trapped between two groups of armored officers. They found three more stuck in a suspiciously malfunctioning elevator. Plus the one merc who made it to her bedroom, that made five.

Not knowing I'm a cop saved them from summary execution on site. She exhaled. *They're probably not going to get death, but they're going to be out of circulation for a while. What the heck happened with that data?*

"Shall I make coffee?" asked Evan. "Or do we want to try sleeping?"

Kirsten laughed. "Sleeping. Yeah. Right."

"I volunteer as teddy bear if you want to try going back to bed." He smiled up at her. "But I won't say no to coffee."

She squish-hugged him. "It's late. We should at least try to get a little more sleep if you want to go to school tomorrow."

"If I *want*?" He raised an eyebrow.

"After what happened?" She whistled. "If you want to take the day off to de-stress, it's fine."

He pondered. "I'm okay. I can go to school. Learning is important. Stuff isn't too scary when I see it coming."

She smirked.

"Okay. I *was* scared at first, but it looked like a nightmare." He laughed. "Besides, those guys didn't scare me too bad. They weren't even demons."

ESCALATION

Kirsten got a nice close look at the kitchen table the following morning.

She sat slumped forward, half awake, half delirious with fatigue, waiting for the coffee to kick in. Evan wandered in, eyes closed, yawning. He crossed the room to the tall closet beside the fridge, reached at thin air a few times, then shoved his pajama pants down before opening the closet door.

"Ev," said Kirsten, not bothering to lift her head. "You're in the kitchen. That's a storage cabinet, not the shower."

He paused with one foot in the closet. "Oops."

She yawned.

He yawned.

A minute or two passed.

Evan took his foot out of the closet. He appeared to be trying to process the meaning of his surroundings. "Can I have coffee?"

"Okay, but not too strong."

"Thanks, Mom." He padded over to the 'sem and poked at the controls.

"Don't leave your PJ's on the floor, please," mumbled Kirsten.

Evan yawned again… which made her yawn. "I won't."

Beep.

He opened the 'sem, took the cup out, then held it to his face and inhaled. Merely smelling the coffee appeared to wake him up enough to open his eyes all the way. He took a tentative sip. "Hot."

"Coffee has a habit of being hot when it's made."

Evan walked over and set the cup on the table, then retrieved his PJ pants, pulled them on, and sat in the chair. He, too, slumped over the table in almost the same pose as Kirsten.

The boy disappeared.

Kirsten sat up, bewildered. His cup was empty and the hall bathroom autoshower thrummed. She stretched, yawned, and pushed herself up to her feet. *Oh, damn. I must've fallen asleep.* "Why am I more tired after getting another two hours of sleep than I'd have been if we just stayed up?"

By the time she had another coffee in hand, Evan walked back in, dressed except for shoes. Feeling exhausted and lazy this morning, Kirsten made 'sem waffles for both of them. The boy loved them, not caring that most people considered reassembled food 'cheap and/or tasteless.' He grinned while eating them—getting syrup all over his face. Still, he looked like a little burned-out zombie.

"Are you sure you want to go to school today? You're going to sleep through most of it."

He yawned. "I'm okay. Are those buttheads gonna try to hurt us again?"

"It's unlikely, but not impossible." She reached across the table to hold his hand. "I'm really lucky to have you for a son. You saved us both."

Evan stared at her for a moment before he started crying in silence.

"What's wrong?" She got out of her chair and scooted around the table, taking a knee beside him.

He sniffled. "Mr. Diaz said my precog isn't really strong. It's only gonna work if someone I really love is in danger."

She brushed a hand over his hair, getting choked up as well.

"I never used-ta have scary visions about bad stuff happening." He looked down, sniffling again. "Even to me."

Did he not care about himself before? A lump formed in her throat. "But, you saw those creeps hurting you last night."

"I guess I really didn't care what happened to me before you found me." He looked up, grinning. "But it works *now*. And since it works, you gotta know I really love my mom."

Kirsten sniffled and hugged him so tight he squeaked. *Nope. I don't really mind Division 9's methods right now. I'd feel sorry for little Jace if his mother is involved, but if the bitch tried to kill my son, she deserves it.*

It took a few minutes for the emotional mood to settle back to normal. After finishing his breakfast, Evan flopped over the table again.

"Would you like another little coffee?" asked Kirsten.

"Umm. I dunno. Coffee is awesome, but if I don't have it I can fall asleep. If I fall asleep, it's easier to get a precog dream."

He's worried someone's going to try to hurt me again. "I'm scared, too, kiddo. Can't let fear control everything."

"Yeah." He sighed. "If the bad guys send more bad guys, they're gonna know you're a cop and they're gonna be way more dangerous than the last ones."

If I had an office job, I'd totally stay home today. People depend on—she grumbled. *People depend on me being at the top of my game. I'm a zombie. I shouldn't go out there like this.*

"Okay, kiddo. Hang on. We're both fried. Let's stay home and take the day. People just tried to assassinate me. That's gotta be a good enough excuse for a 'sick day.'"

He lifted his head off the table, staring hazily past a mop of hair. "Am I s'posed to laugh at that?"

"Yeah. Being serious, but also funny. Gotta laugh at things or they'll drive you nuts." She picked up her NetMini and called Captain Eze.

Evan grunted in agreement and let his head flop back onto his crossed arms.

"Good morning, Kirsten." The captain's holographic head appeared, hovering over the device. "Everything okay?"

"Mostly. Super tired. Barely slept last night. Is it okay if I go emergency notification today?"

"Of course. I wasn't expecting to see you in the squad room this morning." He smiled. "Can't think of anyone who isn't a combat vet with head issues who'd brush something like that off like nothing happened."

"Ack."

"Well, *some* old vets find that sort of thing exhilarating." He rolled his eyes. "Not me. Get some rest. Collect yourself. Take care of that boy. I'll let the school know what's going on."

"Thank you, sir."

He nodded once. "Before you go, following up on what you said last night. You think this is Atmos?"

"Yeah. I can't say for sure what level it came from. There are three possibilities: the CEO, Ryn Tomlin; their director of network security, Lam Orben; or the guy running their board of directors, the first CEO, Chaoxiang Liu."

"Any of them seem more likely than the others?" Captain Eze shifted his eyes left, as if glancing at a terminal on his desk.

"I'm inclined to say Tomlin is the least likely. She had a twenty-year-old son who died to the supposed black ICE…" *I can't tell her I'm helping the ghost who killed her boy, even if the spirit was totally out of his mind and not in control of himself. She won't care.* "I'm not sure she'd be willing to put the company over family. The woman was so upset over losing her son that she had another one, basically cloned him and went to Reinventions to make herself younger so she could take care of him."

"Damn." Captain Eze whistled. "This woman's got some cash."

"Yeah. Weird thing is, I think her former son's ghost came back and hopped into the baby."

Captain Eze stared at her. "You're really trying to give me nightmares, aren't you?"

She chuckled.

"It's not the ghosts." He grinned. "If people start thinking they can bring the dead back, we're in for a hell of a ride."

"Something like this would only work if the ghost happened to be around when the genetics people at Familyperfect synthesized an embryo. Don't ask me at what point the spirit could've jumped in. No clue. And… I don't think he's going to remember his previous life.

Just, basically a reincarnation scenario with the exception that his body is genetically identical to what he had before."

"Way over my pay grade." Captain Eze puffed air. "Nope. Other two?"

"Still not sure Ryn is out of it. I don't know how she'd react if she learned the truth of *why* her son died. She might blame Atmos for it or she might blame the ghost. So, the other two. Lam Orben seemed really upset when I caught him lying about there being black ICE on the company network. H1ghb0rne told me they have a doom pit protected by it. He's the only one involved in this case who actually died to a countermeasure program. He successfully got the data out but it killed him doing it. I don't know if this Orben guy is truly aware of what the doom pit contained. He'd only been at the company for six or seven years. H1ghb0rne swiped the data twenty-four years ago."

"It's the old guy," deadpanned Evan. "You had a bad feeling about him as soon as you looked at him."

Captain Eze swiveled to look at the boy. "Son, go back to bed. You look beat."

"Yes, sir," droned Evan.

"Possible." Kirsten stretched. "I didn't want to point the finger at him right away because of that. Did I get a bad feeling from him because he's involved or would I be inclined to accuse him of being involved because I got bad feeling from him?"

"I can't answer you there." Captain Eze pursed his lips. "However, you do have a little chip on your shoulder toward the wealthy."

"Just a tiny one." She laughed. "But this guy's worse than just rich. He treats the current CEO like some servant underling. Don't usually get 'bad vibes' from people like he gave me."

Evan sat up, smiling. "You hang out with Harbingers so much, maybe you can smell the bad people too."

"Heh. If only." Kirsten tried to drink from her empty coffee cup, groaned, and put it down. "Need a refill."

"I can wait a moment." Captain Eze pursed his lips. "Hmm. You know what? Coffee sounds like a good idea. Let me call you back in a few minutes."

"All right." She set the NetMini down on the table and got up to make more coffee.

Hmm. None of them could possibly know I got the incriminating data… unless Skittles decided to pull a shady move and try to sell it back to them. Eh, that doesn't make too much sense. She said she wouldn't do it. Besides, she knows I have a copy. Atmos' people would be able to tell the file's been replicated and she wasn't selling them the only existing record.

Kirsten rushed back to the NetMini and called Skittles.

A blank hologram—tiny rainbow dots flickering in the air—appeared. The call seemed to have been answered despite there being no one in front of the device.

"Hello?" asked Kirsten.

"Do you know what fornicating time it is?" asked a dazed, sleepy-sounding Skittles.

"Sorry. Yeah. It's early. Just worried something happened to you."

Dark grey cat ears rose into view from the bottom of the holographic display area, soon followed by Skittles' face. Her left ear angled back, right ear perked up, mirroring her eyes—one closed, one open. "Why would something happen to me?"

"Mercenaries paid me a visit last night. Thought they took a contract to kill a data thief."

"Eep!" Skittles ears perked up. Both eyes opened all the way.

"What happened with the NewsNet?"

"I sent the data anonymously to their office. Is it not broadcasting yet?"

"I haven't seen it. Kept looking for it all day yesterday." Kirsten shook her head. "Silence. Not a peep."

Skittles frowned, baring one fang. "Grr. I will check. Maybe NewsNet person see the data and think they get rich."

"Oh, ugh." Kirsten facepalmed. "I never even thought about that happening."

"You are perhaps too nice and innocent to be police." Skittles giggled.

"I suppose." Kirsten shrugged. "Guess that's why I mostly handle ghosts and stuff."

28

EVIDENCE

Her rest day turned into a loud afternoon when Evan's friends all showed up.

Shani, Walter, Shawn, Maela, and Willow arrived unannounced soon after school let out. Apparently, Nila conspired with the kids for the surprise, bringing them over to check on Evan. At least she stayed over and helped supervise. While having six kids in the apartment made anything even close to napping utterly impossible, the positive energy they brought with them did as much or more good.

As an added benefit, no one showed up to kill her.

Aside from Evan wanting to spend the night in her room, all seemed back to normal.

She sat at her desk in the squad room the morning following her day off, expecting chaos. Restless ghosts and/or demons gave her a break and didn't set off any emergency calls. Good chance something crazy would happen today.

Less than five minutes after her butt touched chair, Nicole came rushing over, carrying two bags. She hastily distributed coffee and egg sandwiches to most of the people in the squad room who chipped in on the order, then stared at her.

"What?" asked Kirsten. "Ooh. thanks."

"What do you mean what?" Nicole bopped her over the head with the empty bag. "You're here one day after a team of mercenaries tried to take you out! And no problem. Got your message about the alarm."

Kirsten opened the clamshell containing her egg sandwich. "The alarm worked fine. My brain failed. One day was fine. I'm fine. Only needed to make up for lost sleep."

"Uh huh." Nicole flopped in her chair one desk to Kirsten's left, by the wall. "It's so wrong Div 9 is just going to shoot everyone responsible."

"I... out of my hands. I don't have to like it either, but they *were* going to kill Evan, too."

Nicole rushed chewing her first bite, swallowed, then shook her head. "No, I mean it's wrong because *I* want to do it. Let me get my hands on the piece of shit who wanted to hurt you..."

Being simultaneously amused, horrified, and comforted her friend would be so protective, Kirsten winced, then laughed. "If you did it, they'd at least know why."

"Damn sure they would." Nicole scowled. "Div 9 is too methodical and efficient. Just pop out of nowhere and bang. Gone. What's the point of doing it if they don't know why?"

"I'm sure they figure it out eventually after death." Kirsten took a long, slow sip of her mocha raspberry coffee. "Oh. Chocolate raspberry today. Nice."

"They ran out of strawberry. Sorry. I know it's your fav."

"This is good, too."

They fell into a conversation that, in typical Nicole fashion, changed topics about three times every minute. Sam probably moving in with Kirsten, Evan being good, Nicole's boyfriend Jaden having a name similar to the son of the Atmos Industries' CEO, Nicole and Jaden still dating with no firm plans to do anything but have 'fun sex' whenever they felt like it. Kirsten wanted to tell Nicole about burning that shack to the ground, but not here... not now. A conversation like that might be one of the few things on the Earth capable of making her friend stay focused on a single idea for more than thirty seconds.

"Oh, speaking of Sam..." Kirsten swung her chair to face the terminal. "I needed to ask him something. Give me a minute."

"Sure. Take all the time you need with your lover." Nicole batted her eyelashes. "There's a room on level four over by the filtration processing unit. Storage area 4-03-C. No one ever goes there. You guys could... you know. Trust me. It's safe."

Kirsten felt the blood rushing to her face, but still opened a vid call to Sam.

"Hey there." He smiled from her terminal screen. "I am so sorry I couldn't get there."

"It's fine. I know you were on standby that night."

"Stuck in this room for forty-eight hours, not just 'that night.'"

She cringed.

"My ass print is probably still on a storage container in there." Nicole gazed off absentmindedly.

Kirsten's cheeks warmed even more.

"You're too easy." Nicole made a goofy face. "I'd never have sex in a storage room here."

"Oh. Ugh." Kirsten shook her head and started to take another sip of coffee.

"I'd do it in the locker room like everyone else," deadpanned Nicole.

Kirsten sputtered into a coughing fit—mocha berry coffee went places it did not belong inside her head.

Everyone cracked up laughing except for Nicole's partner, Forrester, who made a 'this is what I have to deal with every day' face. Kirsten grabbed her face in both hands and moaned until the burning stopped. Coffee dribbled out of her nose.

Sam cringed, helpless to do anything but watch from the terminal screen.

Once she could breathe again, Kirsten flung a foam stress ball at Nicole, making her laugh. "Ouch. Don't say crap like that when I'm drinking."

"She does that on purpose." Forrester chuckled. "I've learned not to drink anything unless she's got something in her mouth so she can't talk."

Nicole glanced at him. "Meh. Too easy. Not going to say it."

"Your discretion is much appreciated." Forrester resumed working on a report. His dark complexion made it difficult to tell from this angle if he blushed, though the way he avoided eye contact said he hadn't meant his comment to be such an innuendo.

"Anyway," muttered Kirsten, turning her attention back to Sam. "Can you confirm the cat left the dead mouse where it was supposed to go?"

"Ooh! Spy talk!" Nicole laughed. "Someone's up to something naughty."

Kirsten set her elbow on the desk, face in her hand.

"No problem. Give me a few minutes." Sam gazed into space, shifting his focus from the real world to his GlobeNet connection.

H1ghb0rne manifested by the wall amid a whorl of spectral energy. Even before she looked at him, the alarmed urgency in his presence made his emotional state obvious. Something had to be very wrong. He rushed over to her desk, passing through Kurosawa, making the woman shiver and start glaring at Kirsten.

"You have to see this." H1ghb0rne pointed. "It's Atmos. Gotta be."

"See what?" Kirsten blinked.

"Guy's been killed." The ghost tried pulling at her. "Hurry."

"Okay. Okay…" Kirsten stood. "Has anyone found the body yet?"

"No." H1ghb0rne shook his head so rapidly it blurred.

Crap. It's not going to be a secure scene. She glanced left. "Nikki… mind giving me a little backup?"

Nicole jumped to her feet. "You got it. Give us a sec to armor up and we'll be right there." She rushed around her desk, tapping Forrester on the shoulder on her way past him.

He glanced at Kirsten. "What's going on?"

"A ghost I've been working with just ran in and told me someone's been killed and I need to get to the scene right away."

The room fell silent.

Forrester whistled. "If you were anyone else, saying a thing like that would get the captain sending you to see the doc." He stood. "Crazy world we live in."

Morelli looked around the squad room, seeming oblivious to

H1ghb0rne and Dorian. "We've had Sgt. Marsh's spirit sitting at that empty desk behind Wren for years. Tell me you can't feel his presence in here."

"Yeah... yeah..." Forrester shook his head in an 'I don't want to think about it' manner and hurried off after Nicole. "Go on, lieutenant. We'll catch up after we get our gear on."

"Thanks." Kirsten spun to look at the ghost. "Okay. Show me where."

FOLLOWING H1GHB0RNE'S DIRECTIONS, KIRSTEN FLEW NORTH AND slightly east from the PAC.

Thirty-two minutes later, she arrived in Sector 5479, a little over 300 miles away. From the air, the swath of shiny silver residence towers looked like a clean spot where some great being started to polish West City but soon lost the energy to keep going. A noticeable drop in hovercar traffic plus an increase in the density of advert and delivery bots further called attention to it being a higher class area.

Nicole and Forrester caught up to her around 180 miles into the trip, thanks to pushing their patrol craft to its speed ceiling. If not for all their armor plating—and if they'd been designed a bit more aerodynamic—they could break the sound barrier. Even doing 690-700 MPH made for hazardous flying, so Nicole had gone up high, flying at 2,000 feet until she came within a quarter mile of Kirsten's PC.

"There." H1ghb0rne pointed. "The one covered in green shit with the big ball."

Kirsten looked where he indicated, a residence tower at least ten stories taller than other buildings nearby. The spacing of the windows on the upper quarter or so of the structure indicated expensive penthouse apartments where each floor contained four or fewer separate dwellings. Hydroponic growth tanks bearing various vegetables, fruits, and other plants covered the entirety of the roof except for a giant, spherical white tank at the center, which likely held water.

Penthouses are expensive enough… but a private garden growing real food? Wow.

She didn't want to think about how much it would cost to live in this building.

Kirsten steered into a gradual descending turn to line up on the indicated tower, then tapped a few buttons. A targeting reticle appeared on the forward viewscreen around the high-rise. Two floating holo-panels opened, displaying information about the floorplan, hovercar approach vectors, security status, and so on. Everything appeared calm. No one had set off any emergency alarms, which meant the body hadn't been discovered yet.

On the way up here, she'd opened a separate inquest record for an unknown deceased male. H1ghb0rne didn't say much yet other than she needed to see this dead guy. Command knew she responded to a report of a corpse, though only Division 0 was aware the report came from a spirit.

Since the garden took up the entire roof, hovercar parking occupied the fiftieth and fifty-first floors.

"Going in quiet?" asked Nicole over comms.

"No reason to make a big scene yet." Kirsten nudged the PC downward, following the virtual 'track' guiding her to the parking area entrance. "The killer or killers are either long gone or still there and I'd like to surprise them."

"You think they'd still be here? It took us like an hour." Nicole's hologram rolled her eyes.

"Thirty-four minutes." Dorian tapped the chrono display on the console. "Not an hour."

"Nicole's brain is overclocked. Time works differently for her." Kirsten chuckled.

She lined up at the level of the opening in the wall. Soon after the patrol craft entered the building's interior space, dozens of small floating orb bots, some with spiderlike limbs jutting out in multiple directions, stopped to watch her go by. They appeared to be a mixture of cleaning units, security bots, and convenience bots there to sell products anyone entering or leaving might need in a hurry. Like a pack of curious onlookers turning their heads, the silvery spheres rotated to follow her.

A dead body from a recent murder counted as enough of an emergency situation for Kirsten to land in the yellow-striped zone near the central elevator core. In truth, any member of the National Police Force could use that area if their visit to a building involved official business. It didn't necessarily have to be an *emergency*.

Nicole landed next to her amid a billowing cloud of white water vapor and Cryomil fog.

A cluster of vend-bots approached but kept their distance, not wanting to intrude on police business but making themselves conveniently close on the tiny chance the arriving cops might need to buy something. One opened a holo-panel extra-large, showing donuts and various pastries. A nearby bot bonked it with a thin metal arm as if afraid of getting in trouble.

Kirsten hurried to the nearest elevator. Nicole and Forrester, both in full psi armor, followed. Dorian and H1ghb0rne strolled in and stood on either side of her. The door closed. Everyone stood in silence, watching Kirsten stare expectantly at the ghost.

"Where are we going?" asked Forrester.

"Good question." Kirsten raised her eyebrows. "What floor?"

"Oh. Uhh. Right." H1ghb0rne reached a hand into the elevator console, which beeped.

Awestruck, almost childlike, delight shone clear in Nicole's eyes, obvious despite her wearing a helmet with a visor. Kirsten didn't even have to peek into her thoughts to know her friend watched the ghost via surface thought scanning her.

Forrester seemed unsettled at the elevator apparently activating itself, but remained calm.

H1ghb0rne selected the 104th floor, specifically 104-2, one of three apartments on that level.

The capsule whirred upward in relative silence for a moment before stopping, rotating, and sliding sideways a short distance. Its door opened to reveal a smallish chamber made to look like an outdoor 'front yard.' Hologram projectors created the illusion of blue sky overhead. The lawn on either side of a fifteen-foot walkway up to the door might even be living plant matter.

Kirsten paused, surveying the room. Nothing looked out of the ordinary. The door remained closed. No visible damage. No smoke, blood, or signs of a disturbance broke the peacefulness of the room and its fake bird chirp sound effects.

She drew her E-90 out of an abundance of caution and approached the door. Nicole and Forrester both readied their weapons as well. Her friend preferred the somewhat smaller E-86 pistol since it got about twenty or so more shots than an E-90 on the same e-mag. Also, it produced a green beam which she jokingly claimed to find 'prettier' than the dark azure of the E-90. Honestly, even the E-86 had more power than a cop truly needed when dealing with people. The lasers did, however, come in handy for angry cyborgs.

Upon reaching the door, Kirsten listened to silence for a few seconds before transmitting a police override to the security system. The instant the door opened, a smell like burned meat slapped her in the face. Ahead, a massive living room in white, beige, and silver stretched out in pristine glory. This one room took up more space than her entire apartment. A holo-vid screen easily fifteen feet across shimmered in the air, displaying a screen-saver landscape of snowy mountain peaks in front of a white sectional semi-recessed in a pit. The massive sofa had enough space to hold twenty adults.

It's so damn clean and perfect it looks like a demo unit. Not one where someone lives.

"We got it, Kay," said Nicole. "Hang back."

"Your call, lieutenant." Forrester glanced at her.

Kirsten gestured in a 'be my guest' manner.

Being Tactical instead of I-Ops, they had much more experience clearing potentially dangerous locations. Kirsten stepped aside and let them take the lead. Room by cavernous room, she followed them as they made their way across the apartment. The kitchen showed a minor sign of occupancy, a blinking 'finished' light on the dishwasher.

The smell of burning grew stronger the deeper they went. Other than a fist-sized orb bot gliding along the hall cleaning the baseboards, nothing moved. Every room they passed looked to be in perfect order.

After a painstaking six-minute process checking every corner and opening for potential threats, Nicole and Forrester reached the end of the hall. They stepped through a doorway at the end, Forrester aiming left, Nicole covering right.

"Got him," said Forrester.

"Clear on this side." Nicole swung around to look left. "Got a dead guy here."

Kirsten followed them in. The doorway occupied the middle of the south wall of a giant rectangular room extending at least twenty yards to either side. The facing wall, thirty feet in front of her, consisted entirely of dark tinted window with a view of the city stretching off to the horizon. Silvery-grey carpet only added to the starkness of such a large room having a mere three pieces of furniture: a desk all the way against the left wall, a chair placed near said desk, and a round, blue beanbag style blob on the opposite end of the room that resembled an enormous mochi ice cream. It might have been intended as a soft place to sit or merely an art object.

Smoke still wisped upward from the head of a dead man with short aqua-colored hair in the chair by the desk. His mostly nude body lay backward, mouth agape, arms splayed out to either side. The scent of cologne-infused autoshower soap mingled with the aroma of fried meat. Except for the smoke rising from his mouth and nostrils, no obvious cause of death showed itself from this angle.

Kirsten holstered her E-90 and approached the body.

The man appeared to be in his early thirties, athletic to the point of disbelief. His body looked as if it belonged to a comic book superhero, perfect and sculpted. An off-white bathrobe covered little more than his shoulders, giving her a complete view of everything. No open wounds marred his skin. Lifeless eyes with metallic copper irises— obviously cybernetic—stared vacantly into the abyss. His chiseled jawline and sharp nose further cemented the 'superhero' look.

Blackening and discoloration marked the skin behind his left ear, next to his M3 plug. A wire dangled from his head, looped around under the chair, and plugged into a large, expensive looking terminal on the desk. Insulation had melted away from the wire for the first thirty-or-so inches nearest his head. The four holo-panel screens didn't contain any salacious content and the man did not appear to have been even remotely aroused at the time of death.

"This is why you shouldn't plug in right out of the autoshower," said Nicole. "Shame. This guy was cute."

"Too much. He was trying too damn hard." Kirsten resisted the temptation to tug the bathrobe over his nether regions until proper crime scene documentation took place. "He's obviously been to Reinventions."

"Didn't even have to study him to tell you that." Forrester laughed. "No one as young as this guy looks could afford this place."

"Who is he?" Nicole raised her left arm and activated her holo-panel.

Kirsten did the same. The man had an ImDent chip, essentially the most important parts of a NetMini embedded under the skin, which made it easy to pull up his record. "Zannis Dalvren. Age sixty-one. Looks like he was an executive editor for NewsNet Corp."

"Sixty one?" Nicole whistled. "Damn, he's had work. Any guess as to why he's naked?"

Forrester smirked. "What do you think it means to find a naked guy plugged into his terminal?"

"Not what you're implying." Nicole made an obvious show of checking out the dead man's equipment. "He's completely at rest. Guy worked from home. Probably wanted to be comfortable. I can relate."

Kirsten made it a point *not* to look at the body any more than necessary for her investigation. "Can we maybe try to at least be a tiny bit professional? Making jokes about a dead guy hours after he was killed is…"

Nicole gazed around. "Sorry. Is his ghost mad at me?"

"If he is, he's not here to say anything about it." Kirsten looked at the terminal screens. "Smelled like shower soap in here. He probably rushed out of the tube to answer an email in a hurry. Look at the size of those windows. This guy wouldn't lay here like this in full view if he'd had the time to think about what he was doing."

"Not exactly full view." Nicole glanced out the windows. "This high up, no one would see him."

"He might not have minded being seen." Dorian gestured at some shelving beside the desk. Four small statuettes of the dead guy struck poses like Greek gods—though none were nudes. "Got the feeling he was on the vain side."

Nicole winced at the statues. "Oh, just a little. Okay, he's not so hot to me anymore. Can't stand people who are so full of themselves."

"It's good to be rich." Forrester twisted to look at the big empty space. "Rich and lonely."

The contents of his holo-terminal screens all appeared to be work-related messages, video clips for upcoming news stories, employee records, and so forth. Since it happened to be right there and visible, she read over some of the recent messages. Eleven emails, the most recent, came from someone named Nori, pestering him about 'editorial approval needed' with increasing levels of panic at not getting a reply. The twelfth email had a masked sender.

Your terms are potentially acceptable. Let us meet virtually to discuss your offer. We will be checking the Karsson-Niemand to ensure you have not copied the data. If it's intact, you have a deal.

"Son of a bitch." Kirsten stomped.

"What?" asked Nicole and Forrester at the same time.

"She *did* leave the data where the NewsNet would find it. This guy got a hold of it and the bastard tried to sell it back to Atmos." Kirsten gestured at the corpse. "They lured him into the GlobeNet and black ICEd him."

H1ghb0rne clapped. "Exactly. You're on point. Only got one little thing wrong."

She stared at him. "You knew? Why didn't you just tell me this?"

"I was kinda curious to see how long it would take you to figure it out." He smiled. "If you didn't get it right away, I'd have explained, but you're sharp. Didn't need my help."

He's trying to make me feel better... confident. "What did I get wrong?"

"A minor technicality." H1ghb0rne tugged ineffectively at the wire coming out of the dead man's head. "Black ICE is a type of *defense* program. This guy didn't get fried by that. Another deck jockey attacked him."

Kirsten stared at the body. "Looks like the same thing."

"It is, from a mechanical level. The difference is semantic."

H1ghb0rne made a throwing gesture. "It's the difference between breaking into a place and setting off a bomb or having someone chuck a hand grenade at you while you're just standing there not breaking the law."

"Murder then." Kirsten typed notes into the inquest file, then resumed checking the terminal.

With a little bit of nudging from H1ghb0rne, she discovered some deleted messages showing Zannis Dalvren making arrangements with someone unnamed at Atmos Industries to sell them the compromising data and keep it off the NewsNet for sixty million credits. It appeared as though Atmos made a counter offer: death.

"Did they fry his terminal?" asked Kirsten. "What happened to the data?"

"It's still in there." H1ghb0rne inserted his hand into the deck. "Whoever pulled the trigger and melted his brain jumped the gun. They underestimated NewsNet's security. They are still trying to get in and kill the data as we speak."

"Can you blast this message chain to every single employee at NewsNet and include a copy of the data? If *everyone* has it, it will be really damn difficult for anyone to think of selling it."

"I could, but that would be unethical," said Nicole.

"I'm not asking you." Kirsten grinned at her. "Same reason I haven't done it myself yet."

H1ghb0rne bowed at her in the manner of a high elf from Monwyn. "As you command, fair lady."

She sighed, thankful no one could hear him.

Her NetMini beeped with an incoming call. She answered via her armband terminal.

Samuel Chang's holographic head appeared floating above her arm. "Found something. Kitty left the dead mouse on the doorstep. Someone took it. I'm in the middle of tracing it now."

"I think I'm here already. Standing next to the remains of the guy who swiped it." Kirsten explained the situation—and what she found on the terminal.

"Excellent. Saves me a bunch of time. One second... plucking the TID..." Sam whistled to himself.

Her armband chirped, then the desk terminal screens flickered.

"I'm in. You know I'll have to start an official case about this."

She smiled. "I wouldn't expect you to do anything else. Command has the data already. I really don't know what Atmos thinks it's going to do. They can't keep the truth completely quiet."

"No," said Dorian, "but they can try to downplay it as much as possible in hopes of dragging things out long enough to find a senator amenable to a payoff."

"So cynical." She sighed.

"Says the one who wanted the data sent to the NewsNet because she knew the government would take too long to bring charges." Dorian rested his hands on his hips. He started to smile at her then swiveled to look at the doorway. "Incoming."

Kirsten drew her E-90, spinning to aim at the room's only entrance. Nicole and Forrester reacted to her by doing the same.

This room is shitty, said Nicole via telepathy. *Absolutely no cover. So empty.*

A tall, broad-shouldered man wearing body armor and a trench coat walked brazenly out into view. Everything about him from his long, black hair to his combat rifle, to his silver right eye said 'corporate hitman.' The woman following him sported a metal right arm and right leg. She had the unimpressed air of a former soldier about her, as well as a few facial scars. Like the big man, she also wore body armor. Two submachineguns, attached via flex-cords to her armor, dangled about where holstered pistols would be at belt level. Last, a thin Asian guy, shorter than the woman, strolled in. He didn't have armor or any weapons larger than what might have been concealed under his expensive-looking black raincoat.

For no reason other than she happened to be in the middle of their formation, Kirsten aimed at the woman with the cybernetic limbs. Given a huge guy, an aug woman, and a normal-sized man in ordinary clothing, she instinctively regarded the small man as the biggest threat. He probably had speedware or possibly psionics—something to give him the confidence not to rely on armor or big guns.

The woman glanced casually at the three cops pointing laser pistols at them. "Damn. That's creepy."

"What is?" asked Kirsten.

"A dude old enough to be my grandfather looking hot as fuck," said the woman.

"He's dead," muttered Nicole.

"Nah, I'm messing." The woman glanced at Forrester and Nicole before staring at Kirsten again. "What's creepy is how the shit the cops got here before us."

"Don't discount the idea we might be here for completely unrelated reasons," Kirsten opened a telepathic link to the woman's mind. "Why are you here?"

An immediate response to the question formed in her thoughts. Mr. Liu from Atmos Industries sent them here to torch the place of all evidence potentially tying the company to Zannis Dalvren. The woman knew one of the company's network people killed this dude a bit too hastily before they managed to crack their way into his system. Consequently, she and her two associates had been rushed into action. The reason for H1ghb0rne's urgency became apparent. He wanted Kirsten to get here before the cleanup crew.

"You must be a rookie if you think I'm going to just talk to the cops." The woman laughed.

"You must be a dumbass if you're going to threaten the police." Nicole scowled.

Kirsten eyed the other two, scanning their brains. Sure enough, the small guy had neuralware. Speed boosts, vibro claws in his arms, and hundreds of hours of sim training in hand-to-hand combat. If he got within arm's reach, he could easily kill all three of them in seconds. The big dude appeared to be a run-of-the-mill heavy. A 'just point me at whatever you want to be destroyed' type of guy. Some strength augmentation, targeting systems in his electronic eye, implanted armor as well as body armor. He'd laugh at almost any ballistic weapon, but an E-90 or an E-86 would melt through his defenses without an issue.

"No, I'm not a rookie." Kirsten glanced at Dorian, then flicked her gaze to the speedware guy. "I'm Division 0. You told me what I wanted to know simply by thinking it as soon as I asked. Sorry, but I can't allow you three to burn the place to eliminate evidence. I'm afraid Mr. Liu will need to argue his case in front of a judge. I suggest the three of you leave while the worst thing you've done is enter an active crime scene without authorization."

As soon as she said 'Division 0,' both men became noticeably apprehensive.

The woman gave a sigh. "Oh, he said you might be here. Sorry, kid, but you count as evidence. That means we have to destroy you, too."

"Damn," whispered Kirsten. "Here we go."

29

RESISTING ARREST

A whole mess of chaos happened all at once.

The thin man held his arms out to either side. A pair of twelve-inch metal blades snapped into view from between his knuckles. Before the hair-raising hypersonic screech of vibro-claws could even start, he abruptly flung himself to the floor and began thrashing around like a fish on dry land.

Nicole reached her left hand toward the big guy, grunting as if lifting something heavy. The man's combat rifle lurched out of his grip and flew toward her. Forrester simultaneously fired his E-90 at the same guy, putting a beam through his lower abdomen and into the wall on the far side of the room.

Screaming, the thin guy continued thrashing uncontrollably. His claws repeatedly retracted and extended; no longer in sync with each other, they grew longer and shorter at varying speeds. Foamy drool bubbled out of his mouth.

The woman grabbed for her submachine guns, starting to shoot even before she whipped them up all the way.

"*Stop!*" shouted Kirsten, pounding her in the brain with a hard psionic suggestion.

A look of enraged bafflement twisted her features, but she froze... no longer firing.

Searing pain stabbed Kirsten's right side, just below the ribcage. To her left, a series of loud plastic clicks announced bullets bouncing off Nicole and Forrester's armor. As the realization she'd been shot reached Kirsten's consciousness, fear and anger gathered into a reactive Mind Blast. The whole world briefly turned blindingly white. She fired a stream of random, meaningless sensory input into the mercenary's mind, bombarding her brain with a thousand different images, sounds, feelings, tastes, and smells.

The flash ended. Kirsten clamped one hand over the bullet hole, staggering backward until her butt hit the desk.

Groaning like a zombie with a migraine, the mercenary woman keeled over to the side and fell down on one knee, a heavy tendril of drool falling from her lip.

Green and blue laser flashes lit up the room to Kirsten's left. Nicole and Forrester peppered the big merc with laser fire as he charged in at them, seemingly ignoring the barrage despite the beams coming out his back, lighting his coat and armor on fire. His angry roaring got louder and louder with each step closer.

"Senji, what the fuck is wrong with you?" grunted the mercenary woman, her voice slurring as if she'd gone from stone sober to blind drunk in an instant.

Dorian continued staring intently at the floundering man. "Senji is having some hardware problems."

Senji's screaming momentarily became gurgling as he tried to speak.

The merc woman glared at Kirsten, evidently blaming her for what happened to her associate. "Fucking damn psio freaks."

Kirsten fired.

Fast as a blur, the woman leaned to one side, shifting the laser strike from a deadly one in the middle of her chest to an explosion of sparks, smoke, and molten metal spraying from her artificial arm. She'd moved so fast, Kirsten didn't even see the thrown knife coming until it hit her in the chest. The woman glared at her with an annoyed, droopy expression, as though she'd suffered a stroke.

That's a lung. That's definitely in my lung.

Kirsten fired again as she slumped to the floor, wheezing. Her second shot missed the side of the woman's head by an inch.

The big dude went flying away from Nicole as if punched by a huge cyborg. She telekinetically flung him all the way to the end of the room. Forrester shot the flying man thrice more in the few seconds it took the guy to hit the wall and collapse to the floor.

"K!" shouted Dorian an instant before he blurred into a smear of light and dove into Senji.

The thin mercenary stopped floundering, flipped upright, then sprang at the woman, attacking her in a blur of claw strikes. Her outer jacket seemed to explode in an instant to scraps of fluttering fabric. Dozens of gashes appeared across her armored vest. She moved faster than Kirsten's eyes could compensate for, grabbing Senji by the throat. More sparks crackled out of the laser gouge in her metal arm.

"Traitorous fuck," growled the woman.

Dorian glided backward out of Senji's body.

"Not... me," rasped Senji, a second before his neck disintegrated with a sickening crunch.

His ghost peeled away from his remains and staggered off to one side.

The woman threw the body to the side and faced Kirsten again, stalking toward her. "Damned. Psio. Freak."

Kirsten forced her right arm up, aiming at the woman's face. "Stop! Why don't you give up? Why are you forcing us to kill you!?"

"Heh." She half smiled, but kept walking closer. "We attacked the police. Got two choices. Win or die. Ain't no surrendering at this point. We're dead either way. Best I can do is take you with me."

A green laser beam pierced the mercenary woman's head from the side an instant before Kirsten squeezed her trigger. She convulsed on her feet, teetering.

Kirsten glanced over at Nicole. "Thanks."

"Bitch kinda has a point," muttered Nicole. "Crazies like this might actually give up once in a while if the automatic death penalty for attempted murder of police personnel didn't exist."

"If it didn't exist"—Dorian grabbed Senji's ghost—"a thousand more crazies would try their luck every damn day."

The female mercenary's body collapsed over, leaving her ghost standing in its place. Anger in her glare faltered briefly to confusion when she noticed Dorian and H1ghb0rne.

Kirsten set her E-90 on the floor, grabbed the knife sticking out of her chest, then clenched her jaw before yanking it out. *Oh, fucking hell, that hurt.* Stars danced in her vision. "Yeah... bad idea. Penalty good. Makes them hesitate. At least the smart ones."

"What bitch?" barked the dead mercenary woman. "You calling me stupid?"

"I am." Kirsten glared directly at her. "You are a damned idiot."

Nicole rushed over and stabbed Kirsten in the side with a stimpak. "Yeah to me or did he say something?"

The small red-and-white autoinjector emitted a faint hiss. Coolness spread outward from the spot. In seconds, both the bullet wound and the knife wound shifted from burning to tingling.

"Talking to Dorian," rasped Kirsten. "Damn that itches... inside."

Darkness welled up in the room's only doorway. Dread saturated the air. Thin streams of black liquid raced across the ceiling. A billowing geyser of ink-black vapor burst upward and took on the shape of a Harbinger, which fixated on the woman's ghost.

Whoa. I didn't call them. Kirsten gawked. *This bitch has got some serious problems if they've been waiting for her.*

She turned to face it. "What the fuck is that thing? You expect me to believe it's real? This isn't funny. Someone's jerking with my sim. This whole job's just a goddamned prank, isn't it? Fuck you, Mannheim. End this shittin' sim right now or so help me I'll cut off your balls and feed them to your kids."

Kirsten squeezed her fists, fighting past the pain of her injuries as well as the maddening itch-tickle frenzy of medical nanobots going nuts inside her. "You've done some bad things." She gasped for air. "Just... go with it. Don't fight. Be much easier on you."

"Oh, no." Nicole gave her another stimpak shot. "That's a punctured lung, K. Stimpaks ain't gonna do it. Tank time for you."

"What the hell are you talking about?" The woman backed away from the Harbinger. "Are all you psios crazy? You're making me see this. It's a hallucination! Stop that. Get out of my head!"

"No hallucination, I'm afraid." Dorian flung Senji's spirit to the ground and absentmindedly started to reach for his binders, but stopped himself. "Damn. Well, now I feel dumb. Anyway, hon. Hate to break it to you, but you are dead. You're a ghost. And that's the garbage collector."

Slow, but relentless, the Harbinger kept drifting after her as she backed toward the windows.

"Are you fucking kidding me?" blurted the mercenary. "You're trying to say that hell shit is real?"

Kirsten pushed herself up to sit, then put her E-90 back in its holster. "It's not hell. I honestly don't know what goes on there. Might just be like... I dunno... like sorting souls so the dirtiest ones get washed separately."

The Harbinger paused, twisting its head to look at Kirsten. It didn't have a face, merely two sparkling silver spots for eyes, though somehow conveyed a mood like it raised an eyebrow at her. After a second, it again faced the mercenary woman and glided forward.

She screamed, equal parts anger and fear, and tried to run around the Harbinger toward the doorway. Five more Harbingers swarmed out of the walls, surrounding her in a billow of vaporous darkness. Her screaming grew distant as though she fell down through the floor. The cloud of shadows condensed in on itself until it vanished, leaving the room silent save for the rapid, unintelligible whispering of a dozen spectral voices.

"Stupid." Kirsten shook her head, then tried to stand. "She should've just gone with them."

Nicole helped her up.

"Ops," said Kirsten. "Need a forensics team to my current location. Sergeant Forrester is taking over the scene. I've got to get to medical."

"Copy, lieutenant," replied a male voice. "Do you need a medical team?"

"Ehh, nah. Faster if I get myself to the PAC. Save the medics for someone hurt worse."

Senji stared at the empty floor where the Harbingers had been, then shifted his gaze to Kirsten.

"Guess you got lucky, pal." Dorian stood up off him. "Don't mind me. I keep forgetting there's no way to arrest spirits."

"Dorian, hang on a sec. Don't let go of him yet." Kirsten summoned the Astral Lash. "I'm going to ask you this once. Do you have any friends waiting outside or is it just the three of you?"

Senji jumped back—into Dorian's grip.

"Simple question." Dorian smiled. "You've been a spirit for less than five minutes. If she hits you with that thing once, you're going to cease to exist. You're also dead, so there's really no reason to lie anymore."

"No one else. Just us. Fewer witnesses. Fewer people to pay," said Senji in a shaky voice. "This can't really be happening. Who are you? What just happened to Cora?"

Dorian let go, then patted him on the shoulder. "You're dead. You'll work it out sooner or later."

Kirsten pressed a hand down over the bullet wound in her chest. The stimpak closed it enough to stop external blood loss, but she likely still had internal bleeding. Walking still hurt. She figured the synthetic adrenaline and painkillers in the two stimpak shots would keep her going long enough to at least get to the patrol craft. If she passed out after takeoff, the medical staff could drag her out of the car when it landed at the PAC.

"You okay to drive?" Nicole hurried over and put an arm around her. "Let me take you."

"Can't leave your partner here alone." Kirsten wheezed. "Backup is on the way. I can't wait."

"True." Nicole glanced at Forrester. "I'll just get you to your PC and come back down then."

"Be careful." Kirsten paused to catch her breath. "Big guy isn't dead. No ghost. He might get back up."

"Easy enough to fix that." Forrester raised his E-90.

"Careful. Those guys love to have kill-switch bombs," said Dorian. "The instant he goes brain dead, he might explode and throw shrapnel everywhere."

"Wait," squeaked Kirsten, attempting to yell. "Might have... bomb. Die equals boom."

"All right." Forrester kept aiming at him. "Then I'll stand here like this until he wakes up or backup arrives. Hurry up, Logan. Get the lieutenant on her way to medical and haul ass back down here."

Nicole scooped Kirsten up in a telekinetically assisted grab. "Hurrying. Be right back. Again, are you sure you're okay to drive?"

"Not really. Dorian can handle it. Or Auto." Kirsten exhaled. "Just get me to the car. I'll be fine."

30

THE MINUTIAE OF ETERNITY

The interior of the patrol craft shifted in a seeming instant to a peach-hued, somewhat blurry room awash in thousands of blinking lights on hulking obelisks of technology.

Breathing no longer hurt, though it took effort to push the fluid in and out of her lungs. All the maddening tingles had ceased. Kirsten waited a few minutes for the mental haze of anesthetic to fully wear off, then looked around.

She floated in a gel tank, her hair billowing out around her in a halo of pale blonde. Minor bruising marked her stomach an inch or so beneath her ribcage on the right side. The spot where the bullet went in —and certainly all the way through her—looked more like someone punched her a few days ago. Soreness pervaded the area, inside and out.

Itching resumed in her left lung.

Ugh. Not done cooking yet.

Kirsten absentmindedly rubbed a hand over the spot the knife hit her, annoyed the damn thing had to go through her boob to get to the lung. At least the medical team put things back together perfectly, not even a scar remained. She caught herself a moment later, cringing at having the nerve to be irritated at a non-fatal injury. How could an augmented merc with a digitally precise cyberarm—and no doubt targeting electronics—have possibly missed what should have been a kill shot straight to her heart?

The answer came in the form of a mild throb across her brain. It fell short of qualifying as a headache, but not by much.

Mind blast... She sighed fluid out her nostrils. Despite the power's reputation as being horribly bad, Kirsten preferred it to shooting people with her E-90. The damage caused by her psionic attack would, in most cases, completely fade away given an hour or two. Laser burns tended to be a bit more permanent, especially if they hit the heart or brain. Barring a moment of extreme emotion—like with Evan's bastard of a stepfather—it would be unlikely for her to cause any long-lasting harm using Mind Blast. Mere seconds after suffering the effects of the power, a person would be dizzy, nauseous, seeing spots, hearing phantom sounds, essentially the equivalent of too drunk to walk.

Kirsten had been far more frightened than she realized in the seconds leading up to the fight. She knew she faced three heavily augmented corporate assassins. If Dorian hadn't been there to neutralize Senji immediately, the man would have likely killed her, Nicole, and Forester faster than she could've thought 'oh shit; we're screwed.' Only by virtue of Mind Blast happening at the speed of thought had she even lived. Cora—the merc woman—could easily have shot all three of them in the head from that range with the precision of a robot.

So, yeah. She'd been emotionally charged... leading to a rather potent mental walloping. That the woman hit her at all with a thrown knife so soon after such a forceful Mind Blast was terrifying.

I wasn't entirely stupid this time. I had backup. Didn't go alone. Not like we had any advanced warning of mercenaries on the way. She frowned, wondering why H1ghb0rne didn't warn her. Ghosts could be weird. It's possible he merely knew something bad would happen but couldn't comprehend the specifics of what. He'd acted as if she had to get there quick to find Zannis Dalvren.

He didn't know why the evidence would disappear, just that it would.

Again, she sighed.

After a tediously quiet twentyish minutes, a medical tech entered, checked over some displays, then approached the tank to smile at her. Despite floating nude in peach-colored liquid, having a strange man studying her body didn't stir any feelings of embarrassment or annoyance. He kept it professional, focusing his attention on the injured regions.

"Welcome back to the land of the conscious." His voice carried through the fluid, amplified by hidden speakers somewhere in the tank ceiling. "Everything looks good. Ready to get out of there?"

She nodded.

"All right. I assume you know the drill since your records show this isn't your first time."

Kirsten gave a thumb-up.

He reached out and tapped at the buttons on the fridge-sized computer cabinet beside her tank. Soon, whirring filled her ears. Wavering bubbles of silver appeared above her like mercury spilled on the plastisteel ceiling. They expanded in size, merging, until the entire surface overhead shimmered. Gel drained downward at a rapid pace, sucked out of the tube by pumps somewhere in the floor. She sank with it to sit on the base of the tank, not even trying to stand while coated in such slippery goo. Once the fluid mostly disappeared into the vent grille in the middle of the base, she got up on all fours and emptied her lungs of as much fluid as she could.

The gagging, coughing, and crying that came with transitioning between B-gel and air was the absolute worst part of medical tanks. Kirsten much preferred the green stuff that required a facemask for air… but with a punctured lung, didn't have that option this time. The nanobot-laced fluid had to go where the injury occurred. A brief suction sound accompanied the clear tube cylinder unsealing from the top. It lowered into the floor, leaving her perched on a raised plastisteel pedestal like a life-sized statue in a museum.

The medic draped a huge white bathrobe made of towel material over her, helped her to her feet, and kept her from slipping too much as he escorted her across the room to an autoshower. She thanked him and set about rinsing the slippery mess off.

K̲irsten, back in uniform, stepped out of the medical room and nearly crashed into Nicole.

Her friend stood half a step away from the door, grinning like a fool. "Here."

It took a moment to process the sight of a disposable cup hovering in front of her face. The smell of mocha-strawberry confirmed the presence of coffee. Kirsten accepted the offering, mildly surprised to find it so hot.

"Sensed you wake up." Nicole backed up so she could fully exit the medical room. "Ran off to grab it halfway through your shower cycle. Timing worked perfectly."

"Thanks." Kirsten rolled her left shoulder, grimacing at the tightness in her chest.

"You okay?" Nicole raised both eyebrows, seeming worried.

"Yeah. Just sore." She started to raise the cup to her lips, but paused. "This is too hot to drink yet. How long were you out there?"

"About an hour and fifteen." Nicole waved dismissively. "No big deal. We finished up at the apartment pretty quick. Those Div 2 teams are like piranhas going after meat."

"What the heck is a piranha?" Kirsten blinked.

"It's a kind of fish that eats really fast. There are lots of them so, like, if people fall in the water, there's only bones left in a couple seconds." Nicole fake cringed. "I think they're still around. Don't remember if they went extinct, too. Kinda snoozed through fifth grade science."

Kirsten risked a small taste of coffee. Still too hot, but the awesome flavor made up for it. "Fish, right. So, the techs tore the place up?" She started down the hall toward the elevators.

"Not so much tore, but yeah, they worked fast." Nicole fell in step at her side. "It's all getting processed now. Should be linked to your inquest. Eze is furious—but not with you."

"Ugh. Two hit teams attacked me in the span of a few days."

"Yeah." Nicole swigged her coffee, clearly older—and less hot. "To be fair, those three who showed up at the apartment weren't sent after you personally."

"No, but they did attack three uniformed officers."

"You're the only officer." Nicole crossed her eyes. "And yes, I know… officer is a generic term for anyone in the NPF. It dates back to pre-war times when the police department wasn't part of the military."

"I know." Kirsten fake rolled her eyes. "I didn't miss *that* much school."

Nicole laughed.

"Are you happy now?" barked a man behind them.

The wave of paranormal energy, plus Nicole's non-reaction to the shouting, announced the arrival of a ghost.

Expecting to find the big mercenary assassin who hadn't yet died when she left the scene, Kirsten turned… and blinked at the ghostly figure of Chaoxiang Liu. She narrowed her eyes at him and held her coffee out to Nicole. "Hold this a sec. I'm going to need my hands."

"What's up?" Nicole took the cup. "Ghost? I feel something weird."

"Yep." Kirsten stared at the man. "Happy? No. What did you expect was going to happen when you tried to contract the assassination of a cop? Even if they managed to kill me, Division 9 would've paid you a visit."

Mr. Liu jabbed his finger into her face. "You ruined my company! Everything I built!"

"Your company ruined itself. If your people hadn't decided to ignore the defect to save money, Atmos wouldn't be on metaphorical fire right now. This *situation* is entirely the fault of whoever made the decision to prioritize money over quality and safety. Going to assume that was you."

Mr. Liu snarled, then stomped around in an impotent, raging huff. As soon as he turned to the side, a large gunshot exit wound became apparent at the top rear of his head.

"Oh. Nine didn't get you, did they? You ended it yourself." Kirsten shook her head. "Do you believe in ghosts now?"

He stopped short, spinning to glower at her.

"Not sure Nine would've been involved here." Dorian emerged out of the wall. "This guy isn't big or powerful enough to be able to brush off the legal shitstorm waiting for him. He just didn't want to deal with the public shaming."

Mr. Liu flailed at Kirsten, somewhere between a punch or slap. His hand passed through her head with a faint chill.

"Oh, one more thing." Dorian tapped a finger to his chin, seeming contemplative—then punched Mr. Liu hard enough to knock him flying backward. "That's for trying to kill my partner."

The former chairman of Atmos Industries' board of directors glided to a stop some fifteen feet away, his head an unrecognizable blob of ectoplasm. Over the next thirty seconds, it gradually reconstituted back to his normal face.

"All right." Kirsten stalked toward him. "Do you have any messages or whatever you'd like me to communicate to any living relatives before you go?"

"Go?" Mr. Liu scoffed, glaring at her like a king who couldn't believe the servant girl dared speak to him directly. "Where do you think I would go?"

She examined her fingernails. "Oh, I can think of a few places. One in particular. But…" She glanced around. "If they didn't get you before you came all the way here, you're probably not dark enough."

"Dark enough?" Mr. Liu tried again to ineffectually slap her. "Start making sense, girl."

Kirsten raised a hand to stop Dorian from pounding the man's head into an amorphous blob again. "Maybe you didn't make the decision to continue using the cheap parts. All the people who died to your company's deliberate recklessness might not be on your soul. The NewsNet guy's death is, though. But… apparently killing one guy and trying to kill me isn't quite enough to get *them* seriously looking for you."

"They'd probably pounce on him if he stumbled across one." Dorian glared at Mr. Liu.

Nicole sipped from the wrong coffee. "Oops. Sorry. Oh, hey. This *is* good. I'll have to get this flavor next time."

"I'm still not sure how they feel about suicide." Kirsten tapped her foot. "You're probably going to be stuck wandering around as a ghost until you figure stuff out. Basically, you have three options. One: go through the silver door. Two—"

"This guy isn't going to see that door for a while," said Dorian.

No doubt. She exhaled. "Two: haunt the normal world. Or three: end up being dragged to the Abyss."

Mr. Liu swung through her face again. "You did this to me!"

Dorian pounced, lifting the other ghost up by his suit lapels and pounding him into the wall. "If your hand touches her one more time, I am going to twist you into an octopusine pretzel knot so convoluted it will take you sixty years to untangle yourself. Do you understand me?"

"He's not actually hurting me." Kirsten folded her arms. "And no. You did this to yourself. You ran every little detail at Atmos. Don't think I didn't notice the way Ms. Tomlin looked at you as if needing approval. I don't really believe you didn't know about the defect. Nothing happened there without your say so. You knew about the risk and decided to gamble with people's lives rather than lose money fixing a deadly problem. You did nothing about it until the death toll became difficult to keep quiet. Everything that's happened to you and your company is the result of your choices. Welcome to the afterlife."

"Welcome to never sleeping again," snapped Mr. Liu.

Dorian tilted his head. "Do I need to impress upon you why that is a bad idea?"

Mr. Liu frowned at him. "Since when do you guys have patrol ghosts?"

"I'm special." Dorian smiled in a decidedly threatening manner.

"Fair warning." Kirsten locked stares with Mr. Liu. "If you cause trouble, we will meet again."

"Hah." Dorian laughed. "I doubt that. You'll be retired before this guy's strong enough to do anything but rattle kitchen cabinet doors."

Kirsten raised an eyebrow. "I'm not above slapping the smarm off his face if he makes a pest of himself."

Dorian let go of the guy. "If you hit him once, you'd destroy him."

"That's a sacrifice I'm willing to make," deadpanned Kirsten as she summoned the Astral Lash.

"Ooh, I love that thing," whispered Nicole. "So pretty."

Mr. Liu recoiled from the energy whip, clearly understanding it could cause him great harm. He emitted a nervous gurgle and raced off into the wall.

Kirsten dispelled the lash and took her coffee cup back from Nicole.

"You are such a rotten liar." Dorian snickered. "I have no idea how he believed you'd casually destroy him."

Kirsten wagged her eyebrows at him. "He's a spineless weasel."

"Now what?" asked Nicole.

"Ugh. Reports. Lots and lots of reports." Kirsten hung her head. "Might as well get it over with."

31

NORMAL PEOPLE

P redictably, as soon as they reached the squad room, Captain Eze called her into his office.

Kirsten let Nicole take her coffee to her desk for her and walked up to him. "Sir."

He looked her over. "Good to see you are all right. Please, come in."

"Thanks." She followed him into his office.

Captain Eze smiled, then motioned for her to have a seat before moving around to sit behind his desk. "Division 9 sent over word they traced the mercenaries to a Mr. Chaoxiang Liu, former CEO of Atmos Industries."

"Which mercenaries?" asked Kirsten, semi-seriously. "The ones who attacked me at home or the ones from today?"

"First group." Captain Eze glared at something on his desk terminal screen. "Thought you'd like to know they found him dead in his home two hours ago. Seems he shot himself before they could."

"Yeah… he got in my face on the way up here from medical." Kirsten explained her encounter with him.

"Do you think he will be a problem?" Captain Eze leaned back in his seat.

"Not for at least thirty years, probably more. He's not emotionally wrapped up in anything—except his own sense of ego—powerfully enough to affect the mortal world abnormally fast." She shrugged. "It's difficult to say what effect becoming a ghost will have on any person. This guy was extremely proud, controlling, and a bit of a dick. Spending years being invisible and powerless as a ghost might crack him. It's just as likely he trips over a random Harbinger and ends up in 'the bad place' as it is he has an epiphany."

"Hmm. Interesting." Captain Eze chuckled. "Glad I don't have to worry about that stuff. Be nice if you had a little help, but you seem to be handling things well."

"Thanks." She exhaled, worried about Evan's future. *Command is going to try to recruit him… and he's going to say yes because he wants to help.* The thought of him being shot at made her equal parts furious and anxious.

"You've been in the tube for a while so you've missed the show." Captain Eze gestured at the large holo-panel on the wall to his left between the shelves. "Atmos has been the main story in the NewsNet cycle for the past several hours. Stocks are taking a nosedive. Division 2 has launched a comprehensive investigation into the company. They're auditing just about everything. Some massive recalls are underway as well. I think it will be a while before anyone trusts e-suits made by them. The company's PR team is already scrambling to put all the blame on Mr. Liu since he's dead. I doubt the government will issue a dissolution order. Whether or not Atmos Industries remains a viable company is up to the court of public opinion."

She fidgeted, smoothing her hands down her legs a few times before grabbing her knees. "Feel kinda bad for all the employees caught up in it. Most of them had nothing to do with this."

"Yeah. No doubt." Captain Eze exhaled. "I looked over your notes for this case. Seems solid enough. Nice work. Try not to make a habit of poaching stuff from Two or they'll start trying to jettison all the crap they can't figure out our way."

Kirsten smiled, sensing his mostly teasing tone. "Understood, sir. Just tell them a ghost came looking for help and that should change their mind. I can't pull spirits out of thin air if they've already gone somewhere."

"Yeah. Not a bad idea." He smiled, tapping his fingers on the desk. "They always do turn various shades of pale whenever we talk about that stuff. Anyway, feel free to take the rest of the day to recover from your tank time. Hmm. It's Thursday. If you want to stay home tomorrow as well, that's fine, too. See you Monday."

"Thanks. I'll see how I feel in the morning. I'm available for emergencies, as usual."

He nodded.

She stood. They saluted each other as a matter of protocol, and she returned to her desk.

I could do the reports from home. Evan's out of class now. Yeah. She grinned. *He's gotta be worried about me.*

After securing her terminal, she got into a brief conversation with Nicole about going home to recover—which turned into an un-brief conversation about another thirty random topics. Her friend thought it cute she let Sam keep the Monwyn-themed deck. The thing might be an antique as far as computer hardware went, but it had value to a fan.

"Speaking of Sam…" Kirsten grabbed her NetMini and sent him a text to say she would be going home any minute and might even be off tomorrow—barring an emergency call.

He vid-called back in four seconds. "Hey. You okay?"

"Sore. Mostly fine. Not going to say no to the chance to rest and spend time with the kid."

Nicole leaned into the call. "She's such a good mom, isn't she?"

Kirsten palmed her friend's head and pushed her out to arm's length, both of them laughing. "I'm trying."

"Why don't we do something fun later?" Sam wagged his eyebrows.

Nicole made 'ooh, nice' face at her.

"What did you have in mind?" Kirsten tried not to blush.

Sam held up a tiny toy sword. "Was thinking maybe we could take Ev somewhere fun, like that real-world Monwyn adventure. Not the VR one, the actual place with the synthetic stuff."

"I could be talked into that." Kirsten grinned.

Nicole shook her head and whispered, "Not where I expected that conversation to go…"

"Great. I'll book it now. We'll make a day of it tomorrow. I got plenty of flex time." Sam winked.

An odd, warm, tingly feeling filled Kirsten's chest watching Sam check the GlobeNet site on his other terminal. She couldn't wait to be with her family... and with Sam once Evan went to bed. She had a certain interrupted birthday night activity to make up for.

Is this what normal people feel like?

Merely looking at Sam's holographic face floating in front of her made the stress of the past few days melt away.

I could really get used to it.

---

fin

ACKNOWLEDGMENTS

Thank you for reading Division Zero book 7! Kirsten's story will continue in another book as soon as the muse is kind enough to stop by with a story idea.

Additional thanks to Lee Sheridan for editing and Alexandria Thompson for the cover design!

ABOUT THE AUTHOR

Originally from South Amboy NJ, Matthew has been creating science fiction and fantasy worlds for most of his reasoning life. Since 1996, he has developed the "Divergent Fates" world, in which *Division Zero*, *Virtual Immortality*, *The Awakened Series*, *The Harmony Paradox*, *and the Daughter of Mars series* take place. Along with being an editor at Curiosity Quills press, he has worked in IT and technical support.

Matthew is an avid gamer, a recovered WoW addict, Gamemaster for two custom RPG systems, and a fan of anime, British humour, and intellectual science fiction that questions the nature of reality, life, and what happens after it.

He is also fond of cats.

Visit me online at:
   Facebook: https://www.facebook.com/MatthewSCoxAuthor
   Pinterest: https://www.pinterest.com/matthewcox10420/
   Goodreads: https://www.goodreads.com/author/show/
7712730.Matthew_S_Cox
   Email: mcox2112@gmail.com

OTHER BOOKS BY MATTHEW S. COX

Divergent Fates Universe Novels

Division Zero series

- Division Zero
- Lex De Mortuis
- Thrall
- Guardian
- Harbinger
- The Shadow Fixer
- Neuroshock

The Awakened series

- Prophet of the Badlands
- Archon's Queen
- Grey Ronin
- Daughter of Ash
- Zero Rogue
- Angel Descended

Daughter of Mars series

- The Hand of Raziel
- Araphel
- Ghost Black

Virtual Immortality series

- Virtual Immortality
- The Harmony Paradox

Prophet of the Badlands Series

- Prophet's Journey
- Prophet's Mercy

Divergent Fates Anthology

(Fiction Novels - Adult)

The Roadhouse Chronicles Series

- One More Run
- The Redeemed
- Dead Man's Number

Faded Skies series

- Heir Ascendant
- Ascendant Unrest
- Ascendant Revolution

Temporal Armistice Series

- Nascent Shadow
- The Shadow Collector
- The Gate to Oblivion
- The Queen of Discord
- The Burning Alchemist

Vampire Innocent series

- A Nighttime of Forever
- A Beginner's Guide to Fangs
- The Artist of Ruin
- The Last Family Road Trip
- The Phantom Oracle

- How Not to Summon Demons
- Ordinary Problems of a College Vampire
- A Vampire's Guide to Surviving Holidays
- An Introduction to Paranormal Diplomacy
- A Vampire's Guide to Adulting
- How to Stop a Vampire War in Six Easy Steps
- Ancient Vampire Death Cults and Other Annoyances
- Hunting Vampires for Fun and Profit
- A String of Seriously Unlucky Events
- The Summer of Completely Usual Strangeness

Standalones

- Wayfarer: AV494
- Axillon99
- Chiaroscuro: The Mouse and the Candle
- The Spirits of Six Minstrel Run
- Sophie's Light
- The Far Side of Promise anthology
- Operation: Chimera (with Tony Healey)
- The Dysfunctional Conspiracy (with Christopher Veltmann)
- Of Myth and Shadow
- The Girl Who Found the Sun

Winter Solstice series (with J.R. Rain)

- Convergence
- Containment
- Catalyst
- Catacombs

Alexis Silver series (with J.R. Rain)

- Silver Light
- Deep Silver
- Silver Quarrel

- Silver Crucible

Samantha Moon Origins series (with J.R. Rain)

- New Moon Rising
- Moon Mourning
- Haunted Moon

Vampire For Hire series (with J.R. Rain)

- Moon Master
- Dead Moon
- Lost Moon
- Vampire Destiny
- Infinite Moon
- Vampire Empress
- Moon Elder
- Wicked Moon

Maddy Wimsey series (with J.R. Rain)

- The Devil's Eye
- The Drifting Gloom
- Dark Mercy
- Primal Wrath

Samantha Moon Case Files series (with J.R. Rain)

- Blood Moon

Immortal Operative (with J.R. Rain)

- Broken Ice

Four Elements series (with J.R. Rain)

- The Elementalist

- The Black Rose
- The Wakefield Curse

Witches series (with J.R. Rain)

- The Witch and the Hangman

Zeb Clemens series (with J.R. Rain)

- The Beast of Devil's Creek
- Wanted: Undead or Alive

Young Adult Novels

The Eldritch Heart Series

- The Eldritch Heart
- The Cursed Crown
- The Sapphire Soul

Evergreen Series

- Evergreen
- The World That Remains
- The Lucky Ones
- Nuclear Summer
- The Nuclear Frontier
- The World We Make

Progenitor Series

- Out of Sight
- Out of Mind

Diary of a Teenage Fey

(Short story series)

- Elder Horror
- The Hag of Barrow Falls
- Babysitter's Nightmare
- Lharakki
- Bauble for a Soul
- Simulacrum
- Amorphous
- Manticore

Standalones

- Caller 107
- The Summer the World Ended
- Nine Candles of Deepest Black
- The Forest Beyond the Earth

Middle Grade Novels

The Adventures of Ubergirl series

- My Dad is a Mad Scientist
- Aliens Ate My Homework
- The End of all Halloweens
- Dr. Infinity and the Soul Smasher

Tales of Widowswood series

- Emma and the Banderwigh
- Emma and the Silk Thieves
- Emma and the Silverbell Faeries
- Emma and the Elixir of Madness
- Emma and the Weeping Spirit

Standalones

- Citadel: The Concordant Sequence
- The Cursed Codex
- The Menagerie of Jenkins Bailey

www.ingramcontent.com/pod-product-compliance
Lightning Source LLC
Chambersburg PA
CBHW051951240626
47153CB00005B/1708